HOT BLOODED

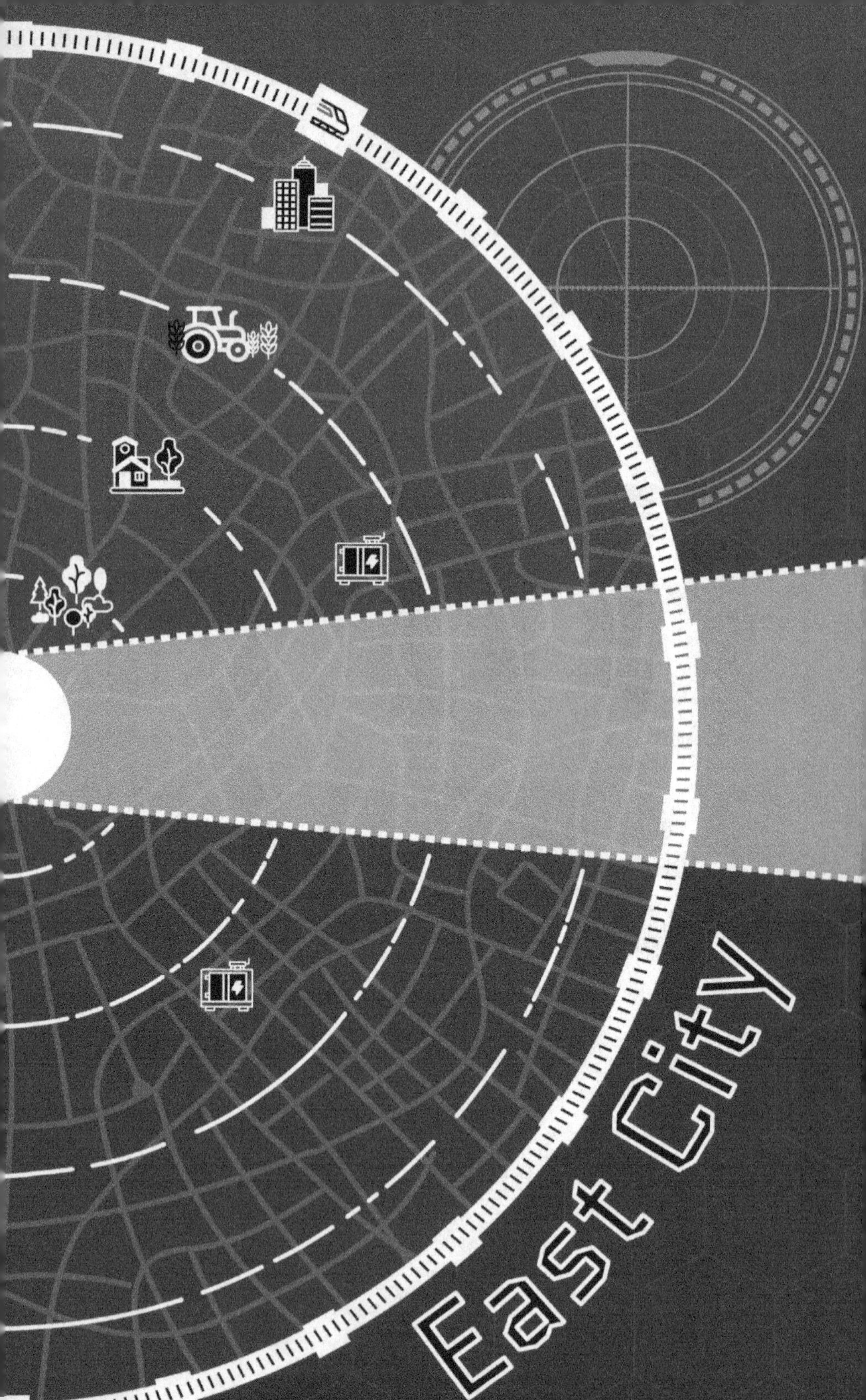
East City

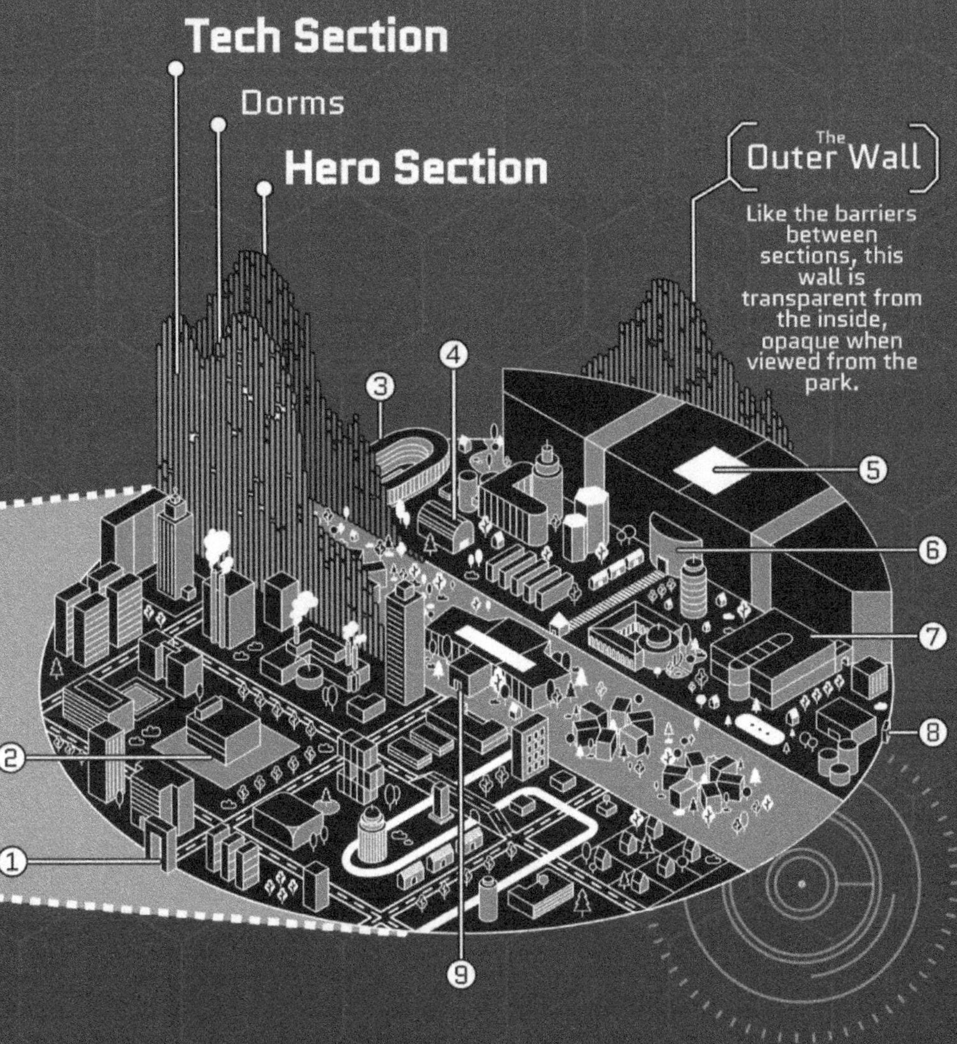

East Technical Institute

1. Campus Main Entrance
2. Armorer's Lab
3. Gym
4. Field House
5. Jet Pad
6. Disaster Simulator
7. Power Gym
8. Service Entrance
9. Dining Hall

014-2087 CLASS ROSTER

PENDING REASSIGNMENT

RANK	ALIAS	MIEN
1	PHOENIX	healing/resurrection
2	KIRIN	corporeal carbon manipulation
3	IFRIT	carbon monoxide manipulation
4	KAPRE	atomic control of landscape
5	ADLIVUN	life force re-distribution
6	KUAFU	nuclear fusion in palms
7	CLIDNA	sonic scream/ echolocation
8	AÏCHA KANDÏCHA	bovine lower forelimbs
9	NESS	phase shift
10	GOLDHORN	zombic blood (plant)/ ram's horns
11	IMPUNDULU	dimensional wings
12	BHUTA VAHANA YANTRA	technopath (golem)
13	WYRM	scapular spikes/ paralytic poison
14	ANTAEUS	compaction (reversible)
15	EN NADDĀHA	vampiric emotional manipulation
16	ENENRA	personal dissipation
17	LILIN	void creation
18	MEDUSA	ocular paralysis

ranks as of completion of first year. miens subject to re-assignment per armorer analysis. class rank 1.

Book Cover by Mariska Maas.

Map by Loona Ginga.

Aquarium Illustration by Loona Ginga.

Character Artwork by Minikyu.

First edition 2025.

ISBN: 979-8-9909492-4-9 (print); 979-8-9909492-5-6 (ebook)

To everyone who has ever felt monstrous. Someone out there will understand.

And to Mini. My creative partner in crime, though the crime is you living an ocean away.

HOT BLOODED

BOOK TWO OF THE CARBON CHRONICLES

J GREENE

With Art by Mariska Maas,
Loona Ginga, and Minikyu

AUTHOR'S NOTE

Note on the use of International Sign Language: as this book is written in English, the depiction of sign language throughout the novel is a *translation* of ISL into American English. Sign is typically shown in *italics*, spoken words through TV/headsets/lip-read are in "*quotation marks and italics*." If you don't already know your country's sign language, consider learning!

Trigger Warnings: Please find a list of trigger warnings below. If you wish to avoid any and all potential spoilers, do not read below the break. Please take care of your mental health; for detailed descriptions of trigger warnings you can go to my website, which will also have short summaries of what was important from each scene so you can skip over potentially triggering moments without missing any critical information.

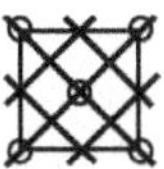

Trigger warnings: child abuse/neglect (mentioned/implied, brief flashback), comic typical violence, cults/extremist groups, death, discrimination based on appearance/abilities, gore (brief descriptions), grief, gun violence, language, murder. For more information on trigger warnings and summaries of scenes in which trigger warnings occur, please visit

jgreene.ink.

0

What's Right

THE QUIET DRIP OF molten metal reminded Force where she was.

She'd forgotten for a moment, somehow, despite the blood on her shoes and the sweat sticking her hair to her face. The world outside of the building— or what was left of it— was still chaos; she'd turned her headset off to avoid the overlapping voices calling out where forces were needed, the climbing fatality count, and the potential locations of the fleeing villains. She had her target; she didn't need to know any more.

Or so she had thought.

Her hand found the switch on her comm and she flicked it on, feeling her anger rising.

"Majesty," she said through gritted teeth, "you neglected to mention that it was a *kid*."

The line crackled for a moment before Majesty's voice came through, calm as ever.

"Would it have mattered?"

Force crushed the receiver so she didn't have to say it out loud.

No, it wouldn't have.

A torn wire sparked above her head as she pressed further in. The air was hot here, hotter than it was outside, but far cooler than the hellfire the city had been when she'd first arrived. This must have been the fifth or sixth floor of the building, though now it was almost level with the ground, the lower floors melted and part of the solid metal foundation. It was cooling slowly, the sinking of the buildings almost imperceptible. The flames causing the destruction had stopped inexplicably, but she hadn't asked why. She never asked why. It wouldn't change anything.

Now, though— now she was beginning to regret that.

From a distance it'd been obvious that the person she'd been told to eliminate was a child. The moment she'd set foot in the building she'd heard him yelling, the shrill pitch of his voice betraying his age. The words were lost as the sound bounced through the space, growing louder as it went. It was like she was surrounded by hundreds of children, thousands of lost little boys, crying out.

Metal parted with a horrific screech as she shoved her way through a partially collapsed wall. Her mien allowed her to walk into such an unstable structure without fear, but sometimes she wished she didn't have to hear how destructive she was. How violent she was.

A buzz in her pocket alerted her that Valor had noticed her headset was offline. If Majesty had talked to him, he'd know she was angry at having the true horror of the mission withheld from her, and that it had been no accident she'd walked in blind. Then again, he already knew it rarely was.

She ignored the persistent vibration as the final barrier between her and her target fell away.

It'd been five years since she'd faltered. She hadn't made a single mistake since graduation, had kept her image perfectly clean. There wasn't a single complaint about her registered with the Hero Commission, not a word against her in any of the main feeds. True, some people in the forums online thought she was hiding something, but they did admit that at least her above board work was flawless. And now, at the top of the world, she hesitated.

The sound of her entrance should've alerted the boy to her presence, but maybe he'd grown so used to the sound of tearing metal that he didn't register it at all. Or maybe he was just too distraught, since he seemed to be holding another dead child.

No, the other child was holding *him*.

The screaming one finally noticed her.

"Please!" The volume didn't decrease, even though he could see her standing only a few meters away. "Help him, please!"

Force, the number one hero in all the world, destroyer of villains and savior of thousands, found herself frozen in place.

The boy didn't notice her hesitation.

"He caught me, he *saved* me! Please, I can't leave him like this!"

There was something desperate in his voice, which wasn't surprising, but the edge to it was... odd. His fear wasn't directed at the prospect of his own death— which he rightly should have been since he looked half-starved and covered in blood— instead far more focused on the fate of this other child.

"I think it's too late for him." Force heard the words, felt them in her chest, but they didn't feel like they were *her* words. It was a script, a set phrase to turn the unthinkable into a nice, neat package. Not something that she should be saying to a little boy. Not something she should be saying to someone she was going to kill.

"What?" The dark-haired boy was looking at her, his eyes a deep, uncanny red. Was that how he was spotted by the insurgents who took him? The very color of his eyes a dead giveaway? "I'm sorry, could you please speak up? I couldn't hear you."

A resounding crack echoed behind her as she couldn't contain her mien, a wave of force rippling backward and destroying a block of concrete. There was just something so *innocent* about this boy. Who the fuck would say *please* when the world was in flames around them?

"I think…" Why was her mouth dry? She had a job to do. Her hands were not meant to console, were not meant to soothe, to fix. They were only good at one thing, and this was not it. All she had to do was kill the target and leave, just another drop of blood on her hands. She'd done it hundreds of times before, never failing, never faltering. So why was she walking forward and falling to her knees?

The dark-haired boy was too thin. His shirt hung loosely, covered in grime that looked too set in the fabric to have been from the past few hours. Had he really been grabbed that very day? Or had Valor misled her again?

"He's breathing." He was still talking too loudly, gesturing at the other boy. Now that she was closer, she realized why they were here, at the very edge of the room. Because this other child, this boy who was so soaked in blood that his hair was dripping red, was *holding up the wall*.

"He lost consciousness only a few minutes ago. I did not see any wounds or lacerations on him and he was able to move very quickly so I do not…" The dark-haired boy wavered, his lip trembling. "I don't know what's wrong with him. Please, *help him*."

When her eyes met red, she found herself nodding.

The boy in the wall was wedged firmly, his head lolling to one side as concrete and metal bore down on what seemed to be *diamond plates* in his back. Blood seeped sluggishly from the edges of the crystal, harsh lines of steel puckering where they met skin. When she couldn't stop herself from reaching out, the metal burned her fingertips the second they brushed it.

"He's fine." These words, oddly, came easily. "The wounds are cauterized, he's just unconscious from the pain."

But when she turned back, the other boy seemed not to have heard.

"What's wrong with him?" Still so loud.

"The metal. It burned him." She was speaking louder now too, irritation mounting. Was she mad at the dark-haired boy? No, she didn't think so. He was still staring at her like he hadn't heard, but the confusion had faded, replaced instead by vague fear.

"I— I'm s-sorry." The realization hit him just as it was hitting her. The dried blood from his ears, the failure to notice her. An explosion that leveled two city blocks. "I c-can't hear you."

"I know." Her voice came out in a whisper.

His eyes widened for a moment, tears building up at his lower lash line. Then, furiously, he wiped them away and regained control.

"Can you show me how to help him?" His chin was lifted, his lip trembled, but he betrayed no other sign of distress. There were dark shadows under his eyes, he was altogether too thin, and he *still* was trying to be brave, to be strong for this other child he didn't seem to know. And through it all, he never once doubted that she was there to help them. He may as well have shoved a knife under her ribs from the way her heart hurt.

She needed to end this. She needed to do her job and leave before the temptation to be a *hero* again took over.

She pulled the diamond boy out of the wall.

The dark-haired child grabbed him immediately, holding onto him and shielding him as the building began to crumble around them. The diamond boy was bigger, but still the malnourished, sickly child that she was supposed to kill tried to use his frail skeleton to shield someone else. She felt bile rise in her throat as the rubble fell down.

When the dust cleared, they were all still alive.

She didn't know why she was surprised. She knew her mien. She *knew* the amount of force she'd sent out would keep the debris from them as well. But after the past few years, she'd almost thought it wouldn't work. That the one time, the *one* time she decided to do what felt right it wouldn't work. Yet the boy she was no longer going to kill was blinking, squinting up at the sun.

The other boy moved now too, shifting in his uneasy sleep. His brows were drawn together, his face pale and damp. From his position on the ground, from the dirt on his face and the jagged edges of crystal along his back, he looked like he'd just been unearthed from a long-forgotten slumbering place, something out of a fairytale. When his eyes slowly opened, she felt like maybe she'd been brought back into the light too.

"It's okay. I've got you." Her hands trembled slightly as she patted him on the head, her palm coming away red. It was a muscle stiff from disuse, but she'd get used to it again.

Her pocket buzzed, reminding her that she hadn't saved anyone yet.

Would Valor help? Her brother had been the biggest factor in things going this far, in her career coming here, to this point. They'd both gone to East Tech with the same dream of doing something worth doing. Maybe he'd remember that.

Yet she could already see photography drones in the distance, closing in. Whatever Valor might be in private, he was a very traditional hero in public. They'd been given orders. It was not her place to question them. The brother she'd grown up with would agree with what she was doing, but the brother she had now wouldn't. As she lifted the blood-stained boy off the ground, she knew that she was alone.

"Wait here." She knew the dark-haired one couldn't hear her at all, but he either read her lips or understood the hand she held out to him. It would only take a few moments to get the unconscious child into an ambulance, and it would be best for everyone if he were not associated with her target. And if she was going to succeed, she needed to take a leaf out of Valor's book. She needed to get the press on her side.

Luck was a slippery thing in her experience, and often too hard to tell if it was good or bad until you were safely away from it. She did think her luck was good that day, having enough time to leave her diamond charge in safe hands and return to the dark-haired boy before anyone found her. And that it was Majesty who appeared instead of Valor.

Her hasty destruction of the building had left a crater in the landscape, the rubble that used to make up the skyscraper piled high in a rim around her and the child. It provided some cover, at least, or made them hard to spot until an intruder crested the ridge and came into view. Likely it was the reason that Force had gotten as much time as she had. That or the other heroes' terror of the child she now held in her arms.

"What are you doing?" Majesty hadn't sounded frightened like that since they'd left school. Maybe even earlier than that, on those first days they'd known each other, when Majesty hadn't been sure what she was doing there at all.

"The right thing." Force tried to keep the conviction she'd gained in her voice. It was hard now, seeing the horror on Majesty's face. "He doesn't deserve to die, Maj."

"We don't decide that." There it was, that slight stubborn edge, the one that always came out when she was too afraid to consider the alternative.

"Why don't we?" It was a relief to finally say it aloud. It had always been there, hiding in the corners of her mind, nagging at her with each mission that felt wrong, wrong, wrong. Yes, she signed up knowing that she would likely have to kill, but she should've had some say in when that ability was used. Where mercy belonged.

"You know why." Majesty's face was turning angry, which was a feat in itself. There were few things that could truly make her composure slip, though Force had thought she'd known all of them. "We're too close to it, we can't make those decisions."

"So people who don't know what it's like should? People who sit back and let us do their dirty work just in case something else might happen? Killing off a child who looks half dead feels one step closer to killing anyone who just *might* do something wrong in the future. That's not something that I can be a part of."

"They're not going to let you get away with this." Majesty's eyes flickered upward, toward where the cameras were undoubtedly closing in. Force had been too close to the center, too close to danger for the feeds to chance sacrificing their equipment before, but now that everything was calm and settled, they wanted to see their hero standing tall. They wanted to see *her*, since she belonged to them.

"Their only option right now would to be to kill me and a child directly on camera. They won't risk it. Not now."

"And your future? They won't let you keep working. They'll arrest you."

"It'll be worth it." It was easy to sound sure about that, because she was. The weight of the past few years was falling away already, replaced with the weight of a head on her shoulder and a still beating heart in her arms. "I don't care what happens next, I just know that if I did what they told me to, I'd never sleep peacefully again."

"But *I* care what happens!" It shocked Force to realize that behind all that anger, Majesty was hurt. "If Force doesn't exist anymore— if *you* aren't there anymore— who do we look to? You're the only hero that's well-known across the globe. You're the first person that the world fully accepted and trusted—

when you're gone, what then?"

"There'll be someone else—"

"There won't." Majesty's voice held a note of pained finality. "There's no one else like you."

Force felt her grip on the boy tighten as she looked up at Majesty. Majesty herself was looking down, but she still had that look in her eyes, that reverence, like she was looking at a saint. Like her god had just come down to earth and told her to stop believing.

"There are so many people like me." Force said slowly, feeling the cracks that had always existed between her and Majesty widen as she spoke. "They just never had a chance because I killed them."

"That's not true. All our targets were—"

"Powerful mien users. Sometimes in the midst of a normal day. Often, yes, party to some petty crime. But also just regular people who one government or another was afraid of. We've got to stop lying to ourselves Maj, we're not helping right now. We're just weapons to them. Something needs to change, and we can start changing things by refusing to do what we know is wrong."

Majesty was backing up, shaking her head.

"You don't mean that. We can't think like that. I'm going to go get Valor and he'll—"

She didn't get to finish her sentence as a wave of force took out her legs and pitched her forward, falling like a marionette with its strings cut. Force felt her heart in her throat as she regarded the crumpled body, the shock of bright blue hair cascading down the rubble. She'd understand, when she woke up. Force would have time to talk to her and make her understand.

But for now, Force had one mission, and one mission only.

"It's okay," she said, ignoring the fact that her charge couldn't hear her at all, "I won't let anyone hurt you."

Then she crossed over the ridge and into the blinding light of cameras, leaving that peaceful body behind.

1

Just Breathe

IFRIT KNEW HE'D FUCKED up.

Knowing didn't make it any less irritating though.

See, the main fault lay with him still being slightly too blunt with his words, but it was also the fault of his fucking annoyingly overprotective classmates. It'd been touching, their concern for him after... after everything that'd happened. They'd been so kind when he came back, and he'd been beyond moved that they'd all been willing to literally lay down their lives for him, but it'd been *two months*. He still needed his alone time and his privacy, neither of which he could get with them all buzzing around like he'd drop dead any second of the day. So he'd finally snapped and yelled at everyone to leave him alone for one fucking minute.

They'd taken it well, honestly. Seemed almost as relieved as he did that things were going back to normal. None of them had begrudged him the explosion; even Phoenix had left the floor for a few hours without so much as a pointed comment about his temper. However, the issue was that Kirin still thought "everyone" applied to him.

It was his own damn fault. He knew that Kirin was... self-deprecating at best. Considering he'd been the absolute worst about hovering, he probably thought that it'd been directed at him specifically, instead of exactly the opposite. But Kirin was usually so good at reading him that Ifrit had naively thought he'd somehow know exactly what Ifrit had meant.

Unfortunately, that meant this was the first time in two months that he was trying to fall asleep alone.

The giant bed that his classmates had made in the common area during his disappearance had remained, and several of them had been sleeping there for the past weeks; Clidna, Adlivun, Invisibitch (*Ness*, Kirin's voice corrected him in his own head), and Yantra had been practically living on their floor most days. Tonight though— tonight he was back in his room for the first time, and he felt like he couldn't breathe.

The window was open all the way, and he knew that Pressure had installed extra air filtration and ventilation in all their rooms. Even so he could barely close his eyes for a few minutes before it felt like the air was settling in his lungs, dense, charcoal-heavy air pressing down, down, down, and his eyes would snap open. He'd sit up feeling like his heart was trying to escape his chest, his mouth dry and head pounding. One time it wouldn't stop until he stuck his whole fucking head out the window and took long, greedy gulps of the cold March air. It was well past midnight and with the first day of classes starting tomorrow, he knew what he needed to do.

Before he could open the door to the hallway, he heard a slight thump outside. With the window open, he knew all too well that it'd been the sound of someone jumping onto his balcony.

Instantly, he rolled out of bed, pulling all the carbon in the air around himself. It wasn't much— see, it *had* all been in his head— but it would be enough should they try to grab him. He breathed out, forcing more into the air, ignoring the way his growing sense of the room made his hands shake. It was odd, the way he could sense the gas, the way he could *feel* the shape of a space through it. The extra supply he'd just channeled butted up against the door, the sensation of glass and metal as real as if he'd brushed it with his own fingers. More intense, even.

Slowly, careful not to make a sound, he crept forward, toward the table at the end of his bed where he'd left his ignition rings. It was too stupid, he'd told himself, to sleep with them on, such a risk of setting himself on fire if they'd accidentally sparked and set his sheets ablaze. Still, a tiny part of his brain that was stuck deep in a tunnel had whispered that he should do it anyway.

The room flickered out of his awareness, and even though that'd been all he wanted mere minutes before, he frowned. He needed that carbon, needed that poison so he could fight his way out, but it was depleting rapidly, far too quickly for it to just be from the window. It was almost like there was a fire outside, greedily consuming it from the air—

He stormed over to the door and wrenched it open, causing Kirin to fall backward into his room.

Kirin looked guilty as he lay on the floor, his golden hair splayed around his head like a halo, made even more enchanting by the way it seemed to capture the wan moonlight. Or starlight was probably more apt, given the way it glimmered. His eyes were slightly red at the corner, a sure sign he was tired, and his mouth had fallen open into a small "o" at being caught.

"What the fuck are you doing?" It took Ifrit's brain a minute to remember how to form words.

"...leaving you alone?" Kirin didn't move off the floor, eyes roaming Ifrit's face to see if he was angry. Ifrit hated how he could see Kirin realizing he hadn't been asleep, hated the way those dark eyes seemed to see everything all the time. "But I was too anxious; I couldn't sleep."

Maybe Ifrit should've been angry, should've been annoyed that Kirin thought he wouldn't be okay after just a few hours apart. But Ifrit was far too distracted by realizing that Kirin was wearing one of *his* shirts.

It shouldn't have been surprising, since Ifrit had ~~happily~~ lent it to him just a week or so before. Kirin was trying to get over his fear of their friends seeing his scars, starting with changing out the ridiculous tank tops he always wore. However, since Ifrit hadn't wanted to leave campus, Kirin hadn't either. And now Ifrit had to deal with Kirin wearing *his* clothes— which barely brushed the hem of Kirin's shorts— when they were truly alone for the first time since getting back.

Ifrit yanked him to his feet and pulled him inside, closing the door with perhaps more force than was necessary. He just hoped his face wasn't as red as it felt.

"Do you want me to go?" Kirin's voice was gentle, non-judgmental. He didn't even step farther into the room, waiting patiently for Ifrit to tell him what to do. Fuck.

"...no."

"Okay." Kirin smiled one of his blinding smiles, and then, for some reason, started heading for the door.

"I just said you could stay, dumbass." Ifrit was suddenly drowsy, Kirin's presence erasing his headache at once.

"I was just gonna get my—"

"Don't bother." Ifrit *knew* his face was red now. "We've been sleeping in the same bed for a month now."

An emotion flickered across Kirin's face faster than Ifrit could gauge it before fading back into his usual pleasant expression. Ifrit only hoped that his face was giving away just as little, that Kirin couldn't tell how hard his heart was pounding, how pathetically hopeful he was. The silence stretched between them, and try as he might not to, Ifrit read a thousand different things into that pause.

"Okay," Kirin agreed, his eyes never leaving Ifrit's face, "I'll stay."

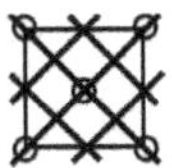

They *had* been sleeping in the same bed, but Ifrit's was much smaller than the large pile of pillows in the common area. There was still enough space that they didn't touch— East Tech provided much roomier accommodations than most colleges— and Ifrit found himself wishing they were in a shitty twin instead.

Kirin wasn't any farther away than he'd been all the past nights, closer still than when he'd frequently sleep on Ifrit's floor. And yet he still felt too far away, like the thin strip of mattress between them was a whole sea that got wider with each passing second. A chasm of things that Ifrit hadn't dared ask about, had been afraid that he'd dreamed carving a line in the sand. The feeling that Kirin was both there and so far away briefly got lodged in his chest and his breath hitched.

Maybe that was why Kirin rolled over and opened his eyes, or maybe it was the uncanny way he seemed to know everything that Ifrit was thinking. His usual open expression eased some of the tightness in Ifrit's chest, and he found himself wishing, not for the first time, that he could bottle that calm and bring it with him forever.

"Do you want to talk?" He always made the invite sound like just that, something that could be turned down without judgment, without anger. There was never any pressure to be *anything* from him. Just *being* was enough, however unpleasant that might be.

"Don't fucking know what I'd say." Ifrit knew that was a lie, and hated even more that he'd turned away to look at the ceiling so he couldn't tell if Kirin knew too. Maybe it was the way he'd moved, or maybe Kirin had shifted closer without him knowing, but his shoulder was brushing ever so slightly against Kirin's chest. The tiny amount of contact steadied him, and he let his eyes close for a moment, thinking that this would be enough. Could be enough.

"I didn't plan on sitting outside, you know." Kirin rarely managed to confess anything when Ifrit was looking him in the eye, and this time was no different. If Ifrit hadn't closed his eyes, they likely would've sat there in silence. "But I couldn't stop thinking about you in here alone and having a nightmare and not wanting to come get someone since you'd told everyone to leave and so I just... wanted to be there. In case you needed someone."

"You don't have to fucking apologize dumbass. You were right." Ifrit pressed the heels of his palms to his eyes, for *once* the gesture being in embarrassment and not because his head ached. The only time he didn't have a headache was when Kirin was around, metabolizing the toxic air that Ifrit created, and Ifrit would never fail to appreciate it. Just another reason Kirin was fucking perfect.

"I wasn't apologizing." There was an undercurrent to Kirin's voice that he didn't recognize and opened his eyes. They locked gazes and Ifrit lost his breath *again*. "I was just letting you know that I'm here for you. Always."

"Good." His brain managed to give him a single word, and apparently it was the right one, since Kirin relaxed fully. One of his legs nudged Ifrit's and Ifrit tried not to react as his heart nearly stuttered. It wasn't like they didn't touch all the time, but now, somehow it felt different. More... intimate.

Maybe it was the way Kirin had been looking at him lately. Before... everything happened there had been some uncertainty in his gaze, some worry, but it was gone now. Now Kirin watched him unabashedly, with... well, if Ifrit had to put a name to it, he would say with longing.

He was terrified to let himself believe it.

"Why weren't you asleep?" Kirin finally came out and asked.

Ifrit ignored him for a minute, instead deciding to study his nails carefully, like there might be a secret hidden in them. Unfortunately, if there was, it was hidden beneath the cracking layer of black nail polish Clidna had painted on a few days before.

Kirin took his hand.

"Hey, talk to me." The *softness* of his voice ran through Ifrit like a knife, the genuine care twisting it in deeper. "I... I don't know how to help if you don't tell me what's wrong."

The fear, that familiar powerlessness, snapped Ifrit back to reality. Kirin's eyes were full of sadness, and it was his fault.

"You are helping. By being here." He wasn't lying, not even a little bit. This was what he needed, all of it. This was enough.

That was a lie, wasn't it? He wanted more.

Kirin was still watching him, still holding his hand so he couldn't use it to hide. Ifrit wished that he wasn't so expressive, that maybe Pressure should've taught him how to *hide* his emotions as well as wear them, but a quiet, secret part of him was glad that Kirin could see right through.

"...it feels like I can't breathe." He gave in under the weight of those eyes.

"When you're going to sleep?"

"Whenever I'm alone." He would've turned away if Kirin wasn't holding him in place forcibly with a single hand. A single gentle touch.

"I was surprised you let us hang onto you for so long."

"Yeah, well, at least you fucking idiots are good for something." He couldn't even muster any heat to his words. Odd how being around Kirin could do that to him.

"I'm here." If it hadn't been exactly what Ifrit needed to hear, he would've scoffed at Kirin for pointing out the obvious. "For however long you need, I'll be right here."

Instead, he just grumbled.

"You fucking better be."

Irritatingly, Kirin smiled at that. Ifrit hated that smile (he didn't).

To hide how much he didn't dislike it, Ifrit started to play with Kirin's fingers. He was always surprised by how rough they were, considering Kirin always moved with such strange grace, like he were a dancer instead of a bulldozer. They were a laborer's hands, calloused in different places than Ifrit's own.

"What did you do, before this?" Ifrit suddenly found himself asking. They weren't supposed to discuss anything about their lives before, but what did it matter now, when Kirin knew everything about Ifrit and Ifrit knew nothing about him?

"Lots of things. But I worked on a farm, mostly, and volunteered with the fire department when they needed it."

That was so fucking like him it was almost laughable.

"Should've known you were from the middle of fucking nowhere."

"You saw me on my first day out in the city, figured that would've given it away." He was quiet for a moment. "Guess you grew up here, then."

"We couldn't find you." The words tumbled out before Ifrit could think if it was a good idea to share. Before he could consider if Kirin wanted to think about when his father had died at all. "I asked Pressure to look for you, but they said you'd already been checked out of the hospital and your family asked the record to be sealed."

Whatever response Kirin had expected, it wasn't that. The surprise on his face was apparent, and when it melted into happiness, he almost seemed to glow.

"You looked for me?"

"You saved my life, dumbass. Of course I did." He couldn't stop himself from moving a little closer. "I never thanked you for that."

"It was hardly saving your life. I was a glorified jack post."

Ifrit closed the gap between them by smashing their foreheads together. Kirin had the fucking audacity to use his mien to not move from the impact, his eyes turning opalescent as he did. It didn't matter how many times Ifrit saw it, he never stopped thinking it was beautiful.

"You stopped a building from crashing down on my head. That's firstly, fucking impressive, and secondly, definitely saving my life."

"I wish I'd stayed awake though." Kirin didn't back away, their noses brushing slightly as he spoke. Ifrit's brain was stuck on the fact that he *didn't move away*. "Maybe if I'd talked to you then we could've... I don't know, kept in touch? Not that my mom would've wanted me to, but I would've tried to find a way."

"I would've beat your ass for talking shit about yourself before you could go and grow a whole ass complex over it."

Kirin laughed at that, and as he did, he wrapped Ifrit in his arms.

Ifrit... Ifrit *melted.*

It wasn't like Kirin didn't hug him, and he was always touching him— an arm around his shoulder, pulling him by the hand— but this was different with no people crowded around, with the moonlight streaming in the window and the pair of them so, so close. And it wasn't like *this* where Kirin was laughing again, and for the first time in months he didn't feel quite so numb inside, where the loss of Pressure was a dull ache instead of a sharp wound, and then suddenly Ifrit was crying.

Kirin didn't let go.

"That's it," he murmured, "let it out."

Ifrit didn't know why he was crying, whether it was happiness or sadness or just *relief*, but he did cry for long enough that Kirin's shirt was damp and his throat felt dry. Kirin was stroking his hair gently, kindly ignoring how much of a wreck Ifrit was, wrapping around him like a shield and creating a tiny space that was just for them.

"Better?" Kirin wiped the remaining tears off Ifrit's face as he looked up, absently running a finger along Ifrit's jaw once the tears were gone. He could've started crying all over again from how *nice* it felt, how *right* it felt.

"Mm."

"You haven't cried once since the funeral." Again, not an ounce of judgment.

"Haven't felt like crying."

"Ifrit, they're your friends; they're not going to be upset with you for grieving."

"It's not that." He struggled to find the words, not because he didn't know what he meant, but because he was ashamed. "When everyone's around... it's hard to even think about it. About her. I've never had friends like that before."

He took a breath.

"Like *this*. Like when we're together there's only here and now and everything's okay."

Kirin, as always, remained quiet, letting him finish his thought. Right now, Ifrit would've loved for him to say something, anything.

"It's just so fucking weird. Everything else feels... perfect. I have friends— though I'll fucking kill you if you tell them I said that— and I have... you."

Kirin didn't react at all, except, maybe, almost imperceptibly, tightening his grip.

"Sometimes I'll... forget that it happened at all. That when we go to class tomorrow, she'll be there waiting, ready to piss me off in a way that no one else'll notice just because she thinks it's funny. She'll joke saying I should bring you home one of these days and I'll ignore her and come back here." The wave of grief swept over him, but he swallowed it down. "And I *thought* it was fine, that the stupid fucking therapy she made me go to for years was actually good for something and I could deal with it, but then you weren't around to make my stupid fucking mien harmless, and I was back in that room and I was choking and—"

He was silenced by Kirin tilting his chin up and pressing their foreheads together.

"Breathe."

Ifrit breathed.

"Keep going."

"...and it feels awful because most days I'm more upset about that than about losing her." Ifrit finished in a whisper. He knew that it was normal. Every therapist over the years had told him it was. Every therapist had said that it was normal that he, as a child, would've been more upset about his own kidnapping and imprisonment than the hundreds of thousands of people that'd died because of him, that it was human. It stood to reason then, that his second kidnapping and imprisonment would be more traumatizing than his mother's murder. Even then, and especially now, Ifrit was certain of one thing. Being human sucked ass.

"I'm not going to tell you that it's normal, or that you shouldn't feel bad because I know you know that. And it won't stop you from feeling that way. But I will tell you that she of all people would've understood and would've slapped you upside the head for feeling guilty about it." Kirin's hand had moved off Ifrit's chin and was instead carding through his hair. "It's just how trauma works. The physical thing is easier to process than the emotional, so you're stuck on it. But you're not alone."

"Mm."

"And it just takes time. You need to feel safe again."

"Kind of hard to when *I'm* the fucking danger to be afraid of."

Kirin let out a hiss of breath, his arms tensing involuntarily, pulling Ifrit closer. Pressed chest to chest, Ifrit could feel how rapid Kirin's pulse was.

"Don't talk about yourself like that." Kirin's voice sounded raw, his hands gentle though he was holding on so tightly. "Don't you dare say that."

"But it's true, isn't it?" The thought had been lurking at the edges of his brain, and finally saying it felt sour. "I fucking destroyed a city *twice* and both times I didn't have to do a fucking thing but *exist*."

"So what, you think you should be dead?"

Ifrit hesitated.

It was the wrong thing to do.

Kirin took the silence as confirmation, and suddenly Ifrit was on his back, Kirin kneeling over him, pulling him up by his chin.

"Don't you *ever* think this world would be better without you." Kirin's eyes were shining, his face set in a mask of desperation. Ifrit desperately wanted to erase the lines of misery that were carved around his eyes and bring back the laughter of just a few minutes before— why, *why* did he always ruin this?— but it was too late. "Do you hear me? My life would be so much worse if you weren't here."

"Your dad would still be alive." He didn't mean to throw it in Kirin's face, the words coming from a dark part of his heart that he thought he'd long since buried. He could tell they'd found their mark from the way Kirin dropped his hand in shock. "Pressure would still be alive. Aether wouldn't even exist—"

Kirin abruptly let go of his chin and walked away.

He didn't go far, just a few steps toward the door, but it was enough to make the space feel cold. If Ifrit had thought the strip of mattress between them had felt far, this was an infinite void of space between them. Already Ifrit felt like the air was heavy around him, like his next breath would be his last. How pathetic was he? Of course he fucked it up, of course he would ruin the only good thing left in his life, of course—

A strangled sound tore him out of his self-pity spiral, and he was on his feet before he knew he had moved. Kirin was facing away from him, his hand over his mouth, his shoulders shaking as he bit back on a sob.

"I'm sorry, I didn't mean—"

"*Stop* apologizing." Kirin turned back to face him with clouded eyes, pushing a hand through his hair as if he didn't know what else to do. "I just hate that you sound like me."

Ifrit didn't know what to say.

"I'm not good at this. You always knew what to do, and I just don't know how to be that for you." Kirin's hand stopped just short of touching Ifrit's face again, so Ifrit moved closer until the palm rested against his cheek. "You deserve so much better than what you've gotten, and it hurts so bad to hear you blame yourself. You were a *victim*. You did everything in your power to stop it, both times, nearly killing yourself *both times*, and if you're guilty then I am too because I *killed people to save you*."

Kirin pressed their foreheads together.

"Because I believe you are worth the world." Kirin spoke so softly, but Ifrit felt like even if his hearing aids had been turned off, he would've heard, just because he knew how every word coming out of that mouth sounded. Because he'd imagined that voice saying a million terrible corny phrases just like it before. "So please don't think I'm better without you."

"Okay." The word took too much effort to say. But how could he not believe it when Kirin looked at him like that?

"Promise?" Kirin was so close that his hair created a curtain around their faces, making a small space that was just the two of them, cut off from the rest of the world. It'd grown back so quickly, like it'd never been cut in the first place. Long enough that standing there, heads pressed together like this, reminded Ifrit of a dark tunnel, of Kirin's tears on his face, and of something else he wasn't sure had truly happened.

"Promise?" Kirin asked again, his eyes anxiously searching Ifrit's.

"I fucking promise, okay?"

Kirin let out a shaky breath, the slight movement knocking their noses together. For a moment, just a moment, Ifrit's heart lurched as he thought Kirin was going to kiss him. But, just as he knew Kirin would, he pulled back, looking mollified. Because when he said things like that, he meant them, but not... not the way Ifrit wanted him to. Not the way that made Ifrit remember, when he'd been barely half alive, his best friend kissing him.

He turned away before he did something he'd regret, getting back into bed without glancing at Kirin. He knew he'd imagined it, he had to have. Otherwise, Kirin would've brought it up, would've said something, *anything*, in the months since. Maybe Ifrit himself, in his delirium, had kissed Kirin and he was just being polite by not bringing it up. More likely it had been just a product of his fevered brain, considering he was too much of a coward to even *ask* Kirin if it'd been real.

He risked a glance at Kirin to see if maybe *he* seemed upset that nothing more had happened, but Kirin was turned away, heading for the door.

"Where are you going?" Ifrit fought to keep the fear out of his voice, worried that he'd been too obvious, that Kirin had gotten uncomfortable and was going back to his room, leaving Ifrit alone in the dark.

"I'm just going to grab a different shirt, okay? This one's wet and I've already stolen enough of yours." Shit, he'd cried that much?

"You don't sleep with a shirt on half the time anyways, just fucking take it off." He hadn't *meant* anything else by it, but hearing his own words made him flush.

"I don't have my scars wrapped today; I don't want to cut you."

"You won't."

"I move around a lot in my sleep, there's a good chance I will." Kirin chose just then to take off the shirt in question; Ifrit *tried* to be polite and look away, but failed. Kirin's scars glittered in the low light as he delicately hung it on a chair to dry.

"You can't." Ifrit had to get up and grab Kirin's shoulder to stop him from leaving. If he was lying to himself, he was so determined because he enjoyed the idea of Kirin shirtless next to him. If he was truthful, it was because he was scared that if Kirin left now, he wouldn't be coming back.

"You remember last time—"

Ifrit slashed his hand across the scar that curled over Kirin's collarbone.

Kirin immediately grabbed at his palm, already trying to apply pressure to a wound that wasn't there. His eyes furrowed in confusion as he realized.

"But before?"

"You haven't fucking wondered how I never seem to get cut very much, do you?" With Kirin briefly distracted, Ifrit was able to subtly lead him further into the room. "The doctors always thought it was because I'm a fucking era two mien-user or whatever."

"Era two?"

"The theory we learned about in History of Heroics?" Kirin stared at him blankly. "For fuck's sake, you got a perfect score on that exam!"

"I probably guessed."

"It was short answer."

"Why do you remember that?"

"Because you came and showed it to me? You were fucking—" Ifrit stopped himself before he said cute "—excited that you'd done so well."

Kirin was looking at him with a stupid smile.

"Stop making that face."

"Era two though?"

"The theory of mien evolution. That we'll start seeing fewer and fewer people who get hurt by their own abilities. Like Wings, right? He said that it hurts if he doesn't release his mien every so often, but you don't have that issue. Well, for me, I have way thicker and tougher skin than most people. And a hard fucking head."

"I can believe that." The corner of Kirin's mouth was tilting up.

"Shut up."

"How did I cut you before, then?"

"My fingertips. They're the only place it's not like that."

Ifrit was suddenly very pleased at his decision to start this conversation as Kirin sat down on the bed and started inspecting his hands.

"I thought they were softer." Kirin had his head down and was running this thumb from the tip of Ifrit's pointer finger down to the base. The touch was so gentle it was hard to notice, until Kirin crystalized his finger on the way back up. The sharp edge traced a very clear path, until it hit the final knuckle and pricked the skin. Kirin turned his hand back to flesh to press against the tiny cut. "I've cut you before, though. And not just your hands."

"If you apply enough force, yeah, you will. But just brushing against me isn't going to do shit."

Sometimes Ifrit could pretend he wasn't desperately in love

with his best friend. But when Kirin gave him that wide-eyed look of wonder all his defenses were gone.

Anything that might have remained was obliterated when immediately following such a look he was crushed into a hug.

Ifrit was pulled so far off balance that they toppled onto the bed, one of Kirin's hands in his hair. Pressed together so tightly, Ifrit could feel Kirin's heartbeat in his own chest, the warmth of Kirin's breath on his ear. The worst of Kirin's scarring was on his back, but the one that curled over his shoulder jabbed at Ifrit's shirt, irritating but not threatening.

"You never cease to amaze me."

It was good that Kirin couldn't see his face, because Ifrit was surely glowing from the praise. How he managed to find all the things that Ifrit was ashamed of, was self-conscious of, and adored them, Ifrit would never know.

"Can you... can you put your arms around my neck?" Kirin very rarely asked for anything, and when it was already something Ifrit was inclined to do, he wasn't about to say *no*. They'd fallen backward onto the bed, but Kirin sat up very quickly, knocking Ifrit into his lap. Ifrit didn't hesitate for a moment, pulling Kirin's face into the crook of his neck.

He'd held Kirin like this once before, but he'd been worried that the scars were too raw a subject to dare touch them. Now he wrapped his arms around Kirin's shoulders, letting his bare forearms scrape across the jagged edges. He didn't miss the shaky exhale, didn't miss the way that every muscle tensed and then relaxed, the tremble in Kirin's hands. How long had it been since someone touched him so freely? How long had it been since he'd been held by someone without fear of hurting them?

"...your arms are okay?" Kirin's voice was muffled from where his lips were pressed against skin. Ifrit barely resisted a shiver from the sensation of Kirin's *lips* against his *throat*.

"I fucking said they would be." Ifrit cleared his throat and shifted so they were both lying down. Kirin moved without complaint, pliant in Ifrit's hands. "It's actually... kind of nice, or whatever."

"Hm?" Kirin's voice had gotten sleepy, his fears for the moment forgotten. Ifrit was sure he'd be dropping off any minute now.

"Like I said. Thick skin. Means I don't feel as much as other people."

"So?"

"Since it's super fucking sharp I can feel it easier. Less dull." Ifrit cleared his throat again. "It's nice."

"Ohhh." It was less a word and more an exhale. Kirin absolutely better fall asleep soon because Ifrit's heart couldn't take much more of this. "We should do this more, then."

"Less fucking crying next time." Ifrit felt himself starting to get drowsy too, the hateful voices in his head suppressed by Kirin's calming presence, and the distraction of Kirin's silken hair. How was it so shiny *and* so smooth? It wasn't fair.

"I don't mind if you cry." The words were being stretched out long now, slurring into one another. "I like... all of you."

With that, Kirin fell asleep. Well, not quite. Ifrit's brain was having trouble processing what might have happened in between, unsure if it was an accident or if he'd just imagined it again, the night having contained so many turns he likely had whiplash. Because *if* his stupid skin wasn't so thick, maybe he could've been certain that Kirin had placed a kiss on his throat.

The thought should've taken away any drowsiness, should've jolted him awake into another round of questions, of doubts. Just ten minutes before he probably would've been panicking, feeling like he didn't deserve it. But as Kirin curled around him, Ifrit couldn't focus on anything other than how happy it made him.

Yeah, he was fucked.

2

Semester Start

KIRIN AWOKE TO IFRIT'S hair in his face.

It was a nice change of pace from his new normal daily routine of jerking awake and frantically looking around, his heartbeat only settling once he saw Ifrit dozing an arm's length away. Kirin breathed in, the now familiar scent of Ifrit's shampoo filling his lungs, the quiet reassurance of Ifrit's breathing rhythmic against Kirin's throat. They were together, they were safe.

The peace of the moment was threatened by Ifrit's (first) alarm, and Kirin was suddenly caught in a conundrum. Ifrit was still sleeping— his head resting on Kirin's arm, body fitted like a puzzle piece around Kirin's— and his phone was on the other side of the bed. Kirin moved gingerly, gently, trying to reach the phone without waking Ifrit, swatting at it until silence took over once again. Kirin breathed a sigh of relief as he looked around, noting that the sun had just barely begun to creep over the horizon. They had hours yet until their first class of second year started; they should at least try to be well-rested for it.

Ifrit's eyes shot open as the mission alarm started blaring from both of their phones.

Kirin had lurched to grab the offending objects, leaving their faces centimeters apart.

"Good morning." Anything more meaningful had fled from Kirin's head the moment those red eyes focused on him. He wasn't sure why he was whispering, especially when it made it harder for Ifrit to understand him, but his voice didn't want to get any louder. "I think we need to run."

Ifrit didn't respond, his brain still foggy from sleep as he studied Kirin's face. Kirin was suddenly warm all over, his heartrate skyrocketing though, somehow, he knew it wasn't from fear. It'd been happening more often recently, or maybe he was just noticing it more with all the idle time they had on their hands. A brush of a shoulder, a too-keen gaze and Kirin could feel his pulse thundering in his ears. Maybe he needed to check in with the school physician.

"Are you going to fucking get up?" Ifrit's mouth twitched into a smile and Kirin felt even the tips of his ears go red. "Your breath smells terrible."

"Yeah, sorry!" He practically threw himself backward, earning a small chuckle from Ifrit.

"Dumbass." Ifrit was still smiling to himself as he got up, putting on his ignition rings. Kirin didn't look away as he pulled the tank top he'd slept in over his head, shockingly few scars dotting his back. There were faded lines across his shoulders, speckled puncture marks along his left side, but Ifrit's back—despite him being the more vulnerable of the pair of them—was far less marked than Kirin's own. It disappeared seconds later, Ifrit pulling on a long-sleeved shirt for their run through the frigid morning air. The halo around his head flared into existence a moment later, the warmth of the fire finally breaching Kirin's mental fog. Kirin got up slowly, thoughts muddled, but hope flickering in his chest as the despondent Ifrit from the night before failed to resurface. Ifrit's good mood only seemed to grow as he looked over their mission alert.

"We're going on a mission with Majesty's assholes." The fire around his head sparked, his eyes flashing with excitement.

"It's finally time we show them up, then?" Kirin found a matching grin unfurling on his own face, feeling like maybe things could go back to normal.

But the way his heart flipped in his chest when Ifrit gave him a cocky grin promised that some things couldn't be put back once they started creeping out into the open.

"We're going to make them look *pathetic.*"

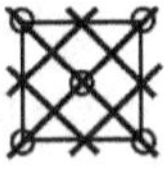

One of the perks of entering their second year was that each class had their own locker room now. Instead of changing awkwardly on the jet, they'd convene on the top floor of the Disaster Simulator to put on their costumes and receive the mission briefing. The schedules they'd received the day before had left the professor for Mien Training conspicuously blank, so this would be the first time they'd find out who was to be Pressure's replacement.

The mood as they walked was odd, a mixture of dread and anticipation, fear and excitement. Ifrit had put it well; there was a part of Kirin that had expected them to walk into the room and find Pressure waiting impatiently, complaining about the hour. But when Goldhorn opened the door, hand hesitating a moment on the handle, there was a collective despondency as they found the room empty.

The minutes ticked by in unbearable silence, the anxiety growing the longer a professor— any professor— failed to appear. A holo screen near the door began blinking, instructing them to prepare to head up to the jet pad and yet still no instructor materialized.

"Could they just not find anyone?" Antaeus broke the silence, his curly hair unruly from their unceremonious awakening.

"I wouldn't be surprised given..." Dulu shot a guilty glance toward Ifrit. "Given what happened."

Ifrit's shoulders bristled, but before he could say anything at all, Shifter dropped out of the ceiling.

"If you wanted to make a grand entrance, maybe *don't* make it an alarming one." Phoenix's voice was tired, lacking some of his usual energy, though he was right. The shock appearance had sent the whole class to their feet, Goldhorn now having to unwrap Shifter from the thicket they'd erupted into existence. It was lucky they had reacted first, since Kirin could taste the thickness of carbon pouring off Ifrit, whose breathing was alarmingly shallow.

"If I could've, I would've, but quite frankly the school would rather I wasn't here at all." Shifter brushed off the last few twigs clinging to him, though he didn't look concerned at the attack. Even if Phoenix was unwilling to heal him, he could reknit his own organs so Kirin supposed there never was any reason to worry.

"Then why the fuck are you?" Ifrit practically bit the words out, and Kirin couldn't blame him. Shifter had been frustratingly elusive in the past few weeks, insisting that they stay out of the Hero Coalition's work until the school year was done. He was probably right, with the increasingly fine line they walked of the good graces of the school and Hero Council at large, but it didn't make it easier.

Shifter had enough sense to look contrite.

"They've kept your new teacher's identity locked up tight—" here a pointed glance at Yantra, undoubtedly because Shifter knew she'd told them the same after being thwarted by the school's increased cyber security in her quest to find out— "and even I haven't been able to discover it. Supposedly they're off island and will be rendezvousing with you after the mission."

"You know nothing useful, then." Surprisingly, it was Clidna who spoke up, her red hair pulled back tightly and matching the orange panels on her costume. Shifter didn't look offended.

"The mission for today is a simple raid on a known mien-user encampment in a dead zone. Keep your guards up; there is some weak intel that Aether has interfaced with them, though none should still be present." Shifter's eyes flickered to Ifrit for only the faintest moment before his face blurred, hiding his expression. It was rare he let them see his mien in action; his tiredness wasn't feigned, then.

"We're going into a dead zone?" Yantra looked worried.

"There will be minimal surveillance since tech won't work, but don't mistake that for nobody watching." Shifter pressed his lips together. "These sorts of missions are commonplace, and they aren't enjoyable. Yet you are expected to see them through."

"Great," Naddāha grumbled under her breath. "Sounds promising."

"Don't react. That's what they'll be looking for." Shifter hesitated again. "You have power by being popular. There will be reporters at the end of the mission, and they'll want to hear what the new heroes think, what you've seen, what horrible things happened where cameras couldn't catch them. For now, that's how you help the Coalition. Tell the public what heroes are expected to do, tell them what crimes are determined worthy of dozens of heroes pouring in."

"You refuse to tell us what you're working on, and you still want our help?" Clidna scoffed. "And just for publicity?"

"While East Tech has many things wrong, the one that they are unfortunately right about is that safety comes not at the hands of the few but the will of the many. If we want to change things, we *need* public support." The previous trace of regret was gone from Shifter's face entirely. He looked painfully serious, and decades older. "The gears of the world move slowly, and though she didn't seem like it, Pressure had far more patience for this type of politicking than I ever will."

Kirin's hand had found Ifrit's, Kirin needing the stability in this shifting air.

"She wanted to wait to bring you all into the fold, wanted to let you focus on being young and learning, and she was right to want you to have that. You deserve it. It's not a matter of trust or of competence but simply that you *should not have to* worry about this. But I'm not her, and I cannot do this without someone at the head of it, someone to be the face of it."

Now it wasn't only Shifter looking at Ifrit, the whole class had turned to stare at the pair of them. Yet when Kirin looked, Ifrit was staring right back at him.

"I understand why you don't want to, I understand that I have made it hard to, but for now, I'm asking you all to trust me." For the first time, Shifter let his mien fall away completely. The bags under his eyes faded, the habitual stubble around his face disappeared, and instead of looking haggard, he looked scared. A man adrift in the world with far too few people to trust. He looked younger, maybe even younger than Pressure's scant thirty-five, too young to be herding eighteen barely adults through a minefield.

"Fine." With the single word from Ifrit, Shifter looked like a weight had been lifted off his shoulders. "But don't fucking expect too much."

"Why shouldn't I?" Here Shifter adopted a sly look. "After all, you are the Institute's top-rated class."

"Wait, really?" Adlivun looked startled.

"By a considerable margin."

There was a beat of silence before Phoenix started laughing. "Oh, I'm *so* going to rub that in."

"Needless to say, you didn't hear that from me." Shifter spoke tonelessly, loud enough to be heard over the commotion that had broken out. "And with only Majesty overseeing you out there today, I'm sure I don't need to remind you that rankings don't mean anything just yet."

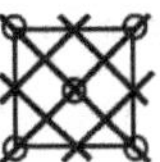

As they headed up to the roof, Kirin realized he didn't know why their ranking mattered at *all*.

Despite having been at the school for a full year now, Kirin felt like he barely knew anything about how their actual jobs would work once they graduated, what the paperwork Pressure had constantly been surrounded with was actually *for*. He knew that the International Hero Council has some power, but power over *what* he didn't know.

"The rankings are just important for post-grad shit." Ifrit answered the question just as Kirin opened his mouth, rolling his eyes as some of the others in the class crowded in to listen. "Before we graduate, they have us fill out a fuckton of paperwork, including what jurisdictions we want. The deal the Council has with the UN means they have to spread out new heroes, so only a few people can be assigned at each location. The reward for being a good little student is just to have more say in where you're stuck for the first five fucking years after you leave."

"How in the hells did we get to be ranked first, then?" Antaeus was practically bouncing, the linework on his suit blurring. His hair had gotten long, curls flopping into his eyes, but no one had made him fix it yet. "Shocked they haven't found a way to rig that, too."

"They have, it just worked against them this time." Adlivun

had managed to get her costume changed after the repeated replacements made it impractical. Instead of white she was now dressed in dark gray, her hair pulled up into a braided bun, leaving the scar across her throat plainly visible. "The first semester we're allowed to go on missions, it's just a revolving schedule of every squad as calls come in. The second, local heroes are allowed to request specific squads. The more missions your squad is chosen to go on, the higher your ranking. Since half the trainees are the children of active heroes, their parents just request them every time. But, since they were all too worried about their kids dying, they were stuck with us."

"It's nice to know that we got *something* out of being used as sacrificial fucking pawns." Kirin fought to keep a straight face, realizing just how much Ifrit was rubbing off on Clidna.

"It's really good if you want to get one of the roving positions, like what..." Lilin trailed off, dark eyes flickering to Ifrit. They were the only part of her face visible as her dark blue suit covered her chin in one seamless piece.

"You guys can fucking say her name. I do remember she's dead whether you bring it up or not." Ifrit *was* trying to be reassuring, but Kirin suspected he might be the only one to know that.

"Ah, right." Lilin nervously tucked a dark curl behind her ear. "Well, um, yeah, Force had one of the mobile positions, and from what I understand, they're the hardest spots to get, usually only two or three open each year."

"Aw, you're getting better at being sneaky, proud of you." Yantra filled the empty space hurriedly. "Though I can be more specific than that and say only two spots will be available at the end of this year."

All eyes gravitated back to Ifrit. Then immediately to Kirin.

"Where *are* you thinking of going after school, Kirin?" Ness appeared at his elbow. Her costume hadn't changed at all, or maybe it had. It was all dark and dappled, and combined with her blurry appearance, he could hardly see her at all.

"After? I mean, I hadn't really thought about it much..." Kirin found his eyes drawn to Ifrit, who was staring at him rather intently. "I guess—"

The door at the top of the stairs burst open.

"Hurry up. We are not going to be late because you were *chatting*." Majesty was there, her bright blue hair shining in the sunlight. It should've looked joyful, but combined with Majesty's expression, all Kirin could think of was ice. Her own class was emerging from the second stairwell on the other side of the building, lining up lazily in front of the still-sealed jet.

"You just got here, don't pretend like we were taking fucking forever." Ifrit had his arms crossed, any vestiges of a good mood obliterated by Majesty's presence. He planted himself just inside the doorway, ready to stay there indefinitely if it'd piss her off.

"But we should get on with it, yeah?" Kirin prodded gently, moving Ifrit to the side just enough that the rest of their class could get through. Majesty and Ifrit were still locked in a glaring match, neither noticing that the roof had largely cleared off.

"You're right." Ifrit took a breath and looked away, though the crease between his eyes stayed. "We wouldn't want to be late, now would we *Majesty*?"

Kirin was instantly sent back a year in time, the way that Ifrit said her name so reminiscent of the way Pressure had the first day in the armory. Majesty recoiled as if she'd been slapped, her eyes widening in the same way they had when her own child had been afraid of her.

Ifrit didn't notice, already on his way to the jet. Kirin hurried after him, and while Ifrit didn't look back, Kirin did. And he was surprised to see Majesty still standing there, looking at Ifrit's retreating back, some kind of horrified understanding on her face. When her eyes met Kirin's, they still bore that vulnerability, a hurt that made her look ten years younger.

In that moment, seeing Majesty standing there in the bright sunlight, Kirin realized something too.

Majesty's hair was the same exact color that Force's costume had been.

3

First Assignment

THEY LANDED ON THE outskirts of an unfamiliar city.

The ride had been short, which was fortunate given the oppressive atmosphere. Majesty's assholes sneered, speaking in voices loud enough to carry with what they surely thought were clever jabs that had all the intelligence of a particularly dull rock. Ifrit turned off his hearing aids once it became apparent his own classmates weren't in a talking mood, wrapped up in their own thoughts. This was the first time they'd set foot on a jet after coming back from Satol. The first time they'd left without Pressure.

When the gate opened to let them out, the outside wasn't much better. The air was thick with moisture, so heavy it almost felt like cotton pressing on Ifrit's face. His breath hitched in his chest, the lurking sensation of choking so close in memory, but then Kirin's hand was in his and with one simple squeeze, Ifrit's lungs stopped tightening. Then they were out in the open and Kirin was forced to let go.

A small group of heroes were waiting at the foot of the ramp, and one of them raised a hand to wave at their class, specifically. He seemed vaguely familiar to Ifrit, though he didn't know why. The man was dressed in a particularly offensive shade of bright yellow, and it was the color that reminded Ifrit. That was Mesmer, one of the heroes from Satol. One of the most outspoken heroes praising Pressure— and the whole class— for protecting the city.

Great. They really wanted to make sure Ifrit didn't forget.

Majesty had gotten off first, striding away to greet the heroes and waving impatiently at the students to group up behind her, her class already lining up in ranks. Pressure's class, on the other hand, stood loosely grouped together, unsure of what to do. On their missions, they'd been the one interfacing with the locals, not Pressure. It wasn't an official rule of her censure, but one she opted into willingly, wanting her students to be prepared for when they were on their own.

Ifrit still didn't feel prepared enough.

He was shaken out of his thoughts when Mesmer broke away from the larger group and strode directly up to Ifrit. He held out a hand, which Ifrit took warily. Only to have his shoulder nearly shaken out of its socket.

"It's good to see you looking well." Mesmer placed his other hand on top of their joined ones. "I was hoping to see you. Your mother was a good woman, and I wanted to let you know that many of us are taking up the mantle she left behind. If you ever need support, you shall have it."

While Ifrit hated his classmates dodging around the topic of Pressure's— his *mother's*— death, he didn't know what to do when a complete stranger confronted it directly. Luckily, by some measure, he was spared the need to respond by Majesty's arrival.

"Show us to the briefing room." Mesmer must have met her before, since he didn't react at all to her bitchy affect. Still, it was always nice to remember she wasn't just like that with *them*, she was just *like that*.

"Certainly. We're still waiting for some other reinforcements, but we can start the students early, if you like." Mesmer stepped back and gestured for her to go ahead, where the rest of the local heroes were already on the move. She did go on, but he stayed back, quietly keeping pace with Ifrit. It was almost... protective.

"Does this mean the Coalition still thinks I'm a target?" Ifrit couldn't decide if he was relieved that someone was actually looking after them or pissed that he was being treated like he was incapable. He settled for a nice middle of the road irritated.

"Not necessarily. But we are just on the edge of the dead zone. You never know who could be hiding in there." Mesmer gave them a knowing look that meant absolutely nothing to Ifrit.

"Right."

Luckily, Tech— *Yantra*, Kirin's voice corrected helpfully in Ifrit's head— was nosy as ever.

"What do you mean by that?" Though she gave Mesmer a smile, she looked nervous.

"Nothing works just past that boundary." Mesmer gestured to a thin chain-link fence that ran parallel to the path they walked. The proximity of it to where they had landed was startling. Ifrit felt that ever present anxiety creeping up the back of his neck, that threat of disaster lurking on the edges. The dead zone looked completely normal inside the fence, the buildings older, true— rundown red brick and dirty glass— but not so different from the ones they walked past now. "No technology, at least. It's harder to tell when the sun's up, but the moment the natural light fades, the difference is stark. The fence is half for show; most people won't stray past that line for any amount of money."

"But it's just that tech doesn't work. Why are people so scared?" Invisibitch— *Ness*, Kirin's voice said, more sternly this time— popped into existence on Mesmer's other side, and Ifrit's mood was buoyed by the way the bearded man fully jumped in fright. Ifrit coughed to cover a laugh, though he noticed Kirin frowning.

"It is less that nothing works, and more than no one can explain *why* nothing works." Mesmer himself looked wholly unconcerned, instead delighted to find an enraptured audience. "When folks live in such brightly lit worlds, the darkness seems scary, even scarier when you don't know *why* it appeared. Lots of people believe the dead zones are growing, though there's no proof of that. You cannot reason with fear. Our whole society hinges on technology, on phones and computers, trains and buses and cars. The very island you live on can only survive with electricity powering the water purifiers, the grow lights for the farms tucked half beneath the streets. They are a living reminder that just a generation ago our whole way of life was destroyed."

He let them sit with that awful thought for just a moment.

"And then there are the people who worry that the very electricity inside our brains will be affected by whatever technological dampening occurs. Worry not, no one has ever been affected by that, it's perfectly safe to go inside."

What a horrible thought to put in the heads of people about to go inside.

"It *is* odd that it knows how to differentiate." Yantra was distracted from her discomfort by the puzzle of it, lost in thought. "Is it because it's so low-level, or is there some device that creates the dead zones and can differentiate organic from inorganic? Dulu, when we're inside, do you think you can..."

Ifrit let her voice fade into the background as they arrived at the briefing room.

It was obvious what it was, since it was decades newer than the surrounding area. Not only that, but there was the quiet hum of electricity coming from this building, the kind that made his hearing aids crackle. The kind that Ifrit only now realized was missing from the other buildings they'd walked past. Inside, the room was covered floor to ceiling in screens, holographic maps being pulled up from tables, groups of heroes standing around and talking in authoritative voices. Ifrit debated turning his hearing aids fully off. He recognized a few faces from events with Pressure, but none that he wanted to talk to.

They were, understandably, among the the last to arrive, so the briefing began just a few minutes after they walked in, leaving them standing along the back wall. Majesty's class was closer to the center of the room, seated and looking bored.

It wasn't a hero who stepped forward to describe the mission plan, but a uniformed police officer. She was standing at the center of the room, which was much like one of their lecture halls if not smaller and rectangular instead of circular. She stood at the bottom of the tiered seats, and when she moved to gesture at the holo map projected above her head, he caught a glimpse of the flag patch on her shoulder. They were somewhere in South Africa, then. He turned his attention to the map, trying to focus on her words instead of the gazes he felt drifting to him from all sides of the room.

The map was both surprisingly detailed and entirely lacking. The old maintenance tunnels beneath the city were mapped in their entirety, color coded for different services, but the buildings were little more than shells. It looked like the only information they had on the buildings was what they could see from the outside, those along the edges more detailed than the ones further inside. The map was perfectly circular, several kilometers in diameter, a blinking red dot in the dead center.

"We've been tracking a loose conglomeration of villains for some time now," the officer began, "and are confident they've set up a base here. The main orchestrators are all mien-users, and they will be using their abilities before we even set foot inside. Their method of operation is a show of miens, flaunting the restrictions and putting civilians needlessly in danger."

Ifrit found himself frowning.

"We expect five to ten mien-users within that group, but there will be a number of other individuals gathered within the building that we cannot account for." She pressed a button on the table in front of her and the map zoomed in to a red dot, to a very rough model of a building. Another press and the walls became transparent, a dozen levels digging into the earth with a central open atrium that looked down onto them all. "They will be gathered here. In order to isolate the organizers from the crowd, we want to attack from the top, pushing them into the tunnels where other troops will be lying in wait. We have it on good authority that they have been using these tunnels to get into the dead zone undetected."

"Is there a contingency plan for any stragglers?" Majesty was seated at the same level as the officer, her arms crossed. Though most of her class was seated behind her, directly to Majesty's right was Bia. Bia's costume was sky blue, just a few shades darker than Force's had been. The matching mask only covered the top half of her face, leaving her smug smile visible. Her blond hair was pulled back into a ponytail, every inch of her a piss poor imitation of Force. Ifrit heard his knuckles pop, earning a concerned look from Kirin.

"From our reconnaissance, the primary targets always move into position a full day early, so any latecomers can be assumed to be civilians. Regardless, they should still be detained, and as always, if they use their mien to resist arrest, can be handled with force." The officer removed a pair of handcuffs from her belt, appearing unperturbed by the interruption. "We will be providing restraints and knockout tablets for ease of transport.

Any bodies accrued during the mission will also need to be transported back to base, so please, keep it as clean as possible."

An appreciative laugh circled throughout the room, and Ifrit felt bile rise in his throat. The disgust was mirrored on Kirin's face when Ifrit looked, an uncharacteristic hardness in his black eyes.

"For the crowd, will the police be handling them? Or can we consider them suspected mien-users and therefore under our jurisdiction?" Ifrit couldn't tell who had spoken, but it was a stupidly necessary question. Heroes were only allowed to deal with "villains," or more accurately, anyone using a mien in public.

"There will be a significant police presence, though per the outlined mobilization, we will be waiting outside to apprehend those who flee to allow the heroes to deal with the more unpredictable elements."

"Cowards," Ifrit muttered under his breath.

"As is typical with these situations, our ability to assist is greatly hindered by the dead zone itself. We do believe that the assembled hero force, however, should be able to neutralize the mien users without great risk to anyone."

"Anyone they care about." Ifrit swung his head to make sure he'd heard correctly. But Phoenix met his eyes evenly, an unusual anger in them. They hadn't talked much, hadn't wanted to in the month that had passed, but now Ifrit was wondering if that had been yet another mistake.

"And what of the potential of Aether's involvement?" Mesmer was seated only one tier down from their class, isolated from most of the other heroes. A flicker of a frown passed over the officer's face, but she smoothed it away quickly. "Is there any plan for that?"

Ifrit hated the way the carbon in the air rose, hated that Kirin could feel it too. It was a name. He didn't need to flinch anytime someone said it.

"At this moment in time, with the intel from our most trustworthy sources, we are inclined to dismiss any possibility that Aether was or has been involved in this organization." The officer's tone had gone from professional to chilly. "The greatest likelihood is that there will be some Aether sympathizers in the crowd, but no active members."

Several heroes looked like they were going to protest, but the officer plowed on.

"We have distributed the assault plan, with the key players in their respective locations. For the rest, take a moment to break into distinct groups and submit your allocations within the next ten minutes. In twenty, we move out." The officer dismissed the map, the lights in the room automatically brightening once the holo was off.

Without any further discussion, the room shifted, the tiers pulling up until there was only one level, and as heroes stood their seats vanished, replaced instead by tables with miniature versions of the holo map. There were six groups total, each taking a different path to the center of the dead zone, the routes tagged with different colors and a list of names that updated as heroes around the room decided which route to take.

"You all." Majesty had deigned to grace them with her presence and even speak with them. How lucky were they. Even luckier, Bia stood sneering at her shoulder. "I have little to no information on whatever it is you do, so come up with a strategy on your own. With your additional training I hope you can come up with something adequate."

And with no other instructions at all, she strode away.

"You know, even though I was hoping we'd be left alone, I'm still somehow pissed off." Yantra sighed. "I guess I'll take it. Also, all of you get your fill of my help now, before I'm completely useless."

"Stop that." Ness swatted her arm, her fuzzy appearance already giving Ifrit a headache. Well. More of a headache. "Just because your mien isn't helpful in this case doesn't mean you're useless."

"But it's something we have to consider." Ghosts— Adlivun— might as well have already been using her mien, since the light from the table turned her eyes from dark brown to the sickly white that usually foreshadowed the appearance of some specter. Maybe she was using that as cover, already spreading her shades out into the dead zone, where maybe they'd feel at home.

"If you want advice on how to be useless but fun, come to me," Phoenix chimed in. Ifrit hated that he could tell he meant it. He didn't want to have to deal with another crisis when he was barely staying afloat of his own. Was there some food that Phoenix particularly liked? He ate everything Ifrit made with the same enthusiasm, so he'd have to ask Adlivun later. It was such a small, pathetically meaningless gesture, but it was all he could give.

"Kirin and I can cover Tech. She can clean up after us." If Ifrit was being reasonable, he would've split them up. Yantra was fine with basic combat skills, nothing terribly impressive, but from the briefing they shouldn't be facing anyone she wouldn't be able to handle, mien or no. Kirin and him were two of their hardest hitters, and there were plenty of non-combat specialists within their class who could've benefitted from the support. And yet, as he stared at those tiny blinking *underground* lines, he knew he couldn't get through this mission without Kirin by his side.

"Who else will need cover?" Wyrm leaned in, struggling to adjust the map with his talons. His name Kirin hadn't ever had to correct Ifrit on, since, well. *Wyrm*. "Kapre will need someone to watch their back, and Phoenix doesn't have any additional combat abilities. Obviously, he can heal himself, if need be, but I'd rather we didn't let it get to that point."

A lock of blond hair slipped from Wyrm's tightly wound bun and Shrink— *Antaeus*, fuck why were there so many of them— tucked it back for him absently. Huh.

"I can cover one or the other, but I'm not able to do much fighting in the meantime."

"I'll stay with Phoenix." Ifrit wasn't surprised Adlivun volunteered, less surprised when she didn't phrase it as a question. He'd been making a fourth serving of food for months now.

"I can protect Kapre and attack," Goldhorn offered. "Could just be the two of us if we need it."

"I don't think it'll be necessary at all, we've got enough to balance each team of three. But what I'm wondering is just... do we really need this many people to stop ten?" Antaeus's voice lowered as he spoke. "This seems... excessive."

Ifrit's gaze was drawn across the room, to the dozens of costumed heroes, the interspersed police uniforms between. Easily a hundred people, all for under two dozen "villains."

"Ears, Antaeus." Yantra gestured to the table and then broadly at the rest of the room. She seemed even more on edge than usual. "Not right now."

"Isn't that your specialty though?"

Several emotions flashed across Yantra's face, made even more difficult to understand with the mask hiding the bottom half.

"I'm not that kind of technopath," she said finally.

"Let's focus, though. We finally have a chance to show Majesty's class that we're not just as good as them, we're *better*. But to do that, we need to run this flawlessly." Ifrit hazarded a glance at Ness and found that for the first time, she was shockingly substantial. He could see the cut of her jaw, the way her eyes narrowed as she regarded the map. Like her determination made her more… whole.

"Who else doesn't feel like this mission plays to their strengths?" Kirin prompted.

"They don't seem to have more information about what we'll be walking into, so I might not have all that much to work with." Antaeus spoke up almost guiltily. "If there aren't things I can use, I'll have to fight hand to hand and that usually doesn't go my way."

"Do you not have any supplies?" Wyrm looked surprised. Admittedly, his weird ass mask made him look permanently surprised, covering his forehead and chin but only connected by a strip down the middle, all in bright orange that matched the— for lack of a better word— scales on his cheeks.

"I had some in the pockets of my old costume, but they replaced it."

"All of ours," Adlivun murmured quietly.

"Do you think they'll let you walk around and grab things?" Wyrm asked.

"I fucking doubt it." Ifrit shook his head. "We got here early and crammed into one fucking jet. They're trying to hide numbers, they're not just going to let him wander around."

"Alright, then." Kirin looked around at who was left. "Aïcha, do you think you could work with Antaeus again? I assume you've gotten used to how his mien works."

"Certainly." Hooves's costume was perhaps the most cartoonish out of their whole class, a tight fitted top with a skirt that was little more than a loincloth, leaving her goat legs visible for all to see. Her black hair was down around her shoulders, her dark skin washed out under the fluorescent lights.

"Everyone else okay?" Kirin looked around, making that face he always did when, for a time, he forgot to be self-conscious at all and just let himself be good at what he did. That serious, determined face. "Alright, I guess we just divide the rest evenly."

He'd hardly finished speaking when the rest of the group devolved into grabbing and pointing and whispered conversations, leaving Kirin, Ifrit, and Ness in a bubble of quiet.

"Ness, what're you thinking you're going to do?" Kirin turned to look at her, Ifrit suddenly feeling awkward. He knew how to act when it was just him and Kirin, or him and Kirin and Clidna, or him and Kirin and Phoenix, but everyone else still felt... weird. Like he was a discordant note played in the middle of an otherwise harmonized orchestra. He went to turn away, but there was nowhere to go, so he just stood there, uncomfortable.

"Hm?" She hadn't noticed Ifrit's distress, instead caught in the act of staring at the backs of Majesty's class.

"Do you know who you want to work with?"

Though just a minute before she had been almost completely solid, now she looked like she was going to fade into the air any second, Ifrit certain he could see the table *through* her. It was worse than when she was just a blur. And new.

"I can hold my own, so it doesn't really matter." Her gaze flickered back to Majesty's head, off in the distance. "But can I ask for a favor?"

Now Ifrit truly felt like he was intruding. She seemed nervous asking, like it was something personal. He went to turn off his hearing aids, to give her some semblance of privacy in this loud, overcrowded room, but she— not Kirin, *she*— swatted his hand down.

"Yeah, whatever you need." Kirin hadn't failed to notice her odd behavior either, his brows furrowed.

"I can't be in the same group as Inanna." The words came out in a rush.

"Inanna?" Kirin sounded confused.

"The woman in Majesty's class who got attacked," Ifrit supplied. There. He wasn't terrible with all names. He was great if there was a tragedy attached.

Ness nodded.

"And one of the people who attacked us right before class started," Kirin said slowly. Ifrit hadn't remembered she was there, but now that he thought about it, he could picture her, the heart-shaped face that would've been pretty if her gaze wasn't so cold. Dark skin, dark hair, but shockingly purple eyes. The only one who hadn't actually attacked them. Though, if Phoenix was right about her mien, maybe one of their classmates had just been weirdly horny the whole time.

"That's the one." Ness was looking at Kirin worriedly, too worriedly. Like she was afraid of him realizing something.

"We can wait to assign your group until we see which one she's in, or we can put you on and then switch you to a different one if it happens to be the same."

"The first one," Ness answered without hesitation.

"Alright, I'll let Yantra know to hold on where you're going then." Kirin moved to go tell her, since she'd taken up residence at the map, inputting the squads as they came up to her. Ness grabbed his arm before he made it more than a step.

"Don't tell her I asked you to. She'll want to know why and I... I don't think I can talk about that yet." Her hand briefly passed through his arm, her whole body blinking in and out of sight. Ifrit didn't like that he recognized the particular flavor of fear that was in her eyes.

"Of course," Kirin said, though his focus wasn't on Ness. He was looking across the room, and when Ifrit followed his gaze, he found the subject of Ness's fear staring directly at them. Or, more accurately, directly at where Ness blurred into the background. "I won't say a word."

4

Following Orders

IF KIRIN WASN'T SO worried about Ifrit, he would've been pissed.

By the time he managed to make his way to Yantra, all but a few members of Majesty's class had submitted their chosen groups, Inanna's name conveniently right at his eye level so he didn't even have to ask. Yantra had their chosen squads up and assigned, though she hadn't submitted it yet. Turns out, she had been waiting for him.

"All of the paths have at least a kilometer underground, but this one is the shortest." She pointed to one of the glowing lines. "I can't help much, but I can give him the least discomfort."

Kirin had agreed, and with that she finally hit send. A moment after their names appeared, another appeared directly below Ifrit's.

Bia.

At the time, Kirin had thought it must've been an unfortunate coincidence. Now, in the tunnels with her, he knew she'd done it on purpose.

"How *lucky* it is that our squad is going in from the top, so we don't have to stay in the dark for very long." Bia's voice, always louder than it needed to be, carried unfortunately well under the earth. She stayed firmly at the back of the group, while Ifrit, Kirin, and Yantra walked at the front, and yet they could hear her every word clearly. "Could you imagine being stuck underground? Oh, how *awful* that must be. Still, only a *child* would be afraid of it."

"Is she six or something?" Yantra forgot her own anxiety in her annoyance. "This is the most schoolyard level bullying I've ever seen."

Kirin only nodded, too focused on Ifrit's face to talk. His expression, or the portion of it visible over his mask, was carefully neutral. Kirin had realized how they were getting to the site just as Ifrit did, and though Ifrit hid it well, Kirin had noticed the momentary flash of panic at the thought of walking for near an hour under packed dirt. He had felt the air turn dense when Aether's name came up, and he had felt the night before, Ifrit's near panic at feeling like he couldn't breathe when he was alone in a room with windows and alarms and a healer just down the hall. Their friends were right to worry about Ifrit's grief, but they were wrong in thinking it was the worst thing he was fighting against.

The forced calm was almost worse than panic. Bia was doing her best to try and dig up the only recently covered graves, and though she had no way of possibly knowing it, was hitting on the worst fears Ifrit had. Yet he kept walking, like he didn't hear her at all.

Maybe they were extraordinarily lucky and the sound of the rest of the group— the more innocent murmured chatter, the sharp footsteps against hard stone floor, the high-pitched buzz of the electric lights— created a stew just right that meant Ifrit couldn't parse the words. And soon, painfully soon, he wouldn't be able to at all.

There was no fence that showed the demarcation of the dead zone down in the tunnels, just the darkness that loomed ahead where the lights— still strung with the same wire— ceased to work. Ifrit was watching the line grow closer, his eyebrows drawing tighter together, try as he might to fight it.

Yantra, however, was looking distinctly sick. Her normally dark skin looked sickly pale, and while Ifrit strode unflinching ahead, her steps grew increasingly hesitant. Every few steps she would have to jog to catch back up, shaking herself and moving forward only to immediately fall back again.

Kirin felt torn, not wanting to draw attention to the discomfort of either of his teammates, not with Bia already out for blood, but not wanting to leave them to their fear. It was easier than confronting the way his heart nearly stopped when someone ahead leaned down to tie their shoe, looking very briefly like they were crumpling to the floor.

But there were no bodies here, nothing to see but flickering light behind and darkness ahead, until suddenly they crossed the invisible line between the two.

The local hero in charge of their squadron called them to a halt, her and a few others lighting and then passing out old oil lanterns. Yantra gladly took the one she was offered, though the light above Ifrit's head was brighter than anything the weak flames gave off.

When the group set off again, it was with a different tone. There was an air of solemnity, even Bia keeping her mouth shut as they walked off deeper into a time without tech.

Your turn to distract me. Ifrit elbowed Kirin to make sure he was paying attention as he started to sign. *Always fucking forget the hearing aids have Bluetooth, but the second Bia got here I knew I didn't want to hear a fucking thing she said.*

Oh.

I can't believe you turned off your hearing and let us deal with that alone.

If you could've, you would've, don't fucking lie.

Slower, please. Yantra was squinting at their hands.

Sorry.

I fucking told you that translation program wasn't going to help you learn fucking faster.

I— Yantra paused, frustrated. "Kirin, what's the sign for realize?"

Realize.

Thank you. She turned to face Ifrit. *I realize that* now.

Ifrit was nice enough to only look smug for a second.

The idiots look even dumber without all their shiny lights. Ifrit paused for a moment. *Your costume looks fine, Tech.*

That got a smile out of her, and not just because she'd been flattered Ifrit had helped her pick out a sign name. He really had been trying to be nicer lately, and perhaps unsurprisingly he found it easier in sign than aloud. Better his second language than a third.

I thought more than just "shiny." Her grammar wasn't perfect, but Ifrit was a forgiving translator and a better teacher. One of the few good things that had come out in the last month was that every single one of their classmates had been trying to learn ISL, and in the giant pile on their dorm floor the secret had been revealed. Ifrit, ever the perfectionist, immediately had everyone start practicing, and his biggest rule was even if you can't say it right, still try. Though only a few were anywhere near proficient, they'd almost started to develop their own language of half formed sentences and bad explanations for lost words.

Without the lights they just look like they're wearing bad tracksuits. Kirin was happy that he earned a smile from Ifrit. After almost a year of interpreting what was happening under his mask, Kirin was completely fluent in the microscopic changes in the tilt of Ifrit's brows, the crease of his eye when he smiled.

Fucking clown suits. The distraction was only momentary though, the worried furrow back as Ifrit looked down the long tunnel ahead. The light carried by their leader barely made it a meter in front of them, the darkness stretching into infinity. Kirin wished it wasn't only Ifrit who had the ability to create light, that he could do *something* to help, but there wasn't anything to do. There was only walking.

Yantra felt the same, her hands faltering and her gaze kept down on the ground. It might have just been the firelight, but Kirin could've sworn that she looked pale. No, not just pale: she looked like there was something missing, like a piece of her had been removed and she wasn't quite whole. He shook his head; he was just projecting. They were alright, nothing was wrong.

Everyone felt it though. The lamps did little to push back the darkness and so Ifrit was the brightest thing in that tunnel and the group crowded around him, moving in closer and closer until they were all nearly touching. Even Majesty's group— even *Bia*, for all her blustering— were creeping near. Kirin felt his shoulders tense, glaring at them angrily for using Ifrit when it served them and demeaning him when it didn't.

"Hey." Ifrit elbowed Kirin in the stomach to get his attention. *It's fine, you don't need to fucking scare everyone.*

Kirin frowned. *I'm not doing anything.*

Not trying to. Yantra smiled.

"...art can't take this shit." Ifrit's voice was low enough that Kirin only heard the last few words.

What?

Don't worry about it. Ifrit sighed. There was a pause and a flicker of reluctance passed over his face before the fire over his head expanded to cover the ceiling.

Are you sure? The carbon in the air was so tightly contained Kirin could barely tell the difference. Normally when Ifrit would expend such a large amount some of it would seep out of his control, and yet there was no extra carbon that Kirin could detect, though the flames licking the stone promised it was there. Now that Kirin knew to look for it, knew how to feel it, he could see just how painstakingly intricate Ifrit's power was. The way the carbon was placed, the control required to keep the sources distinct and unique; it was an art form almost.

It's fine. In the brighter light, Kirin could see the fear that Ifrit was hiding deep in his eyes, and he watched it fade as Ifrit turned to look at him. *You're here. You won't let anything happen.*

Kirin was struck by the entirely irrational desire to pick Ifrit up and drag him back to their dorm where they could be alone, where Kirin could crush him in a hug and promise a thousand times that yes, of course he would always be there. Whenever and wherever he was needed.

But he couldn't. They had a job to do, and if they didn't handle it, someone else would do it with more violence, more force against the people accused. Instead, Kirin linked their pinkies together, hoping that everything he wanted to say could be conveyed in that tiny, fragile contact.

As they darted between buildings, Kirin found his back crystalizing unconsciously. The dead zone was quiet, eerily so, and the broken windows that surrounded them caught the moonlight unevenly, glinting like watchful eyes. Darkness had fallen while they were underground, and though it made them less visible, Kirin still felt horribly exposed.

Ifrit and Yantra were with him every step, the three of them part of the rearguard as their squadron got into position. The moment they had broken free of the tunnel they had started moving in sprints, stalking silently until they reached their target. It was in sight now, noticeable from the dim glow around the doors. The sounds of shouts and cheers poured out; a beacon of life in such a silent and still landscape.

A low whistle sounded, the signal for half their group to peel off, running around to the opposite side of the target. It was a low, squat building— or so it appeared from the outside— with half a dozen doors littering the side facing them alone. It must have been a concert venue or some other community space before the curtain had fallen and cut it off from the rest of civilization.

Another whistle and they were just outside, backs pressed against the concrete walls. Yantra was breathing heavily, one hand tightly gripping a lock of her hair. Ifrit was doing his best not to breathe at all, his red eyes flashing as he focused the cloud of carbon around his body. His halo had been extinguished for the sake of secrecy— not that there was anyone around to watch their approach in the first place— but even then, the air around him seemed to shimmer, the cloud densifying as they all waited for the order to go in.

As the seconds ticked by, Kirin thought he saw Ifrit's hands start to shake.

And then they were inside.

Ifrit's rings clashed together, the spark jumping happily to the prepared fuel source, throwing him through the door in an instant. Kirin was only a step behind, feeling the flames lick against diamond, shredded metal from the door brushing harmlessly over him. The room they'd entered filled the entire top floor, the other half of their squad visible as they flooded in from the opposite side. No walls broke up the space, but a void did, a large, gaping hole in the center of the room, around which most of the crowd was gathered. It went down deep enough that Kirin couldn't see the bottom, but he could see the ledges that continued down, like box seats at a theater. People gathered on those levels too, pressed right up against the railings, though now they turned to flee away from the yawning pit and off into the shadows.

Ifrit was blazing a path straight for the gap, civilians scattering in front of him, so focused on his goal that he failed to notice a fist flying toward his face.

Kirin grabbed the offending party and threw them back over his shoulder, hearing them connect with the ground with a sharp crack. When he looked behind him, Yantra was already handcuffing the man, only glancing up to give Kirin a nod. A hero Kirin vaguely recognized was standing over Yantra and guarding her, ensuring that none of the retreating crowd stopped to help their fallen companion.

Ifrit hesitated for a moment when he reached the edge, long enough that Kirin was able to step up to the railing beside him. The tremor that Kirin had noticed outside was back, Ifrit balling his hands into fists to try to stop it. But when Ifrit looked across the room and saw Bia heading straight for the pit, his gaze hardened, and he threw himself over the edge.

Naturally, Kirin jumped as well.

In the few moments of weightlessness, Kirin breathed in deeply, taking in the leftover carbon from Ifrit's fire and crystallizing every part of his body, making himself so dense that when he impacted the floor, the room shook slightly. His feet were embedded in the ground up to his ankles, so he couldn't move at all when the first attack came.

The knife skittered harmlessly across solid diamond, the woman who threw it stumbling back a step when she saw it had no effect. Her eyes had been overdrawn, made to look larger so her expression could be seen from a dozen meters above, and the effect was sad, showing just how frightened she was.

Ifrit landed next to Kirin, his descent more controlled. The flames beneath him widened into a ring, keeping the two of them separate from their targets, who were spread out in a loose circle around them.

They had landed in what appeared to be a circus ring, lit with old gas lights and torches set in sconces around the walls. The inhabitants of the ring were all dressed in garishly bright colors, the outfits looking quite similar to hero costumes, if only ones that had seen better days. The makeup coating their faces cracked and flaked as they moved, proof it was either expired or simply had been on too long. Their faces displayed more fear than aggression; there was a sense of disrepair that coated these people, of filth and grime, of *despair.*

That despair turned to determination as the rest of the troop pulled out knives matching the one the woman had already thrown. These weren't the dull blades of a juggling act, nor were they the well-kept blades of a collector. These were rusted and dented, unhappy reminders of things that had been done. Still kept reminders of what they would likely need to do again.

"We don't want trouble." One of the people on the outermost reaches of the ring spoke. They were putting their body between Kirin and the two smallest members, who were holding onto each other tightly. The person speaking lowered their knife slightly and took a step forward. "I recognize you."

The sound of combat rang out from above and several of the other people shuffled forward, less innocently. Kirin could taste the carbon in the air, he could feel Ifrit's muscles coiling from where their backs touched. Ifrit couldn't hear what they were saying.

Kirin breathed in deeply, once, twice, pulling as much carbon toward him as he could. The change in the air earned him a split-second glance from Ifrit, just long enough for Kirin to hold his hands out.

Wait.

"How do you know me?" It wasn't the best question, was hardly the most important one, but it was the first thing that came to mind. Of course they knew him, his face had been all over the feeds, his costume unchanged since the year before.

"They showed us a photo of you." She stepped forward again. "They're looking for you."

Before Kirin could ask *who*, a body was thrown down from the top level, landing with an awful crunch in front of the woman who had already thrown her blade.

"Tell them to run." Kirin nodded to the pair of teenagers hiding behind the one person willing to talk. The woman screamed, her voice full of horror and rage, and the rest of the performers pounced.

Like moths drawn to flame, most of them targeted Ifrit. The fire in front of Kirin flared, sending performers stumbling backward to avoid being seared, and Kirin pivoted on one foot to throw Ifrit behind himself as a dozen knives clattered against his skin. One shattered, hitting the edge of his cheekbone just right, sending shards of metal out in a cloud. Two men flanked Kirin, one growing larger as Kirin watched, like he was inflating from the inside. The other lunged, his eyes blinking sideways. Kirin kicked the knife out of the man's hand, letting his momentum twist him until he could kick with his other foot, clipping the man in the temple. Ifrit detonated a blast right where Kirin had previously stood, blasting the inflatable man back a few steps, giving Kirin a moment to restrain the man on the ground.

Ifrit forced the inflatable man further back, his new cumbersome size a problem against Ifrit's speed and agility. A fire-powered elbow to the man's chest knocked the wind out of him, literally. A sudden rush of air forced Ifrit back a few steps, but it blasted the man straight back into the wall. After the collision, he collapsed, unconscious.

The numbers that they'd been given were incorrect, because with two down and two running off, there were still nine more performers fanning out. The faces that surrounded them all bore grim resolve, no sign of backing down. Kirin's eyes found the body splattered on the ground, and he couldn't blame them for thinking this was the only way out.

A moment later Kirin was knocked back into Ifrit, a short woman throwing her hands out as the palm split open and a rope shot out, starting to wind its way around them and tying them together. When their backs collided, Ifrit let out a huff of annoyance, which their assailants took to be a gasp for air as they grew emboldened by this easy success.

Once they were almost within arm's reach, Ifrit lit the rope on fire.

Kirin ripped free of the binding, grabbing one end and swinging it around like a whip. The performers fell backward, most dropping their weapons. For the first time, they looked afraid. Kirin's stomach lurched.

Morals were put aside by a grunt of pain from Ifrit.

Kirin turned to see several needles sticking out of Ifrit's back, connected to thin gossamer threads held by one of the men to their left. The man yanked toward himself, and Ifrit was thrown toward him, the strands pulled taut.

Kirin hadn't even taken a full step toward them, hand outstretched, when Ifrit neatly severed the lines with a rippling burst of flame, another explosion detonating next to the man and blowing him off his feet. Two others were caught in the blast— the two kids who had been meant to run away. They were thrown backward, toward the edge of the room. The girl's head smacked against something sticking out of the ground.

The boy hurriedly covered her body with his own, saying words to her that were lost in the din. Kirin distantly felt something hitting him— little more than brief pressure with his skin still hardened— as the boy got to his feet and squared his stance, not readying for an offense, but instead poised to defend.

A rumbling from above brought Kirin's eyes skyward, and he was greeted with the sight of Bia descending, her eyes flickering gleefully as her blond hair streaked behind her as she fell. Kirin met Ifrit's gaze, and then looked back to where the teenagers now stood, supporting each other. The kids looked at him, looked at the sky, and then turned and fled.

They stumbled into one of a dozen rooms that branched off the central hall, more than the five their intel had shown. They could get away, if only they chose right. They were too young to deserve punishment, not for this. The adults that had been with them were largely unconscious, the few who were upright retreating. As long as no one had seen where they'd gone, it'd be fine, they could escape—

The ground trembled to announce Bia's arrival. The look in her eyes, the greedy way her gaze was trained on the path the kids took made the decision for him. Ifrit didn't need to ask, he understood, and they took off running after the kids, down into the tunnels.

5

Deadly Intent

IFRIT FORCED HIMSELF TO be glad they were underground. True, his breaths came heavier than they should; true, his chest felt like it was wrapped in iron bands keeping his lungs from expanding, but it *was* convenient when he needed to track people.

Especially when he couldn't trust his eyes.

The moment they'd passed through the door, he'd lost Kirin. The reason the kids had charged straight for this room had become apparent the moment he'd entered, since the room was filled with mirrors. Kirin had gone left and Ifrit had gone right, and then the walls weren't where they were supposed to be anymore. The carbon he had in the air was enough to tell where the real walls were, even where the tops of the mirrors were— too close to the ceiling for him to go over without toppling the whole thing— and it didn't match what his eyes were telling him. It didn't match what could exist in the dead zone either.

Instead of a shadowed hall of mirrors with only his flames for light, he was standing in a hospital room. It was so bright he had to squint, sunlight streaming in from large, open windows, curtains hiding the view and rustling in a breeze he couldn't feel. There were electric lights overhead at regular intervals, beds with sliding dividers laid out neatly. His brain almost convinced him that he could hear the beep of monitors, the hushed conversations as he watched nurses move in and out of rooms. But it wasn't there.

He ran face first into the wall in front of him anyway.

Ifrit forced his eyes shut, trying to ignore it, head against the glass to keep himself oriented as the map filled out in his mind. He felt a tremor run through the mirror and a few seconds later found the gap in his mental drawing, the black hole that had to be Kirin. The edges of what Ifrit could sense were fuzzy, but it seemed like Kirin was panicking, lashing out at the wall of glass in front of him. However, clear as day, Ifrit could feel the disturbance of the air as the two kids ran right by Kirin, so close he could've touched them if he'd known.

They were too far from Ifrit's position, but if Kirin could get to them before Bia...

A wave of force rippled through the entrance and Ifrit turned his face away as glass shards sliced through the air. She wasn't tempering her power at all, heedless of the fact that there were people in there. She'd kill those kids in a heartbeat without thinking anything of it. Kirin had to get there first.

Ifrit had already found the door the kids had passed through, but he was hesitating for some reason. He sacrificed some of his carbon, putting it close to Kirin's face, just to get an idea of what he was doing. The briefest impression of Kirin turning his head surfaced before the image evaporated, the carbon consumed. Kirin was *waiting*, looking for Ifrit.

Bia's path was starting to curve that way, maybe out of luck, maybe because Kirin was calling out, but it made Ifrit curse under his breath. He couldn't fucking yell, he didn't want her to know. But could he...

Kirin took one step back toward Ifrit before Ifrit sent a trail of carbon racing off through the maze. Hoping that Bia was just as caught in the illusion as he was, he risked sending a line of fire over the mirrors, the gas he'd sent Kirin's way igniting and illuminating the tunnel ahead. Kirin must have been able to see, or maybe he just felt the heat of the flames, since he took off running. Before he faded from Ifrit's mental map, Ifrit caught one last gesture. Arms crossed in an X and then pulled apart. *Safe*.

Ifrit found himself smiling. Yeah, he'd stay safe. As if he couldn't deal with *Bia.*

She'd stopped advancing for some reason. Ifrit turned his attention back to her and found her on the ground with her hand to her head. She'd been destroying all the mirrors, crushing them into a fine dust, but she'd forgotten that there were *real* walls too. It looked like she'd run straight into one of them and hit her thick skull on the concrete.

The wave of force that rolled his way reminded him that even though *he* couldn't hear himself laugh, she still could. He dodged to the side, ducking into a roll and stopping short of hitting the wall himself as the world around him wavered. The people moving through the illusion didn't notice. Ifrit was at the edge of both the real room and this fake overlaid one, against the window. From this vantage point, he could see a little boy lying in the bed, bandages all the way up his side. A young girl was curled up next to him— like a twin or a sibling from how alike they looked— bandaged just as heavily. The image wavered once, twice, and then blinked out completely, leaving Ifrit staring at his own splintered image in the shattered glass.

The mirrors around him were still standing, a lucky break since the illusion had likely broken for Bia as well. He wouldn't bother lying to himself and saying she hadn't seen him go in, and what would be the point anyway? It wouldn't be the first time she'd used any excuse to attack him. This time though... this time there wasn't anyone else watching to make her pretend to pull her punches.

He could hide. He could even hear Pressure's voice in the back of his head telling him that there was no shame in it, feel the ghost of her hand on his hair. The maze around him still stood, though Bia had already created a sizable hole from the entrance to the center. She was aiming left, not right; she wouldn't notice him.

But she would notice the door.

On the very edge of his consciousness, Ifrit could feel Kirin running, the tiny amount of carbon with him just enough to create the impression of movement. Ifrit didn't know what Kirin was going to do, didn't pretend to have a clue of how to let the kids go without drawing suspicion back on themselves. Kirin would come up with something though, some story that would disarm everyone. If Bia got there first, it wouldn't even be her word against theirs, it would simply be her word. Her parents were co-chairs of the Hero Council; she was bulletproof.

And more than that, beyond just the desire to help two kids who were in deeper shit than they truly knew, there was the fact that Ifrit felt like something was wrong. Something was off here, from the numbers, to how desperate the performers were, to the secrecy surrounding a bust of a fucking circus. Ifrit needed someone who would listen; Ifrit needed *Kirin*. Ifrit needed to make sure nothing ever happened to him.

He started running.

The instant he came out into the open, he felt Bia realize it was him. It only took a second, just the briefest moment, and then her face fell into open excitement. The attack hit him square across the chest.

He was thrown backward, the blast clipping him just right to send him into a spin, shards of glass tearing the fabric on his back as he hit one of the still-standing walls. He angled an explosion behind himself to stop losing ground, the pressure bouncing him back to his feet as he landed. The crushed remains of the mirrors crunched under his feet as he rolled his shoulders and squared his stance, brushing fragments of glass and metal from his hair.

"Oh. You." He couldn't hear her tone of voice, but her face spoke loudly enough. The words were a smokescreen, and a poor one, not that she even needed it. Glimpses of flying bodies behind her promised the other heroes were too occupied to care about what happened in one small, dark room.

Ifrit didn't reply, not sure what her play was. They weren't kids anymore, this wasn't the stupid school Pressure had tried to send him to, but he was confident Bia hadn't grown up even slightly since then.

His suspicion was confirmed when her attention immediately shifted to a hatch in the floor. There hadn't been anywhere near enough time for the kids to get in before she started blasting, but if he thought about it with child logic, *surely* that was where the people he was looking for were. Of *course* they would squash themselves into a hole in the ground and hope no one would look, rather than running into any of the dozen tunnels that led away from the central room. Her smug satisfaction promised that she well and truly believed she'd found them.

He was happy to add to that conclusion by faking a lunge for the trapdoor, like he wanted to open it first. His plan had been to get her to push him away and try to open it herself, which half worked. She did attack him, slamming him back against the wall, but when she walked forward, she stepped straight over it, eyes locked on him.

For a second his eyes betrayed him, checking to see if the thin thread of fire connecting him to Kirin had gone out. The tunnel entrance was still covered by at least two rows of mirrors, which he would've given away if she wasn't too busy *monologuing* to notice anything.

Despite the faint ache in his chest from where her attack had landed, despite the very real and present threat she posed, he felt his nose wrinkle in annoyance. She'd broken his hearing aids more than once in an "accident" and every time she continued to speak like he could hear her. When he'd finally been too pissed off at the fact that she hadn't seemed to grasp what being deaf meant and snapped at her, she'd haughtily retorted that he could just read her lips instead. Which wasn't really true; he could, but only *some* words if someone was enunciating clearly and the lighting was good. Here, with her backlit and speaking quickly, she could've been saying anything and he wouldn't fucking know.

She was going on so long he had time to stand up from the floor and shake the mirror shards out of his hair and his clothes. He caught the words "expendable" and "villains" and could essentially backfill the rest with any of her other petty outbursts through the years.

She noticed he wasn't basking in her presence appropriately and took him off guard with another blast, this one pinning him to the wall and forcing him to look at her— oh wow, she actually remembered he was deaf this time, gold fucking star for Bia— as she continued on. The pressure on his chest increased as she stepped closer, making Ifrit's lip curl in disgust. They'd given *her* Force's color, just because of how "similar" their power sets were, but Bia's power was so laughably pathetic when compared to what Pressure's was. What Pressure's had been. The thought made the scowl drop off his face.

Fuck, was Bia really still talking? At least *that* was enough to keep the grief at bay, just for a little longer. The same shit as always too, there was "disgrace" and "lucky," the same things she'd been saying since it'd been announced he was allowed to join the school. And "dog"— that was so old too. Seriously, he'd take bitch over that. Oh, yes, there was "good" and "us" in close proximity— almost certainly something along the lines of "how *dare* you think you're as good as us"— and he decided to cut off her little self-righteous masturbatory speech right there.

"You're wrong." From the thrum in his chest, he was speaking as loudly as he meant to. "I think I'm fucking better than you."

She opened her mouth to respond, but he didn't let her. He detonated two explosions at once; the first sent Bia careening off to the side, the second threw him up and over her now that the force pinning him to the wall was gone. He darted into the maze again, shattering a few mirrors at random to hide his path as he headed for the tunnel. Kirin had vanished completely from his awareness, but the tunnel ran perfectly straight, he just had to get to the door—

Another wave of force exploded the mirrors in front of him.

It was the last shred of his luck that the mirror in front of the doorway remained intact. Bia was starting forward, walking casually like she had all the time in the world. More of their squadron must have made it to the ground floor, judging from the light spilling in behind her, but still no one came to look.

He turned away from the doorway, anger making his shoulders shake. Of course no one would come looking. They never did. Only one person ever had, and she was gone and now someone else was wearing her color. Someone else was pretending that they could ever fill her shoes, but Bia was *nothing* like Pressure. Not even at her worst. Who the fuck even let her use that blue? Pressure had tried to get the school to let *him* use it, but they had said no, that Force was too important, too iconic to give it to anyone else. And yet hardly a few months after her death *Bia* was deemed worthy of wearing it?

Abruptly, he felt the line of carbon monoxide he'd sent forward for Kirin hit a wall.

Ifrit didn't know anything about the kids they were covering for, only that they didn't deserve to die, which they would if Bia found them, and they didn't deserve to spend the rest of their lives in jail either. Hell, none of these people did. And that was why he was here. To change that. And there were people here who felt the same, people who were willing to run off alone to help kids escape because none of them fucking deserved this. His role, right now, was just to make sure the type of hero who would happily see those kids die wasn't able to get anywhere near them.

Bia strolled forward, ready for another pithy tirade. When she started, he only caught one word.

Crossfire.

She was fucking dumb. The maze around them was in ruins, any shot now would have to be intentional. And did she even need to pretend? He didn't think she'd be punished even if she wholeheartedly said that she'd attacked him on purpose. She was well-connected, well-suited to the hero profession. He was a problem already and posed to become a bigger one. It'd suit them just fine if he died.

Somehow that made him so much more determined to keep on living.

He shot forward, not toward her, but toward the trapdoor in the center of the room. Her attention turned and she dove for it, right as he used a blast to change direction midair. Using the smoke as a cover, he flew straight through the doorway, not daring to give himself extra light until he was halfway down the path. The thin strand he'd left for Kirin still flickered, but there was less carbon in the air than he'd intended, which promised Kirin was alive and still breathing just at the end of the hall.

He forced more monoxide into the air and expanded the thread to a ceiling of fire, building another store of carbon off to his other side, sure that Bia would come sailing through and start a fight any moment. The additional light showed that this wasn't a subway tunnel, nor was it an old maintenance shaft filled with pipes. The walls were compacted dirt, the unevenness of the finish indicating that they were hand dug, and recently too. Had they been warned about the raid?

The air was damp here; a drop of water fell and hit his nose. By the time he reached the turn, it'd steamed away from the heat around him. He hadn't meant to let it, but the fire crawling along the ceiling had crept down the walls as well, engulfing him on all sides, his control fraying as his anxiety grew. The room came into focus slowly, the edges sharper than the tunnel that had led to it. Piles of construction material lay on the floor, rebar and power tools left to molder in the damp air.

And Kirin, holding a piece of metal loosely in one hand.

"Kiri?" Ifrit couldn't tell how loudly he'd spoken, but it must have been near silent since Kirin didn't react at all. He remained facing away, almost perfectly still. Ifrit continued to flood the wall with flames, looking for where the teenagers had gone. There was no illusion, or if there was it fit the shape of the room they were in. Ifrit was peering into the corners next to him when he saw Kirin move out of the corner of his eye.

Kirin's hand went up, the end of the rebar touching the fire over his head. Ifrit lurched forward, but was too slow to stop the metal from piercing all the way through Kirin's thigh.

Kirin fell to one knee as Ifrit caught him, arms wrapped around his chest. Ifrit's cheek was pressed to one of Kirin's scars, and even through the impenetrable fabric he could feel the sharpness, so foreign to the rest of Kirin's warmth. Ifrit hadn't realized his hands were shaking until he almost let Kirin fall, unable to get a grip.

He was pushed back sharply, Kirin lurching away like he'd been stung. All Ifrit could see was the way Kirin's face was rapidly paling, the wound on his leg leaking blood. Kirin turned to face him, and for a moment, Ifrit almost didn't recognize him.

The self-loathing, the misery in Kirin's eyes was too much.

Kirin reached out as if to touch Ifrit's jaw, his hand freezing just a breath away from contact, his gaze darting to the door. Ifrit could barely make out the words Kirin's hands began spelling, too focused on the crimson flecks trapped in in Kirin's hair.

Kirin noticed and pressed their foreheads together, taking one of Ifrit's hands and placing it gently on his chest, letting Ifrit feel the slow rise and fall. Despite the pain he must be in, Kirin's heartbeat was slow, steady. The tips of Ifrit's fingers brushed against the bare skin near Kirin's collarbone, which felt clammy from the drying sweat. There wasn't the faintest tremor from Kirin, not any indication that he was the one injured, not Ifrit. Kirin let them stay there one moment more, the shaking in Ifrit's hands subsiding, and then pulled his own hands back to talk.

I'm sorry. His eyes looked pained, from regret, not from his injury. *People are coming; I need you to collapse the exit.*

They were standing right next to it, tiled walls appearing through a roughly widened doorway. Ifrit could do it, easily, but if he did—

I'll be fine. Phoenix isn't far behind. Though Kirin had removed his hand, Ifrit hadn't removed his, and so he knew Kirin meant it, could feel how steady his heart was even in this. *We just need an excuse for why they got away. They made an illusion and we couldn't see them. They hit me with the pipe and it sparked, causing an explosion. Okay?*

Ifrit didn't respond, and for the first time, Kirin looked worried.

Please.

The explosion threw Ifrit back out into the hall. He hit the wall in a daze, already pushing himself back to where Kirin had been flung away from him, where Kirin had crashed backward the wrong way, the power too great, flying back through a pile of rusted metal. When Ifrit scrambled back into the room, he could see that Kirin had managed to activate part of his mien, the force of the detonation embedding him into the rock. The detritus on the floor had been blown backward too, pieces of metal sticking out of the wall and out of... out of...

"PHOENIX!" Ifrit felt the word rip out of him as he tried to tell himself that it was just another illusion. Or maybe he'd finally hit his head too hard. There was just no way that a sheet of metal was sticking out of Kirin's chest, there was no way that his head was hanging limply, his body only held up by the wall he was trapped in. Ifrit reached up with a shaky hand to check his pulse, refusing to even look, refusing to check where that piece of shrapnel had landed.

His fingers only met sharp diamond, coming away bloodied before the skin started to return to its normal amber. Ifrit pressed his fingers in again, ignoring his own tiny cuts, feeling both the rapid beating of Kirin's pulse and a vibration as Kirin said something.

"Someone get Phoenix!" Ifrit yelled again, not daring to take his gaze away from where Kirin was stirring. When Kirin lifted his head, his mask fell clean away, having cracked from the impact. The explosion had turned the fabric mask underneath to ash, allowing Ifrit to see the wobbly grin Kirin gave him.

I told you I'd be fine. Ifrit trapped Kirin's hands before he could sign more, desperate to stop him from moving. Desperate to keep the blood from leaking from Kirin's sternum.

Stay still. Ifrit resisted the urge to scream again— where the fuck was Phoenix??— afraid that it would come out as a sob. He was grateful beyond words that the only light in that cave was fire, because part of his brain only wanted to think of the color blue when he saw that much blood.

But Kirin was straightening slightly, his brows pressing together and lips pulling into a thin line. He was looking over Ifrit's shoulder, and as he did, he reached up and ripped out the piece of metal embedded just over his heart.

Ifrit froze.

Kirin stood, slowly, allowing Ifrit to see the shine of diamond under a layer of torn flesh. There was still rebar protruding from his thigh, but the worst hadn't happened. Kirin wasn't going anywhere. Ifrit wasn't going to be alone.

And alone they weren't. When Ifrit finally got himself to move, he saw Bia sizing up Kirin, her lips moving quickly, an ugly scowl on her face. She was shouting, maybe, but Kirin stood like a wall between them, crossing his arms and refusing to move even when she tried to get into his face. Ifrit felt a surge of anger, real anger; how *dare* she yell at Kirin when he had a fucking spike through his leg? Where did she fucking get off trying to give him shit when *she'd* derailed their mission by trying to start a fight?

Without intending to, Ifrit had been pumping the air full of carbon, his fingers itching to strike his ignition rings, to finally make her shut up. His thumb and middle finger were already pressing together, the cool metal pushing against his too hot skin, but then the room was abruptly emptying of ammunition. Kirin's back shimmered as he burned through the carbon in the air. The sudden lack shocked Ifrit enough that he stumbled back a step, only to fall back another when Kirin ripped the rebar straight out of his leg.

Briefly, Ifrit could see straight through to the blue of Bia's suit. He thought he might be sick, his stomach lurching so violently he found himself on the ground to steady it. Not even a minute later, the hole was gone, the only evidence of it ever existing the hole in Kirin's pants, and the faint dark stain around the edge.

Are you good? Phoenix had entered without Ifrit realizing, the wet stains on her costume indicating she'd taken the short way down to them. Her eyes were just as haunted as Ifrit felt, her complexion ashen as her eyes flickered to the stone ceiling above them.

Ifrit waved her off as Kirin turned, his expression clearing at once to concern when he saw them both on the floor.

Hey, I'm okay. Kirin dropped to his knees and Ifrit flinched, unable to unsee the damage. *We can leave now, but take your time. Everyone is in custody, we just need to head back.*

Kirin's being nice, let's get the fuck out of here. Phoenix was breathing too quickly, gripping Kirin's arm tightly. The corners of her gray eyes were suspiciously red, and she looked like she might cry. In the weirdest way, it made Ifrit feel better. He wasn't the only one lost, he wasn't the only one remembering the last time the three of them were underground. The last time Kirin had been so hurt. The last time they had been in a world where Pressure was still alive.

Ifrit got to his feet with Kirin's help, still unsteady. Phoenix was worse, shaking slightly as they walked back down the tunnel. Ifrit kept the fire wide, refusing to walk in darkness, and it gave him a glimpse of the dark circles under her eyes.

Her mien hid all their physical scars, but Ifrit was beginning to fear it couldn't do anything for the ones underneath.

6

New Direction

KIRIN WAS AN ASS.

He was a dick, a complete piece of shit, absolutely every terrible thing he'd thought about himself over the years was true. How could he do that to Ifrit? How could he ask him to do that?

He hadn't been thinking, that was how. He never thought. And now he was paying the price with both Ifrit and Phoenix horrified and shaky, on their very first mission of the new year. Great job Kirin.

"Shit, there's press." Yantra had been quiet, only making a sound when they crossed the barrier of the dead zone. Even then she had only gasped, one hand going to her heart, the other to the thin scar over her ear. Kirin almost asked if she was okay, but Ifrit was still clutching his fingers so tightly they were in danger of snapping, and he didn't dare distract himself in case Ifrit needed anything.

This was all his fault.

"Majesty usually doesn't let her class talk, so we should be fine." A circle was hovering around Yantra's eye as she looked up footage of the year prior, biting her lip. "There was no reason for us to come this way; why didn't they want us in the tunnels again?"

"They want to fucking show off." Ifrit spoke for the first time since they'd left that underground room. His breathing had leveled, the pulse in his thumb was normal, but Kirin didn't believe it. He couldn't banish the anguish in Ifrit's eyes from his mind, the chorus of *my fault, my fault, my fault* too loud in his head. "Prove that it was worth calling this many fucking heroes in."

"Was it?" Usually Yantra was the most paranoid one in their group, but they were all so tired he couldn't fault her for the slip.

But now they were too close for casual conversation. There were a few dozen journalists waiting on the other side of the police barrier, cameras already flashing. Kirin almost wished they could stay in the dead zone, away from the world for just a while longer, away from the people who wanted to drag out the worst into the light.

Especially since the cameras had already spotted Ifrit.

"Force's son! What do you have to say about this mission?"

"How is the school treating you now that your mother is gone?"

"Did you agree with her philosophy? Are you planning on going rogue?"

"Was Aether involved in this villain hideout?"

Kirin could see Clidna moving in from the corner of her eye, getting ready to assume their old routine of her taking the questions so Kirin could get Ifrit away, when Ifrit stepped up to the barrier almost nose to nose with one of the reporters.

"What we raided today was a circus." His tone was flat, angry. "If you look to your left, you can see that the people we were told to capture dead or alive are wearing *clown costumes*. The youngest of their troop couldn't have been more than eighteen." He paused. "The two teenagers got away."

Despite the shittiness of everything, despite the way that Kirin's heart felt like lead in his chest, he couldn't help the smile that was unfurling under the extra mask he'd been given. Ifrit was so brilliant. The tone, the casual dismissal of their escape, it didn't prove anything. But there was just the tiniest, smallest note of pleasure in that last statement.

"Aether was involved." Just like that, the tiny flicker of hope was blown out by the sound of Bia's voice.

Some of the cameras seemed loathe to move away from Ifrit, though plenty immediately swapped to her. Kirin could see Majesty marching up angrily in the background, but she had been bringing up the rear, and Kirin couldn't imagine her ever breaking out into a run.

"How do you know Aether was involved?"

"Were there Aether agents captured during the mission?"

"Do you have any updates on the location of the woman in white?"

"There was stolen technology that can easily be traced back to Aether hidden in a compartment in one of the rooms of the villain hideout." Bia paused for dramatic effect. "Beyond this, there were cartons of pamphlets with Aether propaganda in that compartment as well. We have no doubt that many of those taken into custody today will rapidly abandon their allegiance to Aether and tell us the whereabouts of the larger group."

"How do you feel knowing that this troop was involved with the people who killed your mother?" One of the reporters who hadn't taken their drone off Ifrit's face finally became brave enough to shout.

Ifrit stiffened, turning to look back.

"Aether didn't kill my mother," he said. "The police did."

Though the reporters shouted more and more questions after him, Ifrit didn't look back again.

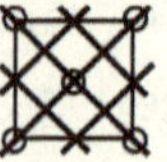

The jet ride home was nightmarish. Kirin was jealous that Ifrit could turn off his hearing, rest his head on Kirin's shoulder, and fall blissfully asleep, while Kirin had to hear Bia crowing about how *she* had discovered the troop's Aether association. It hadn't mattered that Majesty had gone in front of the cameras and pulled Bia away, noting that the materials Bia had found were sealed and covered by the troop's equipment, indicating they might have not even known it was there, and that they were not the only organization that used the dead zone for a base; Bia was still gloating.

Even worse, her smugness had rubbed off on the rest of her class. While Pressure's class sat quietly— some of them sleeping, others like Medusa simply meditating— Majesty's class was alive with jeers and laughter, as if they'd all just come from a particularly incredible party and not a place where people had died.

Though it felt like a full day had passed since they set out, the sun was still far above the horizon when they landed back in East City. Kirin felt like he could lay down and sleep until morning anyway— Phoenix's healing always left him slightly tired. Yet there was no rest to be found, as there was someone waiting for them as they disembarked.

Kirin would've missed him if Ifrit hadn't ripped his hand away. When Kirin turned to ask what was wrong, he'd noticed Ifrit's horrified gaze and followed it. And there, standing far too close to where the jet had landed, was Valor.

He was half in the costume Kirin knew— a dark blue mask that covered the bottom half of his face— and half in old army clothes, the sort the United States' soldiers were always wearing in his textbooks. He wasn't as tall as Kirin might've expected— nearer to Dulu's height than Adlivun's— with short cropped brown hair and blue eyes. The half of his face uncovered was as Kirin remembered: blocky and angular. The contrast between his crisp and clean army fatigues and the grime-covered hero costumes they all wore was made sharper as they walked closer.

"Head to Lecture Hall D for debrief." He didn't even wait to see if they'd heard, turning on his heel the moment he'd finished speaking. Even his steps were precise, his boots clicking out a steady rhythm until he made it to the rooftop door.

"They replaced Force... with Valor." A muscle was going in Clidna's jaw. Her face was usually pale, but as her anger rose, so did the color in her cheeks.

"How could they think getting her old partner was a good idea?" Wyrm's voice was gravelly as always, but the outrage made it feel more dangerous.

Majesty's class filed by, uncaring as theirs was stuck in disbelief. Pressure was going to be replaced— they'd known that. Shifter had confirmed it just that morning. But bringing in her old hero partner? That felt too much like they were trying to replace her entirely, like they'd gone and found the closest thing to her. It would hurt a lot less if it was just some random hero they'd pulled off the street.

It took Kirin a few moments to master himself, and when he did, he immediately looked to Ifrit. This wasn't going to sit well with him, surely. Valor was— by all accounts— a much worse hero than Force had been, and hardly even in the public eye for the last six or seven years.

Yet when Kirin turned to face Ifrit, he didn't find rage in the other man's face. No, the expression Ifrit wore was plain to see, but it wasn't anger.

It was fear.

The silence in the lecture hall was unbearably tense. Kirin ached to move, the dried blood on his suit crusted over and itchy where it poked his skin. He'd eventually crystallized the patch of skin directly under the ripped fabric, since Valor was reading something at the desk while they all just... sat there.

Ifrit had insisted they head straight to the lecture hall, Adlivun seconding that decision. That meant they were all sweaty and tired, shoved into rows of desks, with only the sound of Valor tapping on his keyboard now and then to fill the hall. They had been there for nearly an hour at that point, just watching Valor *read*.

If he was considering ditching, Ifrit was doing the exact opposite.

He didn't think Ifrit had moved at all since they'd sat down, posture ramrod straight. His back must have been aching, but he didn't slouch at all, no matter how many minutes ticked by. His hands were on top of the desk, palms down. It oddly reminded Kirin of when they'd been accosted by Reverb the year before. Like he was trying to prove that he wasn't up to anything.

Valor finally stood up and the whole room snapped to attention. The anxiety from the mission compounded with the hour of silence left them like a taut string, ready to snap.

"I have been specially selected by the school to reform this class and address the deficits in your schooling." Valor even mimicked military posture, walking back and forth slowly with his hands clasped behind his back. "I have reviewed the mission report and have found unacceptable weaknesses in this group, which will be addressed."

No one in the room dared say a word.

"Bhuta Vahana Yantra. Phoenix. Ness." He gestured sharply for them to come down and stand in a line, consulting a list once they began to move. "Antaeus. Clidna. And... Kirin."

As Kirin stood, he noticed the faint whitening of Ifrit's knuckles.

The six of them lined up silently. Ifrit was keeping his expression carefully blank, and they were all taking cues from him to do the same. Only Ness couldn't hide her anxiety, her face even, but her image becoming more transparent as Valor looked at her with disgust.

"All six of you are, from this moment on, back on probation."

There was a gasp from somewhere in the room, and Valor turned around sharply to try to catch who it was. Lilin's mouth was mercifully hidden from view, so after a few moments he turned back to face them.

"Bhuta Vahana Yantra. That name is too long. You are to go to the marketing professor and change it." Kirin hadn't thought Yantra's name was hard to say, and yet Valor managed to butcher each word. "You were also completely useless in this mission. If that happens again, you will be expelled."

This time multiple people broke out in disbelieving, angry whispers.

"QUIET." Valor slammed his hand onto the desk as he yelled, and it cracked in two. The sound of it resounded throughout the hall, silencing everyone. "You will also do a shift cleaning the locker room to pay for your failure. Dismissed."

Kirin expected her to argue, to point out that she *hadn't* been useless in the first place, and even if she *had* been they were in a region where there was no tech so there was absolutely nothing she could do about it. But she was silent. As she walked away, she even looked guilty. Bent over from the weight of the shame, for the first time since he'd known her, she looked like she was trying to make herself small.

"Phoenix." Kirin's attention was brought back to Valor as he stopped in front of their flame-haired healer. "You're too flashy and too slow. Have them dye your hair. And next time, jump faster."

Valor was about to dismiss Phoenix when she cut him off.

"Can't dye it, the second *I* die it comes right back." Phoenix rarely got angry, and never for long. Yet she'd been looking at Valor with contempt the whole time. "And *Pressure* specifically worked with marketing on this image to assist with an offensive strategy."

Valor *scoffed*.

"What did she know about strategy? She died. Dismissed."

Kirin felt blood on his palms as his fingertips crystallized, his hands balled into fists. His gaze shot up to Ifrit, who was watching him with intensity. The rapid rise and fall of his chest gave Kirin enough clarity to uncurl his hands, to get his own breathing under control. As he did, Ifrit let out a shaky breath.

"Ness." Valor's mouth was covered, but the disgusted curl of his lip could be *heard*. "Speak to someone about this issue—" he waved at her generally— "and fix it. It's disgusting. Dismissed."

She headed back to her seat next to Yantra without a word.

"Antaeus." Here, Valor spoke with a slight, disparaging chuckle. "Another marketing mistake. You're practically *adorable*. It's disturbing. Fix it."

Antaeus started to head to his seat, but Valor grabbed him by the collar and threw him back into place so hard he crashed into Clidna.

"I didn't say you could go." Valor's eyes flashed, looming over Antaeus, more than a head taller than him. Clidna still held him up, the small man shaking with what could have been either fear or anger. They stayed locked there for a moment, frozen in a silent war of attrition. Only once Antaeus stood on his own did Valor say he could go.

"Clidna."

She wasn't planning on taking whatever insult was coming lying down. Her chin was lifted in defiance, a dangerous glimmer in her eye. Ifrit noticed it too, his fire skittering outward from his head before he could get his anxiety under control.

"The limits on your power are unacceptable. Either get used to working through the pain or give up. If there is no improvement in a month, you will be expelled. Am I clear?"

Stiffly, like all her muscles were protesting, she nodded.

"I said, *am I clear*?" His meaning was, at least.

"...*yes*." Kirin flinched at the sound of her voice, which was so raw it sounded closer to Wyrm's than her own.

"Good. Dismissed."

That left Kirin as the last one standing.

Clidna, brilliant woman that she was, didn't go back to her previous seat, instead taking the now empty one next to Ifrit. She lightly touched his elbow to let him know she was there, but Ifrit's eyes never left Kirin. He was doing a poor job of concealing his worry now, knuckles wholly white. He'd even put out the flames above his head to hide the fact that he couldn't control them.

"Kirin." Valor came to a stop before him, and Kirin couldn't help but be unimpressed. The way he held himself made Kirin think of small birds that puffed up their chests to look bigger, and the false military attired looked even more like a costume up close. His eyes were a watery, almost colorless blue, which left Kirin to absently wonder if all the posters he graced had artificially saturated the color. His pride seemed large enough that he'd insist on such a thing. "Do you know why you're here?"

"If I had to guess, sir, it's because I was unable to stop two of the villains from escaping." Kirin was proud of himself for keeping his voice level and calm. "In addition to that, I wasn't quick enough to activate my mien and was injured, leaving me doubly incapable of pursuing."

"Hm." Valor looked like he accepted the answer for a moment. And then, almost seeing it happen in slow motion, Valor swung at him.

In that span between breaths, a few thoughts went through his mind.

Pressure wouldn't have believed he'd been tricked so easily. She knew that he trained with Ifrit, and a detonation of that scale shouldn't have been able to even move him. Could he have convinced her to look the other way? Almost certainly. But if Valor knew the extent of what he was capable of, any chance of hiding what they'd done was gone. This was a test. If Kirin blocked it, Valor would know he was lying.

For the second time that day, his back crashed against the wall.

The lecture halls weren't nearly as sturdy as the Disaster Simulator, or even the power gym, and the whole building shook from the force. He'd given himself the luxury of protecting his head and back, but still his chest ached from where Valor's fist had landed. He released his mien almost immediately and fell out of the wall, able to keep himself from buckling through force of will alone. He didn't want to touch his chest, since it was already aching, but when he did later, he suspected he'd find that a rib was fractured, if not outright broken.

Phoenix had the same thought, already making his way down to Kirin, when Valor held up his hand.

"Pain teaches better than anything," he said to the dead silent class. Half of them were on their feet, yet Ifrit was still pointedly sitting. His eyes were large, practically begging Kirin to say nothing, to stay still. "Let this be our first official lesson."

Valor walked over to Kirin and kicked out one of his knees.

It wasn't enough to truly make Kirin fall, but he'd dealt with enough men like this. He leaned into the momentum and let the blow carry him to the floor. Valor leaned down, blocking out the light above him.

"There will be no healing without my approval. Do I make myself clear?" Though the statement should have been directed at Phoenix, Valor said it so quietly that only Kirin could hear.

"Yes sir." Kirin did his best to keep his expression neutral.

"Dismissed," Valor shouted, which did make Kirin flinch. Judging from the amusement in his eyes, it had been intended to. He turned away without a second thought, leaving Kirin to get back to his feet slowly, coming to an infuriating realization.

The school hadn't chosen Valor because he was the closest thing they could get to Pressure.

They'd chosen him because they wanted to destroy any trace of her.

7

Mending Bridges

KIRIN WAS HURT, BUT he was trying not to show it.

Ifrit should've known Valor wouldn't come for him directly. He'd stopped trying that once Pressure started to suspect something. Why would now be different? While outwardly he seemed so cocky, so confident, his mien was simple strength augmentation, and he knew it. There was a reason his sister had been the popular one of the pair, a reason he'd fallen into obscurity once she wasn't attached to him anymore. And Ifrit was the reason she'd abandoned him, at least in his mind.

When they'd gotten off the plane and it'd been Valor waiting, Ifrit's blood had gone cold. He'd expected for his name to be called, to have to relive some of the worst days of his life, to be the one who was hit. After all, if Kirin was responsible for the teenagers getting away, so was he. And then he'd gone, blinded and stupid by anger and the humiliating afterburn of fear, and mouthed off to the press. But only Kirin was the one limping, only Kirin was the one in pain.

"Phoenix—"

"Not outside." Phoenix's eyes were dark too, her rage simmering close to the surface.

"It's really not that bad," Kirin protested.

"Shut up." The whole class spoke in unison.

"Yantra can you—"

"I have access to all the cameras they have in and around the dorm. I keep them running, but I have the footage a day behind so I can edit it when we need to, as well as a script running to filter out when we're places we're not supposed to be." There was a holo screen pulled up in front of Yantra's face, but she wasn't touching it. Instead, she seemed to be coding with only her eyes, words appearing as they slid side to side. It had to be her mien, since he'd never seen *anyone* do anything like it before. "I just need to update the program to check for Phoenix healing us."

"Can you fake a cracked rib?" Ness was on Kirin's other side, looking as angry as Ifrit felt.

"I think so, the only thing I worry about is if he hits the same spot again. It's a lot harder to fake a broken one." Kirin shrugged, and Ifrit didn't fail to notice the wince that rippled across his features.

"I'll kill him before it comes to that." Phoenix didn't sound like she was joking, her face serious as she held open the dorm door. So serious in fact that Ifrit took a second look at her.

Ifrit hadn't known what to make of Phoenix during those first days of school. She was annoying, certainly, and enjoyed getting a rise out of people. She did care, in her own way, and when the two of them were alone on the fifth floor, some days she'd even seemed bearable. But that was before.

Now she and Ifrit were closer, entirely by virtue of having spent so much time dying together. There was a point at which someone saved your life enough times to earn permanent amnesty. It gave you some level of insight into who they were as a person, too. Ifrit understood Phoenix a lot better than he used to, and that meant he couldn't dismiss some of the things Phoenix said as easily as everyone else could. And when

Phoenix met his eyes as Ifrit walked into the building, there wasn't a shadow of doubt in his mind that Phoenix would try to hurt Valor. Somehow that scared him even more.

Ifrit's thoughts had left him distracted and he struggled to catch back up in the conversation, especially with multiple people talking at once. His headache was worsening; not even Kirin's presence at his side could make it go away.

"What're we going to do about him, though?" Naddāha was looking calmly at Kirin. "He hates us, and we haven't done anything yet."

If there was one good thing that had happened that day, it was the genuine confusion that crossed Kirin's face when he realized everyone was looking at him for an answer. Kirin, per usual, seemed uncomfortable with the attention. His gaze then turned to Ifrit.

"What do you think we should fucking do?" The words were out of his mouth before he knew he was speaking. There was a tiny, childish part of Ifrit that wanted Kirin to tell him it'd all be okay, and even if it weren't for that, he wanted to know what Kirin was thinking. He was so solid, so steady; surely he could find a way to make sure they finished the year without anyone dying. Without anyone else dying.

There was a faint shift in Kirin's eyes, and he stood up marginally straighter.

"Obviously, he's going to be looking for any excuse to hurt us," Kirin spoke slowly, like he was piecing together his thoughts as he verbalized them. "Unfortunately for him, we're really good at what we do."

A few smiles broke out around the room.

"We're not perfect though, and that'll be what's hard to deal with. Any infraction, no matter how small, he'll come for us. I can take a hit, I'm happy to cover, and I think that's what it's going to come to. The school picked Valor because they want to try to take away the most dangerous idea that Pressure gave us: that we deserve to be treated like people. And while Valor is going to try to make us feel worthless, we don't have to listen to him. We can cover for one another and that'll get us through this year. It's just one year, and then they can't control us."

"We just have to make sure not to lose our souls in the process." Aïcha was nodding along.

"Which means one of the things we need to cover for is sometimes letting our targets go." Kuafu spoke gravely, his eyes finding Ifrit. It was remarkable how far he'd come in only a year. Ifrit's heart panged as he thought of how proud Pressure would be to see him now.

"Only if you're comfortable." Kirin didn't sound ashamed or surprised.

"You let him hit you." A slightly incredulous smile appeared on Wyrm's face. "Oh. *Oh.*"

"He wants to think we're terrible?" Kirin openly smiled himself. "Well, it stands to reason a few villains would escape every now and again, right?"

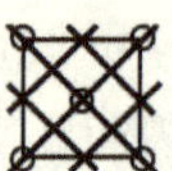

Ifrit was playing with Kirin's hair instead of talking.

It didn't matter how long he took to find his words, Kirin just lay there, one arm behind his head. His hair still wasn't as long as it had been, but it was almost all the way down his neck again, long enough for him to pull into a tiny ponytail. He didn't seem to mind that the gold clashed with almost everything he wore, but it drove Ifrit insane.

"It's getting fucking long again." They'd been awake for a while, having fallen asleep so early. The sun was above the horizon, but none of the rays had made it above the dense thicket of trees. Kirin turned to look at him, his hair moving just out of reach. Ifrit found himself frowning.

"Should I cut it?"

"Not if you're going to do what you did last time. Looked dumb." He was lying, of course.

"Whatever you say." Kirin rolled over and touched a few of the curls that lay over Ifrit's forehead, matted down after being pressed against Kirin's back for the last several hours. His hand traveled up to the roots, which Ifrit knew had to be redyed. "I know you hate it, but I do think the red looks so nice."

Any words Ifrit had died in his throat as Kirin's hand rested on the side of his face.

It was so casual, so natural, and Ifrit's heart felt full to bursting. Kirin's eyes were barely open, he was still half asleep, and yet he was smiling ever so slightly. The first ray of sunshine broke above the tree line and passed across Kirin's face, revealing that as black as his eyes appeared, they were opalescent too. Combined with the way the light caught in his hair, glinting like diamond, he looked ethereal, like a dream.

Unfortunately, all dreams have to end.

A sharp knock on the door slammed all of the anxiety back into Ifrit's chest. Kirin was on his feet before Ifrit had even begun to move, the darkness of Kirin's eyes changing to pure white as his posture stiffened. Phoenix wouldn't have bothered to knock and no one else ever needed Ifrit this early in the morning, which meant...

Go back to your room. Ifrit wallowed. It'd been naïve to assume that Valor was going to continue to ignore him. But Kirin grabbed his shoulder when Ifrit tried to turn away, to hide the fear plainly on his face.

I'll stay. If he tries anything, I want to be here. Kirin looked annoyingly stubborn.

You can't be here. I can't have him realize that I—

"Ifrit. I know you're there. I need a moment of your time."

Ifrit's hands fell still as he registered that it was Majesty's voice he was hearing, not Valor's. What the fuck could she possibly want? She usually ignored him even more than Valor was trying to. It wasn't likely she was there on Valor's orders— the thought was fucking ridiculous— but if she saw Kirin in his room, when both of them had obviously just woken up, there was no chance the information wouldn't make it to Valor.

Luckily, Kirin seemed more malleable now.

Just fucking climb into your room and pretend to wake up and go to the bathroom. Ifrit had only just finished signing the words when Kirin reached out and squeezed his hands. Kirin's eyes were still worried, searching Ifrit's face to make sure it was okay to leave. He lightly brushed a knuckle under Ifrit's chin, and then he was gone, leaving Ifrit blinking after him. It took a solid five seconds for Ifrit to remember where he was, let alone what was going on.

Feeling distinctly cheated, he wrenched the door open.

"What?" Kirin hadn't been gone for even thirty seconds, but Ifrit could feel the headache building. As if summoned by the thought, Kirin opened his door, offering Majesty a nod. He gave Ifrit an encouraging smile behind her back, walking to the kitchen to turn on the coffee maker. Fuck, Ifrit really did love him.

"I... apologize for the hour." Majesty sounded like the words were dragged out of her, which was understandable since Ifrit had never heard her apologize to anyone before. She was probably trying to remember how to say the word. "However, I need to speak with you in my office."

For the second time that morning Ifrit felt like his brain stopped working, though for a completely different reason. She was *asking*. Not only was she asking, she wasn't wearing her hero suit for once, instead wearing a professionally fitted pantsuit. It still wasn't anywhere close to casual, but it proved that she did own some real clothes. She'd traded her typical boots for stiff loafers, though her bright blue hair was still pulled into her signature painful bun.

"...fine." He wasn't sure who was more surprised, her or himself. Kirin even briefly lost his affected calm, eyes jumping to them. "But can I get fucking dressed first?"

"Yes. Of course." Something was definitely up as *Majesty her-fucking-self* looked embarrassed. "Do that."

Her awkwardness grew as Ifrit stood there, shocked, not sure what weird parallel dimension he'd fallen into. Kirin stepped in to fill the silence.

"I'm starting coffee, would you like a cup?"

Ifrit didn't hear the rest of the conversation as he closed the door to hurriedly change. Even though Majesty drank her coffee at a frankly alarming pace, Ifrit still had time to brush his teeth and hair before she'd finished.

"Should I plan to go for our morning run alone?" Kirin's voice was casual, but there was an intensity to his gaze.

"This won't take more than thirty minutes." Majesty was getting back to her usual imperious self, whether it was from the coffee or from getting to leave the dorm, only she knew. "It's just a conversation."

Kirin's eyes still followed them until the elevator doors closed.

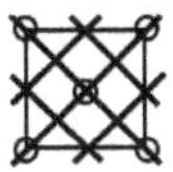

Ifrit was going to blow up Majesty's clock.

Why she had such an old-fashioned one made no sense, since it clashed with the high end furniture in the rest of the room, yet even its incongruity couldn't stop it from ceaselessly ticking. Her office was larger than Pressure's had been, one of the best ones on campus. Pressure had been given a tiny postage stamp sized room, quiet punishment for her disobedience. And on her death, it had been quickly packed up and sent away, like she'd never been there at all.

Majesty's office was spacious, with a pristine white desk and matching upholstered chairs, a small sitting area in one section of the room, and a marble coffee table that had carefully stacked beige books. The only color in the room was the dark stained wood of the grandfather clock behind Majesty's desk, and the bright color of her hair.

The swing of the pendulum behind Majesty felt egregious in its motion when compared to the rigid board that was Majesty. She hadn't moved a muscle since she'd sat down, hands clasped so tightly that her knuckles were pure white. Her mouth had opened a few times as if she was going to say something, but no words came out, leaving the only noise the interminable ticking of that fucking clock.

"Just fucking say what you want so I can go back." Ifrit finally couldn't stand it. Her eyes jumped up and she seemed, if anything, more nervous. Which was bizarre. She was never *nervous*.

"I..." She cleared her throat, switching the clasp of her hands. "I just wanted to check in with you and see how you were doing."

Now it was Ifrit's turn to be at a complete loss for words.

She didn't notice his surprise, focused on arranging the pens above her plotter in a perfectly straight line.

"I reviewed all of Force's records and it seems that she would have weekly check-ins with you. I took it upon myself to resume these." When she looked up, there were creases around her eyes. She looked tired.

"We met every week because she was my *mom*." Ifrit struggled to keep his fire under control as his temper rose. "And her name was *Pressure*."

He'd been expecting to get a rise out of her for that, but she only looked... guilty?

"I don't pretend that I could ever fill her shoes." Her voice was sincere. Or so he thought. He'd never heard her speak without disdain before, so maybe he was just mishearing. His hearing aids probably needed to be repaired; he'd taken enough hits to the head lately. "But I... I am the head of your cohort, and it is my job to help students who are suffering."

Ifrit had had his ankle crossed over his knee and the shock made his foot slip to the floor.

"Pressure's loss—"

"Murder."

"Pressure's loss—" her eyes flickered to the smoke detector by the door and he rolled his eyes. Of course, her office was bugged too— "was sudden and unexpected. I think in my own grief I forgot that she touched more lives than my own."

In less than an hour, two apologies. Incredible. He had to still be fucking sleeping.

"You actually fucking expect me to believe you're *grieving*? You hated her and it's pretty fucking shitty to drag me down here first thing in the morning thinking that we'd what, bond or some shit over her?" He was leaning forward in the chair, voice rising.

"I have been mourning Force for ten years." Majesty's tone was icy, and it was the first time all morning Ifrit felt comfortable with her. This was how they interacted, not niceties and platitudes, but with that veiled distaste for one another. "I also did not expect to be quite so affected. However, I have been forced to acknowledge these past months that in being too caught up in who she used to be, I failed to appreciate her for who she was."

Then it was gone. Majesty was tired and sad and all too human. Ifrit slouched back in his chair, eyes narrowed.

"And in doing so, I suppose I've failed to understand you." She cleared her throat again. "You're very like her."

A year ago, that would have been an insult.

"So you're coping with losing her by trying to find her in me?"

"Yes." Majesty didn't sound the least bit ashamed. "I feel that you embody a lot of what she was striving for. I never listened to what she had to say before, and I thought it was too late to do that now. After this last mission, I realized how much you shaped her, and I would like to understand that better."

She didn't look like she was lying. She seemed genuine, her countenance severe and focused, like Ifrit could peel back the veil of time and show her what she had missed for years. As she leaned forward, her chair twisted just enough to allow him to see the single photo on her desk, tucked behind files and books. A photo of her and Pressure, much, much younger. Pressure was looking at the camera, smiling brightly behind her bright blue mask. But Majesty was looking at Pressure. The look in her eyes was almost... reverent.

When Ifrit met Majesty's eyes, there was something else that he could see too. Behind the bravado, behind the icy façade, there was someone who had been working toward one goal all her life. Someone who had never dared to question it until now. Someone who could never understand the people she hurt, someone who had never tried to.

Yet here she was, trying. Clinging to someone who was gone by finally trying to figure out who they had been.

"What do you want to know?" Ifrit didn't look at her, opting instead to find the ceiling fascinating.

"What did you talk about with her, usually?" There was faint scratching as she began to write. That was familiar at least, since Pressure was almost always doing paperwork when they talked. But she had still made the time. The coalition *had* been underway for some time, but Pressure had wanted to make sure it was perfect when they premiered, everything planned down to a T.

The coalition.

Ifrit's eyes narrowed as he looked at Majesty, but she met his gaze expressionlessly. If this *was* a ploy to find out more, she was shit out of luck. Pressure hadn't allowed him to look at anything; she hadn't wanted him involved in case it went sideways, or worse, if it distracted him from his classes. He pinched his nose to stop the prickling in the corners of his eyes.

"We talked about how shitty your class is." He settled for honesty.

He didn't expect Majesty's mouth to twitch slightly with the hint of a smile. It was smothered immediately, but it was there. She covered the moment by returning her attention to her paper.

"I suppose she always did think legacy admissions were a poor decision. Unsurprising, considering her background."

"Her background?" Ifrit hated how eager he sounded. He knew Pressure, probably better than anyone did except for Shifter, but she never talked about her past. He'd tried to ask her when she'd first taken him in, and while she was happy to tell him little things, he didn't even know what country she'd come from.

"She was...embarrassed, I suppose. The confidentiality requirements were less enforced back then, but she adhered to them rigidly." Majesty paused, her eyes briefly rising to consider Ifrit. "I will never know her reasons for withholding this information from you, and though it might not have been her wishes, if it would help bridge the divide between us, I am willing to share."

"Why do you fucking know?" The sentence came out angrier

than he'd intended, but Majesty didn't bat an eye.

"That is not what I'm offering to discuss." The iciness crept back into her tone.

"Well, what *do* you know?"

"Likely not much more than you. I know she grew up poor, yet she was well cared for and well loved. She rarely mentioned her parents, and Valor never did. I know they came from somewhere in west Asia, though never what country. She worked impossibly hard to earn a spot here, and was livid when she discovered that some people were simply allowed in because of their parents. Even angrier when Valor used her name to get his own admission. She was naïve, far more than you would ever believe her to be, when she arrived. There was an earnestness to her that even the Hero Council could not fail to see. It was why they made her into the hero she was."

"She wasn't made into anything, she was just an incredible fucking hero on her own."

"We are all made, one way or another. They gave her the most prominent assignment, had her on billboards worldwide. She was a fresh start, no family pressures to consider, no righteous ideas of how she should look. She was their perfect canvas, and even they forgot what she was capable of when she wasn't trying to be what they wanted her to be."

Ifrit knew Majesty had said too much the same moment that she did. A quick burst of light flew to the smoke detector, even though Majesty hadn't appeared to move a muscle.

"If that's taken care of, I want to fucking know what you meant by that." Even with the suspicion that Majesty had temporarily knocked out the bug in her office, Ifrit kept his voice low.

She sighed, her perfect posture faltering. She pressed a hand to her temple, right above her eyebrow, the spot where Ifrit usually got headaches.

"I understand she was trying to protect you, but I will never understand how you couldn't have pieced it together. Surely, you knew she was more powerful than she let on?"

"She was just holding back to avoid collateral damage." The words were empty to his own ears.

"At some point, when you are powerful, it does not matter how well you adhere to the rules. There is always the fear of you and the threat you possess. Force was stronger than the Institute knew, and even then they asked her to hold back. The strength she showed to the public was only a fraction of her real ability, and no one had ever seen her at her full potential until she went to rescue you."

Ifrit was still processing the last few words, but Majesty steamrolled forward.

"Had she still possessed a license, I have no doubt in my mind that they would have still cut her down. I believe that she let them, in hope that they would be so distracted by their apparent success that they would ignore the new threat looming on the horizon."

"What do you mean?" Ifrit's mouth was dry, and he knew what she was going to say before she said it.

"I mean you." He wasn't expecting the follow up though, nor how casually she said it. "Or that classmate of yours, the one who cannot die."

8

Mission Two

KIRIN'S KNEE WAS BOUNCING as he waited for Ifrit to come back, sitting and staring at the elevator like it would make time move faster. Majesty hadn't seemed like she was there to start a fight with Ifrit or to punish him, but that meant Kirin had no idea what she'd wanted, and that was far worse.

He was distracted from his vigil by Phoenix slipping out of their room.

They didn't notice him at first, closing the door ever so gently behind themself. Adlivun was probably still in there, since she never left their side for long. In the few moments that they were unaware of Kirin's presence, he was able to study them, and it made his frown deepen.

Phoenix had been... quiet since they'd gotten back. They would still joke and cause mayhem, but not with the same regularity. And most of their jokes had turned inward, like what they'd said on the mission. That all coupled with the way their posture slumped, like it was too hard to even hold their head up, made Kirin worry that something hadn't healed quite right.

They jumped when they finally noticed him.

"Listen, I thought being dark and broody was Ifrit's thing. I'm not sure how he'll feel about you coming for his brand."

The easy smile was back, their posture going from defeated to casual in a single second. Kirin wasn't buying it.

"Do you want me to make breakfast?" He was already standing, happy to have something to do with his hands.

"Nah, that's okay." Phoenix never turned down food.

"If I don't make you breakfast, I'll mention to Ad that you skipped." His back was facing Phoenix, but he could still hear the way they paused. A few moments later there was the squeak of a chair being pulled back from the counter.

"This is blackmail and I expect better from you," they grumbled. "Mind if I turn on the TV?"

It was likely an excuse to avoid talking, but Kirin hummed his agreement anyway. If he knew anything about Phoenix, it was that if they did not want to talk, they did *not* want to talk. Kirin would just make sure to mention it to Adlivun later, to see if she could get them to open up.

"*China made headlines today for being the first major nation to sign onto the Mien-User Summit, a meeting of nations to propose and adopt sweeping reform to current mien-user laws.*" Kirin's head snapped up at the headline. Phoenix had been in the middle of changing the channel, but they paused too, eyebrows coming together. "*The move was spearheaded by a number of both heroes and politicians who have announced that they are members of the independent Hero Coalition that was formed by the late hero Force. The move has been met with widespread public approval, counteracting conservative lawmakers' original assessment that associating with the Coalition would be political suicide. The summit is intended to be the culmination of the Coaltion's past year of advocacy for not just political protection but acceptance of mien-users as well.*"

The image onscreen changed to show smiling faces standing shoulder to shoulder carrying a banner between them with something written in Chinese. The auto translator caught up a moment later and the phrase "gone but not forgotten" appeared over the text. Who it was referring to was made perfectly clear by the brilliant blue of the banner itself.

Which reminded him of something.

"Hey, have you noticed that Majesty's hair is the same color as Pressure's costume?" *That* got Phoenix's attention back right away.

"Oh, no *wonder* they hated each other." They smiled broadly. "I never really thought about it before, but now that you say it, yeah they really are the same."

"You think it was a competitive thing?" Kirin frowned.

"You think it was something else?" Phoenix tilted their head, half of their fiery hair slipping out of their bun. "Hm. How old do you think Majesty is anyways?"

Bán immediately crossed Kirin's mind. They couldn't be more than twelve, and one of the requirements for starting as a hero was that you couldn't have any children. He'd be shocked if she was over forty, which meant she had to be somewhere between that and thirty.

"I'd guess mid-thirties?" He shrugged. "Why?"

"How old was Pressure?" Phoenix leaned back on the stool, making it tilt.

"Probably about the same."

"So they would've been in school together." They tapped their chin dramatically, which brought a smile to Kirin's lips. At least that was more like them. "I think you're right that it was probably something more. There's way too much drama there for it just to be college rivalry, unless Majesty's particularly petty. And while Bia would be, Majesty feels more... pretentious than that. Pressure's power doesn't really have a color association, and there was nothing about her complexion or eye color that would mean they'd go for that color *specifically*. She probably picked it."

"That's what I was thinking." Kirin's eyes slid to the elevator again.

"Did they date, do you think?" Phoenix was absently twirling a strand of their hair, but the thought startled Kirin enough that he dropped an egg directly into the pan. He cursed quietly as he crystallized a finger to not burn himself while he pulled the eggshell out. "What? It would make sense why they hated each other then."

"And why she knew about Majesty's kid." That thought wasn't meant to be said out loud, and the way Phoenix perked right up meant it hadn't been missed.

"What's this now?"

"Phoenix—"

"I give you *so* much information, the least you can do is return the favor."

"Technically Adlivun tells everyone."

"But I still find it out!"

Kirin sighed.

"Yes, Majesty has a kid. I helped rescue them at the end of the school year. When..."

"When Ifrit and I got forcibly kidnapped and imprisoned?"

Kirin winced.

"Yeah, right before then."

"And you didn't think that was the *first* thing I'd want to know upon being rescued?"

"I thought you'd want to find Adlivun, but maybe I was wrong."

"Well, you're correct that I wanted to kiss her beautiful face, but finding out that Queen Bitch had a kid should have been the *second* thing you assumed I wanted to do."

Oh. Kirin paused in flipping the omelet for a moment.

"You two *are* dating, then?"

The legs of Phoenix's chair fell back down with a thud as

they used both hands to push themself all the way across the counter, scrutinizing Kirin's face. The intensity of their gray eyes made Kirin squirm, which brought a real smile to their face.

"You are being genuine, huh?" They settled back into their seat, kicking their legs up on the counter now. Kirin paused again to pointedly move their feet *off* where they ate, which earned a laugh. "Kirin, baby, what did you *think* was going on?"

"Friends can sleep in each other's rooms," he protested, though his voice sounded weak to his own ears. Maybe that was just because they were burning though.

"Is that what you and Ifrit are doing?" Phoenix's tone was joking, but when Kirin didn't respond, their expression dropped. "Kirin. Why are you making that face?"

"Because we are just friends?"

"Then why did you say it as a question?" Phoenix slammed their hands down on the counter and stood up so quickly their stool toppled behind them. "I *saw* you two kiss!"

That left Kirin speechless, and Phoenix rightly recognized the silence as confusion and not avoidance.

"At Satol? When you rescued us? Hello??"

"Oh." Kirin turned back to the eggs, pulling them onto a plate and frowning at the side that was slightly too brown. He'd just have to eat that one and make a fresh one for Ifrit. "No, I can release oxygen when I breathe. It was... it was just to wake him up."

It was the truth, but why did it feel like a lie?

When Phoenix was silent for a beat, Kirin looked up, surprised to see them with such a devastated expression.

"Does Ifrit know that?" they asked softly.

Kirin was spared from answering by the newscaster's voice.

"Breaking news: we have just received word that the hero Mesmer has been murdered."

Phoenix recognized the name too, and they both turned at

once. An image of him was onscreen, a broad smile under his bushy black beard that contrasted so sharply with his vivid yellow costume.

"He was reported missing last night after he failed to report to his home jurisdiction of Satol. He was one of the several dozen heroes at the successful joint raid on an enclave of villains located in dead zone N30-22."

"Did you see him on the way out of the dead zone?" Kirin asked.

"I was a bit focused on you." Phoenix was distracted by the sound of their door opening, Adlivun coming to join them. But Kirin felt the words sharply.

"Viewers are encouraged to use discretion before watching the next portion of this segment. The images provided by police are graphic in nature and may be upsetting to younger audiences."

That was an extreme understatement.

Mesmer was hardly recognizable, even in his yellow suit. His body was crushed and broken, blood splattered indiscriminately around the alley he lay in. It looked like there wasn't a single bone in his body that remained intact, the remains too thin for his ribcage to not be entirely crushed. It almost looked like he'd been stepped on from above.

"No." Phoenix was focused on one detail of the image, one that Kirin had managed to overlook as he had tried to match the man he knew with the stain on the ground. But now he could see the message left behind what used to be Mesmer's head.

The sound of the elevator opening had Kirin rushing to intercept Ifrit before he could see what was on the screen.

"What the fuck's going on?" Ifrit wasn't oblivious; whether it was the way Kirin was placing himself between Ifrit and the broadcast or if it was his expression alone, Ifrit knew something was wrong.

"I just don't know if you'll want to see it." Kirin had instinctively put his hands on Ifrit's shoulders, just to reassure himself that Ifrit was still there. If Majesty hadn't interrupted, maybe they'd still be in bed. Maybe they could've avoided seeing the news for hours yet.

"He'll want to see." Phoenix's voice sounded angry. When Ifrit pushed past, Kirin could see Phoenix's face mixed between fear and rage.

"That's just fucking great." Ifrit seemed less affected, only glancing and then moving to get himself coffee. Yet his lips were pressed into a fine line, and there was a faint tremor as he took out a cup.

Phoenix didn't look away from the screen at all, and Kirin felt his own fear rising as he looked at the stylized A reflected in their eyes.

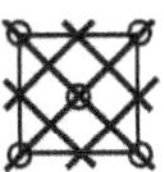

Faking a cracked rib was going to be harder than Kirin thought.

Their previous mien training classes had been mostly self-guided, as Pressure wanted them to explore their limits and to experiment with their miens. She only stepped in to offer advice or suggest a different approach, insisting that what was most important was to get the most practice time that they could. It was critical, she had said, especially in the early stages of training when they were locked out of the power gym outside of class hours. Even as they got better she still never hovered, saying they knew their miens better than she ever would.

Valor had a very different opinion on the matter.

Instead of training throughout the period, they spent most of the time sitting. Valor instructed one student at a time, everyone else forced to watch the person being "taught." It felt all too much like public humiliation, especially with Valor's booming commentary.

"Now this is just pathetic. No one would be taken down with a strike like that." He stepped to the side and hit Medusa on the back of the head. She fell to the ground, her goggles snapping with an audible crack. Out of the corner of his eye, Kirin could see Adlivun grab onto the back of Phoenix's t-shirt and hold them in place, their hands balled into fists on their knees. Their posture didn't relax until Medusa started to push herself up from the floor, holding the now broken goggles against her face.

"I don't understand how you haven't died already when your physical abilities are so lacking. It's a wonder that you passed your final exam and were granted a license at all. Whoever allowed you through should be ashamed."

The subtle digs at Pressure were testing Ifrit's patience, but he was holding it together well. His hands were splayed on the ground, the muscles along his arms taut as he pressed down against the floor to release some of his aggression. He was playing with the ring of fire around his head, making it rotate and lazily spiral, only losing the nice, tight shape once or twice in the whole hour they'd been "practicing." It was probably for the best that he was managing so well, since he'd immediately shaken off Kirin when he'd tried to take his hand.

Kirin was trying not to think about that, and Valor being a complete and utter dick was helping. So far, he'd only called up their physically weaker classmates to insult— Antaeus, Ness, and Naddāha already having gotten special attention. Lilin was on deck after Medusa was done, and she was nervous, if the shaking of her leg was anything to go by.

They were thankfully interrupted by the simultaneous ringing of their phones.

While they were all immediately on their feet, Valor looked displeased at having been interrupted.

"We'll have remedial class once we return," he yelled at their retreating backs. "Don't assume you're all free. Be at the jet in three minutes."

"He'll fucking forget about this after the mission," Ifrit muttered, his voice low enough to only be heard by Kirin. "Once he has something else to insult us for."

"We're not going to give him anything to fault this time." Kirin managed to catch Ifrit's fingers and squeeze them, Ifrit keeping hold even when Kirin tried to let go.

"Are we?" Ifrit's eyes were searching, and it only then occurred to Kirin that he hadn't found a moment to talk with Ifrit about the mission. About what those kids had told him. But maybe, after this mission, it'd be taken care of, and Ifrit never had to know.

But they'd reached the top of the disaster simulator, already in their costumes from class. Majesty's group was jogging into view from the other side of the disaster simulator, and even though they were too far away to hear anything, they were still too close for comfort.

"Of course not," was all Kirin said instead. "Since we're going on a mission to find an Aether cell."

Sweat dripped down Kirin's nose and onto the floor. His legs and back ached from being hunched over for so long, but there was nothing he could do about it. Ifrit had been assigned to this section— likely an assignment direct from Valor— and that meant Kirin sure as hell was going to be there too.

He just wished the ceiling was taller and there were fewer

heating pipes.

"Team four are you in position?" Majesty's voice came over the headset and Kirin could see Ifrit grit his teeth. They'd been the first *in* position and they'd been there for over an hour already. The maintenance tunnel was so short that even Clidna had to duck, let alone Kirin.

"Yes, we're in position." Somehow, despite not unlocking his jaw, Ifrit managed to speak.

"We'll be starting momentarily. Ensure you are oriented correctly." Majesty's voice cut out as the 3D map pulled out of Ifrit's phone. The positions of the teams were shown in blinking red dots and the spot they were supposed to burst through the wall was dead ahead, as it had been for *an hour*. If hunching over hadn't left Kirin's muscles shaking, the strain of waiting and not plunging ahead alone would have. The last of Majesty's class were finally falling into place, which made Clidna roll her eyes.

"Can you *believe* we're paired with these amateurs?" she muttered, in a halfway decent impression of Bia.

Even that wasn't enough to make Ifrit crack a grin. He remained scowling as he put his mask back on; if Valor hadn't been there, Kirin almost thought Ifrit would've kept it off the whole time. It wasn't like Aether didn't know what he looked like. Kirin himself only had a cloth mask made of the same material as his shirt for coverage, since he hadn't had time to see Nwabudike to replace the one that had broken the day before.

Their target was— yet again— underground. Ifrit was putting on a brave front, but Kirin could taste the carbon in the air, could feel the current as it churned with Ifrit's discomfort. Phoenix had looked horrified during the briefing as well, likely less to do with the location and more to do with their target.

The International Hero Council had received a tip that an

Aether cell was hiding out in an old, abandoned hydro-electric plant. Several witnesses had noticed people coming and going, and a few of the heroes from Satol had claimed to recognize some of the photographed suspects as those who had escaped the city. But the bigger catch was the single reported sighting of the woman in white.

It felt odd that she was so easily found, after months of searching. Yantra, however, was convinced that it was a good sign, that public opinion was turning against them. She didn't think it was a coincidence that the tip had come in the same day that the images of what they did to Mesmer leaked.

And even if she wasn't here, someone was. The pipes were blistering to touch, water pumped up from the hot spring below turning the mechanical space into a sauna. Clidna and Kirin were sweating buckets, yet the only discomfort that Ifrit showed was from the enclosed space.

They seem really fucking confused about what momentarily means. Well, he was more pissed than usual too, but he had good reason to be.

Neither Clidna nor Kirin had time to respond before the go signal went out and they sprang into motion.

Ifrit blasted the wall in front of them open, propelling all three forward with a smaller blast from behind. Kirin shielded them from the front by turning his chest, thighs, and face into diamond, Clidna whistling at a high enough frequency to shatter any debris that would be falling their way. Gunshots went off, pinging harmlessly off Kirin's chest as Ifrit and Clidna darted out from behind and knocked out the two sentries. So far, their intelligence had been good.

They were coming up from the rear, along with Yantra, Ness, Wyrm, Aïcha, Antaeus, and Dulu. The other two groups had taken marginally longer to break through the walls— they *were* reinforced concrete after all— and Ness vanished to scout ahead the second they caught up. Yantra produced some shock cuffs from one of her pants' pockets and secured the two downed sentries before Ness returned.

"Our floorplans are shockingly accurate." Despite the positive news, Ness looked skeptical. Or maybe she just looked transparent. "We should converge with the others once we go through the service corridor around the main generator."

They set off down the stairs, Kirin going first. There wasn't anything to note as they took the tunnel at a run, just unadorned concrete walls and a concrete ceiling. Every now and again there would be a light attached to the wall, safe from damage in its metal cage, or peeling signs for safety regulations. Nothing out of the ordinary.

At least on their end.

More gunshots could be heard filtering through their comms, but from Majesty's class. There was some difficulty in subduing the guards on their end, though it sounded like no one had gotten hurt yet. If they didn't hurry though it would mean—

"*Teams four, five, and six, you are moving to engage.*" Majesty's voice betrayed a hint of frustration.

"Acknowledged." Ifrit was echoed by Yantra and Aïcha, who were their respective squads' leaders, at least for the moment. Valor had arrived late, and Majesty had once again told them they could organize themselves however as she had briefed them on the jet. Kirin had been surprised Valor didn't rescind the order once he'd appeared, but all he'd done was select their routes. He hadn't even bothered to watch over them, the coward.

Now that they were all in motion, Ifrit's discomfort had faded away. He was somehow managing to run *and* check the positions as they headed forward, and he didn't like what he saw.

"Everyone else is going to be stuck up there for a fucking

while, if these numbers are accurate." He'd turned off his comm to make sure Valor couldn't hear. "We've only got us nine and an unknown number of hostiles in there."

"I can scout ahead, even through the wall." Ness appeared in front of them, jogging backward.

"And if I can get a sightline, I can sabotage any tech they've got on them," Yantra added.

"What were the numbers for the main room again? And do we need to worry about a detonation from the generator at all?" Aïcha was definitely slowing herself down to keep pace with them; Kirin had seen her move easily twice the speed.

"The schematics indicate that if there's power, the emergency subroutines are running, so there shouldn't be any explosions to worry about except the ones that help us." The ring around Yantra's eyes grew as she pulled more information into her view. "Our original intel suggested that the largest number of people would be congregated at the main entrance, where everyone else is stuck, and it at least *sounds* like that's true. We should be looking at even numbers once we get in there."

Wyrm put his hand in front of his face in the agreed upon signal and they all dropped comms immediately.

"Should we be worried that they organized a whole international party for a raid on ten people and are comfortable sending in *nine* of us with unknown numbers?" He spoke quickly, which made his usually rough voice almost unintelligible. Kirin signed the message along to Ifrit, glad Yantra had a quick answer.

"Theoretically, they didn't *know* what was going on in there. And here, we both know what's going on, and who's in there, roughly."

Wyrm nodded and turned his comm back on, satisfied at least for the moment.

Kirin was less sure.

What if this was a trap? What if they wanted Ifrit back? They weren't done targeting the class, even if he was the only one who knew it. The fear was coating the back of Kirin's throat just as heavily as the carbon was, his breaths far too quick. As his eyes flickered to Ifrit, whose face was scrunched in focused anger, he decided it didn't matter if they were targeting him.

Kirin would protect him no matter what.

"Three inside." Ness confirmed, reappearing on their side of the wall.

"Anything to indicate what they're doing?" Yantra asked.

"They've got a whole ass computer set up in there, but I have no idea what they're doing on it. It's all code."

"Any potential entry points?" Kirin was bouncing on his feet, shaking out his shoulders to get some of the energy out, Wyrm also stretching as best he could. They were at the end of the corridor, a door to the left leading them into the generator room itself, the door ahead heading to the service tunnel they were originally supposed to take to meet with the rest of their forces. The central room their targets sat in was only accessed through the generator room, or by smashing a hole in the wall.

"If we break through five meters down the wall, we'll miss all the main equipment. There are two scouts guarding the door to the generator room, and then someone at the desk."

"*Describe them*." Valor's voice crackled through their headsets, making Ifrit wince.

"Dark blond hair, mid-height. I would guess one hundred and seventy centimeters, probably. Wearing a gaiter pulled over her face, brown eyes. Wearing some kind of tech I was unable to identify on her belt, looked like a small box with blinking lights."

"*Could that be our woman in white?*" One of the local heroes cut in, the sound of combat in the background. Gunshots were echoing, though Kirin couldn't hear anything from where he stood. They really were far from any backup.

"Potentially. She is your primary target. Be cautious, we do not know what sort of mien she or either of those two guards have." Majesty's voice was half drowned by the fighting around her. There were fewer guns, but a scream passed through to them with such clarity that its owner must have been standing right next to her.

"Understood." Ifrit was hard at work, though to anyone else it would've looked like he was standing still. Kirin could feel the air around him densifying, Ifrit careful to only let the carbon drift into Kirin's airspace to keep the others safe. Wyrm carefully ran his hands down the spikes on his shoulders, tracing the shape of a door with his hands once they were coated. The moment his palms made contact, the surface began to hiss, steam rising as the concrete corroded away.

They managed to enter the room without being noticed.

The two sentries had their backs to the group, facing the window wall that overlooked the generator. On the opposite side of the room was a bank of computers, the sound from the generator pouring in so loudly Kirin couldn't hear the click of the keyboard, though the seated figure's hands were flying back and forth, her head moving between screens with a dizzying pace. Her back was to the group too, though Kirin hadn't made it more than a few steps before Yantra held up her hand. Kirin had to activate his mien to keep himself from running headlong at them anyway, biting down the urge to scream at the further delay when their targets were *right there.*

Her lips were pressed into a tight line as she stared at the computer screens, the ring around her eye doubling and tripling as she zoomed in on the words. A second later and her eyes widened, just as she was shot in the chest.

Ness vanished and Kirin was sprinting for the sentry that was further away, the one who still had his gun raised and was now targeting Wyrm. Ifrit detonated an explosion behind the other guard and he flew clean across the room and landed in a crumpled heap on the floor, Aïcha already there and securing him.

A shot went off, Kirin only feeling the slightest pressure on his chest from the impact, even the second bullet at point blank range doing nothing to slow him down. He crushed the barrel of the rifle with one hand as he kicked the woman in the chest, sending her through the very door she had been guarding. Wyrm was there like a shadow and followed her through, paralyzing her.

"No!" Ness screamed. Kirin's head snapped up, afraid that Yantra was bleeding out. She was staggering to her feet, however, Ness grasping where the woman had been seated just seconds before. He caught the afterimage of the woman fading, a smirk playing across her face. "She wasn't even really here!"

"But she was *at* the computer!" Yantra rubbed her shoulder as she stumbled over to the computers, staring at where the woman had been. "She had to have been here."

"*Team five, report.*" Valor's voice came through breathlessly, like he was running.

"Sentries at main generator secured." Aïcha gave the report as Ifrit didn't look like he would be able to speak without screaming. "Woman with them just… vanished."

"*People don't vanish.*" The noises behind Majesty had ceased, leaving only her icy tone. "*Sweep the building, she must be there somewhere. Teams four, five, and six, maintain positions.*"

Momentarily dismissed, Yantra took a seat at the computers, skimming through the code the woman had been working on. As she did, the color drained from her face so quickly Kirin worried that maybe she *was* losing blood, that the armor in her suit hadn't fully stopped the bullet.

"What was she doing Yantra?" Kirin tried to cover for their silence over the comms, worried that Valor would rage at Ifrit for ignoring the order to report.

"She was..." Yantra cleared her throat. "She was modifying a code to redirect the energy output of the generator, as well as creating a new subsystem in the emergency protocols that would redirect alerts to a mobile unit before going to the onsite computer. The third program would be to automate which of those emergency alerts would be allowed to pass through. She didn't finish the code, but it's easy to assume it'd be everything except the redirection notice. There's nothing in here that poses a threat to those of us onsite right now."

None of that explained why her face was so pale, nor why she was motioning for him to come closer. Wyrm was watching one door, Aïcha the other, and Ifrit stood with a wall of flame blocking the opening they'd made. Satisfied they were safe, at least for the moment, Kirin crouched down next to her. She put her hand in front of her face and they both shut off their comms.

"Kirin," she whispered, "I know who wrote this."

"Who?"

She looked around again, as if someone would've been able to sneak in.

"I did."

9

Returning Defeated

"REMIND ME, WHERE WAS your team positioned?"

"We were coming from the f— from the tunnels." Ifrit felt his fingers tapping along his arm and scowled, realizing he was fighting a losing battle. How could he *not* fidget when he could see Kirin pacing through the window to his left? Kirin couldn't see him, since it was one-way glass, and Ifrit wished it was his side that was mirrored. His traitorous eyes couldn't help but follow Kirin back and forth, back and forth, when he was right there in view.

"Separate from the main forces?"

The question made his eyes narrow. They'd made it sound like such an unofficial briefing, bringing them one by one into a sitting room instead of the police interrogation room just down the hall. Ifrit had almost gone into it by mistake, purely out of habit at this point. But no, they were in a bright and sunny room, in plush chairs, with a one-way mirror overlooking the regional hero headquarters' lobby. Valor— of fucking course— hadn't given them any explanation for why they weren't returning to campus immediately, leaving it to Majesty to tersely tell them that the police would be taking individual statements on the mission.

Likely to try to figure out how the fuck the head bitch of Aether got away.

"There were nine of us. We held our position for an hour and then went in alone once it became clear reinforcements weren't going to make it through in time."

"And you didn't see anything suspicious en route to the target?"

If Ifrit could've narrowed his eyes any further, he would. But he wanted to be able to still *see* the detective, to watch them as they asked their questions.

"Suspicious how?"

"Any pieces of technology that looked out of place, any places where the schematics of the building did not match what you were seeing?"

"No, it matched."

"To clarify: no additional entrances, exits, or openings other than the one created?"

"Definitely no openings." He was sure of that, since his chest had tightened the more they walked into the enclosed space. Though Kirin's back had to still be hurting from how hunched over he had been, thank fuck he was there, otherwise their team wouldn't have made it out alive. Not with Ifrit losing control over how much poison he spewed into the air as his fear grew. "I didn't notice any odd tech but our technopath would've."

The detective nodded, painstakingly writing down every word Ifrit said.

"Was there any point that you lost contact with the other teams?"

"Our comms cut out for a few seconds after we received the order to move out."

"All of them?"

"All of them." Ifrit returned the bland stare as impassively as he could.

"And could you tell which direction the villain fled in?"

"She didn't flee." For the first time since they'd left the field, Ifrit felt panic bubble up in his chest. It wasn't overwhelming, but insistent, present. Familiar. "She vanished."

"Could you give more detail?"

Ifrit struggled to maintain his temper. He was the very last member of his group to go in, which meant they'd heard all of this before. They'd heard everyone say the same thing but for some fucking reason kept making everyone say it again and again and again. It was all just a great fucking waste of time, but if he said that, there'd be hell to pay for being *rude*.

"I didn't see much. She was there. And then she wasn't."

"If you had to describe it like anything, what would you say?"

He didn't roll his eyes. He really wanted to, but he didn't.

"Like switching off a screen."

The detective nodded solemnly, like those words held a lot of weight.

"And do you happen to know what time this occurred at?"

That gave Ifrit pause. The time? He'd never bothered to check.

"No more than five minutes after the call to move out." Ifrit's gaze was drawn to Yantra, who flitted in and out of view as Kirin passed in front of her. He'd had to do a double take to make sure it was her at first, since her normally rich skin had paled to a near white. She was always paranoid, but now she looked like she'd seen a ghost.

"Thank you for your time. I'm sure this was frustrating, but it truly is helpful." The detective stood, offering their hand for him to shake. They seemed genuine, at least, and so he returned the gesture. "Please do know that we don't do this to punish you, or to imply we think you're being dishonest. Only that the more eyes we have on the scene, the more we can confirm what happened."

Ifrit found his eyes narrowing again, though the officer was already moving away. They knew what was going on. The villain could teleport, a never-before-seen mien, and one that posed significant risk to them all. And yet that wasn't the point that the detective had seemed most interested in. No, they had only once betrayed a true flicker of interest, and that was when they wanted to know *when* she vanished.

Ifrit looked back toward his classmates, to Kirin, pacing back and forth, and to Yantra, eyes haunted. Two people who knew something about this mission that they were trying to hide.

A week later, and Ifrit *still* hadn't found time to interrogate Kirin.

It was really remarkable how much of a dick Valor was. Despite Ifrit and Kirin sleeping in the same bed, spending nearly every waking moment together, Valor was keeping them busy from dawn to dusk with "remedial training," which was really just the polite way of saying "beating the shit out of them intermittently." Each day after the ill-fated Aether mission, they went to bed exhausted, Ifrit passing out the moment his head hit the pillow, or more accurately, the moment his head hit Kirin's shoulder, since he now had the tendency to use that as a cushion instead.

But today, today it would be okay. Because today Valor had actual responsibilities to attend to instead of just hitting them, which meant class would end on time and Ifrit could drag Kirin into a corner and ask him what the fuck had been up with him. They just had to make it through this last combat class and then they were free, for a few hours at least.

Even with the end so near, Ifrit found his hands curling into fists on his knees as he watched Kirin and Valor fight.

He knew, logically, that Kirin was going to be okay. That Kirin was faking having trouble, that Valor wasn't even half the fighter that Kirin was. He knew that if it came down to it, Kirin *would* defend himself, that Ifrit didn't need to step in, didn't need to worry. But it was so hard to accept that when he watched Kirin get hit in the face again and again.

When Valor knocked Kirin to his knees and walked around behind him, Kirin even had time to shoot Ifrit a casual grin. He was a brilliant performer, maybe a missed calling, since just a second before he'd been grimacing and panting like he was fighting with all he had. Ifrit couldn't appreciate it though, because all he could see in his head was Valor somehow noticing, somehow seeing and taking out his *real* temper on Kirin. Brutal as he'd been up until now, Ifrit knew it was just vague disgust, and not true hatred.

That, Ifrit would never forget.

"Get *up*," Valor growled, grabbing Kirin's collar and pulling him to his feet. He was more on edge lately, which was odd. They'd expected some sort of repercussion after their mission had once again failed, but there had been nothing. No warnings, no threats from Valor or the school, just the interminably long practices. The police hadn't called them back in, there had been no reports that Yantra could find, nothing. The mission was considered a success, the site roped off and analyzed for any further clues or traces of where the woman in white went. It must have just been the shame rubbing off on Valor, the smell of failure lingering in the air.

Valor hated failure.

Kirin dodged to the left clumsily, avoiding the worst of Valor's punch but still letting himself be spun off-balance. He'd been up there for an hour, and the clock was ticking down with just fifteen minutes left in the period. He'd gotten impossibly good at making it look like he was just barely getting out of the way, had learned quickly which hits would actually do damage and which he could take, and though he had to be getting tired, he was still putting on a good show. And Ifrit *still* found his heart in his throat as he watched Kirin dance backward, his back to them.

Ifrit didn't realize that he'd let his mien get out of control until Kirin turned ever so slightly to look at him. Their eyes locked, and in that second, Valor grabbed Kirin by the face.

Valor threw Kirin down onto the floor, flat on his back, hands splayed out against the concrete from the force of the hit. Ifrit could see the diamond ridges creeping back out of sight as Kirin tried to hide his quick reaction, and Valor was too distracted launching himself into the air to notice anyway. The rest of the class relaxed while Ifrit found himself on his feet, watching Valor drop in slow motion, down to where Kirin was slowly turning to crystal.

The impact vibrated through the floor.

Yantra was the first to notice, her strangled gasp the first indication that anything had gone wrong. Kirin reacted not a moment later, throwing Valor off himself and clutching his left hand to his chest, covering it with his right as if that could stop them from seeing. As if it could stop them from noticing that his left ring finger was missing.

Ifrit felt like there was static in his ears, like his hearing aids had suddenly turned the background noise up to ten. There was no blood, no pain on Kirin's face, so maybe he'd been mistaken, maybe it was a trick of the light. Maybe Kirin's finger had still been made out of diamond and so he couldn't uncurl it just yet.

Valor grabbed Kirin's wrist and dragged the hand out into the open, his lip curling in disgust.

"They let you in with this?" He shook Kirin's arm once for emphasis before dropping it like he couldn't stand to touch Kirin for a moment longer. "Pathetic."

"Yes sir." For the first time, Kirin seemed like he was actually taking Valor's words to heart. He'd resumed cradling his arm to his chest the second he'd been released, right hand firmly wrapping over the left, covering the metal implant that must have been the interface for the now smashed prosthetic finger. It lay on the ground in pieces, faux skin torn and revealing the tiny metal parts that were crushed beyond repair. Without the nerve interface, the skin had lost its color, defaulting to the gray of the base material instead of blending seamlessly into Kirin's hand.

"Go to your armorer and have it fixed at once. It's unsightly." Valor had hardly given the order before Kirin was standing, moving quickly toward the door as if he'd like to do nothing more than have it repaired and out of his own sight. Ifrit's mouth was halfway open to tell him that was a mistake before Valor beat him to it. "Wait."

Kirin stopped in his tracks. He didn't turn around, like he was ashamed to face them. The last time Ifrit had seen his shoulders hunched like that had been the day his father's ghost had appeared.

"You're only approved to have your mask repaired." Valor's smile grew as Kirin's shoulders tensed. "Leave the finger until you've proven yourself useful for once."

Ifrit wanted to argue. He wanted to shout at Valor and tell him to shut the fuck up for once. He wanted to scream and rage and throw things.

Instead, he watched as Kirin, head bowed, walked out the door alone.

10

New Tech

Kirin was hesitating outside Nwabudike's door.

He felt sick to his stomach, his skin clammy and his mouth dry. He'd felt like he'd finally made a place here, made connections with his classmates, proven himself to be reliable, trustworthy. And now they all knew that at least some of that bravado was entirely a lie.

No, they don't dumbass. A voice that sounded suspiciously like Ifrit's echoed around his head. *It's just a fucking childhood injury. What, you going to judge all of mine?*

It couldn't get him to uncurl his left hand, but it was enough to let him reach out and knock with his right.

Nwabudike opened the door immediately, though he stood off to the side with his gaze down as if he were waiting for Kirin to come storming in. When Kirin just stood there blinking, Nwabudike looked up with anxious eyes, before all the fear melted away.

"Oh, Kirin!" His whole countenance brightened, his smile relieved. "I didn't know you were coming today! Come in— I have some new designs if you'd like to review them, I've been thinking about the ways we could adapt the fabric from your shirt to help give the pants a little more durability..."

Kirin let the chatter wash over him, grateful that he didn't have a moment to think as Nwabudike dashed around, shutting a door further into the room and pulling up schematics on his worktable.

"It's a slight pain to try to create a blend with this new material, but I *think* if I do it as the standard fabric for the warp and our custom strands for the weft, we can potentially..." Nwabudike trailed off, finally noticing Kirin's arm clutched to his chest. "Are you hurt? I don't have any of the healing supplies the med office does, but I can whip up a sling easily, my fabricator is right over there."

His bright eyes were wide with concern, making him look even younger than he was. He really couldn't have been more than eighteen could he?

"No, no, I'm alright." In his desire to reassure, Kirin had instinctively held out his hands, and then cursed as he saw Nwabudike's eyes zero in on the missing finger.

"Oh! Did your prosthetic break? No worries at all, I already have several spares based on the scans we did last year. Figured it wouldn't be as resilient as you were." Nwabudike was moving, pulling out one of the many drawers on the wall and taking out a half dozen spare fingers to drop on the table. "They should be identical though, so if we're looking for upgrades, I'll have to make new ones. I actually *should* look into creating a secondary underlayer of skin from this fabric, that could help with its resilience now that I think about it..."

"I, uh, I'm actually not allowed to replace it right now." Kirin forced past the lump in his throat to speak. "We can definitely talk about upgrades later, but for now I just need to have you make a new mask."

He tried his hardest to sound casual, to force a smile even under his mask, but his heart just wasn't in it.

"Just the mask?" Nwabudike's eyebrows came together. "Are

you sure?"

The word no was trying to push its way past his teeth, but he forced it away.

"Yeah, that's fine."

Nwabudike's leg braces screeched as if to share in the disbelief on his face.

"Your file said that the prosthetic was part of your acceptance requirements."

Despite the shitty day, Kirin found himself smiling. He'd missed how sharp the kid was.

"Valor's orders."

"He doesn't have the approval to do that." Nwabudike marched over to his desk computer, tapping away on the keyboard for a few moments. He enlarged the screen and sent it to the worktable, spinning around quickly enough that his braces gave another whine of disapproval. "See here? These are the Dean's requirements, which is the highest level of authority in the school. If they want you to have that prosthetic, you get it."

"But Valor—"

"Is a blowhard high on his own shit." Nwabudike looked so serious as he said it, Kirin couldn't help the laugh that escaped.

"Yeah, he definitely is. I still don't know if being overridden by bureaucracy is going to do me any favors with him though."

"I'll note it in your log that I was unable to comply with his request due to prior higher level orders. He'll have to take it up with Reader if he wants to say anything." Nwabudike held out his hand confidently, though there was the slightest shake in his fingers. "Can I see your hand please? I want to make sure the coupling isn't damaged before I attach it."

Kirin sat down on Nwabudike's stool, placing his hand on the worktable where the scanner could enlarge the joint for Nwabudike to look at it.

"One side is definitely bent, which is annoying but not impossible to deal with." The younger man rummaged through his drawers briefly and then pressed a button on the side of the wall, which flashed a few times. "Do you want me to try to add the reinforcing to the prosthetic? I can take the faux skin off and get a sleeve to go under it in just a few minutes. Won't add any bulk either since I can re-skin everything with the fabricator."

"If it's not a bother, that'd probably be for the best." Kirin couldn't forget the smug tone in Valor's voice when he left, how Valor *knew* that was something he could target moving forward.

They both looked up as the door opened.

It was another armorer, if her badge was anything to go by, brown hair pulled up into a messy bun and carrying a box of tools with her.

"What're we doing today?" she asked brightly, setting the box down on the end of the worktable and taking a seat. Nwabudike didn't look concerned, immediately rifling through the metal implements laid out neatly in the box, but Kirin quickly checked that his mask was still in place. He normally took it off when he was alone here, and it was only his own distraction that had led to him keeping it on.

"Need to fix his coupling joint for a finger prosthetic. Got dented." Nwabudike spoke absentmindedly as he rummaged, before triumphantly pulling out a small, thin tool from the pack. He hardly even looked at the woman, instead immediately going to prod Kirin's hand. The instrument he'd picked up had a mechanical clamp on the end, it seemed, grabbing one side of the circular joint and, at the push of a button, expanding a third leg to press against the rest of the joint to straighten the offending piece. Kirin flinched as he felt the light shock of the coupling coming back online, more concerned that he hadn't noticed the absence of the faint tingling sensation. He knew it somehow powered itself with the same energy that ran through his muscles; that must have been why it still worked in the dead zone, now that he thought about it.

"That was all!" Nwabudike turned brightly back to the woman, holding out the tool for her to take back. She returned his smile with her own and gave Kirin a polite nod before heading back out the way she came, taking the toolbox with her. Nwabudike was already onto testing the fit of his pre-made prosthetics before the door even finished closing.

"I really thought that you could fit every tool in the world in those drawers, but I guess even you have to ask to borrow some from someone else, huh?" Kirin was finding the tension draining from his shoulders as he watched the skin flicker from gray to a matching tan. He clenched and unclenched his hand, wiggling his fingers to make sure the false one was moving in concert with the others. Satisfied that it was functional, Nwabudike took it back off, gently peeling off the layer of synthetic skin and an old sample scrap of the custom fabric of Kirin's shirt to bring to the fabricator.

"Oh, those used to be mine. But I'm not allowed to have them without supervision." Nwabudike spoke absentmindedly, his gaze too focused on the bed of the fabricator as it stitched the two materials together.

"Supervision? You really that young?"

Nwabudike looked back at Kirin like he'd forgotten he was there.

"Yeah, I suppose." The shrug felt forced, but the moment was passed over as the machine beeped cheerfully that it was done. "But more importantly, lets make sure this still fits like a glove."

The connection always felt odd, like his knuckle had somehow gone numb for a moment before his brain registered the metal appendage as something it could control. He flexed the fingers again, happy to note that it didn't feel any different when he interlaced his fingers or pressed them together. The sensation in his left finger was always duller than the rest, but it was there.

"We should test the enhanced durability." Nwabudike's eyes were gleaming with excitement again. "You could just try to smash it on the table I suppose, that could work."

"I don't want to break the display." Kirin ignored the little voice telling him it was wasteful, hardening his upper thigh and placing his left hand on it. Before he could think too hard about it, he crystallized his right fist and smashed down as hard as he could.

Something definitely gave in the joint, the curling of the finger now moving more robotically than smoothly, but the skin was still in one piece, and the finger itself still attached.

"That's certainly better." Kirin felt the faint whirring as he ran his thumb along the side, the prosthetic trying to fix itself if it could. He gave it a few seconds more and the finger flexed as if nothing had ever been wrong with it. "Yeah, much better."

"I think we can get it perfect with just a little more tweaking." Nwabudike had a faraway look, already moving to pull up the scans of the original model. "They're using you as a heavy hitter out there; we need to make sure that you don't have any problems with it in the field."

"It hasn't actually been a problem until now," Kirin confessed. "I... I kind of forgot about it."

Nwabudike paused in his work for a moment.

"Really?"

"Yeah, it's weird. The finger was gone for fifteen years, but once it was on, I felt like it was never missing."

Nwabudike was quiet for a moment and when Kirin looked up at him, he was surprised to find the younger man's eyes filling with tears.

"Sorry, did I say something wrong, I—"

"It was my design," Nwabudike blurted out. "One of the first things I created when I got here."

"I shouldn't be surprised. You're insanely good at what you do."

"I thought it's why you got assigned to me. So I could make sure it was still functioning." Nwabudike picked up one of the extras he'd made. "I never got to see it go out to clinical trials. Wasn't sure if there would be any issues over time."

There was a sad undercurrent to his words, one of his hands absently straying to his braces, right where they disappeared under his shirt.

"Did the school just not want to put the money into it?" Kirin tried to choose his words carefully, sensing that, for once, this was a topic that Nwabudike wouldn't want to pursue.

"I got moved to here." Nwabudike shook himself, like he was resetting his thoughts. "And now that I'm here, I'm going to do the best that I can for you. We need to update your mask as well, right?"

His voice wasn't as bright as it should've been, a faint shininess under his eyes from the remnants of the tears, but his expression looked so fragile Kirin didn't want to push him any further.

"Right. It's broken a couple of times in the last few fights." Kirin gestured to the cloth mask he was wearing. "I've been getting by with this since I haven't had time to stop in."

"Hm." Nwabudike swapped the display to show the original mask design, exploding the view to see the components. "I was just using a metal base, but if that's not sturdy enough I suppose I could switch it to carbon fiber."

He rotated the 3D view, hovering it in front of Kirin like he was wearing it.

"Do you remember where it's breaking? Like is there a specific weak spot?"

"Mostly the front is cracking in half and falling off. Right over the mouthpiece."

"Interesting, I wonder if..."

As Nwabudike became distracted with the minutiae, taking apart and restructuring the design again and again, his sadness bled away like it had never been there. His eyes twinkled as his hands sped over the keys, his smile genuine again. Despite what he'd said before, he truly did look happy here, like he'd been meant to be an armorer his whole life. As Kirin finally walked out the door, he wondered what he would've picked instead, if he'd been given the choice.

11

The Past

Ifrit ambushed Kirin outside of the armorer's. Kirin must have been expecting it since he didn't fight back at all when Ifrit grabbed him by the collar and steered him through the residential section, through the hero section, and out the delivery entrance, which Yantra had conveniently turned off the shield for. They were completely out of the park by five or six blocks before Kirin even questioned what they were doing.

"This isn't the way to the grocery store," he said lightly, not even sounding concerned.

"No." Ifrit shoved his hands in his pockets, fighting the urge to grab onto Kirin. "It's the way to my house."

Kirin was quiet for a beat. Technically, it wasn't Ifrit's house at all. Students at East Tech weren't allowed to have property or even outside bank accounts. Officially, the house now belonged to Shifter, along with everything in it. But Shifter had given Ifrit a key a few days after the funeral, along with two pieces of paper. One was a short note from Shifter, promising that once he graduated the house would go back to Ifrit. The other, which was still unopened, was a letter addressed to him in Pressure's handwriting. It was in his pocket even now, pressed against his chest.

"You want to talk about something?" There was an edge to Kirin's voice that Ifrit wasn't expecting. When Ifrit looked at him, there was the faintest line between Kirin's eyes, the smallest hint of anxiety. For the first time, Ifrit wondered if he was going to like what Kirin had to say.

He had planned to respond, but the sight of Pressure's house— his *home*— took away all his words.

It was the oddest thing, coming home when the person who'd made it more than a house was gone.

He hadn't been back since the funeral. Hadn't had a reason to, or the chance. Now that he was there, outside the door, his chest squeezed. There were so many memories here, even just standing outside. All the days he dreaded walking in and telling Pressure that he'd been attacked *again* in school, that he needed to switch school districts, or that he needed a new backpack because his had been ripped and stolen. The anticipation grew as he hesitated before turning the key in the lock, familiar enough that it brought a stinging feeling to his eyes.

Kirin gently placed his hand over Ifrit's to turn the key and the stinging grew worse as the door swung open. The lights flickered on automatically, welcoming them in. For half a moment Ifrit couldn't breathe, expecting to smell burning rice and hear Pressure cursing in the kitchen. Without meaning to he'd stepped inside, removing his shoes and placing them on the ledge inside the door. There was his winter coat, still on the hook, Pressure's favorite leather jacket hung up beside it, keys to her car in the dish below. The dish itself was cracked in every direction from her constant frustration when she'd misplaced them, Ifrit having spent countless hours painstakingly gluing it back together for her. It stood in stark contrast to the one next to it that didn't have a single scratch, despite being significantly worse quality. But Ifrit had made that one, so she'd left the old damaged one there to take out her annoyance on.

The quiet click of the door alerted Ifrit that Kirin was standing next to him again. Ifrit hadn't meant to get wrapped up in his emotions, but it felt like if he moved a hair he'd dissolve into tears, wanting to stay in that moment for a second longer. To stay in the memory of when Pressure was alive.

"I'll go wait in the living room. You take your time." Kirin's voice was gentle, as was his hand when he squeezed Ifrit's shoulder.

And Ifrit had fully intended to let him do just that, but when Kirin's fingers trailed down his arm, when they lost contact with each other, suddenly Ifrit was reaching out, pulling him back. And Kirin was wrapping his arms around Ifrit, resting his chin on Ifrit's hair, blotting out the rest of the world for a moment. Ifrit's hands were balled in Kirin's t-shirt, and with his knuckles pressed to Kirin's sternum he could feel the steady beat of Kirin's heart. They stood there for a few moments, Ifrit breathing in and out slowly, counting his breaths. The burning in his eyes grew less and less, until he cleared his throat and pulled away.

One of Kirin's hands went to his face, but there were no tears to wipe away. Even so, Kirin's thumb stroked back and forth, his eyes painfully soft, which made Ifrit feel like his heart was going to tear in a different way until he took a step back.

That worried Kirin more, however, and the crease between his eyes reappeared, deeper than before. But they weren't here for Ifrit to worry about his stupid fucking crush.

"I'll make some tea." He was running away and he knew it, trying to hide desperately before Kirin could read his every thought on his face. He cursed himself in the back of his mind as he made his way to the kitchen, rummaging through the cabinets until he found a tea he thought Kirin might like. He'd managed to get the water on the heat and wash two mugs before he realized that Kirin hadn't followed him.

Panic flared as he checked back in the hallway, but Kirin hadn't left. He was just walking very, very slowly, eyes roaming over the dozens of photos that were hung on the wall. Ifrit felt his cheeks start to go red, which finally reminded him that he was still wearing his mask. He ripped it off and grabbed Kirin by the arm to pull him away from the embarrassing record of his teenage years.

"Don't fucking look at those." He heard his tone too late and cringed, feeling Kirin tense under his hand.

"I'm sorry, I—"

"No, it's fucking fine. Just embarrassing." Ifrit sucked in a breath, glad the kettle was already boiling. It gave him a reason to let go of Kirin too, though he desperately wanted to hold on tighter. He didn't want to talk anymore; he just wanted to curl up inside Kirin's chest, to spend their precious free time tangled up in each other. But who knew when they'd get away from campus again?

"You let those kids go." He pushed the mug across the counter. "You said you'd fucking explain why."

Relief swept over Kirin's face.

"Oh, yeah. Sorry, it's been such a horrible week." Kirin pressed the heels of his hands to his eyes, and Ifrit's attention immediately fell to his left hand— which wasn't missing a finger anymore.

"Wait, you replaced it?" He grabbed Kirin's hand, his ears ringing. "Valor said not to."

"Apparently the requirement that I have it was from Reader, so it overrode anything he said." Kirin shrugged, far too casual. He didn't *understand*, they couldn't just ignore what Valor was saying like this without consequences.

"You need to take it off." Ifrit was clutching Kirin's hand too tight, and when he realized, he forced himself to let go. "You're already on his radar, you don't want to bring any more attention to yourself; you don't know what he'll fucking do."

He'd expected Kirin to put up a fight, to argue back. Instead, Kirin simply twisted his finger, and with a faint click, it came right off. Kirin set the prosthetic on the counter wordlessly, looking at Ifrit with those sincere black eyes.

"If you're that worried about it, I can keep it off during classes." Kirin's voice was soothing, hand offered to Ifrit for him to take. "It's not like everyone doesn't already know, anyway."

"How'd you even lose it?" Ifrit wished he was stronger, but he'd already grasped Kirin's fingers, lightly running his fingertip over the joint where the prosthetic connection was nested. It was a clean amputation, the barest nub of flesh coming out of the knuckle. The metal here was neatly inserted, nothing like the angry ridges on his back. The stump had plainly scarred over before the coupling had been inserted, so smooth and worn was the flesh around it.

"I was little. Three or four. Someone had heard there was a kid made of diamonds in our village. Came right up to the gate of our house, asked me to show him. I didn't think anything of it, so I changed a few fingers to show him. He cut one off and sold it to a pawn shop in town."

"What?"

"It was funny last year when my armorer was saying that he thought it wasn't real diamond at first. I knew it had to be because that piece was passed back and forth for years, always appraised by professional jewelers until the police were able to track it down." Kirin went to rub at the missing finger, ending up stroking Ifrit's hand instead. "We moved after that, and my dad insisted I keep my mien quiet. If anyone asked it was just the hair. If anyone questioned things too much we just moved again."

"Is that why he..."

"Why he didn't want me here?" Kirin cracked a smile. "Yeah.

He was scared, and scared people will do a lot of terrible things. But he wasn't only scared for me."

His expression grew troubled again.

"Why'd you let the kids go?" Ifrit suddenly wanted to change the subject. He wanted a problem he could put his hands on and shake, not the echoes of the past.

"Oh. Well, originally it was just what you'd expect, and what I told everyone else. They didn't deserve it. They were *kids*. Maybe we could've pulled strings and gotten them off, but we don't know how far we can push before we're cast out too. Even more now that Valor's breathing down our necks every day."

"What changed?" Ifrit was holding onto Kirin's hand tightly now, his thumb nervously tracing the metal circle.

"I caught them."

"No shit. You're way too fucking fast."

A ghost of a smile flickered across Kirin's face.

"Only you think that."

"Everyone else did too." Ifrit wasn't even being biased; it was true. Not a single one of their classmates had believed *Kirin* could've been injured by some random teenagers.

"Mm." Kirin looked troubled. "I guess they did."

"Or they just couldn't fucking believe you'd get a pipe stuck in your leg."

"Rebar."

"*Kiri*."

"You're right, you're right." Kirin gave their joined hands a squeeze. "I'm stalling."

"Why?"

Kirin's eyes flashed up to meet Ifrit's before turning down to the counter again.

"I'm not going to..." Ifrit cleared his throat. "There's nothing you could say that would bother me."

Now Kirin really looked sad.

"Again? I get the shit with your dad was fucked up, but it wasn't even your fault—"

"I have four siblings." The words came out in a rush. Kirin's eyes flickered to Ifrit before he extracted his hand to trace circles on his mug. "I'm the oldest."

"So?" Ifrit was genuinely baffled.

"The youngest are ten, or I guess eleven, now." Kirin took a sip of his tea, wincing since it was still too hot. "Twins, in fact. They never really got to meet our dad for... obvious reasons."

Maybe it was the only child in him, but Ifrit was really struggling to figure out where this was going.

"And then there's my sister, and she's fourteen. I think you'd like her a lot." It was strange. There was a world of difference between the sadness Kirin had talked about his dad with, and how he was speaking of his siblings now. The former was mixed with guilt and regret, some measure of hatred and anger. Now, now it was closer to how Ifrit felt about losing Pressure. A wound without complications. "And then my oldest sibling. They'd be... nineteen now. I think you'd get along with them too. Adlivun reminds me of them, now that I've gotten to know her more. That same kind of quiet humor."

"What about your mom?" There was a gap in this family history, a hole Kirin was dancing around.

"She..." Kirin's jaw tightened, and Ifrit suddenly got a nasty suspicion that he would *not* like Kirin's mother. "She tried. I think she really did. But she went from a happy, stable marriage, to the sole breadwinner for five kids. She was halfway across the country from anyone she knew, had just had twins, and suddenly she was alone."

Ifrit felt anger prickling up his spine. Unbidden, and for the first time in years, the image of his own birth mother was conjured. A woman on her own, with a son she didn't want.

"When my dad died, we didn't have a lot of money, suddenly. She worked constantly, but that only went so far. So... I helped."

"Helped how?"

Instead of speaking, Kirin pricked his finger and a tiny, blood-red diamond dropped down between them.

Blood-red was correct, in fact. When Ifrit picked it up, the inside... moved. Because it wasn't solid, but liquid in the center.

"Is that—"

"My blood?" Kirin sealed the tiny prick with a diamond patch and picked his mug back up. "Yup."

"Who would want to buy—"

"You'd be surprised. I got better at it, with time, so now I can make ones that are perfect diamonds, though a number of jewelers *preferred* the red. I'd only sell a few here or there when we really needed the money, and no one ever questioned where we were getting them. Or maybe they didn't want to know. It helped, though."

"We should've looked for you more." Ifrit had forced himself to walk around the counter instead of jumping it, grabbing Kirin's hand. "I should've insisted that Pressure—"

"You wouldn't have found me." Kirin spoke gently, shifting how their hands connected so their palms pressed together. "The *school* didn't even know I was there. My mother had my father's death listed as an accident, my stay at the hospital erased. The only injuries the school knew that I had were my finger and my top surgery scars. They didn't know about the scars on my back, I only told them about the things they didn't care about or could be easily fixed."

He let go of Ifrit to reattach the finger, the seam blending in like it was never there. It was Ifrit's turn to examine Kirin's hands, and if he hadn't just seen the finger missing, he would've never known it was gone.

"Why are you telling me this *now*?" Ifrit was afraid of where

Kirin was going.

"The boy we were chasing, he set up an illusion when we first walked into the mirror room, right?"

Ifrit could still see the room, the two kids curled up together on the hospital bed.

"When I caught up to them, he set up the illusion again. I knew it was fake, so I wasn't really paying attention at first. But then they pushed me back, and I could see the final bed in the room." Kirin's voice broke, ridges appearing on his face as a wave of emotion made him briefly lose control of his mien. "It was *them*, Ifrit."

Ifrit's heart thudded.

"How—"

"I don't know." Kirin shook his head, looking miserable. "I don't know if it was real or just something he pulled out of my head, but it was the twins. And they..."

Ifrit pulled Kirin into a hug, Kirin clinging right back on like Ifrit was the only steady rock in a savage sea.

"They look like I used to. Like they were being carved up for parts."

"It wasn't real." Ifrit didn't know of course. It had felt real to him, had looked real. But it needed to not be.

"How could he have known what they looked like otherwise? That they'd sleep like that?"

"They were pulling images out of your head. Your worst nightmares."

"I talked to the kid." Ifrit pulled back, trying to gauge Kirin's expression. "He said he had a message for me."

"What did he say?" Ifrit didn't need to ask who the message was from.

"He said if I let them go, he wouldn't tell Aether where the rest of my siblings were."

"The rest?"

Kirin finally met Ifrit's eyes.

"It means that Aether has at least one of my siblings."

12

Hold On

IFRIT HAD BEEN QUIET the past few weeks.

Valor had gone back to keeping them occupied, ordering them to stay and practice until he got out of meetings instead of letting them leave on time.

From the outside, it could've seemed like Valor was working them hard *because* of the looming threat of Aether. After the mission at the power plant, there had been no further leads, much to the growing despair of the media. It couldn't even be kept quiet, since another gruesome murder had taken place after the woman in white made her escape. Yantra almost always had the TV on in the common room, and though Kirin would've liked to avoid any mention of the organization, he was forced to hear about them every morning as they left for class.

Maybe that was why Ifrit was quiet. Ignoring for a moment what it brought up for Kirin, how must Ifrit be feeling, knowing the people responsible for his own kidnapping were not only at large but just being... evil? The news feeds would sometimes mention his abduction casually, as if it were something to be brought up over dinner and not something unspeakably horrific to go through. And much as Ifrit pretended he was okay, the ever present twitch in his jaw when they were mentioned promised he was not.

Kirin wasn't faring much better. He spent the precious few minutes free from schoolwork trying to see if there were any viable leads on Aether.

The extent of the school restrictions on his laptop had begun to reveal themselves, since he'd tried to search his own last name, only to have the computer refuse to let him finish the characters. Even his siblings' first names wouldn't go through, nor the name of the town he'd grown up in. His phone too refused to let him dial his mother's number. He'd entertained the thought of trying to send a letter to her to ask, but the one time he'd tried to sit down and write it, the words had failed entirely.

What could he say?

I know one of them is missing, and I know who took them, but not where they are or if they're okay. Actually, I know they're not okay. You know what dad feared would happen, the reason he desperately wanted me to keep my mien hidden? Well, I started showing the world what I could do, and now someone is being carved up in my place. Could you please tell me when they were taken so I can start looking for where they could be? I almost captured their leader, but I let her get away. Also, I saw dad's ghost and I hit him until he vanished. I'm sure you're glad to hear about that.

No, it was for the best that he didn't try to speak to her. And maybe it was for the best that Valor was keeping them so busy. At least then he could pretend that his failure to find anything was due to not having enough time to properly look, and not that he was once again completely and utterly powerless to save the people he loved.

Therefore, when Valor canceled their late night remedial class again, Kirin felt simultaneously relieved and horribly guilty.

Being Valor, he'd called them all into the disaster simulator to make the announcement that class was canceled. They'd all already changed and had been waiting for him to arrive— fifteen minutes late, as per usual— when he stepped through the door.

"Something more important than trying to fix your inadequacies has come up." He was distracted. Even the insult was weak. "Report to your dorms. Anyone attempting to leave campus will have their funding pulled for a month."

And just like that, he was gone.

"What a fucking *dick*." Clidna rubbed her face, her voice permanently sounding raw these days. She turned away Phoenix's healing more than she accepted it, not willing to risk Valor finding out and stopping Phoenix from healing more pressing injuries.

Medusa was standing next to Clidna, her mouth pressed into a thin line.

"I wasn't even considering leaving, but now staying here is thoroughly unpalatable."

"He has that fucking effect." Ifrit's posture was relaxing again, the muscles along his shoulders loosening now that Valor was gone. "But he's probably got half the fucking school watching out for us, so we're stuck here."

If anyone had the energy to argue, maybe one of them would have. They weren't even halfway through the semester, yet everyone was starting to flag. Only Ifrit was unaffected, and that was simply because he was used to being chronically exhausted from being poisoned by his own air in his sleep.

The lack of rest was catching up to Kirin, and he found himself nodding off as they walked back to the dorm. He was lagging behind the rest of the group, and twice he almost straight up fell over. After the second time, Ifrit cursed under his breath and swung Kirin's arm over his shoulders.

"You don't have to do that." His words were thoroughly undermined by the yawn that interrupted them.

"It's fucking fine." Ifrit didn't look tired, his eyes looking around nervously. Since they were standing so close, Kirin felt all his muscles tense before he had the presence of mind to follow Ifrit's gaze across the green.

"What are they doing out so late?" Kuafu had lost his rigidity around rules for their class, but he had no qualms about critiquing Majesty's. "Our classes are supposed to attend all missions together; why are they being briefed?"

"I don't think it's a mission." Ness flickered into existence next to Yantra. "I could hear Majesty yelling about something when I got closer, but I couldn't tell what."

"Where's Bia?" Yantra was zooming in on the group with her digital display, her frown deepening.

"She's not there?" Adlivun sounded surprised, which was rare enough that it woke Kirin up. He managed to get his tired eyes to focus, and it was true that he only counted nineteen.

"If *Bia* got called to a private mission with Valor, I really hope it ends terribly." Clidna shook her head. "I wouldn't want to be there for all the world."

"I fucking wouldn't either." Ifrit hadn't meant to speak so loudly, judging from how his eyes widened when Kirin turned to look at him.

It was a normal enough thing for him to say, and Kirin was so exhausted that if Ifrit hadn't reacted the way he had, Kirin might have overlooked it. But somewhere in his sleep-addled brain, he was forced to remember that while Ifrit only spoke of Majesty derisively, he only ever spoke of Valor with fear.

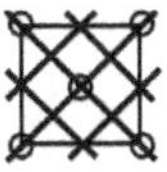

One of the things Kirin had grown to appreciate was how well he slept beside Ifrit.

Even when they'd just been sleeping in the common room, not touching, just near each other, it'd helped. Long before Satol, but ever worse since, Kirin had struggled to *stay* asleep. His nightmares would trick his brain into thinking his body it was in danger, his mien activating without him knowing. He'd wake up when the carbon ran out, the sudden lack of protection jolting him awake in a cold sweat. With a portable source of carbon monoxide, Kirin could rest easy, knowing that if someone were to attack them in their sleep, he could just roll over and they'd be protected until dawn.

Sleeping directly *next* to Ifrit, well that was even better. Kirin's nightmares these days were about waking up and finding Ifrit gone again, taken somewhere Kirin couldn't reach. With Ifrit tucked safely against his chest, he could sleep soundly, knowing that if anything were to happen, he'd know immediately.

Which, of course, meant his eyes shot straight open when he felt the pressure of Ifrit's head on his chest disappear.

Ifrit had insisted they go straight to sleep once they got back, shoving Kirin into his room and onto the bed before Kirin could suggest they try to do some homework. Ifrit didn't look tired, but he must have been coming down with something since his face had been unusually flushed. He hadn't been planning on sleeping himself; he'd made Kirin lie down and then turned to leave. Kirin had responded by wrapping his arms around Ifrit and flopping back onto the bed, and that had stopped the argument right there.

It had to have been midnight, and Ifrit was clearly trying to sneak away without waking Kirin up. He was moving very slowly, gently shifting Kirin's arm off his back, delicately transferring his weight off the bed. Kirin's eyes had closed again against the bright light of the moon, and any attempt to open them again was halted by the sensation of Ifrit softly touching his face. Even so, Ifrit *had* to know he was awake, since Kirin's heart was beating so loudly it must have been audible two rooms down.

"Why do you never fucking ask for help?" The words weren't angry, they were almost tender. Kirin wasn't sure he'd ever heard Ifrit sound so openly affectionate, and his chest felt warm, a tingling sensation crawling down the back of his neck. One of Ifrit's nails scratched ever so lightly against the edge of Kirin's jaw, eliciting an involuntary shiver. Ifrit pulled away immediately, the loss of contact an open wound.

Kirin opened his eyes, half chasing after that feeling of comfort and security. He was met by Ifrit's concerned gaze, and an expression of... well, guilt.

"I didn't mean to wake you." Ifrit's usual gruff tone was back, his face turning away. "You can go back to sleep; I'm just going downstairs for a minute."

"I'll go with you." Kirin was already swinging his legs over the side of the bed, though sleep still clung to the edges of his mind, making his movements sloppy.

"You're fucking exhausted, just go back to sleep." There was the faintest undercurrent of worry in Ifrit's voice that banished all chances of Kirin staying.

"You need sleep too. If you're going somewhere, I'm coming."

Ifrit sighed and stepped back, giving Kirin space to stand. The shorter man leaned back against his desk and scrubbed the heels of his hands up and down his face.

"I'm not a fucking child, you know."

Kirin stiffened. He *had* been treating Ifrit like he couldn't be trusted, hadn't he? When was the last time they were apart for longer than an hour? Kirin couldn't remember.

"I know."

"And you know you don't have to fucking babysit me."

"I know."

"Then why can't you fucking wait here?" There wasn't anger, only quiet pleading. When Ifrit looked at him, there was a raw edge of desperation. The warmth in Kirin's chest had evaporated and something heavy settled in its place.

"I can't lose you." The words came out as a whisper. They struck too close to the big issue, to something Kirin had absolutely no power to do anything about. "I... can't sleep when you're not here. I just keep feeling like I'm going to open my eyes and you'll be gone again and... I can't do it again."

Ifrit's expression was frozen. He hadn't restarted his fire since he'd only just gotten up, and it was only by the rise and fall of his chest that Kirin could believe he wasn't made of stone. The fear of Ifrit insisting that Kirin leave, of Ifrit deciding that they should *prove* it'd be okay if Kirin wasn't there, made the tips of Kirin's fingers go numb.

"It won't fucking happen again." Kirin wished that Ifrit would ignite the air around them, so he could see more than the gleam of Ifrit's eyes. A cloud must have passed over the moon, because suddenly it was so dark.

"It's *already* happened again, though, hasn't it?" He hadn't meant to say it, not really. Because then he was thinking again. Thinking about how two— or maybe *all*— of his siblings were in Aether's grasp. Were being cut apart, just like their father had feared. And it was all Kirin's fault.

"Then let's go fucking do something about it." Ifrit cut right through Kirin's self-pity spiral, grabbing Kirin by the shirt and pulling him toward the door.

"What *can* we do? I had one chance to grab her and she's gone. There's no other word of Aether, nothing. None except..."

Kirin stopped himself both because he realized what an idiot he'd been and because it wasn't his secret to tell. *Yantra*. There *was* a lead for what Aether might be doing, where they might be going, however slim it seemed.

Ifrit, despite knowing everything, had the same idea.

"Tech can access more than the fucking news feeds." Ifrit seemed to have some sense of how late it was, considering for once he didn't kick open the stairwell door. "She'll know where to look."

If Kirin had been in Yantra's shoes, he wouldn't have felt inclined to help people showing up at his door past midnight. But not only did she stand back and let them inside, she seemed like she'd been waiting for them to show up.

"Yeah, yeah, get in here you two." The TV was still on, split screen between a mainstream newscaster and one of the more paranoid feeds, her laptop adding a cool glow to her bed. It was messier than Kirin remembered, even when Ifrit and Phoenix were missing. There was a pile of laundry in the corner, and scattered pieces of circuit boards and wires spilling off the desk and onto the floor. Somehow, she'd even gotten a pair of kinetic gloves, and microscopic lenses to boot. It was funny, in a way, thinking of her building things with her hands when her mien allowed her to create golems out of spare wires and metal. "I was wondering how long it'd take for you to come."

"He fucking told you?" Though Ifrit's phrasing was always rough, his voice sounded sharper than usual.

"What do you mean told me? I told *him*." Yantra hadn't failed to notice his tone either.

"Actually, you're both thinking of different things, but they might be connected." Kirin hurriedly stepped between them. "Yantra, I didn't tell him because it wasn't my place to say anything. And Ifrit, no, you're the only one who knows."

Though there was no fire to see, Kirin could taste the carbon at the back of his throat. Oddly though, the crease between Ifrit's eyes had eased immediately, and he looked at Kirin, his lips parting slightly.

"A third murder has been committed by Aether, no less gruesome than the first two. The victim is one of the council members of our own East City, killed in her home."

Ifrit's head swung to the screen, his face paling. Yantra's earlier irritation vanished as she took stock of Ifrit's expression, quickly muting the TV and standing in front of it.

"What did you want to talk about?" Her cheerfulness was forced and she wasn't quite tall enough to block the whole screen from view as the image of the unfortunate woman's remains appeared. It *was* just like the photo of Mesmer, wasn't it? And, unbidden, Kirin realized something else.

The body looked the same as the people Pressure had killed in Satol.

"We're hoping you could find a lead the police missed." Kirin forcibly pulled his own gaze away, though he could still see Ifrit out of the corner of his eye fixated on it.

"For Aether." Yantra nodded slowly. "I know there's a very obvious reason for you two to want them found, but why *now*? I get their supposed leader escaped, but that was weeks ago."

"Supposed?" Ifrit's attention was at least momentarily diverted.

Yantra shrugged as she moved to sit down, pulling her laptop closer to her on the bed.

"I thought she was in charge for a while, but then the mission at the generator felt... odd. Why would they have the head of their whole organization out in the field like that? I'd be convinced she was in charge if it *had* been a trap, but I still can't tell what they got out of being there."

"What do you mean?" There was only one chair apart from the bed, so Kirin guided Ifrit to it before sitting on the floor himself.

"The program she was working on, it was pretty simple; it hijacked a power source and circumnavigated the protocol to alert anyone it was happening. It's not super complicated, but even so you'd want to test it on a newer facility, not something old enough to be out of commission. And then they were spotted so much."

"So?"

"If it were worth the risk for them to be there, then I wouldn't think anything of it. Or if it had been a trap. And sure, I don't know what they're planning to do, but it doesn't *feel* like it's enough." Yantra looked up from the computer, shaking her head. "The only way I could make it make sense in my head was that she's working mostly on her own. Like Satol was a disaster for them, right? Even Futurus' human testing has been swept under the rug— I mean, *yes* all company assets have been seized and the corporation disbanded, but there's not much media coverage— since Pressure is the main headline."

"That still works to their fucking advantage though." Ifrit hadn't bothered to sit until just then, instead of taking the chair, stubbornly joining Kirin on the floor. Kirin didn't mind, since it meant he could play with Ifrit's fingers to get rid of some of his discomfort.

"Not as much as you would think. People are really good at compartmentalizing when they want to be, so Pressure being killed has been relegated to an issue with the police, and there's still faith in the hero system. The fact that most of the people who've come out in open support of her are heroes— and those opposed, police— has only reinforced that. I also expected to see a bigger hit in public confidence of the hero system, but it just didn't happen."

Mesmer's words came back to Kirin.

"Do you think that's why they're attacking people?"

"What do you mean?" When Yantra turned, Kirin noticed that there was an extra glint in her hair. He had no idea when she'd had time to get another piercing.

"When we showed up for that first mission, Mesmer mentioned that he supported Pressure. And that photo of the woman, I think she was one of the people advocating for the new committee on mien regulations. Maybe they're trying to remove the less extreme option, so people have to choose between oppression or them."

Yantra's fingers stopped moving as she looked at him, eyebrows coming together.

"You really think they would rather make things worse if people don't support them?"

Kirin felt Ifrit's eyes on him.

"I think they're willing to use us just the same as anyone else if it suits them." Though he'd been the one playing with Ifrit's fingers, Ifrit gripped tightly onto their joined hands. "And that's why we're here."

"You don't have to explain that to me." There was a soft smile playing on Yantra's lips as she looked at them, but her eyes looked sad.

"Actually, I think we do." Kirin shoved his guilt down, ignored the shame pooling in his stomach. "Because I'm not talking about what happened last year."

Yantra had fully abandoned her laptop and was pacing back

and forth.

"They must have gotten into East Tech's system. That's the only thing I can think of." She wheeled back around to face Kirin. "Your siblings never used the power gyms or anything, right?"

"No." Kirin shook his head. "We didn't really have the money and quite frankly it was always... harder for them than it was for me."

Yantra nodded but didn't stop pacing.

"And did people from your hometown know? Obviously, it would've been logged in the gym's database— and you would be *shocked* to know how much information they keep on you from those— and were you registered?"

"Registered? I didn't officially have a record, if that's what you're asking."

"Officially?" Ifrit's eyes narrowed at the wording, but it wasn't enough to distract Yantra.

"Yeah, did you have to register your mien with your country or anything?"

"I don't think we did. We moved around a lot and changed our last name twice, but I don't remember ever having to fill out mien related paperwork."

"If I were slightly less nice a person I'd demand more information about that, so remember this next time I ask for a favor. Were you open about your mien to the people around you? Like would Aether have been able to get information about you from your old friends or anything?"

"No, I didn't talk about it with anyone. I only went to the gym at night when there weren't usually other people there."

"Okay." She drummed her fingers along the edge of her lip. "I mean it still doesn't rule out the possibility that one of your friends or something was able to put two and two together, since you're pretty recognizable, and they would know that you'd just vanished without warning."

"Didn't have any friends so that isn't really an issue. I told my coworkers I was joining the army to cover for being gone."

Both Yantra and Ifrit looked at him.

"Okay, I guess maybe the army was kind of obvious, but it seemed like a good idea at the time?"

When they both continued staring, he felt his cheeks grow warm.

"But isn't it also more likely that they got in through the school with what *you* told me?" He didn't want to say anything more without Yantra's permission. He trusted Ifrit with his life, with more than that, with his *family's* lives, but it wasn't his trust that mattered.

Yantra's face went slack.

"You're so right." It was strange, he could've sworn that relief flooded her face. "Yeah, that would make more sense."

"So, can you fucking check to see if someone got into the school's system or not?" Ifrit's tone wasn't quite hostile, but there was still an edge to it. Kirin squeezed his knee in a way that he hoped was reassuring.

"I'll do my best, but it's honestly way easier to get into the police database than the school's. I can mess with the cameras because those have actual hard wiring I could access and tap before it's reported to the server, but things like our personal information are really locked down." She bit her lip.

"You're saying the Aether bitch is a better hacker than you?"

Knowing Ifrit, he'd probably just said it to try to make her competitive, but it had the opposite effect. She seemed to shrink back, folding in on herself.

"They're fucking not." Ifrit noticed too, and sometimes Kirin thought his blunt way of speaking was really nice, because you knew he meant what he said. "You're the best fucking hacker this dumbass school has ever seen."

That did earn a smile.

"Not the best Pressure's seen though." She finally sat back down at her laptop and her fingers started moving, though slower than usual. "Listen, I'll do my best, but it'll probably take a few days. I can't risk setting off any security pings, and that means this is going to be slow and painful."

"Yeah, of course. It's already more than enough that you're willing to try." Kirin gave her smile and turned to tell Ifrit that they should go, but found the other man's expression to be thunderous.

"What did you mean about Pressure?"

Yantra winced.

"Not much. Just... I know we can trust Shifter, but at the same time I *really* wanted to know what they're working on at the coalition, so I tried to get in. But I hadn't even started probing at the network before it bounced me right out."

"When the fuck were you doing this?"

Yantra really looked guilty now.

"Well... like I said, having physical access makes it easier and I assumed it'd be hosted on her computer to keep it away from the school, so..."

"At the fucking funeral?" Ifrit was on his feet. It was lucky he hadn't rekindled his flame or the whole room would've been ablaze.

"Only after Shifter told us he wouldn't give us access to anything?" she protested weakly.

Ifrit looked like he was going to start yelling, but then, for some reason, he looked at Kirin. With great effort, he snapped his mouth shut, so hard that Kirin winced at the sound. Without another word, he stormed from the room, the door slamming behind him.

Feeling dazed, Kirin got to his feet.

"I'm really sorry about that, it's just been a lot, lately." Ifrit's reaction wasn't unexpected, but the fact that he'd stopped himself and left was. Yantra herself looked confused as to why Ifrit wasn't berating her.

"Firstly, Kirin, you don't have to apologize for him. He's absolutely right that it was a fucked up thing to do, especially since that was a safe space for him." Yantra's fingers had stilled, and she looked up at Kirin with sad eyes. "But secondly— and more importantly— are you okay?"

"Are you?" He wasn't trying to deflect, not really.

"Me? I'm fine. Honestly, if they just got into the system here that's... better." She winced. "For me. There isn't anyone they can use against me, back home."

Kirin opened his mouth and then closed it when none of his words felt right.

"You should check on Ifrit." Yantra filled the silence easily. "I'm sure he's just worried that the one person *he's* got left is being targeted."

"What do you mean one person? Clidna's his friend too, and everyone else in the class supports him."

"Kirin." Yantra gave him an exasperated smile. "It's okay. We're all happy for you, really."

She took his continued silence as confirmation, not confusion.

"Go check on him. I'll come find you both once I have more info."

As Kirin closed the door behind himself, he tried to figure out what they were happy for. His mind landed on the conversation with Phoenix from weeks before. Did everyone think they were dating? Phoenix wasn't known for being subtle with gossip, and clearly she'd thought that was the case. Maybe that was why Ifrit was upset too, and why he'd been pulling away recently, not wanting to be touched in public. Maybe the idea that everyone thought they were together was just... repulsive to him.

Kirin knew he should open the door and tell Yantra that she was mistaken, and he told himself the only reason that he didn't was because she needed privacy and quiet.

And it certainly had nothing to do with the strange, unexpected happiness when he thought of everyone considering Ifrit to be his.

13

Avoiding Harm

IFRIT FELT TIME SLOW as Valor raised his fist to strike Kirin.

The posture was familiar— *too* familiar— the malice in Valor's face clear to see. But only Ifrit was looking. Everyone else was flowing around him, battling in what was supposed to be a simple exam.

Maybe it was just the glow of the neon lights reflect on the slick black walls of the maze making everyone look stark and sharp, maybe it was just because Ifrit could only get glimpses of Valor's face between bodies and bursts of light from Majesty, but Valor didn't just look angry. He looked *excited*.

Where were the others? Goldhorn and Wyrm were supposed to be with Kirin to take down their teacher, since they were all pretending to be too weak to take him alone. From Ifrit's vantage point on one of the obsidian hills, he could see over the whole course, but neither blond was anywhere to be seen.

It would give away the game, wouldn't it? He couldn't go down, because if he went down, if he deviated from their plan, Valor would *know* he'd found something he could use against Ifrit. Someone. Kirin could take the blow, could take Valor at his worst without hardly trying, it should be fine.

But Kirin wasn't trying.

Even from a dozen meters away and three above, Ifrit could *feel* the power charging in Valors' swing. It reminded him of when Pressure would use her mien, that sudden contraction of the air, like the whole world was holding its breath. Kirin was on his back, hair splayed out, eyes black. He wasn't using his mien. He wasn't going to block it.

Ifrit's feet were moving before he meant to, carbon swirling behind him ready to throw him forward and close the distance between them. But then Kirin's eyes met his. Even without seeing his mouth, Ifrit could tell Kirin smiled from the creases that appeared around his eyes as they turned white.

One of Phantasm's ghouls appeared in front of Ifrit and he detonated an explosion with hardly a thought, using his arm to clear the smoke so he could see what was happening below. The haze disappeared just in time to see Kirin use Valor's momentum against him, pining one leg and throwing their teacher to the ground. Kirin was up in one smooth motion, their positions now reversed as vines sprouted from the ground to hold Valor in place.

When Kirin looked up and found Ifrit still staring, he winked, before turning and heading back into the maze.

"Come on." Clidna's voice was nearly gone. She'd appeared beside him without any noise, presumably done taking care of the fucking bee teacher. "Ness found where Phantasm's hiding."

With a final look over his shoulder, Ifrit followed her down and into the maze.

This was one of the more ominous settings the disaster simulator had conjured, which was a high bar considering it had once turned into an erupting volcano. But at least that had been a straightforward rescue, and not something that felt like a fever dream. It felt like moving through a digital landscape rather than a physical one, and the disorientation was hard to fight. He almost wished fucking Sunshine was nearby, just to stop the world shifting every time he blinked.

"This way." Clidna pulled him around a sharp turn he'd almost missed, the orange panels on her suit glowing under the foreboding red light. Even his own fire wasn't helping much, just another thing flickering in the corner of his eye as it was caught and rebounded by every shiny, slick wall.

And of fucking course the path they had to go down was getting narrower and narrower. Clidna turned down another path, this one barely wide enough for Ifrit's shoulder. He gritted his teeth and followed, thinking it was lucky Kirin wasn't there, since he wouldn't have fit at all.

She ducked down a— luckily— wider path, and for the first time in the past hour, they were far enough away from Majesty that the world was just the lit edges of the walls and the flames over Ifrit's head. Even Clidna seemed to recede into the darkness, the panels on her suit looking more black than orange. Wait. No, they *were* black now, as was her hair.

"Fucking Shifter." Ifrit sighed, exhaling more carbon monoxide to give him enough supply for a quick explosion to subdue the man and then get him the fuck out of this awful little back aisle. "Aren't you supposed to be on fucking leave or some shit?"

I am, and that's why I'm not here now. Ifrit frowned. He hadn't even known Shifter knew sign. This could be a trap to lure him into a false sense of security to stab him in the back. He could've done that when he first appeared though, or when he'd grabbed Ifrit's elbow to show him the way. *I'll show you where Clidna is, just act normal.*

Shifter glanced at him up and down.

Or I guess, normal for you.

Ifrit ignored the barb and crossed his arms, refusing to move closer.

This whole fucking exam is students against teachers, why should I trust you're not going to attack me when I'm distracted?

Because I could have done that already. And what would be the point of keeping up this charade— he gestured to his appearance, which still looked more like Clidna than himself— *if I wasn't trying to hide the fact that I'm here.*

You've forgotten the part where you explain why *the fuck you're hiding.*

Shifter glanced around like there were people watching them, as if the whole area was controlled and monitored by the school. The walls were practically mirrors; there could damn well be cameras hidden on the inside for all they knew. This exam was scored by a panel of judges and not the supervising professor alone— thank *fuck* for that or Valor would've failed them all out of spite, the little bitch— so it would be almost *reasonable* for them to have done so.

Someone's trying to kill me.

Ifrit uncrossed his arms and started to follow.

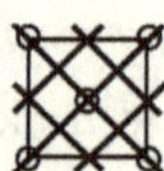

"I'm glad you decided to talk." Majesty poured Ifrit a cup of tea and straightened the coaster beneath it. "I was unsure if you would take me up on the offer. It's been weeks."

Even when she was trying to be nice it came across as condescending.

"It's not like I have a lot of time to fucking chat." Ifrit bit back the urge to remind her that Valor was the reason for that, but he knew he shouldn't try to antagonize her. He was there for information, after all.

"I understand. Valor is indeed keeping you busy."

"Yeah, he fucking sucks."

The corner of her mouth lifted into a tiny smile, which was so shocking that Ifrit almost poured his tea into his lap. It was such a normal facial expression, and he'd been quite certain that Majesty didn't know how to make those.

"That's not a very polite way to speak about your uncle."

It was lucky he'd put the cup down because he physically recoiled at the word. That prompted what sounded like a hiss from Majesty, and when he looked up, he found that she was stifling a laugh by biting her lip.

"Forgive me, I knew you wouldn't like it, but Pressure always made the same face when it came to her brother. I couldn't help testing to see if you two really were so similar." A full smile unfurled on her face, and it made her look less severe, kinder. Ifrit had never seen her look *gentle* before. "But what did you come to talk to me about?"

Ifrit forced down all the comments he wanted to make about Valor, all the things he could tell her to make that smile freeze on her face, but he had to be polite. He had to be *nice*. Because Majesty knew the backend of the school far better than he did.

He just had to figure out how to get her to talk about it.

"It's just been a fucking lot." He settled for the truth, until his brain could come up with a better plan. Shifter explained in a rush what was going on, but it hadn't left Ifrit with much concrete information. He also wasn't sure how much he could trust Shifter, never had in all the years they'd known each other. Pressure had trusted him, that was true. She'd trusted a lot of people though, and look where that had gotten her.

"Being here without her?" Majesty was seated calmly, her posture rigid and perfect, but her hands were fidgeting with one of the many sleek, black pens that were placed in a perfect line across the top of her desk. If she started taking notes, he was going to scream.

"Yeah." Ifrit leaned back and stared at the ceiling, unable to deal with her expression. "It's like they're trying to fucking erase her."

There it was; that was a good start. Maybe if he could find out what the university thought about her legacy, he could figure out who within the walls would want Shifter dead.

Majesty was quiet for a moment, and he gathered the courage to peek at her face. She looked troubled, her eyes flicking to the smoke detector near the door, and then back to Ifrit. A small burst of light escaped her fingers and flew to the device, so quickly he would have missed it if he hadn't already been watching.

"That is because they do." Majesty's tone was gentle, like she was speaking to a wounded wild animal. "They fear that she was too radical and had become something of a symbol for extreme change. I'm sure you've spoken to— to the marketing professor. She would've mentioned that we cannot afford for public opinion to turn away from the school. They do not like to take risks."

"Well, I'm still fucking here, aren't I?" Ifrit resisted the incredibly strong impulse to put his feet on her desk, just to see her composure break.

"Shifter spoke very convincingly on behalf of your class." The first hint of distaste crept into her voice. "That is the only reason you're still here."

"And here I thought it was because the public loves us."

"They like your classmates." She didn't have to say the *"and not you"* out loud.

"Yeah, still don't know how I snuck through. Guess they just can't kill me."

"You are very good at your job, Ifrit." Her nose scrunched when she used his name. It wasn't his real name, and it certainly wasn't what he'd have picked if given a choice. He suddenly wondered if he'd ever hear his real name again, since the only person who'd used it was gone.

"Why do you think they brought Valor in?" The sudden question threw him. He narrowed his eyes at her, since she should know better than anyone.

"Just to fucking torment me, probably."

She shook her head stiffly, the movement so precise it felt practiced.

"They brought him in because he represents a very old-fashioned take on heroism. Strength before all, and pride in what you do. The older generations tend to favor this cult-like reverence for the profession, seeing themselves as saviors and saints rather than what we are, people doing a job."

"You act like you aren't fucking one of them."

Her lips pressed into a thin line.

"I was, once."

The clock ticked loudly, but not loudly enough to fill the space.

"I can't..." Majesty started and then halted, forcibly putting the pen in her hand down. "I cannot do much to help you, unfortunately. I know there is some... tension between you and Valor, and each professor only has say over their own class. Everything that Valor is doing is well within the bounds of the profession, cruel as it may be."

"I think you could do something more than that if you were fucking willing to."

"You know how he is." She spoke so casually, like it wasn't a horrible thing to say. Like Ifrit's dislike was just that, dislike, and not a fear born from being eleven and facing those fists looming out of the dark. "I don't think I could say anything to change his mind."

"Yeah," Ifrit forced the words out through gritted teeth, "I know what he's like."

"There is one thing I could do, if you were so inclined."

Majesty sounded unsure as she pulled out a pristine blue folder from a drawer. When she opened it, there was only one paper inside. "It's unorthodox, but there is precedent after unusual circumstances."

Ifrit tried to ignore the fact that she'd referred to Pressure's death as an "unusual circumstance."

"I do not expect you to accept right away, but feel free to hold onto this and take the time to consider it." With a moment's hesitation, she held it out to him.

He only had to glance at the heading to know that there was no way in hell that he was taking it.

"You want me to transfer into your shitty fucking class?" He was standing, though he didn't remember getting up. "No, no fucking way."

Majesty sighed, like she was dealing with a child who didn't understand. He really needed to sit back down before the fire above his head touched the ceiling.

"I understand your reticence. However, I do not believe that you will get the support and education you need under Valor's tutelage. You have a different... personality and outlook than my students, I know, but there is more to school than making friends."

"I'm not worried about having friends, I'm worried about getting fucking killed in my sleep!" Through the haze of his anger, a quiet voice that sounded like Clidna whispered in his head that this was an easy way to find out if she knew anything. "Could you honestly fucking say you have eyes on them at all times of the day, on every mission? Can even the fucking school?"

"Campus is well monitored, including the dormitories. There is little chance that anything untoward would happen to you on school grounds."

"Firstly, that's a fucking lie because five of your shitheads assaulted us on the first fucking week in *our own goddamn dorm* so fucking forgive me if I don't believe they wouldn't do worse in their own. Secondly, we spend a lot of fucking time outside of campus. You've really managed to keep an eye on all twenty bastards under you every single fucking second of every single fucking mission? What's to stop Bia from flattening *me* like what happened to that hero at the dead zone? That woman in Chile?"

He heard his own words at the same time Majesty did, their faces almost mirroring one another in shock. The Aether murders. He'd thought it was a copycat Force, but maybe it was just an egomaniac with a shittier version of her power.

Majesty recovered first.

"I am in constant communication with my students, and due to their... low threshold for risk they move in larger groups than your class is wont to. Were anything to go awry, I would be able to hear and respond immediately." There was something distinctly guarded in her gaze now, but whatever she was hiding, it seemed like she was now *more* convinced that he needed to switch. "Valor is a much more hands-off professor than I am, and Pressure had no choice in the matter since she had no license. The risk to you would be far less."

Ifrit was still stuck on the unintentional connection he'd made and almost failed to hear her. Could it really have been Bia? The first had happened during their mission, in the same location as their mission. The other had been within East City, and he knew personally how easy it was to sneak off campus if you knew the right tricks.

"At least take the form and consider it more. I think it would leave you with less immediate stress." Majesty took his silence as contemplation, which it was, just not on what she wanted. "And, now that I think of it, our dorm is full. You would even be able to stay where you are."

His eyes flickered to hers, trying to figure out what her game was. It did feel like she genuinely wanted to help him, he'd at least give her that much credit, but now there was something more to her expression. Something he couldn't read. Was she worried that if he stayed with his own class, he'd tell them of his suspicions? No, she had no reason to worry about that. Her word would outweigh any of theirs. Did she suspect Bia too, and think that his presence would be a deterrent for any future violence? If so, she was stupider than he could have ever dreamed.

He wasn't going to figure it out now. He just needed to find more excuses to speak with her, to get her to slip up again.

"Fine." Ifrit grabbed the piece of paper, feeling the crisp sheet crinkle under his tight grip. "I'll think about it."

Relief flooded Majesty's face. He didn't think he could hold his temper much longer and turned to leave before he set the page on fire. He'd almost made it to the door when she spoke up again.

"These murders." She licked her lips nervously, pressing them together in a thin line. "They seem to be following you."

He felt his shoulders rise, and she noticed too, since she rushed to finish her thought.

"I fear that you may be a target soon, if you aren't careful." As she raised her chin higher, he realized that despite how imperious the posture looked, she was using it to hide her worry. "I will do my best to keep an eye out for you, but I can only do what you allow me to."

"Thanks," he wrenched the door open to avoid looking at her, "I'll make sure to avoid anyone who wants me dead."

14

Calculated Risk

KIRIN NEARLY JUMPED OUT of his skin when Ifrit rounded the corner.

He knew he shouldn't have been waiting outside Majesty's office, knew that nothing was going to happen in the middle of campus, but that didn't stop his brain from running through all the things that could go wrong. Perhaps the threat that Shifter was convinced of *was* real, and maybe it *was* Majesty— maybe it was even the reason that she'd been trying to get closer to Ifrit after all— and Ifrit tipping his hand would make her act decisively and cull the threat right there. After all, the school hadn't lifted a finger when Ifrit was taken; if it were her word against his corpse, who would disagree? Or maybe the *real* threat had bugged her office and was going to intercept Ifrit on the short walk back to the dorm and then Kirin would never see him again.

When the voice whispering that something terrible was going to happen grew too loud, Kirin found his feet taking him to Majesty's office. He had at least managed to keep himself from going inside, though he'd been thinking about it when Ifrit materialized.

"Fuck's sake, I'm *fine*." Ifrit's tone was terse, and Kirin couldn't tell if he was finally annoyed with the hovering or if something had happened. But out in the open he couldn't ask yet. The sun wasn't at its peak in the sky, and on the first day of break there were several students milling about between buildings on the hero side of campus. There were people lying out on the lawn or in the shade of the flowering trees, relaxing on the first warm day they'd had in months.

"Figured we'd walk back together; I left something in the disaster simulator after our exam." He tried for a smile and was happy to find it was easy. Knowing that Ifrit was there and safe had soothed most of the fear gnawing at him.

"Whatever." Ifrit started trudging in the direction of the dorms, his hands balled so tightly that Kirin thought he heard Ifrit's knuckles crack.

No, that wasn't it. There was a piece of paper in his hand that'd made noise as it crumpled.

"What'd she give you?" The anxiety that'd just settled resurfaced, clawing at his throat. It was only made worse by the added pressure of his mask as they crossed through the shield into the dorms.

She wants me to join her stupid fucking class. Ifrit's hands moved so quickly he ended up throwing the paper, which Kirin caught wordlessly. *Seemed really fucking dead set on it too.*

What do you want to do? Kirin fought to keep his face neutral. Maybe getting away from Valor would be good for Ifrit. But the idea of Ifrit in different classes than them, of only seeing him during joint missions, made Kirin feel like he was going to throw up.

I would rather fucking die.

To cover his relief, Kirin decided to smooth out the paper instead of replying. It was a simple form and had already largely been filled out. In fact, alias was already entered, and Kirin rapidly folded it over when he realized that legal name was too.

You might want to burn this. Even as Kirin said it, he fought the urge to tuck the sheet away. A small, selfish part of him wanted to keep it, to hold onto part of Ifrit that would help Kirin find him if something ever happened again.

Probably will. Ifrit rolled his eyes before he noticed Kirin's expression. *Why?*

Your name's on it. When the crease between Ifrit's eyebrows remained, Kirin slowly signed again. *Your real name.*

Ifrit's eyes widened and for some reason the tips of his ears went red.

You fucking saw it then?

Kirin shook his head and pressed the paper against Ifrit's chest. Ifrit was slow to take it, so it was a minute before Kirin could sign again.

I read slow, remember? I saw the section header and stopped. They'd made it back to the dorm now, and Ifrit was hovering back, likely to avoid the inevitable ambush from their class. *I didn't see it.*

Ifrit was watching him, brows pressed together. It wasn't his usual angry furrow, instead a soft crease as he thought.

Do you want to know?

Before Kirin could decide if he was going to tell the truth, a pair of hands yanked him backward through the door.

Adlivun was lucky that Nwabudike had made Kirin some extra shirts out of the same material as his costume, otherwise she would've sliced her hands open on his shoulders as he crystallized them out of habit. She didn't seem to notice, however, since Goldhorn fared worse with Ifrit nearly blasting them into the common room.

"What the *fuck?*" Ifrit was more than a little shaken up, tearing his mask off. "I could've fucking killed you!"

Goldhorn was fine, having surrounded themself with a cocoon of vines. The plants were falling apart now, charred and withering even as Kirin watched.

"My idea, not theirs." Adlivun was on edge, which was unusual for her. She was almost always expressive, but she hid her fear better than most. "What happened?"

"As if you don't already fucking know," Ifrit scoffed.

But from the look on her face, she didn't know, for once. Neither did Yantra, who was seated at the main table with her computer, most of their classmates scattered around nearby.

The blinds were drawn— which didn't look suspicious at *all*— leaving the space in almost total darkness. The glow of Yantra's laptop was the main source of illumination apart from the neon stripes around the practice room, which at that moment decided their pattern would be an ominous, pulsing red.

"I have news, which I'm sure won't be shocking to any of us." Yantra looked tired, but then again, they all did. They'd expected they'd be able to relax during their break between semesters, to appreciate the time away from Valor, and here they were working on a new problem dropped in their laps. "Remember when the police questioned us a couple weeks ago after the Aether mission?"

A few people nodded their agreement.

"It's because the timeline doesn't match up." She flipped the screen around, tapping on a graph of all the events of the mission. "The murder that happened nearby, it couldn't have been her. She disappeared *after* they were killed. It could still be another Aether agent that we weren't aware of, but it wasn't our woman in white."

"Shifter might be right then." Kapre was huddled in a chair, looking like they could be part of it. Their hair was usually up and out of their face, but today it hung down freely, melding them with the gloom.

"We should not jump to conclusions. That is how we miss important information." Kirin was grateful for Kuafu, for his dogged adherence to the things he could touch and see. "Ifrit, did you find out anything from Majesty?"

"Not much more than Tech— Yantra has." Ifrit casually tucked the form into his jacket pocket, disguising the act by crossing his arms over his chest. "She *suspects* something, but didn't give me much fucking more than that."

He hesitated, hands tightening where they gripped his arm.

"And she was fucking worried that whoever-it-is is going to target me next."

The room broke out into chaos as half the class started talking at once, everyone clamoring over each other. Ifrit visibly winced from the sudden noise, turning down his hearing aids, and Kirin struggled to follow a single thread as the voices overlapped.

"Okay, okay! Everyone shut up!" Kirin couldn't remember ever hearing Ness yell before, but perhaps the novelty was why it worked. "Yantra, do you want to say that again?"

"Sure." Yantra never used to look uncomfortable being the center of attention, but now she cringed when they all looked at her. "Do you... do you know if she thought it was just you? Or our class generally?"

Ifrit's frown deepened as he thought.

"Just me, but when fucking isn't it."

"Well, that's a good sign in a way." Yantra licked her lips. "That does naturally lead to the broader question, do we think the other murders are associated with us, then?"

"I don't see how they could *not* be." Aïcha had started pacing and fiddling with a piece of her hair, her hooves clopping loudly on the floor. "They've been following us, haven't they? Sometimes it's reported immediately, sometimes days later, but it's *always* suspected to have been somewhere we were, and the day we were there. And *we* go where the school tells us to go. If these attacks are targeting members or even just supporters of the coalition, I fail to see how they could be so attuned to our movements if they weren't being committed by someone traveling with us."

"And Shifter did confirm that all the victims have— so far— been people that he had personal contact with. I don't know if it's just his paranoia that's made him think he'll be next, but until he talked to Ifrit last night, he was the only coalition member that *I* knew of. The murderer has to have a lot more information than we do, or they've been getting very, very lucky." Lilin looked ghostly in the odd lighting, her dark curls making her skin look even fairer.

"I don't believe in luck," Yantra said tartly. "But all of them had, at one point or another, explicitly and publicly expressed support for the coalition. That combined with meeting with Shifter could've been enough to give the murderer enough cause to attack. Shifter himself said he's stowed away in the outer storage compartment of the jet to get off the island without being seen; who's to say someone else couldn't too?"

"If what my armorer's told me is correct, there aren't a lot of stealth based heroes out there." Ness materialized right next to Yantra, which was the first time in months she'd made Kirin jump. He'd been looking right at Yantra, but he hadn't seen Ness at all. Even now she looked less substantial than usual. "We get out of the jet almost immediately after landing. If someone was sneaking off, we'd see them."

"We're ignoring the elephant in the room, aren't we?" Clidna straightened, shifting her body so Medusa was almost hidden from view. "The murders look like they were committed by someone with a mien just like Pressure's. We know someone like that, who has *also* been on all the missions we have, and who is frequently the reason we start late."

All eyes jumped to Ifrit, who had a muscle twitching in his jaw.

"Yeah." Warring expressions passed across his face in a

heartbeat, and Kirin resisted the urge to take his hand. "I noticed that too."

When the suggestion wasn't met with violence, Medusa stuck her head out again.

"That just leaves the question of what do we *do* about it?"

"I don't fucking know what we *can* do." Ifrit ground his teeth. "Her parents are on the damn board; she's practically fucking bulletproof."

"Was Majesty covering for her, do you think?" Antaeus tapped his fingers along the edge of the table, brow furrowed in thought.

"I don't think so, she seemed to realize it at the same fucking time I did." Ifrit rolled his eyes. "Has been working with the bitch for a *year* and didn't even notice the similarities."

"Would Bia really, though?" Wyrm had been braiding and un-braiding a strand of hair the entire time. "Like she sucks, I get it, but this isn't a murder of opportunity. These are pre-meditated murders in cold blood, against someone who wasn't fighting back. Do we think she's capable of that?"

"She tried to fucking kill *me* during our first mission together; I have no doubt in my mind she'd kill people for fun."

"What?" Kirin hadn't meant to speak but the exclamation came out instinctively. Ifrit only then realized what he'd said, his eyes flickering to Kirin guiltily. "When?"

"When you went to get the fucking kids." Kirin almost missed the words with how much Ifrit mumbled.

"You need to tell us these things, so we know about them!" Clidna jabbed Ifrit in the chest. "Yes, she sucks. Yes, she's a great suspect. The problem is *proof*. And do we think she's acting alone?"

"It'd be harder to hide multiple people disappearing, but they do have multiple technopaths." Yantra was scrolling through a list, nodding to herself. "I would guess that if she's our culprit, at least one of them has to be in on it too, to forge her comms signature so no one would notice she's been missing."

"Alright, that's two. How far away can she attack from?" Clidna prodded Ifrit again.

"Not far. She's pretty fucking weak."

"Do we think she'd need someone to clean her off afterwards? That'd be three."

"Blood spatter was contained at all sites. There wouldn't be anything on her." No one bothered to ask how Yantra got access to that.

"Bia's bulletproof," Clidna nodded to herself, "that doesn't mean our technopath is."

"How are we going to get anything on them though? They're not going to talk to us, and even on missions we're almost always kept separate." Aïcha shook her head and looked up, like the answers might be written on the ceiling. "I never thought I'd miss having other classes with them."

"I..." Ifrit took a breath. "I can fucking get into their classes."

"Absolutely not." Kirin felt eyes on him from his tone, but no one looked more surprised than Ifrit.

"People could fucking die if I don't; I can deal with Bia during the fucking day." Ifrit rushed into his next words, trying to cut off the arguments Kirin was already opening his mouth to say. "Majesty even said there wasn't room in their fucking dorm so I wouldn't be staying with them, I'd just have to be in fucking class with them."

"If you think I'm going to let you fucking risk your life—"

"Wait, wait, wait, what?" Clidna stood between them, arms up to get into their lines of sight. "*What?*"

"Did Kirin just swear?" Phoenix had clearly meant to whisper, but it carried all too well before Ifrit managed to respond.

"Majesty asked me to switch into her class. She didn't give me a real fucking reason why, only that she thought I couldn't 'learn enough' under Valor or some shit." Ifrit was trying to focus on Clidna, yet his eyes drifted back up to Kirin. "She... she said she couldn't do much to help me, but this might be something."

"I thought we couldn't switch after the program started." Yantra had stopped looking at her laptop, which was rare enough in itself.

"Yeah. You usually fucking can't." Ifrit's eyes were shining in a way that meant he was dangerously close to crying. "She said that because of the 'circumstances' there might be an exception. That was my fucking *mom* and that's what she's been reduced to. *Circumstances*."

This time Kirin couldn't help reaching out, touching his hand. Ifrit grabbed on tightly, like it was a lifeline.

"You don't need to worry about us finding a way to get to their class. I can get any information we need." Ness broke the silence, though her voice sounded odd. "Just leave it to me."

"Ness, I know you can get in, but you'd have to hang around for hours before someone said anything. With all the work Valor's got us doing, I don't think you'd have the time." Aïcha had finally stopped moving and was standing between Antaeus and Wyrm, each of them holding one of her hands.

"Dammit, why do they all have to be such dicks? If we could just *talk* to one of them, I bet we could get them to slip up." Clidna rubbed at a spot above her eyebrow.

"As much as I appreciate you thinking I could successfully hide in their dorm for days on end, talking was what I was suggesting." Ness's voice *did* sound strange, like it was coming from far away.

"Who would talk to us?" Lilin was perched on the edge of the sofa, knitting needles clacking away feverishly.

Something was absolutely wrong, because Ness wasn't just hard to focus on, she was *transparent*. Kirin could see the hem of Yantra's shirt straight through her, see how Yantra's hands were gripping the edge of the table so tightly her knuckles turned white.

"You know someone in their class." A small, almost insignificant piece of information clicked in Kirin's brain, all the way from the beginning of their time at the school. "When you and I checked in, you were looking for someone."

Ness actually vanished before she spoke again.

"Yes." She didn't seem to be whispering, but the sound was so quiet Kirin doubted Ifrit could hear it. "Phoenix's met her too."

"Inanna." Phoenix's eyes narrowed.

"That's the one."

"How do you know her, Ness?" There was a brittleness to Yantra's tone that hadn't been there before.

"Oh, you know." Ness tried for a disarming smile, but it came out nervous. "I just dated her for four years."

"*Excuse me?*"

"I don't think we have any better options right now, do we?" Ness was regaining color quickly, her voice becoming more business-like as she clapped her hands together. "This is a good, low-risk chance to get more info on Bia. It'll take a couple weeks at least, but Inanna loves to talk. I should be able to get something."

"How do we know Inanna's not going to do anything to you?" Yantra's lips were pressed together tightly, and small lines had formed at the edges of her eyes.

"That's not really her style." Ness smiled again, and this time it seemed rather sad. "After all, she never means to hurt me."

15

Almost There

THE VIBRATION FROM KIRIN hitting the wall *again* was what finally made Ifrit lose it.

Somehow, he'd made it through the entire first semester without ever having to talk to Valor one on one. At first the pointed avoidance was the best gift he could've asked for, since Pressure was too obvious and raw a wound to give Valor access to. Ifrit had been convinced that it was just disgust that kept Valor from talking to him at all, from so much as looking at him, but as the weeks went on, he began to believe that it was something else entirely.

Valor knew Ifrit wasn't a little kid who could be beaten so easily now, so instead he was targeting everyone that Ifrit cared about.

Kirin had made the right call by pretending to be weaker than he was. Valor loved to have a victim and Kirin could take it, even if Phoenix wasn't secretly healing him. All Ifrit had to do was stomach watching Kirin get beat down again and again and again.

Valor was in a particularly awful mood today, working his way through Goldhorn and Adlivun before finally taking out his anger on Kirin. Kirin could tell something was off, since he was actually making a meager attempt to fight back, to keep Valor's attention on himself for longer. The show of resistance was just making Valor worse though.

Clidna was standing next to Ifrit, and if it weren't for her forcing him to keep his hearing aids off, he would've been over there hours ago. It was his own fault really, that he'd turned and seen Valor pick Kirin up and repeatedly slam him into the wall until enough blood ran into his hair to turn the bright gold into orange.

Ifrit didn't remember moving, yet somehow he was holding Valor by the shirt, his fist centimeters from Valor's face.

"You're going to stop *now*." Shit, he'd forgotten to turn his hearing aids back on. His brain was buzzing too much to even remember how the words felt; he could've yelled them for all he knew.

And Valor, Valor had the decency to look scared for a moment. Just a second. But then the reaction that Ifrit had been dreading appeared. Valor looked... *excited.*

Ifrit was too focused trying to read the words on Valor's lips and the punch to the gut took him by surprise. He'd been momentarily horrified seeing that smile that used to haunt his nightmares again; he'd forgotten what came next. Valor hadn't held back any more than he had years before, and Ifrit was thrown back into the very same wall Kirin had been. Only his own thick skin saved him from breaking a rib.

Strangely, that made Ifrit smile. Valor, strong as he might think himself, was weaker than Kirin— and Ifrit had beaten Kirin plenty of times.

Valor was in front of Ifrit a heartbeat later, but Ifrit blasted up and over the shorter man, kicking him in the back. It shoved Valor face-first into the wall and from the spurt of blood, likely broke his nose with the impact.

When Valor turned around, there was hatred in his eyes, far

too familiar hatred and fury. It made his swings wild and easy to dodge, and Ifrit felt like he was in a dream the way everything just... missed. He didn't even need to hit back, since Valor seemed to be hurting himself in the wild way he was moving. The blood from his nose was dripping over his mouth which meant Ifrit had to turn his hearing aids back on to understand what Valor was saying.

"...you're the reason she's dead." An easy to avoid punch caught Ifrit in the shoulder and sent him stumbling a few steps backward. "She was stronger than you knew and yet she's dead now and you're *still here.*"

When Valor's fist connected with his face and sent him to the ground, Ifrit was suddenly thirteen again, holding his face and looking up at the same person with the same face contorted with rage.

You're going to be the reason she dies.

A kick to the ribs didn't make the sick feeling in Ifrit's stomach go away.

Valor crouched down so they were almost nose to nose, his eyes— the same color and shape as Pressure's— filled with disdain.

"If you'd listened to me then, my sister wouldn't be dead."

The shame and self-loathing flooded in so strongly that when Valor lined his fist up with Ifrit's face, Ifrit couldn't even get himself to move.

But before the blow landed, Valor was grabbed by the throat and slammed up against the wall.

"If you hit him one more time, I will tear you limb from limb." Kirin didn't raise his voice, speaking so coldly Ifrit barely recognized him. Valor struggled pointlessly, pulling at the single hand Kirin used to hold him off the floor. Valor punched and kicked Kirin with all his strength, but he might as well have done nothing for how little Kirin reacted. Kirin must have been using his mien, finally, since he didn't move a muscle despite Ifrit's flames flickering from the force of one of the hits. "Do I make myself clear?"

After a few more moments, Valor's face started turning blue. He grabbed uselessly at Kirin's arm a few more times, but when his mouth opened and closed without being able to pull in air, he finally gave a single stiff nod. Kirin dropped him, Valor's knees failing under his own weight as he fell to the floor. Kirin didn't look back, walking over to Ifrit and helping him off the floor.

Are you okay? Despite how emotionless he had been seconds before, Kirin's gaze was now full of so much concern it made Ifrit's chest hurt.

Ifrit's eyes flickered to Valor who was slowly getting to his feet.

Can we go? It felt cowardly, but the thought of being around Valor for one more second was making his chest tighten and his breath come faster.

Of course. Kirin still didn't look back, gently turning Ifrit around, away from Valor. *Whatever you need.*

Ifrit tried to banish the memory of Valor's eyes burning into Kirin's back as they both walked away.

They made it to the door of the dorm before Ifrit realized he really didn't want to go in.

"Hey." It might be a stupid idea, but maybe that meant it was actually a good one. "Do you want to... I don't fucking know, go to like an arcade or something?"

Scratch that, it was a monumentally idiotic idea. Arcade, really? That sounded so childish. It also sounded like a date, which Kirin probably wasn't interested in, and if Ifrit ruined this, if Ifrit ruined what he was able to have with Kirin, he didn't know what he would do.

"I'm down to do whatever you want, but are arcades really your speed?" Kirin took Ifrit's gym bag off his shoulder and tucked it just inside the door before heading toward the main entrance to campus, willing to ditch the entire rest of their day just like that. Ifrit's heart squeezed again, but this time it wasn't from anxiety.

"Anywhere that's not fucking here is good right now." It was a beautiful day, the sun shining and the temperature mild. Students were milling about the green spaces on campus, and Ifrit was shocked by the pang of jealousy for how normal their lives seemed.

"Should we go to your house?"

It was tempting, but only for a moment. Valor could find them there, and Ifrit couldn't stand any chance that he'd show up. Not after what they'd just done.

"No, not there." His anxiety must have shown on his face, since Kirin squeezed his shoulder lightly.

"Come on, you've lived here for years, and I've hardly gotten to explore." It was a crime that they had to wear masks, because Ifrit could tell that the smile Kirin was giving him was blinding, and for Kirin he'd go blind willingly. "There isn't anything you think I should see?"

An immediate thought popped into Ifrit's head, but he shoved it away hard. This wasn't a date, it wasn't. He shouldn't give himself any extra hope, any reason to pretend that it was, because the crash back to reality might just shatter him. Besides—

"I don't fucking know what you like to do." Ifrit felt his cheeks heat as he admitted it. "If it's not fighting or watching movies or fucking homework, we don't do much else except play games."

They passed through the gate to the tech side of campus, and Ifrit wondered if Kirin was going to respond given the number of people milling about. There *had* been an uptick in the number of visitors recently, hadn't there?

"There's an aquarium here, right?" Kirin spoke so quietly that Ifrit almost missed it.

Ifrit's heart skipped a beat in his chest.

"Yeah." He tried to shove aside the feeling bubbling up in his chest, but it was painfully persistent. "I've never been. Let's go there."

It wasn't a date. It wasn't.

Why, then, did Kirin's eyes crinkle into half-moons, and why did he take Ifrit's hand?

It wasn't a date. Right?

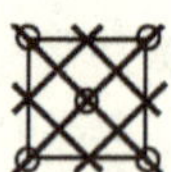

Ifrit was going to combust, he really was. He could only hope the tanks of water around them would shatter, dousing him before Kirin noticed anything. But he was still glad they came. He only wished he could rip the mask off Kirin's face to see how much he was smiling as he dragged Ifrit from tank to tank. Which he could do, since he was still holding Ifrit's hand.

"Look at them!" Kirin was pointing to a sea lion that was swimming in lazy circles. Ifrit was finding it hard to look away from Kirin though, as the speckled light from the water played in Kirin's hair. "You can't tell me that's not the cutest thing you've ever seen."

"It's not the cutest thing I've ever seen," Ifrit deadpanned, and it wasn't a lie, since Kirin was way fucking cuter than some big sea otters.

"Well, that's cause you're not looking." Kirin's smile fell slightly as he realized Ifrit wasn't watching the exhibit at all. "If you don't want to be here, we can go somewhere else—"

"No!" It came out far louder than he'd intended, Kirin's eyes widening. "Shit, sorry."

"It's okay." Damn it all, Kirin was just too nice. He'd dropped his excitement fully and was now looking at Ifrit with no small amount of concern. "It's been a rough couple of days, and—"

"It's just nice seeing you enjoy yourself. Or fucking whatever." Forget what Ifrit had thought about masks just minutes earlier, he was so glad that his hid how bright red his cheeks were. And thank fuck the aquarium was practically empty apart from the two of them, so it was only Kirin who was observing Ifrit's complete and utter mortification.

"If you'd rather do something else, we can though." There was some guilt, oddly, edging into what Ifrit could see of Kirin's expression. From the way his eyes were crinkled, his lips were probably pressed into a thin line, the muscle in the side of his jaw tense— stop.

"I like seeing you happy." Idiot. Nothing to do now but double down. "It makes *me* happy."

"Oh." Kirin, the fucking dumbass, sounded like he'd never considered that.

"Okay?"

"Okay." Kirin rewarded him with a squeeze of the hand and by absently brushing some curls that had fallen into Ifrit's eyes out of the way. Ifrit had been considering getting a haircut, but he decided right then it was a terrible idea and he would never cut his hair again. "But if there's anything that you *do* want to do, tell me. We've got the whole afternoon off, after all."

"Can you tell me about yourself?"

Whatever Kirin had been expecting him to say, it wasn't that. He stopped walking altogether and tilted his head as he looked back at Ifrit.

"There's not much left to say that you don't already know, but whatever you ask I'll answer."

"What's your favorite color?" Damn he sounded childish, *again*. But somehow, he'd done well since it made Kirin laugh.

"Red." Kirin pulled down his mask so Ifrit could see his lips and make no mistake of the words. "Bright fucking red."

"Oh."

"Yours is black, I'd guess? Wait no, black's a shade, not a color." Kirin pulled his mask back up (dammit) and adjusted the straps as he thought.

"It used to be blue."

"Bright blue?" Kirin was sharper than most people realized.

"Yeah."

"But you said used to."

"Gold's not terrible." Ifrit hid his embarrassment by actually looking at the tank next to him and recoiled immediately. "What the fuck is that?"

"Oh, it's a spider crab." Kirin didn't seem phased at all, despite the thing being easily a meter tall, which was, in Ifrit's opinion, far bigger than any fucking crab should be.

"That's a fucking nightmare, don't just 'oh it's a spider crab' me." Ifrit didn't even like standing near it and tugged on Kirin's arm to move away. But Kirin irritatingly stayed where he was.

"Ifrit... you're not afraid of crabs, are you?" Ifrit didn't need to see Kirin's lips to know he was trying and failing to keep from smiling. His tone said it all.

"I'm not fucking afraid of crabs." When Kirin still refused to budge, Ifrit clarified. "I'm afraid of specifically *that* crab."

Kirin laughed at that and let himself be pulled away.

"How do you fucking know about that monster anyway?"

"I wouldn't say they're common in Japan, but they're not unknown."

"You're Japanese?" Ifrit resisted the urge to curse. He'd

searched what culture "kirin" came from, and with the Romanized spelling being what it was that only left Korea and Japan. He'd *guessed* Korean whenever cooking for Kirin when he was upset, but Kirin was far too polite to say anything except thank you, no matter what Ifrit made.

"No, I'm Korean. But my dad used to go to Japan on business trips a lot and he'd take me with him sometimes."

Ifrit was quiet, filing the information away.

"I take it your family is Arab?" The question was hesitant.

"Both sides of the family, going back hundreds of fucking years." He hadn't thought about that in ages. "Pressure offered to move us to an Arabic neighborhood, thinking I'd like it better. But I grew up in Satol, which had people from everywhere, and even then I don't think I would've wanted to. I wanted to forget everything from before I moved in with her."

"There wasn't anything you missed?" Strange how Kirin sounded so sad. It gave Ifrit pause and he found himself answering truthfully.

"I missed the food." As Ifrit spoke they drifted toward a wall filled with silvery fish, which glinted with rainbows whenever the light struck them. "My… birth mom didn't want me around much. But whenever we had a big family gathering, she needed help in the kitchen. I think… I think when she was cooking, it was the one time she wasn't worried. It was the only time she'd ever laugh, or at least the only time she laughed in front of me."

Kirin was leaning his head against the glass, but he wasn't looking at the fish anymore. He was watching Ifrit, looking as relaxed as Ifrit had ever seen him.

"I don't know if I made up the memory or not, since I must have been so fucking little when it happened, but I asked her once, why she was so happy cooking for fucking *hours*. She said that the hours seemed to pass by so quickly when she thought of how happy the food would make everyone once it was done.

And that a little extra effort, especially when it's not needed, is never forgotten."

"Is that how you learned to cook?"

"Partially. Pressure was just a really fucking shitty cook." Ifrit joined Kirin in pressing his head against the tank. "In a weird way, that helped. Home used to smell like spices and meat, but suddenly it was burnt rice and clean laundry."

"So I should burn the rice more often?"

"Or just wash your clothes, dumbass."

Kirin just laughed and pulled Ifrit to the next room, which was impressive even by Ifrit's standard, who honestly couldn't care less about fish.

"Where do you think home will be, after school?" Kirin had stopped walking in the middle of the space. It was a giant circle, the walls and ceiling made of glass that held back the tropical fish swimming overhead. A shark was patrolling the edge of the room, but even it was moving leisurely, gently. The light was scattered further by the creatures swimming by, making it feel like Ifrit really was at the bottom of the sea, held in this bubble with Kirin. Every time a beam of light dared make it down, it glinted off his hair like a stray sunbeam had worked its way down just to illuminate him. "After we graduate, where do you want to go?"

Ifrit used to have a plan. He was going to go to the worst city he could find, and he was going to show all the stuck up assholes on the Hero Council and the whole damn world that he could be a good hero *without* killing anyone, that he wasn't some villain they should've killed when they had the chance, that he could be relied on to take a terrible situation and turn it around. Just like Pressure had. But suddenly, it wasn't important if everyone thought that, just as long as one person did.

"Wherever you go." He felt like he was being too obvious,

that he was staring at Kirin too intensely, that his emotions were written on his face. It didn't matter that half his face was covered because those dark eyes could see through him like he was the one made of crystal. Maybe he could've hidden if he looked away, but he couldn't, he never could. Kirin always met his gaze, always held it; he was never afraid to look Ifrit in the eye.

Their hands were still linked, and Ifrit's palms felt sweaty. Sometimes Ifrit wondered how Kirin could ever be so cruel to himself when he was practically perfect; his fucking hands didn't even get clammy. Meanwhile, Ifrit was busy sweating enough to drown a village, thinking that he'd made a mistake.

Kirin wordlessly pulled down Ifrit's mask, his eyes roving over Ifrit's face, looking for something. Usually Kirin was the one who was still as stone, but Ifrit hardly let himself breathe, afraid to shatter the moment as Kirin rested his thumb just under Ifrit's chin.

"Yeah." He didn't seem to be speaking to Ifrit, his words were so quiet. "We'll be together."

Kirin tilted Ifrit's chin up slightly, his eyes flickering to Ifrit's lips, and Ifrit's heartbeat was in his ears, his own free hand going to pull at Kirin's mask and—

Kirin threw them both to the floor, pinning Ifrit beneath him. Ifrit was a moment too late to extinguish his fire, but he didn't need to as he heard the glass shatter all around them and the flames were drowned by hundreds of liters of water pouring down. Kirin's eyes practically glowed white as he activated his mien, locking himself in place against the force of the water. The second the tide ebbed, Ifrit's ignition rings clicked together, and they were blasting back in to the room they'd just come from. A second blast had them around the corner before Kirin could even deactivate his mien to stop clutching Ifrit to his chest.

"How many?" Ifrit concentrated on sending out as much carbon as he could, feeling the room unfurl in his brain through the changes in the way it flowed. His control at a distance had gotten far, far better since Satol, but he had so little to work with since Kirin consumed what was put out almost as fast as Ifrit released it.

"I only saw one." Kirin's eyes were drawn to the ominous crack in the tank across from them, the remnants of the blast they'd only just avoided. "If I hadn't seen them they would've had a clear shot—"

"But you did." Ifrit stopped him from continuing the thought. "I'm right fucking here."

Kirin couldn't nod since the back of his neck was still crystalized, taking in a long slow breath instead to show he was doing his best to remain calm.

"Can you not do that actually?"

"Breathe?" Kirin looked confused for half a moment and then realized, stopping mid-exhale.

Ifrit closed his eyes, focusing on releasing carbon from every pore. It wasn't as easy without his costume, but the baggy shirts he favored helped, and the space gradually came into his head. There was a bench at the center, the two exits, and, through the circular room, almost at the exit, he caught the impression of someone running away.

Ifrit shoved himself to his feet and threw himself around the corner to catch a glimpse, but just as a shape resolved itself in his vision, the passageway collapsed, blocking sight entirely.

"Just one. And they fucking ran away," Ifrit spat. "You can fucking breathe again."

Kirin stubbornly held his breath for just a moment more before Ifrit punched him in the stomach and all his air rushed out.

"Hey! That was uncalled for." The momentary levity was broken as Kirin looked around the room, his face draining of color.

"What?" Ifrit readied himself to find more assailants but was only greeted with shattered glass and water rapidly running into drains that ran around the whole perimeter of the room.

"The fish..." Kirin was looking at the flopping forms on the ground, his eyes sad.

"They'll be fine, there's that fucking thing in the middle we can get them into." It certainly hadn't been there before the walls shattered, but now there was an open pit in the middle of the room where the floor had peeled back. All the water from the drains was filling this new, more secure tank, a failsafe for— it seemed— this exact situation.

"Let's move the shark first." Kirin must have been convinced that the danger had passed since he didn't hesitate a second longer, heading straight for the thrashing tail of arguably the only animal in the room that could hurt him.

"Wait—" People suddenly rushed past Ifrit and his rings clashed together before he knew what he was doing. A halo of fire ignited around him, scattering the people; the light from the flames illuminated the aquarium logo on their shirts, as well as the fear on their faces.

"It's alright, it's alright." Kirin was back in front of him again. "Your hearing aids must be malfunctioning; they were calling out to let you know they were there."

Ifrit's chest was rising and falling rapidly, though Kirin's eyes were calm.

"We're okay, okay?" Kirin's hand was on the back of Ifrit's neck, his thumb stroking a comforting rhythm as the workers edged cautiously around them. Ifrit almost wanted to hold on to the fear, because it was better than the sour taste building in his mouth as he watched each staff member shoot him the same suspicious look. The same watchful eyes that wondered when he'd explode again. "I'm going to help them move the big guy; it'll only be a moment. Are you good to go sit on the bench over there?"

Ifrit managed to nod, and Kirin squeezed his hand before he was off and asking how he could help.

How was it that Kirin, despite being monstrously tall, could put everyone around him at ease? Though Ifrit sat awkwardly in the sea of busy people, Kirin was able to say a few words and integrate himself into the recovery effort with ease. The staff smiled and nodded and laughed to words that Ifrit couldn't hear. When his hand went to turn up the volume on his hearing aids, he found the left one shattered and pulled it out, cursing.

"...this side better?" Ifrit looked up to see a face that was familiar, but difficult to place. It was the uniform that finally made it click; this was the single kind officer he'd ever run into in East City, the one who had warned him, Kirin, and Yantra about the rising attacks against children with miens. Fuck, that felt like years ago. Had it really only been six months? "I'll take that as a yes, since you looked up."

It was hard to place how old she was, her face marked with smile lines and age spots, though she seemed spry enough. She was surprisingly short for an officer, coming up only to Ifrit's chest when he stood. Her black hair was cut short, which revealed that the scar which started at the corner of her left eye continued back along her scalp until it reached her ear.

"My hearing aid got fu— got shattered." He didn't feel like going into more detail, but if she was here, he was going to have to.

That's no problem at all. She switched to sign. *I'm guessing* he's *alright; are you injured at all?*

It took Ifrit a moment to remember he had to respond to that.

No, he pushed me out of the way.

Did you see your attacker? He wondered if she was recording the conversation somehow, since she couldn't take notes while she signed.

Not physically. I got the impression that they were around 180 centimeters and had a stockier build, but they were running away so that was all I got.

That's alright. It's more than we've had.

Ifrit went cold. A wave of force. The Aether murders.

I'd like to talk more, if you have the time. She was offering him a tap card to import her contact data, and he almost reached for his phone before hesitating. The school likely wouldn't have an issue with inputting an officer's contact, yet he felt... worried about it.

Right. I forgot how strict the school is with your phone usage. Here, you can take this instead. It took her a moment to find what she was looking for, but a moment later she presented him with an old-fashioned paper business card. It read "An Nguyen — Mien Liaison."

More to distract himself than anything, he pointed to the title and asked *what does that mean?*

Right now? Not much. But someday, maybe something. She shrugged. *Your friend seems busy. How about you both come down to the station in a week and I can get your formal statements then?"*

Though her posture was casual, her eyes slid to the aquarium staff and the other uniformed officer who was inspecting the damage to the tanks. Now that Ifrit thought about it, the tap card hadn't been the standard police issue. His eyes narrowed as he looked at her.

We can come to the station next Wednesday. Ifrit signed slowly as his mind whirled. *You need to contact the school to request we be excused from class.*

But not today?

Ifrit felt his shoulders tense.

We got out early. If she sensed anything off in the statement, she didn't react. She just nodded, like she understood, and went to collect her coworker.

That left Ifrit free to finally look at the extent of the destruction. The circular room that had been so beautiful and peaceful minutes before was entirely shattered, large chunks of glass being carefully lifted by the staff and carelessly by Kirin who could crystallize his hands and not worry at all about cutting himself.

"Hey." He stepped into the path of one of the aquarium workers who was leaving. "Is there camera footage of this whole place?"

The worker looked startled that Ifrit was talking to him, his eyes widening and even looking to the side for assistance. All the other staff members were too occupied with their own tasks to rescue him.

"Th—there are cameras, but the police said that they'd all been kn—knocked out by the assailant as they passed through."

"So you can figure out what way they came through." Ifrit was doing his best to not be intimidating, but if anything, he seemed to be scaring the man more, since he was shrinking down into himself.

"I—I guess so, yes."

"Do you know which entrance?"

"I don't know, I just overheard them talking!"

"You don't need to be so worried, he's just trying to help figure out what happened." Kirin was there, though Ifrit hadn't heard him coming up from behind. His presence alone seemed to reassure the man, who immediately regained the color in his face. "Is there anything else you can tell us?"

"No, I don't work in security, I usually only prep the food for the animals." The man wouldn't even *look* at Ifrit now that he could avoid it.

Kirin's demeanor, previously gentle and inviting, turned cold.

"Thank you. We'll see ourselves out." Kirin's voice was wintry as he took Ifrit by the shoulders and started to guide them away. The staffer's ashen face made Ifrit realize that Kirin didn't seem nonthreatening naturally, he did it on purpose. And he could take it away whenever he wanted.

"What was the fuck was that for? We should go find some-one in security and look at those fucking tapes ourselves!" Ifrit struggled to keep his temper in check, the sensation of their lead falling out of his hands almost enough to make him explode again.

"We can look at them later." Kirin's eyes swept the room. They were forced to walk slowly as the staff moved around them. "I told them you had a special use license, but—" he switched to sign— *I think they realize we're East Tech students. We should leave.*

Ifrit almost went along with Kirin's neat handling of his temper when he caught a reflection in the cracked glass. He stopped in his tracks, waving away Kirin's questioning look.

From the reflection, he could see the temporary tank in the ground had sealed itself away again, all of the fish deposited safely inside. Now that the floor was back in place, Ifrit could see the line of attack clearly. It tore across the floor in a per-fectly straight line until it crashed into the tank on the other side.

Kirin had reacted quickly, knocking them both to the ground, but the attack should have hit anyway. The only reason it hadn't...

What? Kirin noticed the change in Ifrit's expression. The sign had made him spread his arms out, leaving him open, exposed, and making the rising fear in Ifrit's throat feel like it was choking him.

The only reason the attack had missed was because it wasn't aimed at him.

It had been intended for Kirin.

16

Again, Again

IF IT WEREN'T FOR the fact that Valor had no control over when they were assigned missions, Kirin would've thought the three a.m. call was intentional.

Valor was still angry. It was obvious in the way he was watching from the corner of the jet, not speaking. Phoenix had been forced to heal him, apparently, because there was no bruise on his throat despite their fight only two days prior. Yet there was no doubt it had happened, as much as it felt like a hazy dream to Kirin. Where there had only been mild indifference before, now there was hatred, and not just a little disgust.

That was fine. There was nothing to do about it, and honestly, if Kirin could keep Valor's attention on himself instead of on Ifrit, he'd be happy. Kirin still couldn't get the fear in Ifrit's eyes out of his head, the haunted look that made him look years younger. Just thinking about it made him return Valor's stare, his own anger now simmering just below the surface.

His thoughts were interrupted by Majesty clearing her throat and walking into the center of the cabin.

"While all our assignments should be handled with utmost care and attention, I will request that today you be at your very best." She looked tired, even her blue suit feeling less bright. Whereas Valor was radiating rage and violence, she was exuding an air of exhaustion. Even... sadness. Like she'd just been told something that crushed her entirely.

"Some of you may have already been made aware of this—" was it Kirin's imagination or did she look irritated at the thought?— "but this is another call where we have strong suspicion that Aether is involved. If they are not personally present, they have certainly had a hand in inspiring those we are to apprehend."

The change in the atmosphere was palpable. Majesty's class still looked bored to tears, Bia even yawning broadly, but everyone on Kirin's side of the plane stiffened. He didn't have to look around to know the grim determination on their faces.

"This is very similar to the last call we had for an Aether cell." Majesty tapped a panel on the floor with her foot, causing a holo hub to rise. She pressed a few buttons and a schematic spread out in front of her: a winding complex of buildings and thick metal pipes, fenced off areas where the voltage was too high to enter. Multiple buildings held clusters of red dots, some even resolved into rough humanoid shapes. "We'll be heading in immediately upon landing, which is why the ground team has sent ahead scans of the area. Once again, they are camping in a generator, but this is an active generator serving a large metropolitan area, roughly the same size as East City."

She paused and cast a severe look at her own class.

"I am sure we all remember what happened when that exploded, don't we?"

Not many of her students looked chastised, though one, closest to the door, looked ill at the thought. Her dark skin turned sickly pale, and it was then that Kirin recognized her. Inanna. He glanced over at Ness, just two seats to his right, and she'd noticed too.

"For the sake of efficiency and coordinating with the local

heroes, we have already gone through the trouble of dividing you into teams." With a swipe, the roster flew from the hub to the air, each group hovering above their entrance location.

"No fucking way." Clidna was two seats to Kirin's left, just on the other side of Ifrit, but Kirin could still hear her clearly. Even if she hadn't spoken, Kirin would've known something was off from the way Ifrit tensed. His hands clenched in his lap, but when Kirin reached to take one, Ifrit pushed him away. His eyes nervously flickered to Valor, who Kirin noticed was watching them closely.

Majesty went on talking, which made it even harder for Kirin to read the words as they blurred together with the background. He finally found Ifrit's name, and his own brows came together as he read further down and failed to see his own.

He did, however, see the reason everyone was immediately irritated. They were broken up into groups of five or six, and yet he didn't recognize several of the names coupled with Ifrit's. Majesty's class didn't look any happier about it, leering through the projected landscape.

"You're with Bia." Ifrit's mask covered his neck and chin entirely, but Kirin could *hear* how tightly clenched his jaw was.

"I'll ask to—"

"There will be no switching assignments for this mission." Majesty sensed the thought before he could fully say it. "Aether does not show themselves often and we cannot afford to let anyone escape. We were only called in for this mission due to your familiarity with Aether operatives, and it will reflect very poorly on any students who fail to do their duty."

It might have been Kirin's imagination, but her eyes seemed to single him out.

"Regardless of what you might consider to be the best allocation of personnel, this has been discussed with those most familiar with the situation. We will be watching all of your whereabouts for the duration of the mission from the control building here." A short structure at the edge of the map lit up in blue. "It is essential that we remain in constant contact with all of you so we can track the location of all Aether agents, and— more importantly— where they attempt to flee to."

Valor ducked into the cockpit as the descent started and their class began to unbuckle.

"Hey." Ifrit grabbed Kirin's hand as they stood. "Promise me you're going to fucking watch your back?"

"Yeah, of course—" Kirin was cut off by Ifrit yanking him down by his mask. Their foreheads almost slammed together as Kirin was dragged to Ifrit's eye level.

"Don't give her a fucking opportunity." Ifrit's hand was in the corner of Kirin's vision and he could see the way it was shaking. "Don't turn your back, don't go into any rooms first, you fucking run away if she's in danger, do you hear me?"

Maybe Kirin could convince Majesty to switch the teams. But Ifrit was with Clidna and Phoenix and Wyrm, who were already forming a protective shell around him. And their entry point was the farthest from the Aether cells, farthest from the generators. It didn't matter that Kirin's was the closest.

I'm coming right back to you. Kirin signed rather than spoke as more people were crowding around. *I promise.*

Ifrit didn't seem convinced.

The fact that Ness was nearly invisible meant she could get away with mocking Bia every time the other woman spoke.

There was a lot of material available, from the fact that Bia had led them to dead ends multiple times, to Yantra having to remind her what they were doing repeatedly, to her not even knowing what a generator *did*. Not that she said any of these things to them directly, since she seemed to think that speaking to any of them was beneath her, instead directing all her idiotic comments at her two classmates. One of them Kirin recognized from their botched attempt to recruit Phoenix, a shorter man with limp blond hair and deep-set eyes. If Kirin remembered correctly, he had some sort of ice ability. The other was a woman about Yantra's height, and if the muscles were anything to go by, her mien had something to do with strength.

If Ness hadn't been making light of the whole thing, Kirin might have just run ahead and left Bia behind, especially since Bia was making so much noise that Kirin wouldn't be surprised if the whole *complex* had heard them coming. His knuckles had cracked from how tightly he balled his hands, resisting the urge to knock her out for threatening the mission.

They were inside, but unlike the previous generator complex, this building was fitted with dozens of windows, though they weren't doing much now that the sun was down. The emergency lights overhead were spaced too far apart, which lead to them passing through sections of shadow before they emerged into clinical illumination again. The moon was half full, but with the clouds hiding it from view every few minutes, it provided weak and untrustworthy light.

"She does remember this is a stealth mission, right?" Yantra had a glowing circle around her eye, likely watching their progress along the map. Even though they'd entered near a cluster of glowing dots, the wrong turns had made them slower than anticipated. Some of the other groups were already in position.

"She didn't even remember that we're looking for Aether agents, *twice*." Ness's edges smoothed slightly as she spoke, even though none of them were speaking louder than a whisper. "Not that us reminding her of that got her to shut up."

"If only one of us were big enough to knock her out and then we could finish this without complications." Yantra sighed.

Kirin didn't think he could respond without betraying his own impatience. Aether was *here*. They'd know more about his family, he was sure of it. He just had to get there without Bia alerting the *entire world* that they were coming.

Maybe he should hit her into a wall.

Bia was still talking loudly when the ring around Yantra's eye blinked once and vanished.

"No." Yantra was suddenly pale.

"What is it?" Kirin immediately turned around, watching their back. He felt Ness appear at his elbow, facing away and watching for Bia's group ahead. "Did you see something on the map?"

The answer became clear as the lights overhead winked out.

"Yantra, what just happened?" Kirin tried to keep his tone calm. Ifrit would be *fine*; he could handle himself. There wasn't more carbon in the air than usual. He was imagining things.

"I think..." Her voice trembled. "I think they just made this whole place a dead zone."

"How could they do that?" Ness was pressing against Kirin's left side, Yantra touching his right. The hallway hadn't appeared to have any doors until much further down, but no one was supposed to be able to shut off all tech in a three-block radius, either.

"I don't know." Yantra sounded genuinely scared. Right. She was entirely powerless now. "It started from... from the room we were heading to."

"Then we better get there." A cloud drifted away from the moon just as Kirin turned to press forward. The added light made him crystallize his entire back and chest, which Ness noticed immediately.

"What now?" She followed his gaze and sighed. "Well, shit."

Bia and her two classmates, who had been suspiciously silent since the lights flashed out, were gone.

17

Unexpected Meeting

IFRIT NEEDED TO HANG around Wyrm more, if only because it kept Majesty's class at a safe distance. Neither of the two assholes in their group would even *look* at him, let alone come near. Wyrm knew it too, and whenever one of the pricks tried to undermine what Ifrit suggested they do, Wyrm conveniently placed himself in the way, effectively forcing them to choose between shutting up or admitting he existed. Altogether very convenient.

Frustrating he didn't know what he was working with though.

He'd sent a thin pulse of carbon into the building ahead of them, getting a feel for the two guards holed up in the security room. The unmoving bodies on the floor were likely the real employees, who were happily still alive. Their breathing was weak, hardly moving the carbon around their faces at all, but it was still there.

One of the seated infiltrators, however, was worrying Ifrit immensely. The picture he was forming in his head was that this person must be *huge*. Every time they breathed, it sent massive ripples through the air, more than three times larger than those of their companion. Only Kirin ever disrupted his mien this much—

Ifrit's heart skipped a beat. There was no way. *No* way.

What's the plan, boss? Clidna had to wave her hand in front of his eyes to get his attention. *We're not going to find out what those two can do, they're giving us fuck all.*

He stared at her blankly for a few moments before remembering where they were. What they were doing.

What's wrong? Clidna signed, moments before Phoenix narrowed his eyes.

"Why do you look worried?" He had the good sense to keep his voice low. The sounds of the generator were large enough to mostly hide his words, but Majesty's students were standing just a few meters away, watching all of them suspiciously.

Of course, the one fucking time Kirin wasn't in Ifrit's group this had to happen. The *one* time. Had Valor known somehow? Was this their punishment from the day before?

Ifrit, you need to communicate. Clidna might have looked angry to someone else, but Ifrit knew her well enough to know she was just trying to stare at his face long enough to divine what had gone wrong.

If that was Kirin's sibling in there, how would Ifrit prove he wasn't going to hurt them? Should he take them into custody so Kirin could talk to them? Should he let them leave so that they wouldn't be sent to jail without so much as a sham trial? Fuck Valor for restricting their comms so they couldn't talk to each other on private channels— was there any way to get Kirin over here?

"Ifrit." Phoenix was looking at him too sharply now. "Are you good?"

It'd be way fucking easier if he was just having some kind of anxiety attack, because then he'd know what to do, at least in theory. It couldn't be Kirin's sibling in there. It didn't make sense. The intel that Kirin had gotten implied that they were being chopped up for money, not working for Aether. Or maybe this was a way for them to keep themself safe? If only he could get them to *talk* to him, or stall them long enough for Kirin to get there—

"I don't mean to alarm you, but I don't like the way they're looking at us right now." Anyone who hadn't seen Wyrm fight would have assumed he was running his hands up and down his shoulders out of nervousness. Instead, it just meant he was getting ready to paralyze whoever was stupid enough to try to hit him.

Ifrit looked over his shoulder to see Majesty's fucking idiots watching with open curiosity. And— in the taller one's eyes— excitement.

"Don't fucking worry about them. If they try any bullshit I'll blowtorch the motherfuckers." Even as he spoke, Ifrit sent out extra carbon in their direction, so they wouldn't be able to attack without immediate retaliation. "Clidna, do you have the map up?"

Clidna pulled out her phone without question, the complex blinking to life with glowing dots. Kirin was in group four... there. It was far, but maybe Ifrit could draw him over without words after all.

The dots on the map representing Kirin's group were still moving, however, farther away from where Ifrit sat. What were the chances that Ifrit could reach him before they all had to move out?

Clidna's phone shut off and she frowned, but then the lights in the security room went off too.

And Majesty's students lunged.

Ifrit genuinely almost fried them. His rings were clashing together before he realized what he was doing, the fire streaking back toward them instantly. In slow motion, he felt their bodies hit the larger cloud of monoxide, felt the stream of heat moving closer. And then Wyrm threw his hands forward, dropping them as the cloud of flame roared over their heads.

It was lucky that he'd kept a steady supply of carbon by the security room door since he couldn't hear it burst open anymore. A cloud had just moved from in front of the moon, bathing the few meters between them and the door in pale light, illuminating the rather mousy woman watching them with wide eyes.

Ifrit felt the squeeze around his heart lessen. This woman looked nothing like Kirin, midnight skin and tightly coiled black hair. She was small and thin, almost malnourished, her mouth falling open in a comical "o." The fear in her eyes quickly took over, and she darted back inside the building, pulling the door closed sharply behind her.

I can't reach anyone, can you? Clidna was signing and speaking at the same time, head looking between the three of them rapidly. Wyrm shook his head. He was crouched down, adding extra paralyzing agent to the students on the ground, both of whom looked up with anger burning in their eyes. Phoenix was saying something, but he was turned away from Ifrit, his mouth hidden.

Do we regroup? If they just lost power too, I don't think Aether is going to be doing anything from this room right now. Clidna ran a hand through her hair, looking over to a building that held the nearest squad. *It looks like all the buildings lost power, not just this one.*

Is the generator running? The ground still felt like it was thrumming, but maybe it was just his heartbeat thundering in his ears.

...it is. Clidna's hands had raised and then frozen as she realized. *How is it still running?*

And why are they still inside? Clidna translated as Wyrm spoke.

What do we do? Phoenix hadn't mastered sign yet, but at least he could certainly ask the simple question.

It's your call, boss. The way Clidna was looking at him made Ifrit feel like his face was giving slightly too much away. Half of him wanted to run headlong to where Kirin's dot had last been blinking, to grab him and drag him back to this corner where it was, at least for the moment, something close to safe. But the other half couldn't fail to notice the supply of carbon by the door swiftly vanishing. Couldn't ignore the fact that he had no idea who else was in the room with the woman they'd seen, since the air churned and disrupted his sense of the space whenever the Aether agent shifted.

We should deal with the people ahead of us. His hands were steady. The chances that he would be assigned to the one building that held the one person they were looking for were slim, but not zero. And if it *was* Kirin's sibling, he'd think of something. He would. *Let's go.*

Do you want to try smoking them out? Clidna joined him in approaching the door and Phoenix and Wyrm covered their rear.

No, I want us out of sight for this. If Clidna thought there was anything odd in the statement, she didn't react in the slightest.

I can give them a headache before we go in, if that's helpful. They were right against the building now. Ifrit was surprised Phoenix was willingly staying back, since he usually used himself as a human meat shield during combat.

Can you tell me where everything is inside?

Clidna couldn't know there was anything odd about the request. They'd been on dozens of missions together by now, but always with Kirin too. She had to be the one to scope out their environment since any carbon Ifrit tried to put out was consumed before it made it more than a few meters away.

*There are two people moving. Two laying on the floor, I'm assuming the actual guards.*It was a little frustrating being told things he already knew, but that wasn't her fault. *Our two moving targets both feel thin, though there's something strange about one of them. They don't sound... like flesh.*

Ifrit willed his face to stay neutral.

They're trying to do something with the wall, I think—

She broke off abruptly and wrenched the door open, Ifrit nearly stomping on her ankles in his rush to stay behind her. A flash of movement at the edge of his vision told him that Phoenix was moving too.

The reason Clidna had rushed in became apparent the moment they entered the room, the darkness outside meaning their eyes didn't need to adjust to the gloom indoors. The short woman who had come outside before was even holding a candle, the flame making her eyes seem even wider as the light flickered across them. Her companion was partially covered with a jacket that looked like it was just draped across their back, one arm occupied with pushing a large portion of the wall inward. A hidden escape tunnel, for exactly this situation. They only looked up briefly, eyes widening, before they grabbed the woman and darted inside. Not even a second later, they vanished from sight.

Ifrit was going to follow them anyway, but it turned out he didn't have a choice in the matter. He *had* felt Phoenix move, and now he was crashing into Ifrit with enough force to knock him down, and they were rolling across the floor of the room and down into the dark gap the moving wall had left. The pair they were following hadn't vanished at all, they'd simply fallen. Just beyond the wall, the floor gave way to a pit, a fact that Ifrit was only aware of when he felt his stomach fly into his throat.

It shouldn't have been a problem, he could fly through the air just as easily as he could walk or run, but the moonlight was out again and the bright red on Clidna's face made his brain sluggish. He felt Phoenix's arm wrap around him weakly, just moments before they hit the ground. He felt a sickly crunch as his full weight landed on Phoenix, who he hadn't realized was quite so thin until it was too late.

He rolled off immediately, able to see that the blood on Clidna's face hadn't been her own. There were torches here, placed like someone had known the power would cut out, that flashlights or phones would cease to work. And they illuminated a ghastly sight. Phoenix was bleeding from a deep laceration on his back, which cut up and around his shoulder, beyond the now crushed ribs.

It should've killed Phoenix instantly. Should have easily killed him, which meant he should be healing now. But he lay on the ground, gasping. Or at least Ifrit thought he was, since sound was still far, far away from him. Phoenix's eyes were open wide, like he was seeing something up above, one of his hands reaching out for someone, something. Ifrit found himself grabbing the hand, and suddenly Phoenix's eyes were on him, sharp as ever. A moment later, her grip grew stronger, and Phoenix was pulling Ifrit to his feet looking with wary eyes behind him.

Ifrit turned and was met with a pair of teardrop-shaped black eyes level with his own. He instinctively loosed a small explosion, one that would only push back the stranger, not harm them. He watched, horrified, as instead their eyes changed from black to opalescent. It wasn't the same as the swirling silver he was used to, more like the slick of oil on asphalt, but it was familiar enough. The explosion only threw the jacket off their shoulders, revealing that one arm ended just below their shoulder in a diamond stub.

"Can you heal others?" They spoke slowly enough and enunciated like they weren't used to the language, so much so that Ifrit could read their lips easily. They weren't looking at Ifrit, focused on Phoenix who was noticing all the same similarities

that Ifrit had. She glanced upward, probably hearing something that Ifrit couldn't, but her gaze was pulled right back down as the stranger moved closer still, hand outstretched plaintively. "*Can you heal other people or only yourself?*"

Phoenix made her decision quickly.

"I can heal you, if that's what you need." She signed the few words she did know, enough for Ifrit to string the sentence she must have said together.

But the stranger shook their head, eyes wide and hopeful. It was a painfully familiar expression, though their face was rounder and the hair that fell across their eyes dull instead of full of starlight.

"Not me," they said, beckoning with their one good arm farther down the tunnel, *"but please help my brother."*

18

Blinding White

Kirin didn't let himself think about where Bia might have gone. If he did, if he considered it all, he might abandon Ness and Yantra completely and run to where he had last seen Ifrit on the map. He could only hope that Bia was exactly as hopeless with directions as she had seemed to be and couldn't find her way there before the power came back on. Because it *would* come back, and Ifrit would be fine. He had to be.

Maybe trying to find the group of Aether combatants with only Ness and Yantra was a bad plan. Maybe he really should've been going the other way. But someone here would know how many of his family members were compromised, where they were, and how Kirin could get them back. And they would tell him. One way or another.

Yantra was busy unravelling something from a pocket of her suit as they ran, Ness flashing in and out of view as she ducked through walls to check for any unpleasant surprises waiting for them. So far, there was only a somehow still humming generator on the opposite side of the wall, and not a single living soul to be seen.

They were closing in on their original target now, the only door down this interminably long corridor. It stood out in the gloom with the clean and bright steel wheel that kept it firmly closed, all the computing equipment for the complex held behind that one door. The record logs for the power created, the communities it served, the internal temperature of the reactors— all of it in one room that was inaccessible from anywhere except this door. Kapre's team should have been coming in from the ground in the back corner, a local hero team from the side, breaking through the solid concrete in unison as their team burst in through the door, but there was no guarantee that either of them were in position now. Kapre could still easily cut through rock and stone to make it, but Kirin had no idea what the other heroes could do.

The door sprung open when they were still ten meters away.

Half a dozen lumbering shapes came out, but Kirin's eyes were latched on the smallest silhouette, the one that lithely and almost casually slipped through the door before the swarm of mien-assisted muscle swarmed around her. The white uniform was back in place and almost *glowing* against the grim background of stark concrete walls.

A bundle of wires ripped itself out of the wall and Kirin realized that she didn't seem to shine because of the contrast, but because, suddenly, the lights were back on. And that meant Yantra was back too.

Just in time, since the first wave of muscle had noticed them and began to charge.

One was caught in wires as another golem started to form out of the wall, an amorphous, writhing shape of sparking cables that wrapped the legs of a charging woman and pulled her back through the concrete. There had been two others right behind her; one barreled forward, crashing into Kirin, while the other paused and pulled the woman out. That pair had just righted themselves when the man who had beelined for Kirin was thrown backward into them, sending the whole group down like bowling pins.

As they fell, Kirin was granted a clear line of sight on the woman in white.

She had to have been expecting the attack, she must have known, since she wasn't the least disconcerted by the turn of events. True, it was hard to tell anything behind the flat, white sheet that covered her face, but her posture was calm, her pace unhurried as she continued forward even as her protection got to their feet.

"Ah, hero of the hour, is it?" Her hand went up and Kirin instinctively crystallized his entire chest and legs, Yantra and Ness falling into place behind him. But she only moved her mask slightly, so that Kirin could see her lips. She was smirking. "How *have* you been, Kirin? No trouble at home I hope?"

Kirin only noticed that he'd moved when he felt the hands grabbing his arms. The woman was no longer meters away, instead just an arm's reach. The fallen muscle had gotten up and were holding him tightly, the pressure clearly meant to intimidate, but he felt nothing apart from the building anger in his chest.

"What have you done?" His voice sounded distant.

"I merely offered an opportunity. After all, losing any income with so many mouths to feed must be so *hard*." With a perfectly manicured hand, she slid the mask back into place, sealing away any human likeness. "You wouldn't be having second thoughts now, would you?"

A flicker in the air behind the woman in white gave Kirin half a second's warning. There were three people holding him back, two hands on each of his arms, and one on each of his shoulders. He reared backward, catching the guard standing directly behind him unaware. A crack alerted him that their nose was broken, and they stumbled only a few steps, enough for Yantra's mechanical snake to coil around them, holding onto their limbs so tightly they couldn't move. Ness flashed into existence in the doorway behind the woman in white, landing a few quick strikes on the rearmost man's throat, stomach, groin. She was gone again in an instant as the man folded.

The two holding Kirin's arms were easy to deal with. Kirin used their grip against them by throwing them forward and into each other, so hard their teeth rattled, and however strong they might be, they weren't used to feeling pain.

There had been two more standing behind the woman, but they were suddenly not there. Not just strength; Aether had gone for speed as well. Ness vanished again, but even behind the partially opaque goggles of her mask, Kirin had seen the fear in her eyes.

He felt like he was moving through molasses as his head turned and he heard Yantra scream. Only one of the two had reached her, the other a blur to Kirin's left. He managed to shoot a crystallized arm out, his shoulder taking the punishment when someone hit the spiked bar moving at full speed. Kirin refused to think about the red now staining his white shirt.

Another heartbeat later, he didn't have to will the thought away because he was focused on the blood streaming down Yantra's face, her *exposed* face. The one guard who had managed to sneak by Kirin had hit her right in the temple, cracking the purple plate that went across her jaw. As Yantra fell, so did her assailant, Ness's shocked face appearing as she removed her bloodied hand from his side.

There was stillness for a moment. Silence. Ness dropped to the floor, momentarily forgetting the target of their whole mission in her hurry to check on Yantra.

"No," she muttered, pushing the long black hair out of the way, trying to get a good look at the wound causing blood to sheet down the side of Yantra's face. "No, no, no, don't you dare close your eyes."

"Hey doc," Yantra murmured, only one of her eyes opening as the other was covered in blood, "I think I might have a concussion. You're looking a little blurry to me."

Ness smiled weakly, before she was bodily thrown into the wall.

The woman in white was there, and she yanked Yantra upright by her hair. Kirin started to move forward, but suddenly he heard a ringing in his head, so high pitched it drowned everything else out. The pain of it was blinding, sending him to his knees. White spots crawled up the side of his vision, and when he was able to get a glimpse of his hands, he idly wondered where the blood spattering them was coming from.

Somewhere, deep in his brain, something reacted, crystallizing his ears and even the eardrum, anything to stop the noise from making its way inside. It wasn't a perfect block, but he gasped from the relief, wiping the blood from his ears as he tried not to vomit from the realization of how close to dying he had just been.

"...DEAD!" The word was so muffled he almost missed it, but he looked up, squinting from the overhead light to see Yantra shoved against the wall, Ness nowhere in sight. Yantra was still bleeding, one eye closed, but she was conscious. Her mien was still working, pieces of metal working themselves toward her on the ground, sluggishly, disjointedly. She hardly even seemed aware of the coming aid, trying to grapple with the hand that was against her throat. When she found no purchase there, she tried for her assailant's face, bright red staining the blinding white.

"How are you not dead?" Clearly the woman was shouting, since the words came through, even when half of Kirin's head was pure diamond. "They said you were dead!"

Yantra's good eye widened a fraction, but before she could

respond, Kirin tackled the woman in white to the ground.

His own blood now colored her clothes, and he heard a strangled yelp as his body weight landed on hers. She didn't seem to be used to fighting, flailing to try to shove him off, yet she still landed a lucky hit to his throat that made him jerk backward instinctively, leaving her to scramble away. He thought that she would make a run for it again, but instead she reached for Yantra.

Yantra had collapsed to the ground; the woman grabbed her by the hair and *pulled*, dragging her along the floor. Ness materialized and reached for her, but suddenly she was on the ground too, clawing at her ears before vanishing again entirely. The only sign that she'd been there at all was a spot of blood that had dripped from her nose to the floor.

Kirin had assumed Yantra was going to be held hostage, since Kapre and Enenra had just burst through the door behind him, others in their wake. But she hardly seemed to notice anyone else at all, violently grasping at the hair just above Yantra's ear and yanking upward. The movement revealed a perfectly level scar that traced back along Yantra's skull, a thin, precise thing that wasn't noticeable when her hair was down.

"I *saw* you die!" The old, now exposed wound incensed the woman further. "If you weren't dead, why the fuck didn't you come back for *me*?"

Even through his clogged ears Kirin heard the grinding of stone and knew Kapre had sealed their group off from their reinforcements.

"You think they'll stick up for you? You think *they'll* support you once they know?" The woman shook Yantra again, and Kirin noticed that mixed in with the blood on Yantra's face were tear tracks. "In this whole fucking system, you're the biggest fraud of all. Are they going to protect you once your little secret is out?"

The woman ripped the stylized A pin from her chest and it molded under her fingers to become a knife barely longer than her thumb. She pointed that needle-like blade at Yantra's one good eye, suddenly going still and calm.

"You chose wrong," she said.

Before she could make good on her threat, she dropped into a hole, arms pinned to her side. Her grip on Yantra hadn't slackened, and Yantra was pulled by her hair to the ground, her forehead hitting the edge of the new crevasse.

Ness appeared to blink in and out of existence, but when she disappeared this time, she somehow pulled Yantra with her too. They rematerialized only a few seconds later, several meters down the hall, Yantra turning and vomiting on the ground.

"*No!*" Kirin looked behind him to see Enenra frozen in her tracks. Ness had yelled to stop her from advancing. "Don't get close— her mien's deadly."

But Enenra advanced anyway, the light flickering through her. Small motes of smoke drifted upward from her neck and ears, and she crouched down in front of their captive with no trouble at all.

"What were you doing with our friend?" Enenra's voice couldn't have been loud, but then how could Kirin hear it? Just like the smoke she turned into, somehow it was finding the smallest crack and making its way.

It was impressive that a blank mask could look disgusted, though perhaps Kirin was projecting his own emotions, seeing the white smeared with red and knowing it was the blood of his friend.

The woman made some kind of response that Kirin couldn't hear, and if Enenra wasn't being affected by the ringing, surely she couldn't either. But before anyone who *could* hear could respond, or even begin deciphering what might have been said, the ground rumbled, and the lights went out.

Kirin lunged forward, knowing consciously that Kapre's mien would hold, that they didn't need sight to keep her in place, yet his hands found the edge of a belt, of a small box. Whoever it belonged to was running away, Kirin being just barely too slow to stop them. The box came away in his hand, his grip so tight he felt it dent before he could remember to let go. A chunk of something hit his shoulder and he looked up, only to realize he could see the moon clearly now, as the ceiling was falling in.

Kapre could hold themself, so he tucked Enenra under one arm as he ran for where he'd last seen Ness and Yantra. The nearly uninterrupted moonlight gave him a path, but a narrowing one, as larger and larger chunks rained down. Ness appeared amidst the dust in his vision, shielding Yantra with her body as best she could, but she was so small, so fragile against the coming force.

He threw Enenra into them, Ness understanding immediately what to do. She pulled Enenra down, and together they tucked Yantra's head in as Kirin threw himself over all three and braced, crystallizing everything he could as the building rained down. Piece after piece fell into place, settling against his back and adding more and more weight. His arm nearly gave way and he mentally apologized to Ness and Enenra as he crystallized the inside of his arms too, opening thin cuts wherever they brushed up against him. His legs were next, after a blow felt like it had come dangerously close to shattering his femur. His back was crystallized, the first thing he'd done, but if he did both his back and his chest he would hardly be able to breathe. When a piece crashed into his spine, he took one final deep breath and held.

Kapre would pull them out quickly. He just had to hold out for a few seconds. And maybe a few more. It would be hard for Kapre to find them in all the rubble; he could deal with the burning in his chest. The headache building in his head. Ness's face seemed to swim in his vision more than usual, her mouth moving with words he couldn't hear. Her face was streaked with dust and she turned to look down at Yantra, who had both eyes closed. Ness wasn't talking to him now, but to her, one hand moving to touch her face even though it meant brushing past Kirin and opening a gash on her arm. Enenra was half smoke, the top side of her body mist in the air to give the others more room in the tiny space carved out beneath Kirin's body. The lights on her suit were all that illuminated the four of them, and the dust that filled the air.

Ness was yelling something now, and Kirin decided it was safe to unplug his ears, if only to give him something to focus on other than how little time there was left before he had to breathe again.

But when he did, all he could hear was the sound of the ground giving out beneath them.

19

All Lies

Kirin's sibling kept a brisk pace in the tunnel, which kept Ifrit from thinking too hard about how far down they were or where the nearest source of fresh air was. Phoenix was jumpy at his side, her eyes scanning their surroundings for a possible way out. The torchlight didn't help, especially not when it jumped as Ifrit passed, sensing the extra food for the flames.

"*How much further?*" Phoenix signed the question as she spoke, her face drawn. Ifrit couldn't blame her. It felt like they'd been walking for hours, though it was probably a cruel trick of his mind.

Not much. Phoenix translated Kirin's sibling's response since they hadn't even bothered to turn around to give it. They hadn't turned once since the trek began, half-limping, half-jogging as if they were eager to get it over with. There was something jumpy and anxious in their demeanor that both felt alien and familiar at the same time. Kirin was deeply anxious, but he almost let it fortify him, used that fear as a bulwark against true despair. But his sibling had all their fear on the outside, wrapped around them like a shroud.

They held themself similarly to how Kirin did. The slight hunch forward to not seem so tall, the way their hand tapped against their leg every few steps as they walked. Ifrit could even believe if he'd seem them out of the corner of his eye, he would've stopped and looked up, thinking it was Kirin instead.

For the first time they turned off the main path, and Ifrit actually stopped for a moment before he could force himself to keep moving. The tunnel was narrower, much narrower, and the torches were spaced even further apart. The air was stagnant, stale, and he could feel the carbon in the air from the machines above. But his guide was still moving. Phoenix was still following, though Ifrit could see the anxious frown she wore, her mask only hiding the creases around her eyes.

Abruptly, Kirin's sibling stopped. If Ifrit hadn't been watching them so closely, he likely wouldn't have noticed the way they hesitated before they turned to face them.

"*In there.*" They pointed at a heavy steel door with a round window. There was no light from the inside, the torchlight in the tunnel reflecting in the glass even as Phoenix cupped her hand over her eyes and peered in.

No see anything. The signs were quick, trying to match the speed with which she spoke. *How in?*

"*...can't... door.*" They looked openly anxious now, whereas before there had been some attempt to hide it. "*Please... too long.*"

Phoenix looked to Ifrit for help. He had a bad feeling about this, but how much of his fear was just from being underground again? How much of it was because he didn't know how to act, how to respond to this person who he felt like he almost knew but didn't?

"Stand back." He could find the cracks in the doorframe; it wasn't airtight. A detonation would be harder, but doable, as long as he pushed the carbon in the tunnel far, far away from where they stood. Phoenix knew how far back she needed to be, but she had to pull their guide away to make sure they didn't get flattened when the door blew off its hinges. They both pretended not to notice when Kirin's younger sibling jumped when Phoenix touched their arm.

Ifrit was glad his hearing aids were still offline when he saw Phoenix flinch from the sound of the explosion. The door shot across with such force that it embedded in the concrete boundary of the tunnel. The impact shook the floor and Ifrit winced as dust from the ceiling fell into his eyes. When he finally rubbed them clean, their guide was already through the now empty doorway, vanished into the gloom.

He and Phoenix looked at each other, hesitating on the boundary. There was no way to get locked in here, the fucking door had just been blown off. But still the dark room loomed large in front of them, like an open maw.

Phoenix started to move first. Ifrit wasn't sure if it was because of something that was said that he couldn't hear, since her eyes widened before she went in, but she lurched into motion as if she'd broken free of a spell. He took a deep breath before he followed her inside.

His eyes took a moment to adjust, not because of the sudden lack of light, but because of the shocking brightness. It was like there had been a curtain across the doorway to hide the fluorescent lighting that filled the room, which Ifrit realized with dawning horror that he recognized.

Kirin wasn't here. Instead, their guide was headed to a bed in the back corner, winding through trays of medical equipment and monitors to a corner that, when Ifrit had last seen it, contained a pair of heavily injured children.

"Please." This *had* to be Kirin's sibling, there was no doubt about it, not when they got that very same pinched look around their eyes as Kirin did when he was about to cry. The room wasn't real, was it? Kirin said he knew it, but the hospital had been *above* ground last time, hadn't it? Maybe the space itself

was the key, maybe it moved, and they were really there now, close to not one but *three* of Kirin's siblings, able to take them home.

Phoenix was looking around with her eyes narrowed, moving forward slowly, cautiously. Ifrit stayed where he was, forcing himself to put more carbon into the air. His brain screamed at him to stop, his throat already starting to feel choked, like the air couldn't make it to his lungs, but as the room filled out in his head, he knew there was something wrong.

Kirin's sibling must have been breathing shallowly because the air wasn't disturbed as much now as it had been before, or at least the carbon was building up easier. He could feel the open doorway behind him, the few wisps vanishing as they passed the doorway into the more diluted tunnel air. The hospital room they were looking at was open like this one seemed to be, but he could sense no equipment, no beds, no nothing. There was only a built out section in the corner that didn't even go to the full height of the room. It felt like a recording booth, especially with the counter he could sense built right into its side.

To enter that section of the room there was a doorway, and through that doorway Ifrit's senses started to fizzle out, as the carbon was once again displaced by Kirin's sibling breathing. Dread crept up Ifrit's spine as his search of the room finished.

They weren't alone.

He'd known the moment the room didn't match what he was seeing, the moment they'd seen the hospital to begin with. He didn't dare look behind himself, toward the back wall where someone was standing next to a row of candles that nibbled at the extra fuel in the air.

"Phoenix, what's wrong with them?" He tried to stall for time, especially when he looked back up and found Kirin's sibling watching him with guilty eyes. Did they know that he'd figured out this was a trap?

Phoenix's reply was lost amidst a loud crash that shook the whole room.

Wait. A *loud* crash. That Ifrit had heard.

His momentary distraction cost him, since it meant he didn't react in time when he felt the person behind him move. They shoved him forward, toward the invisible doorway, but no, now he could see it. Not a sound booth. A prison. A block of concrete with a thick steel door.

The illusion must have dropped for Phoenix too as he could hear her cursing and the sounds of a scuffle. This truly must have been someone that Kirin was related to, as Ifrit could hear them apologizing even as they kept Phoenix from leaving.

A blow to the back of his head reminded him that he wasn't alone.

He hadn't been too concerned about the teenager behind him, since the shove had only made him move from the shock of it. The kid had looked scrawny then and felt it now, no power behind the punch, someone unused to trying to attack.

When Ifrit turned, he was greeted with the teenage boy from their first mission, his hands shaking as he held out fists to defend himself.

A pair of arms wrapped around Ifrit, and he realized too late that his supply of carbon had dropped.

"I'm really sorry about this." The words were barely audible, but the regret was palpable.

When they started dragging him back toward the concrete box, Ifrit lost all sense of rational thought.

He couldn't be put back in a dark room, couldn't be forced to live through that again. *Phoenix*— where was Phoenix?— couldn't live through that again. His blood rushed in his ears, feeling his chest tighten and his breathing start to go ragged as he was pulled slowly, inexorably toward the door that he could now see was twice as thick as the one he had destroyed. Ifrit felt the tips of his fingers go numb, the sensation flee from his legs as he kicked and flailed and tried his hardest to summon even the smallest explosion, but his hands were pinned to his chest with a single arm, his ignition rings useless. Why, *why*, hadn't he bothered to rekindle the flame around his head after they'd fallen into the abyss? Why was he so *weak* as to be put through this again? He should be able to break free, he *would* be able to break free, he just had to keep trying because he couldn't— he *couldn't*— be locked in the dark again.

But this was Kirin's sibling, and though Ifrit thrashed in their grip, it only served to slice open his arms. Blood ran freely from the cuts he earned, the crystallized flesh that kept him pinned in place glazed red. Ifrit was dimly aware that they were apologizing still, crying, even, but it sounded far away. There was someone yelling, and it wasn't until they were at the threshold of the doorway that Ifrit became aware it was his own voice. His face was hot and damp, the room fracturing into pieces before his eyes as tears distorted the scene.

His distress was so complete that when wires reached out from the wall and grabbed the boy, he wasn't sure it was really happening. When Yantra appeared, she looked like a ghost, covered in a white film. The only parts of her that weren't chalk-pale were her eyes and her face, which was slowly turning crimson as blood dripped from a wound at her temple. She hardly made it two steps before she went down in a heap.

Ifrit was unceremoniously dumped to the side, his limbs shaking too much to hold his weight. He collapsed to the ground, just outside of the room that was to be his prison. Phoenix was on the ground inside, unmoving. But then she wasn't there.

The hospital room was back, the same as when they'd entered, blinding white and bright. Ifrit looked back toward the entrance and couldn't even take comfort in being alone, since he knew that his eyes could be lying, they could be anywhere around. The thought that they were there, just out of sight, horrified Ifrit so much that he released carbon, too much carbon, just to try to see where they might have gone. He didn't realize *how* much until he heard Phoenix gasp and sit up, until they were crawling toward him and gripping his shoulder tightly.

"*Stop*." Their voice was hoarse, raw, but their grasp was firm when they shook him. "You need to *stop*."

But Ifrit couldn't stop. His breath was tight in his chest and the room wasn't what it should be and they had almost been trapped *again* and he still couldn't see what was real, he couldn't see anything through the illusion. It wasn't *real* and they were going to make him go back in the dark and leave him there and he couldn't do it again, he couldn't—

The air around the door moved and Ifrit wrenched himself out of Phoenix's grip even though the headache slammed into existence immediately, even though his head collided with the wall, hard. They were back and they were going to send him in; that was why he couldn't see them, that was why they were charging forward and grabbing him and pulling him toward them and holding him with both arms— wait.

The air was clearing rapidly, but Ifrit was still shaking. His face was pressed into someone's neck and there was something sharp poking through their shirt and scratching at his face, and the hands that were stroking his hair were familiar, so familiar. Phoenix reappeared in the corner of Ifrit's vision, and when he saw their mouth move, he realized his hearing aids were off again, and the rumble against his chest were words that he couldn't hear.

It's Kirin. Phoenix was reaching around something that neither of them could see, resting their hand on Ifrit's head to help him focus on them. *You're okay. He's here.*

Kirin. Ifrit had to tell Kirin who had just been there, had to tell him to get up and go after them, had to warn him about what they'd been trying to do. But he couldn't move. Kirin's hand on the back of his head was the only thing holding him together, the only thing keeping him from shattering entirely as he shuddered with the thought of how close they had come.

And if he spoke up, Kirin would leave.

Kirin would get up, he would go to follow them, to find them and get them to safety. Because Kirin had a family. There were people out there who he loved and wanted to protect, people who he was worried for and dreamed about. And Ifrit only had Kirin.

So he would let himself shatter.

"Your family..." Ifrit managed to get his breathing under control just enough to start speaking, but Phoenix covered his mouth. Ifrit very nearly bit their fingers, but he saw their mouth moving.

"*He knows,*" they said. "*He's not leaving.*"

Ifrit buried his face in Kirin's chest and wept.

20

Scrubbed Clean

Kirin's palms could've been mistaken for the night sky with how many diamonds dotted their surface. He kept subconsciously crystallizing the tips of his fingers as he curled his hands into fists, and the only way to stop himself from getting blood everywhere was to temporarily crystallize each and every puncture wound. He'd thought he'd run out of fresh places to stab after a few hours or so, but it seemed like his hands were getting bigger, just to give him new sources of pain.

The door opened and Majesty came out, Valor a veritable storm cloud behind her. While his expression was one of disapproval and disgust, hers was one of mourning.

"It is time to head back." Her voice was cool, yet brittle, like the first ice over a pond. If the brightness of her eyes was anything to go by, her composure was hanging on by a thread. The fragility of her tone seemed to incense Valor more, as his anger transferred from the dirty and bloody students in front of him to the immaculate woman at his side. "Your debriefing will happen tomorrow. For now, we will return, and you will all rest."

There was no mention of the abysmal failure of their mission, nor of the horrifying revelations it had included. And, mercifully, no mention of the personal crisis that Kirin was going through, either.

Ifrit had pulled himself back together before Ness and Kapre had made it to them, Clidna and Wyrm in tow. The woman in white had gotten away, as well as... as well as...

He forced the thought away.

One thing at a time. Ifrit first.

If Ifrit would let him help.

Even as Kapre had slowly pulled them to the surface, Kirin had been holding Ifrit, but the moment they reached the air, Ifrit had refused to let Kirin touch him. There was fear in his eyes, fear and guilt. Each time Kirin had reached out again, Ifrit's eyes had gone bright. He'd backed away, just far enough that Kirin couldn't do anything unless he started to chase him down. When they'd all reassembled, Ifrit had seated himself across the room, head down, eyes closed. Distant.

The ride back to the school was silent. It was only then that Kirin noticed an empty seat on Majesty's side of the plane. He almost asked her about it, but the look on her face stopped him.

When they arrived back on campus, they were instructed to head straight for their dorms. They weren't even allowed to change out of their costumes, though the day had well progressed and students were milling about in the residential section, visible even through the barrier. Covered in dirt, dust, and not a little blood, Kirin felt eyes on his back— on all their backs— until the dorm door shut firmly behind them. Adlivun pulled Phoenix into her room not a moment after they got inside, which meant it was only Ifrit and Kirin left as the elevator chimed to let them know they had reached the fifth floor.

Ifrit didn't notice that they were there. His gaze was haunted, hollow, even now that they were home. When Kirin put a hand on Ifrit's shoulder to move him forward, Ifrit flinched.

"It's okay." The words felt like they were caught in Kirin's throat, sharp-edged and ill-fitting. "We're just here."

There was another beat before Ifrit registered the words and stepped out into the hall, the lights flickering on farther down. Once he was out of the elevator, Ifrit broke out of his stupor and headed straight for Kirin's room, halfway inside before Kirin caught back up.

"We should get you cleaned up first, okay?" Kirin was proud of himself for not letting his voice shake. He'd seen the fine latticework of cuts on Ifrit's arms, but his back was far worse. The material of his suit was in tatters, blood flaking off with every step Ifrit took. The pattern of the cuts was familiar, disgustingly familiar, the pits and valleys creating a mirror to the way Kirin's own chest crystallized. He shoved the thought to the very corner of his brain and kept it there.

"I can't." Ifrit's voice was little more than a whisper.

"If it hurts too much to lift your arms, we can cut it off; I don't think they'll be able to salvage this one anyway—"

"I *can't.*" Ifrit was a little louder this time, sounding like he was going to cry. "The water... makes it hard to fight."

Kirin finally processed Ifrit's posture. Shoulders tense, hands stiff at his sides, eyes flicking from one thing to another. On edge, waiting for another attack. Waiting to find out that his sight betrayed him.

"You won't need to. I'll be right here; you can just yell if you need anything." Even as he spoke, Kirin could see Ifrit's breath start to come faster, his eyes widening in fear. When Kirin straightened up to think for a moment, Ifrit's hand shot out and gripped Kirin's shirt, which was now stained brown with dried blood. *Ifrit's* dried blood.

"How about this," Kirin spoke slowly, unsure if Ifrit would like the suggestion at all, "we can just do a little at a time. Just using the sink, not the shower. We'll clean out your cuts and your hair, since it's more white than black now from all the concrete dust that was on me."

Ifrit didn't agree, but he also didn't release his grip on Kirin's shirt. When Kirin went into Ifrit's room to get new clothes, to grab his shampoo, to his own room to get a washcloth, Ifrit followed, tugged on by his own hold. He didn't do anything to help, but he didn't do anything to hinder, either.

When Kirin put the chair in front of the sink, Ifrit sat down wordlessly, watching Kirin intensely. For his part, Kirin couldn't make eye contact at all, and instead focused on filling the sink with warm, soapy water.

"Can you lift your arms, or do you want me to just cut it off?" Kirin sat across from Ifrit, in the hard chair from the kitchen. Ifrit was perched on one of the stools from the counter, just to give Kirin access to his back.

Ifrit started to lift his arms, but immediately the thin scabs started to pull and bright red lines appeared, like thread that wound from his biceps all the way to his hands. Kirin grabbed him by the wrists as gently as he could, giving a light squeeze before he pulled away in search of the fabric scissors. Once he had them in hand, he hesitated for a moment, eyes flickering to Ifrit's face. Ifrit was watching him back, not in distrust or discomfort, but almost with... confusion.

"I'm going to cut this at the shoulders and down one side to we can get it off." Ifrit had been in the same paramedic class Kirin had, of course he knew what Kirin was doing. But saying it out loud was helping Kirin stay calm, even as the fabric peeled away to reveal that it had been plastered to Ifrit's body with even more blood, cuts shallow and deep mapping his struggle to get free across his chest.

They were all likely superficial, or at least that was what Kirin was telling himself as he started to gently wipe off Ifrit's shoulders and down his arms. When he turned over Ifrit's arm to wipe down his palm, he almost lost his composure as he saw just how close a deep gouge had come to hitting the artery that ran through Ifrit's wrist.

Maybe he hadn't hid his own fear as well as he'd hoped, because he felt a light touch on the side of his face, dragging his eyes up from the now red washcloth in his hands to Ifrit's crimson eyes.

"You have a cut there." Ifrit's voice was odd, but perhaps it was just because he was whispering. His fingers were brushing a spot just above Kirin's ear, no doubt a section that had remained uncrystallized as they fell. "And so much fucking dust in your hair that it doesn't look so shitty."

Kirin felt a ridiculous grin spreading across his face at the insult, the small sign that Ifrit was starting to come back to him.

"Yeah. I kind of fell through a floor. Surprised that's all there is." Even though it was just the two of them and the sink dripping lazily, Kirin found himself whispering too. He didn't need to speak loudly. He'd been leaning forward to focus on his work and when he'd looked up, it had left their faces only centimeters apart. With the heel of Ifrit's hand resting on his cheek, it was almost like the room had contracted to just the two of them.

"You need to fucking wash your hair." Ifrit bit his lip, eyebrows drawn together. "Can't fucking get clean when every time you move you create a damn dust storm."

"I can go shower quickly if—"

"I can wash it." Ifrit was avoiding his gaze, looking at the ground instead. "You're... doing a lot for me and it's going to take a fucking minute, so I can do it."

Kirin could've said no. Could've pointed out that the whole reason he was helping Ifrit was because Ifrit had been too scared to get his hands wet, and washing Kirin's hair would require doing exactly that. He could've quickly showered now that the exhaustion and emotional weight was setting in, but instead he let himself be turned around and leaned back until his head was in the sink.

"Take off your shirt, dumbass." Ifrit still sounded strange, though he wasn't whispering anymore.

"Mm." Kirin did just that, ignoring the pain that shot across his back as he pulled it over his head.

While he did, there was the quiet click of Ifrit's ignition rings and the halo of flames that encircled his head reignited. Ifrit only hesitated a moment before taking them off and placing them on the shelf above the sink, and Kirin pointedly didn't comment on the way Ifrit's hands shook as he did. The shaking only got worse as Ifrit turned the sink on, only one finger under the stream of water to wait until it got warm, the other trembling at his side.

With the knuckle of one finger, Kirin brushed the side of Ifrit's free hand, unsurprised when Ifrit grabbed on and laced their fingers together tightly. His lips were flattened into a straight line, turning them almost white.

"You don't have to get your hands wet if you don't want to." Though Ifrit had stopped, Kirin couldn't make his voice louder than the scarcest whisper.

"I want to." Ifrit's voice was stronger; Kirin could feel his pulse where their thumbs touched. It was starting to slow, finally. "I just... please let me fucking do this for you."

Kirin nodded, and they stayed like that until steam started to come off the water.

"Shit, it's probably too hot now," Ifrit muttered, finally disentangling their hands. He turned the temperature down slightly and then went to the shower, coming back with, oddly, Phoenix's shampoo.

"That's not—"

"Yours, I fucking know. But I just ran out of my shit, and

you buy the three-in-one, and I'm not fucking putting that in your hair." He was definitely feeling better, since he used the fire above his head to create a small explosion to knock Kirin back against the sink. Yet, when he guided Kirin's head back to start rinsing off his hair, he was attentively gentle, putting the second clean washcloth under Kirin's neck.

It gave Kirin a perfect view of Ifrit's face, which was scrunched in concentration as he started to rinse all the grime out. There was still the slight furrow between his brows, but it was softer than when he was angry or upset. In the strong light from the bathroom, it was easy to see that his lashes weren't black, but a deep, dark red. When Ifrit looked down from above, he had to look through them, since they were so long. The shaved sides of his head glowed faintly scarlet as the light passed through the hair, which should have made his skin look pale, but instead just made him look like art.

"You're staring." Though Kirin hadn't once seen Ifrit's eyes slide to his own, he'd noticed.

"You're just..." Kirin swallowed. "Pretty."

Ifrit's hands stopped moving for a moment, and Kirin worried that he'd made him uncomfortable. A second later, Ifrit was tilting Kirin's chin up to get his roots under the faucet.

"...focus." The water rushing past Kirin's ears drowned out most of Ifrit's words. He only caught the last because Ifrit had turned off the tap.

"What?"

Ifrit cast him a withering look, his face red.

"Just shut up and stay still."

Any will that Kirin might've had to argue shriveled up and died as Ifrit started rubbing the shampoo into his hair, all the tension fading out of his body. It was such a simple thing, but the pressure on his scalp and the clean smell of the shampoo let the last of his stress fall and pool at his feet. It was like Ifrit had a map to every snarl and tangle, carefully tugging them apart. When the water turned back on to wash it out, Kirn almost asked him to do it again, just to hold onto the peace a little longer.

But when he opened his eyes, Ifrit was still covered in grime. Some of the cuts along his forearms were weeping again, only small tears but still tears nonetheless. Kirin didn't let Ifrit dry his hair, guiding him back to the chair and starting to wipe down his arms again.

"It really fucking looks worse than it is," Ifrit grumbled.

"I don't believe you." Kirin didn't look up from what he was doing until he found what must have been a particularly deep cut and Ifrit sucked in a breath through his teeth. "Sorry. Should I go get Phoenix? I think they'd understand."

Ifrit shook his head.

"This is... better. Feels... real." Both of Ifrit's arms were now clean, and yet Kirin hesitated before starting on Ifrit's chest. Despite all the things they'd been through in the last year, the new superficial cuts were the only additions to the faint scars that crisscrossed his upper torso. It made sense, in a way, that the physical marks brought comfort. Some small measure of proof that the terrible things had in fact happened, and that he was still alive despite it all.

Though there was no reason for it, Kirin scooted his chair closer, pinning Ifrit between his legs. Kirin found that his own heart was racing as he used one hand to turn Ifrit's chin, lightly wiping the grime off Ifrit's neck. Ifrit shivered from the touch, and Kirin used his thumb to stroke the side of Ifrit's jaw to soothe him. Kirin had cleaned off most of Ifrit's neck and collarbone before he felt wetness on his fingers.

"Hey, hey, it's okay." Kirin dropped the washcloth to cup Ifrit's face with both hands, wiping the pouring tears with his thumbs. "Do you want me to stop for a bit? We can dry you off so you can put your rings back on if that'll help."

Ifrit just leaned and pressed their foreheads together. One of Kirin's hands slid down to Ifrit's collarbone and the other ended up resting on the jut of his hip, where the skin felt overly warm.

"I don't deserve you." Their noses brushed as Ifrit spoke.

"What on Earth are you talking about?" Kirin tried to pull back, to get a better glimpse of Ifrit's face, but Ifrit had a hand wound in Kirin's still damp hair and held them in place.

"I don't deserve you." Ifrit spoke firmly, yet softly. Their faces were so close together that Kirin could feel the ghost of Ifrit's words on his lips. "I didn't want to tell you that your sibling was fucking there. I didn't want you to find them because I thought you'd leave."

Kirin didn't have any words, but his muscles tensed, pulling Ifrit just a little bit closer.

"I just kept thinking..." Ifrit had to pause to take a breath. "I just kept thinking about how you have a family out there, a family who loves you, and I just... I just have you."

It was Ifrit's turn to try to pull back, and Kirin stopped him.

"I'm fucking selfish. And you are so fucking good, and I didn't even want to give you a *choice* because I didn't want to know if you would pick me. And I have no fucking *right* to want you to pick me, but goddammit I do."

"And you still told me." Ifrit let Kirin tilt his face up so they could look each other in the eye, though Ifrit's gaze was now red-rimmed. But the color red suited him. "How can you think that when you were having a panic attack, when you just wanted to be comforted, and you *still* chose to make sure I knew?"

"Why didn't you go after them?" Ifrit's bottom lip was trembling, though his words still came out clear. "You should've fucking gone after them."

"They didn't need me right then. You did."

"That doesn't fucking matter when you could've found out

why they were there!"

"It matters. *You* matter."

"I shouldn't."

Kirin was at a loss for words. It wasn't that he didn't have anything to say, it was simply that he didn't know where to *start*. How to convey the emotion that was bubbling in his chest that made him want to grab Ifrit's face like he had at the aquarium and... and...

"Your family should matter more than me." Ifrit shook through Kirin's thoughts, through the sharp memory of a sudden impulse and what it might mean. "That's only fucking normal, right?"

"I don't think either of us really know what normal means. But I don't think I should choose them over you, and I don't think I'm ever going to."

Ifrit had been preparing to launch himself into a rant, but he hadn't expected such a solid resistance, apparently. His mouth opened and closed, though no words came out.

"I know you never had siblings, but I don't... I *didn't* have a great relationship with mine. It wasn't their fault, and I don't even think I could say it was mine. There were five of us, and we needed money and food and without our dad, funds were running low. Mom couldn't afford childcare after the grieving period ended, so I changed diapers. I made dinner. And when I was old enough, I went to work to help pay the bills." Kirin ran a hand over the back of his neck, pricking one of his fingers in the process. Another scab to add for the day. "I tried to be the adult they needed in their lives, but how could I be? I was still a kid.

"I can't even lie and say I didn't resent them at points, because I did. I had to pause my transition for a few years, even went off hormones once or twice because even the tiny amount the medication cost was too much. I wasn't even able to have surgery until I applied here and the school covered it. The little ones never did anything wrong; they were just... kids. Kids who would be rude and irritating and stubborn. Because they were *kids*. And I shouldn't have been the one taking care of them."

Ifrit looked confused but didn't interrupt.

"For the most part, I could hide it. The frustration, I mean. I don't even think the younger ones ever realized, or maybe they just lied to me as often as I lied to them. But I think Hyeon-soo could always tell. Mostly because I resented them the most."

"Hyeon-soo?" From the look on Ifrit's face, he knew who Kirin was referring to, and just wanted to make sure he'd heard the name right.

"Hyeon-soo's only three years younger than me. Young enough that they didn't fully understand what was going on, but close enough that I used to get so angry that they weren't helping me. That they would just go off and be a kid again." Kirin leaned back on the stool, staring at his hands now instead of Ifrit. "That I didn't get to. And for a long time, I thought *that* was where the anger came from. Just... jealousy."

"I mean, that's pretty fucking understandable." Kirin flashed Ifrit a grin, but it faded quickly.

"I don't think I was angry that I was taking care of them while they got to be carefree. What I realized today was that I was angry that I didn't have a *choice*."

Ifrit's lips parted slightly.

"I chose to come here for a lot of reasons. I love helping people, I do. But I like to get to choose that I do. When I was back in Korea? They all looked at me like I was the parent, even when our mom was there. I was the caretaker, the person who solved arguments and helped with homework. And leaving... it meant I only had to do that if I wanted to. Not because it was expected, or because it was what I'd always done. But you... I got to choose you."

Ifrit's expression was frozen but the fire over his head grew.

"I like helping you because I know you don't expect it. I know that if I'm dealing with something, I don't have to shove it away and pretend to be okay. I can be myself with *you*. And if you're selfish, so am I, because I saw Hyeon-soo. They saw me. But I also saw you. They were standing. You were on the floor. You were bleeding. You were panicking. If I could only reach one, it was always going to be you."

Oftentimes emotions flew across Ifrit's face like sparks, there for a split second and then gone in the wind. Now there was only one, and it was an easy one to recognize. Disbelief. Or maybe incredulity was a better word. Like he'd just been given a gift for the first time and wasn't sure it was really meant for him.

"I don't think—" Ifrit began to speak but had to pause since his voice came out hoarsely. "I don't think it has the same weight because I don't have anyone else left, but I will always, *always*, fucking pick you too."

It was so strange that Kirin found himself smiling now, but he felt... light. Buoyant. He was still dirty, Ifrit was still dirty, but ignoring all that, Kirin pulled Ifrit into a hug. He was perhaps overeager as the force of it sent the two of them toppling to the ground, a crunch indicating that the chair had been broken from the combined weight of them both hitting the floor. It was so ridiculous, so mundane, that Kirin wasn't just smiling, he was laughing, and after a moment of grumbling about how filthy Kirin was, Ifrit was laughing too.

How long they stayed in a pile on the floor, broken wood poking into Kirin's back, Kirin wasn't sure. It was long enough that his ribs hurt, not from having a building fall on him, but instead from mirth, and both he and Ifrit were entirely out of breath. Ifrit was the first to pull himself together, pushing up off Kirin— why was Kirin vaguely displeased about that?— and holding himself up on his elbows to see Kirin's face.

"We should probably fucking wash up now, right?" There was an uncertain note in his voice, and if Kirin wasn't mistaken, a hopeful one too. That was better, much better.

"Mm." Kirin was going to say something more eloquent, but Ifrit had chosen that moment to move hair out of Kirin's face and tuck it behind his ear, and suddenly Kirin's brain wasn't working quite right.

"I think... I think I'm good to shower now." Ifrit hesitated, blush rising in his cheeks. "Maybe we could—"

The door to the bathroom banged open, startling them both. Ifrit was more than spooked, practically *flying* off Kirin toward the door. From the murderous look on his face, Phoenix was about to need her regenerative abilities.

It wasn't Phoenix at the door. Instead, it was Yantra, with Kapre close behind.

"We can come back later." Kapre spoke after a few moments of awkward silence. They didn't look surprised, but then again, they probably had felt what was going on through the floor before Yantra had unceremoniously tried to come inside.

Kirin registered how it must have looked from the outside, and suddenly he was as beet red as Ifrit's eyes.

"It's fucking fine." Ifrit, presumably having already done the math that Kirin was only just catching up to, recovered quickly enough to respond. "Can this wait a fucking minute though so I can get dressed?"

"Why don't you... why don't you shower and then come down to my room?" Yantra was uncommonly nervous, and Kirin suddenly remembered why: the woman in white, everything that had happened before he heard Ifrit screaming. He'd totally forgotten. "I'll... I'll get Ness as well since I'm sure she has questions too."

“I think,” Kirin winced at the sounds of breaking wood as he sat up, “that would be a great idea. Should only be a few minutes.”

“Great.” Ifrit stormed away from the door, shoulders nearly to his ears. “And next time, fucking *knock* first.”

21

Real Power

IFRIT COULD'VE STAYED IN the shower for three years and not gotten rid of his frustration and mortification. The embarrassment was clinging to him more furiously than the grime, though anger was eating away at its edges. Kirin *had* been looking at him the way he thought, right? He had been. Ifrit was sure of it. Seventy-five percent, at least. Ifrit had thought he'd moved past looking for signs, trying to give himself hope, but this wasn't making it up. Kirin, dumbass though he was, had been looking at Ifrit like he loved him.

And maybe something would've happened. Maybe if it had been a few more minutes there might have been something more, suddenly. But no. There was always some fucking bullshit that they were wrapped up in and had to go running off to deal with anytime Ifrit thought that Kirin might be considering kissing him.

His foul mood wasn't invisible, and when they arrived at Yantra's room on the first floor, she practically shrunk away from the doorway when she saw him there. It was impressive that she could do that, since the space behind her was packed.

Ness was already there, though she was hard to see. Ifrit was certain it wasn't a trick of the light either; she was becoming more and more see-through the longer he knew her. He'd never really talked to her one on one, but maybe Kirin could check in with her and make sure she was alright. The short one was there too, with their long dark hair and big eyes. They'd used their mien to make a seat for themselves, since Ifrit was positive Tech's room hadn't had a random rock sticking out of the ground last time he'd been there. Kapre, that was their name.

Then there was Smoke. She sat on the floor next to Kapre, looking unsurprised to be there. Ifrit remembered her name— Enenra— only because it'd turned up when he was trying to figure out if Kirin was Japanese or Korean. She used to give off small puffs of smoke every time she moved too quickly, but unlike Ness, her substantiality had increased the more she trained. Now her almond shaped eyes were watching Yantra attentively, just like the other two. In fact, the only person who didn't seem to know what the fuck was going on was Ifrit.

There was only one space on the bed remaining so Ifrit had decided he'd just stand the entire time— Yantra looked like she was going to anyway— but when Kirin sat on the bed, he pulled Ifrit with him, wrapping his arms around Ifrit's waist like it was a totally normal thing for him to do. Which it *was,* though only when they were falling asleep or completely *alone*. Not in front of a bunch of their friends who were politely and pointedly not saying anything.

"Are you doing okay, Yantra?" When Kirin spoke, he seemed oblivious to the reaction everyone was having to his behavior. Meanwhile, Ifrit briefly lost track of what else was going on as he felt the rumble of Kirin's voice against his back. "Were you able to have Phoenix heal you?"

"Ah, yeah." Yantra rarely seemed nervous, except when she had bad news to share. And never this nervous. She had a few thin gold rings on her fingers and was twisting them constantly, hardly able to look anyone in the eye. "I'm fine."

"Yantra." Ness spoke up now, her edges sharpening as she spoke. Oddly, it was only when she said Yantra's name that she was clearly in view, maybe because of the exasperation in her tone. "We don't have to talk about it if you don't want to. It's been a long day."

"And none of us hold grudges about wanting to keep your own secrets," Enenra chimed in.

"Whatever the woman in white might think, we know who you are, and that's far more important than who you've been," Kapre added.

Ifrit really was lost. The woman in white? She'd been there?

"I... really don't think that's the case." Yantra drew in a breath shakily. "But I appreciate it."

There was a long drawn out pause as Yantra continued to fidget, and finally Ifrit couldn't take it any longer.

"Okay, what the fuck did I miss?"

Ifrit really didn't think it was funny, but for some reason it made Yantra laugh. And her laughing set off Ness, which got Enenra to start giggling, and though Kirin had buried his face in the crook of Ifrit's neck, Ifrit could still feel Kirin's chest heaving with forcibly suppressed mirth.

"Sorry, I just... I'm so used to you being wherever Kirin is that I honestly forgot you weren't with us." Yantra gave him a genuine smile once she was finally able to get her breath under control.

"Wasn't by choice." Ifrit probably would've grumbled more if Kirin hadn't leaned their heads together and squeezed him lightly.

"You're right, sorry." Yantra's smile was fading, but she looked less nervous, at least. "We, uh, we almost managed to get the head of Aether."

"We did get all six of her bodyguards though." Kapre had probably been the one to hold them until reinforcements had showed back up, if Ifrit had to guess. Which he did. Since he *hadn't fucking been there.*

"I don't know how much they'll be able to tell us." Yantra cut back in. "Because... well... and I've talked to Ifrit and Kirin about this but—"

"You don't fucking think she's in charge of anything." Ifrit scrubbed his face. He was too tired to limp through a conversation. "What about it?"

"I don't know why she's with them." Yantra went to bite one of her nails, but they were all bitten down to the quick.

"But you do know who she is." Ness finished the thought. Correctly, too, if the way Yantra's eyes darted to her was anything to go by.

"Yeah."

Another irritatingly long pause filled the space.

"So fucking what?" Everyone looked at Ifrit. "Do you think it'll help the police find her if they know her name?"

Yantra hesitated, considering.

"I don't think so, no."

Well, that was interesting.

"Then you don't need to say shit until it would."

"Why wouldn't it help?" Ness was nosier than Ifrit was, or at least more willing to be so outwardly. Maybe she just never had a secret that felt like it would be the end of the world if everyone knew.

"She's too good. Already cleared all images of her face off the web, all records scrubbed. She's just as good as I am..." Yantra's voice faltered, and she cleared her throat. "She's actually probably better than I am. I couldn't find anything when I looked a while ago."

"You've suspected this for a bit." Kirin didn't phrase it as a question.

"Since the first Aether mission this year."

"We should all get our stories straight, then, for when we have to do mission debrief tomorrow." Enenra was businesslike, typical for her. Great at keeping everyone organized, Ifrit respected that about her. "It would be better to pretend that she didn't have time to talk to us at all, because we don't want to have to memorize too much or it'll sound fake. We'll need a different reason why Kapre sealed us off from reinforcements."

"That'll be easy. Her mien was deadly, nearly took Kirin out. He shouted back to let Kapre know to keep people clear of the area and they did just that." Ness was nodding. "Other people in your squad should've heard him yelling, so they'll corroborate."

"I don't know if they were close enough to hear; I ran ahead when I felt the building shake. Regardless, I think they'll buy it." Kapre was as amiable as always, a small, pleasant smile hanging on their lips as the group discussed perjury.

"Alright, that makes things simple. The only question is how she got away." Enenra's eyes weren't accusing as she looked at Kapre.

"I don't really know." Kapre's placid expression flickered for the first time. "I had her firmly pinned, and then she just wasn't. Maybe her mien had something to do with it? What do we know about what she can do?"

"She was emitting some high-pitched noise that hurt like a bitch, and I assumed that was it." Ness frowned. "Could she have used that somehow to get out? We'd have to ask Clidna if she can do anything like that, since her mien is closest."

"Do we really want to drag someone else into this?" Enenra shook her head.

"I don't think—" Yantra was holding onto her elbows tightly, not looking at any of them, so it wasn't surprising that Kapre didn't hear her.

"Let's just keep it to those of us in the room. The fewer who could get implicated if things ever get uncovered, the better." Kapre cast a look at Ifrit. "Since we've already dragged in one person."

"She doesn't have a mien." Yantra spoke up decisively, her hands falling to her sides in fists. "We don't need to talk to Clidna. She probably had some kind of tech on her that was doing it."

She was shaking. Kirin noticed as well, leaning slightly forward and taking Ifrit with him.

"Something like this?" One of Kirin's hands left Ifrit's waist to dig through his pocket, and he produced a partially crushed, small metal box. It was unassuming, flat, unadorned and so small it didn't entirely cover Kirin's palm. Yantra picked it up with a furrowed brow.

"Maybe." She turned it over. "We'd have to turn it on to figure out what it does, and I don't see how to do that. Maybe a fingerprint scan to access the mechanism, or just a digital display that's broken now..."

"I feel like *that* we should turn over to the police." Enenra nodded, a wisp of black curling off her hair. "If they find that on one of us, it'd be bad."

Yantra's eyes flickered up to them, clearly reluctant to part with it.

"I don't know if the police are our best bet." Ness was the first to disagree though. "I just... after what happened to— what happened last semester, I don't trust them."

Ifrit bit back the comment that rose to his tongue, about how she should've known not to trust them *before*.

"We definitely shouldn't have it ourselves though, I think we can agree." Kapre chimed in.

"Agreed." Yantra hadn't lost the hungry look in her eye, and she looked pained as she handed it back to Kirin. "Is there anyone we *would* trust with it? Someone who'd get it to the *right* people?"

"Shifter." Ifrit offered. "He's already got one fucking target on his back, what's one more?"

"Can we get to him? I haven't seen him on campus in a while. Not that I blame him." Enenra had a point.

"The other fucking option is Majesty."

The silence in the room was irritating.

"You think we can trust... Majesty?" Kirin was the one who asked, slowly.

"Why not like Phantasm or, I don't know, literally *anyone else*?" Ness sounded incredulous.

"I fucking know, okay, but she's been... weird." Kirin had replaced his hand on Ifrit's waist and Ifrit focused on playing with his fingers instead of looking at everyone. "I don't know if she's fucking for real or not, but she says she wants to understand what Pressure was trying to do. She *seems* genuine, and Phantasm would just turn it right over to the fucking cops."

"If you think it's a good idea, I trust you." Despite being the one to object, Ness shrugged and accepted his explanation so easily. The rest of them did too, nodding.

"We should give it to her soon, so it doesn't look like we were hiding it." Kirin pulled out his phone and checked the time. "It's just a bit past the end of classes, do we think she'd still be on campus? I can bring it to her now."

"No." Ifrit stopped Kirin from getting up. "She'll listen to *me*, but I don't fucking know if her newfound acceptance extends to anyone she doesn't think of as family. I'll bring it to her."

"Family?" Yantra was so surprised that she forgot to be worried. "Were she and Pressure—"

"What the fuck? No." Ifrit ignored the way that Majesty talked about Pressure. He did *not* want to even consider that. "She has a fucking kid with Valor."

"*What*?" Kirin grabbed Ifrit's shoulder and turned him around. "Valor's Bán's father?"

"How the fuck do you know Bán?" Ifrit tried to sort through his memories, wondering if he'd mentioned it before.

"We rescued them at the end of last semester. Right before everything happened." Kapre filled in when Kirin only stared, horrified.

"But what does that have to do with *you*?" Ness pointed an accusing finger in his direction.

"Valor wasn't just Pressure's teammate." Ifrit shoved down the memories, pushed them far away. "He's her brother."

"Oh *shit*." Yantra sat down on her desk with a thump. "They didn't just pull him because he was her partner— they really tried to find the closest person *to* her."

"He's nothing like her." Ifrit couldn't help himself from snapping.

"You don't say." Ifrit had never seen Kapre look angry before. "How could they let him teach here?"

"Why the fuck wouldn't they? He's the exact type of asshole this place usually churns out."

"But how he treats his own kid..." Kapre broke off, burying their face in their hands.

Kirin didn't look any less devasted, his breathing shallow and mouth parted. They'd seen something, something that Ifrit didn't know. Something that had changed since the first and only time he'd seen his cousin.

"I'm going to give this to her fucking now." Ifrit snatched the box from Kirin, stumbling slightly as he stood. "All of you go do something fucking normal so it doesn't look suspicious. I'll say that I found it in the rubble you all fell through."

Kirin opened his mouth, probably to insist that he go with Ifrit, or maybe just to tell him what happened with Bán, but Ifrit couldn't take any more stress, any more new revelations about the horrors that surrounded them. He'd give Majesty the stupid thing, come back, and curl up in Kirin's arms until sleep overtook him.

Anything more would be too much for one day.

22

A Realization

Kirin watched Ifrit walk away with a horrible feeling of dread. What if Majesty didn't believe him? What if she decided he'd been withholding evidence? What if—

"Hey, stop that." Ness appeared at his side, now that they were all slowly leaving Yantra's room. "You're making the face."

"What face?" Kirin hardly glanced at her, eyes locked on Ifrit as he passed through the front door and beelined for the hero section.

"The I'm-about-to-do-something-stupid face."

Ifrit was finally out of sight as he ducked behind one of the other dorms, but it was several seconds more before Kirin could look away.

"I don't make a face for that, that's my default."

"No, no self-deprecation after a super shitty day." Ness was more transparent than usual, and yet the frown on her face was perfectly clear. "What's up with you lately? You've been..."

Her voice trailed off and her eyes widened.

"Oh, of course." She shook her head. "Ifrit isn't doing okay, is he?"

There was something sad in the fact that when Ness thought about other people she grew more solid, but whenever she spoke of herself she seemed to disappear. Right then, her face settled, dark eyes, splash of freckles, sharp nose all in clear view.

"He's..." Kirin sighed. "He's doing better than I am, I think."

"Do you want to talk about it?" Ness threaded her arm through his and rested her head against his bicep, the highest she could reach.

"No."

She flickered.

"But there is something else, if that's okay?" Kirin felt her grip strengthen.

"Sure!" There was palpable relief in her voice, and she didn't waste a second steering them toward the elevator. While she didn't look back, Kirin did, as if he could catch one final glimpse of Ifrit through the windows. Instead, he was left with the image of Yantra, standing in her doorway, watching them leave with sadness in her eyes.

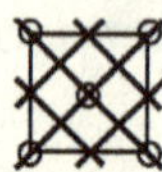

"Alright, you've eaten all my chocolate, now comes the part where you tell me why we haven't talked in months." Ness was wrapped in three blankets, which was understandable given how cold she kept her room. Kirin appreciated it though, and rather than making it feel uncomfortable, it made the room feel cozier. She had pillows and blankets thrown everywhere, which was why smaller movie nights always happened in her dorm room. It didn't hurt that she kept a large stash of candy in her closet either.

"I've talked to you." Kirin knew what she meant though, and he thoroughly deserved the wrapper she threw at his head.

"Fine, we haven't *hung out* in months, is that better?" She was pressed into the corner where her bed met the wall, Kirin leaning against the window and appreciating the cool glass on his skin. If it hadn't been so cold already, he could've used the excuse of wanting to cool off, instead of obsessively watching out for Ifrit.

"You're definitely right." Kirin sighed as he reluctantly tore his gaze from the ground and up to her. "I didn't mean to, I swear, I just—"

"You're afraid to leave Ifrit alone," Ness finished. He pulled the blanket around him tighter as he nodded. "He *can* take care of himself, Kirin."

"I know." He couldn't stop himself from glancing out the window. "But what if they target him again? They know how to use him and how strong he is, so they could easily try to do it again and—"

"Kirin." Ness's voice sounded so firm. "Don't you trust him?"

"Of course, with my life."

"But not his own life?"

Kirin opened his mouth and closed it again.

"I know it's hard, especially since Pressure's gone, and I'm sure he's still grieving that, but he's *really* strong. And he's not going to get caught unawares again." Ness stuck her hand out from underneath her blankets and he took it gratefully. "Even if they were to try anything, we're all looking out for him. Honestly, I think *you're* the only one who would even stand a chance at beating him."

"That might be the problem." Kirin couldn't keep the words from slipping out.

"If you attempt to lock him up somewhere to keep him safe, I *will* be having words with you." Ness frowned.

The image of Ifrit sobbing, of his chest heaving at the thought of being locked in a room was abruptly conjured.

"I would never." He hadn't meant for the words to come out

so harshly, and he rushed to say more as Ness's eyes widened. "We just realized that Aether *does* have something like me."

Now her eyes narrowed.

"That's a pretty rare mien, isn't it?" She spoke slowly and then shook her head. "No wonder you two looked like hell when we got on the plane. But that still doesn't explain what's been going on in the past few months because that happened *today*."

"I've… suspected for a while."

Again, she got his meaning without him having to say much at all.

"I get why you didn't, but you should've told us. We can help."

"I told Yantra."

"If you hadn't, I would've beat your ass." She looked so serious that he couldn't help but crack a smile, though he lost it quickly.

"I thought… I thought they weren't doing anything for Aether. That they were just being held to taunt me. But… they tried to put him back in a little box, Ness." He felt tears start to fall, his free hand covering his face. "And when I got there, when I heard him screaming from the hallway, I almost killed them."

Ness was so much smaller than him, but when she pulled him into a hug it made him feel like a kid again.

"And then upstairs… all those cuts, they look like *I* made them. How can he feel safe around me when he was hurt like that? How can he feel safe around me when I've hurt so many people, when I've *killed* people? But all he kept saying, all he was worried about, was that *he* didn't deserve *me*."

Ness kept quiet and kept stroking his hair.

"I don't deserve him at all, but whenever I can't see him, whenever he's not nearby, I feel like I can't breathe," Kirin whispered, so softly that he wasn't sure she could even hear.

"Oh, you dumb boys." Ness pulled over a tissue box so he could wipe off his face, rubbing gently between his shoulder blades. "Why do you have to deserve something freely given?"

"He deserves someone who doesn't remind him of everything bad—"

"Kirin, I don't think I've ever seen him half as happy without you as he is if you're around. It's hard to find a time when you're not together, but the few times he's alone and you walk into a room, it's impossible not to notice how much happier he gets."

"Really?" Kirin hadn't ever noticed.

"Well duh, why wouldn't he be happy to see his boyfriend?" Ness flicked him in the head, laughing, but it just made him frown.

"Boyfriend?"

Her smile faded.

"Kirin."

"Yeah?"

"Tell me you're joking right now."

"If you mean boys who are friends, sure—"

She got up and started to pace.

"To be clear, you went absolutely catatonic when he was gone, have been sleeping in each other's rooms for half a year, and stare longingly at each other whenever you can, and you *still* haven't gotten your shit together?"

"I don't— well, I mean we do just *sleep*, it's not much different than when we were all in the same bed—"

"Kirin, are you two sleeping in the same goddamn bed and you don't realize your feelings?"

"I mean, that's what I was coming to talk about!"

She froze mid-step and sat back down on the bed.

"I'm listening."

"It's... odd."

"You don't say."

"No, I mean... I've never... dated anyone."

She raised an eyebrow.

"I was busy!"

"No one's that busy, Kirin."

"I was!" When she rolled her eyes, he continued. "I just... I never had friends, before this."

At that, her gaze softened.

"And while *we* are friends, Ifrit's different, you know?"

"Yeah, you guys spend almost every second of the day together." She wasn't upset, smiling at him.

"I just thought that was what having a best friend was like." He rubbed the back of his neck. "I knew I liked guys, but I'd never actually *liked* a guy."

"Aromantic?"

"I thought so."

"What changed?"

"I think... I think I tried to kiss him?"

Ness threw a pillow at him.

"What?! And you didn't TELL me??"

"We got shot at! I was distracted!"

"KIRIN, WHAT THE HELL?!"

"We were fine!"

"I can't even believe you."

"And earlier today, we were just talking and he looked so pretty and then we were sitting there and I just... just wanted to..."

"If you stop talking right there, I *will* kill you."

Kirin buried his face in the pillow so hard his voice came out muffled.

"I was thinking of kissing him and using the excuse that I was giving him air."

"What? Why would you kissing him give him air?"

"Well, back when we rescued him and Phoenix at Satol, he needed oxygen and I, um, well I gave him some."

Ness stared at him.

"So you've kissed him?"

"I don't know if it counts—"

"Did your mouths touch?"

"Well, yes, but—"

"And what did Ifrit do while this was happening?"

"I mean, he was unconscious at first and when he woke up he pulled himself closer, but that could've just been—"

"Kirin, sweet darling boy, I'm going to murder you."

Kirin peeked up from the pillow to look at her.

"You're such a gay disaster, babe."

"I don't think you get to say that."

"Touché." She lightly patted him on the head. "But that doesn't make it any less true."

"I wish I didn't figure it out, though." He rubbed at his eyes with the heels of his hands. "Now it feels like I'm taking advantage of him, but he said he can't really sleep if I'm not there."

"You two are disgustingly cute, and I hate it. But if he *asked* for you there, you're not taking advantage of anything. And can *you* sleep if he's not there?"

"...no."

"Then it's a win-win, all other feelings aside."

Kirin groaned and knocked his head against the window, while Ness laughed softly.

"Yeah, that sounds about right for realizing you're crushing stupidly hard on a friend."

"Is that what happened with you and Innana?" Kirin immediately regretted asking as her face fell. "Sorry, I shouldn't have—"

"Kirin, you only need to apologize if I say 'hey, that hurt my feelings.' Otherwise, it's fine, really." She pulled her blankets closer, though. "But if we're on the topic of things we're not supposed to be talking about, it might actually feel good to tell someone."

He offered his hand, and she took it gladly.

"We didn't even go to the same school." The words came out as a sigh, a regret. "I went to public school, or more accurately, often *skipped* public school, since the teachers would mark me there even if I wasn't. Only perk I think I ever really got from my mien. And it was a terrible school, so I managed to keep straight A's despite only going to class a quarter of the time."

She faded so much that the blanket started to droop into her silhouette.

"I used to just... wander into places I wasn't supposed to be, see how far into a restricted section I could go before I started to get scared that I'd get caught. And that was how I found her." Ness flickered completely out of view for a moment, the blankets and Kirin's hand falling through thin air. When she came back, she rearranged her cocoon like nothing had happened. "I thought it was just supposed to be a rich, preppy school, but it was actually a school for the kids of heroes."

"I didn't even know those existed."

"Well, that's because we peasants of the general public are never supposed to, of course. Like I said, it just looked like some rich kid school, and in a way, it is. Not all of them go off to be heroes, but if any of them decide to, they just get in."

"Like Majesty's class."

"Exactly. As long as they don't blatantly flunk out of school or have a record, they're guaranteed an in. So, if you *can't* get in, it's a horrible embarrassment, and everyone knows it. Enter me."

"She didn't get in?" Kirin frowned.

"No, she did. Because of me." Ness squeezed her arms. "But she never, ever should've."

She looked so haunted that Kirin almost asked her to stop, but her words were coming almost automatically now.

"I was just wandering around the halls, middle of the day,

and almost everyone walked past me like I wasn't there. Everyone except her." Though Ness was barely visible, the tears in her eyes were clear. "It was the first time in my life that anyone actually *looked* at me, and Kirin, to be seen for the first time, by someone that beautiful? I never stood a chance."

Her mouth moved but no sound came out for a few seconds before she realized. She cleared her throat and started again.

"I didn't know, at the time, that it was partly because of her mien that she could see me. She can vaguely sense emotions, like Naddāha, and she noticed that there was someone new there. I'll never know if she started using her mien on me right then, or if that just came later, but it doesn't matter. The moment she saw me, I was gone."

Kirin reached out again, but she only gave him a single finger, the rest of her still firmly wrapped in her blankets.

"I'll admit I ran. She was so stunning it was scary, and being acknowledged, for once? I was sure she was going to call for someone, to get me arrested for trespassing. I didn't even know how big of a deal it would've been if I'd been caught, hadn't realized anything was different about the school. And that should've been it. I just needed to lay low for a while and it'd be okay. Instead, I went back the very next day.

"She was waiting for me. Or maybe she just felt me arrive and came out to meet me. But I hadn't been there for more than a few minutes when she walked right up to me, took my hand, and dragged me into her dorm room." Ness cracked a smile. "Do you want to know what the first thing she said to me was?"

Kirin nodded.

"She said 'no one else in the world notices you, but I see you.' I admit, looking back, that should've been such a red flag, but I'd waited *years* to hear that. I see you." Ness's face shone with the memory of being wanted, if only for a moment. "I don't know if me actually falling for her was part of her plan, but she didn't complain."

"What was her plan?"

Ness actually laughed.

"It's so stupid, really. She strung me along for years, and for what?" She snorted. "Straight A's."

"Really?"

"At first, yeah. I'm not Yantra; there was nothing high tech about what I did. I just walked into an office, changed a grade in the system, and walked out. That was it. She wasn't dumb, just didn't want to do the work. She had so many excuses too; she had headaches, it was stressing her out too much, the pressure from her parents was so paralyzing she couldn't do her work, anything and everything she could think of to pretend she would've done it, if it weren't for all these horrible things coming up. And, once or twice, when I needed to break into a police station, it was always to clear up a 'misunderstanding.' She needed the clean record, remember. She told me she loved me, so she could get into the school."

Ness's smile fell.

"I did love *her* though, and I think I would've even if she'd done nothing to me at all. Her dorm... it was the only space that I didn't make someone jump when I spoke, where I wouldn't get ignored. She liked the same movies I did and listened to the stupid playlists I'd make her, and when I made her a bracelet for her birthday— probably the cheapest thing she's ever owned— she actually *cried.* She gave me a hug, and for the first and only time in the years we were 'together,' she let her mien drop. It was..."

Ness looked startled when a sob burst from her.

"You don't have to—"

"It was so sad because it was the only time that loving her didn't make me feel sick." Ness wiped off her mouth with her sleeve, briefly vivid with dark brown eyes— he'd never been able to see the color of her eyes before— and her bright red nose. "And I *hate* that she took that away from me. That I could've loved her— *would've* loved her— on my own, but she never gave me the chance."

"Ness..."

"My own grades finally started taking a hit, and my parents didn't notice a thing. But she was like an addiction, and if I spent a full day away from her, I'd get shivers, and aches, and sometimes my heart would race so badly I thought it was going to explode. I don't... I don't know if she knew what was going on, but I don't think she would've stopped even if she did know."

"You don't have to be around her now. We'll find another way to get to Bia."

Ness just waved her hand.

"It doesn't hurt, what I'm doing now. It feels good, that *I'm* the one using her for a change, and not even for myself. And..." Ness hesitated. "And I owe it to the class."

"You don't owe us anything."

"I do. Because it's my fault they attacked us last year."

Kirin found himself speechless.

"The way Sh— Inanna's power works, is that it only lasts for 36 hours maximum, and only that long if you've had it used on you repeatedly. It also works better if you've never been in love before, and can't tell the difference, but that's beside the point. Once she got in here, she stopped bothering to talk to me. Legacy students find out almost immediately after they apply, so she knew months before I did. I hadn't even told her I'd applied, because I was so convinced that she'd be heartbroken if I told her and then didn't make it. But after a week of her not talking to me, even with her power worn off, I broke back in to tell her.

"She laughed at me." There were no more tears, and somehow that was worse. "She said they wouldn't even remember my name after they talked to me, so I'd never make it in. I'd almost convinced myself that she was just grieving in her own way, since she knew the odds better than I did, but then she called security on me."

"You're not just in our class because of your mien."

Ness laughed.

"No, I've got a record. Breaking and entering, stalking, harassment. What's worse is that it's all true."

"It's not—"

"It is. I got caught on school grounds three more times before the semester was up. And then I thought I'd never see her again— until I got a call from Reader."

"The dean?"

"The one and only."

"You've met them?"

"I talked to them over the phone. Pressure did my interview, just like everyone else. But Reader was the reason I made it there. They had reviewed my application, and my police file, and noticed that they'd never taken a statement from *me* about what happened. The police had just taken Inanna's word for it. I didn't think it'd really matter, since I didn't know who they were then, but I told them, though I didn't think it'd do much. Next thing I knew, I was sitting in front of Pressure for an interview." Ness smiled wistfully. "The reason I was so shocked that she *wasn't* Reader when I got here was because I walked in the door and she gave me the biggest hug. She told me I was worth so much more than I'd received, and the school would be lucky to have me if I decided to join."

Kirin found himself rubbing at his own suddenly watery eyes.

"She was right."

"I don't know if she was. I'm still working to earn that." Ness faded again, her smile eerily lasting longer than the rest of her like an afterimage. "I was waiting for Inanna on that first day. I thought I'd just sit there until she walked into the gym, to show her that I got in on my own power, whereas she'd needed me to even get a chance. Or at least that's what I told myself I was going to do.

"When I saw her walk in with the rest of Majesty's class, it was like I'd never gotten out from under her thumb. I felt small and pathetic, especially when she walked right past us without looking up once. The one person who had always noticed me, suddenly didn't care enough to look. I went to find her right after. Snuck in right behind her, followed her all the way to her room. I don't know what I was planning on saying or doing, honestly. It felt so surreal seeing her. I'd convinced myself that she wasn't as beautiful as I remembered, and I was right." Ness looked down at her hands where they rested on her knees. "She was more beautiful."

"What did she do when she saw you?" Kirin felt like he really didn't want to know.

"She laughed." Ness looked up at him, eyes tired. "Said she couldn't believe her mien was so powerful to make me follow her across continents. That it was pathetic of me to think I wouldn't go to jail for breaking into the school."

"But you got in."

"She didn't believe me. I had to show her my ID, and instead of finally taking me seriously, she got angry." Ness pushed away a stray hair that had fallen into her face away. "She screamed at me. Accused me of cheapening her acceptance merely by being here. That if I got in, what was it worth to be there herself? After all, I'm so worthless that if I could be accepted, the program must be nothing special at all."

"I'm going to punch her."

"*You* probably could." It felt like a very high compliment indeed. "But I didn't even fight back. And when she told me to prove that I wasn't completely useless, I did."

"You told her about Phoenix." The realization hit Kirin like a punch.

"Yeah." Ness vanished again, this time reappearing underneath the bed instead of on top of it.

"Oh, Ness."

"You shouldn't sound sad for me, you should be mad."

"I'm not."

"You should be." She was crying again, the tears faint shimmers on her fading image. "That was an awful thing to do. I should've known they'd do something cruel like that; I'd seen how Bia treats her 'friends.' Even Inanna's afraid of her."

"You were abused for years. It's hard to shake that, especially when the person who did it is right in front of you." Kirin helped her back onto the bed, pulling her against his side. "That need to be loved is hard to ignore."

"Still. Luckily though, I felt guilty enough about what happened that I didn't go back to see her the whole rest of the year. Not even when she was injured." Ness sniffed. "I was kind of sad to hear that Phoenix stabilized her. It's not that I wanted her to die, I just... didn't want to think about her anymore. I just wanted her *gone*."

"Unfortunately, death has a way of making wounds like that deeper, instead of letting them heal."

Ness regarded him for a moment before settling back against him.

"I'm busy talking about *my* traumatic backstory, so I'll let that slide for now."

Kirin tried to smother the chuckle that escaped, but failed.

"I really don't mind now, being around her. I know what it feels like when she's using it. I know what to look for. And..." Ness suddenly became very interested in her nails. "I know what liking someone without her interference feels like now, too."

Kirin grabbed her by the shoulders and looked her dead in the face.

"Have you been holding out on me?" He did his best wounded look, which was apparently highly effective, since she shoved a pillow in his face to make him stop.

"It's not holding out if you haven't been around to talk to," she protested, but there was laughter in her voice now. "And it's new. Kind of."

"Kind of? That *does* sound like you've been holding out on me."

She laughed again, and Kirin was happy to see the color in her cheeks become stronger, more alive.

"While we're on the topic of personal questions, can I ask one about your mien?"

The newly gained color stayed, though Kirin's attempt to focus on her eyes entirely failed.

"Sure, there's not much to tell though. What you see is what you get."

"Sometimes when you think of certain things you seem... less there."

"Ah, that." She licked her lips. "Yeah. That is a thing."

"Why?"

She shrugged.

"Your guess is as good as mine. It's always been vaguely like that, and I thought with practice it'd get better, but..." She stared at her hands. "It just hurts less now. Maybe because I'm less *here* now, and more *there*."

"It *hurts*?" Suddenly Kirin understood the abject horror Ifrit must have when they'd talked about his scars the year before. That wasn't usually the part of the night that Kirin played over and over in his head, but it was just as burned into his memory as the rest.

"Yeah." Unlike Ifrit though, he got no reassurance. "It used to be worse, like tearing myself in half or ripping my skin into shreds. Now it's just a faint itch, like being dragged against a bed of nails."

"That still doesn't sound pleasant."

"I was so excited when I realized it was getting better. I thought it meant I was just getting better at controlling it, that I'd be able to turn it off, eventually. But I think it's just because the more I use it, the more I fade."

"Where do you go, Ness?"

"Nowhere. Somewhere between. Maybe I don't go anywhere at all." She didn't seem troubled by the lack of a real answer, lifting a shoulder casually. "I just don't exist for a minute. If I stay like that for too long, I start to forget who I am, too."

"You need to talk to your armorer." Kirin had resisted the urge to pace the whole time, but he couldn't fight it anymore. "They might not've had answers the first time, but surely they will now if you just—"

"Kirin." The sadness in her voice stopped him in his tracks. "The only thing I didn't tell her was that it hurt. Everything else I did."

"And she still wouldn't help?"

"She thought it was in the best interest for my hero work that we didn't do anything about it."

Kirin thought of Nwabudike, taking his time to test the material, to fully understand Kirin's mien before even settling the costume design, his insistence that they not rush through anything to make sure it was the best it could be. How could Ness's armorer not have done the same?

"We should—" before he could finish the sentence, the door burst open, and Ifrit was standing there, still holding the crushed cube he'd gone to talk to Majesty about.

"Is something wrong?" Kirin was at the door in a moment,

looking Ifrit over for injuries.

"Your armorer." Ifrit nodded in apology to Ness before turning his focus entirely to Kirin. "We need to go talk to him."

"*My* armorer?" Kirin had actually been about to suggest the same thing, but he hadn't the faintest idea why Ifrit would want to go. "I mean, I'm happy to take you guys there, but I haven't been granted access since my mask was fixed—"

Ifrit wordlessly pulled Yantra out from behind himself.

"Just lead the way." She offered a strained smile. "I can do the rest."

23

Prepped, Armed

MAJESTY'S OFFICE ALWAYS PISSED Ifrit off, even on his best days. And today was decidedly *not* his best day.

At least she hadn't kept him waiting. He'd barely pressed send when her reply came that she would be available in a few minutes and he could head right over. Maybe that should've made him less nervous about revealing whatever it was that Kirin had found, but it hadn't. He'd almost wished she'd said she had already left campus and they'd have to talk tomorrow, so he could go back and lie down and pretend nothing had changed.

It was a small mercy that Valor wasn't in his office. Ifrit had previously thought it was annoying that Pressure's office was right down the hall from Majesty's, but now that it had a new occupant it'd become a source of dread. Valor hadn't done anything, really, since Kirin threatened him, yet it had to be coming. It always did.

Majesty looked similarly relieved, after she cast a nervous glance down the hall. Ifrit's eyes narrowed. A lover's quarrel, then? If he could even call them that. He didn't know what the fuck their deal was, and he really, really didn't want to.

"I'm glad you reached out." She settled behind her desk with ease, her shoulders coming down after the lock clicked quietly into place. "It was a harrowing day. What did you want to talk about?"

He almost felt guilty, seeing how excited she was, how the corner of her mouth twitched in the barest whisper of a grateful smile. He'd known her for years and had never seen her act like this, like a kid happy to make their first friend.

"One of my teammates found this." He put the cube on her desk, the quiet clunk proving it was heavier than it looked. "He grabbed it off the woman in white's belt."

A crease appeared between Majesty's eyes.

"Why didn't he turn it in immediately?" Perfectly following protocol as always, Majesty retrieved a pair of gloves from her drawer before picking it up.

"It was a tough mission." Ifrit's throat felt tight, the terror lurking just out of sight, even now. "We were all a little fucking preoccupied."

She looked up at that, her lips pursed. Her eyes flickered to the smoke detector, so innocuous on the ceiling, as she put the cube down and did something that shocked Ifrit. She began to sign.

I know what happened. Majesty never looked concerned, but she did now. Pressure had been in her mid-thirties and Majesty was around the same age, though sometime in the last few months she'd developed lines around her eyes which made her look older. *I did not tell them to attack.*

Even the way she signed was awkward, stiff. The words fell haltingly, unpracticed. When had she even learned?

And yet they fucking did. Ifrit's reply came a beat late, since he'd had to comb back through the shitty day to remember what she was even talking about. Of course she hadn't told Kirin's sibling to attack. But her own class had.

It was smart of you to not take my offer earlier, and I apologize for being so short-sighted. Her eyes flashed up again, and she started speaking out loud, the words completely out of sync with what her hands were doing. The disorientation was so jarring Ifrit had to turn off his hearing aids to not lose the thread of conversation. *I did not realize he was talking to them.*

Valor? Ifrit's eyes narrowed.

We both know that he was put here because of you. To punish *you. I am sure the school thought that some of your classmates would side with him, and yet I have no knowledge that he was meant to do anything other than scare you. But he's been more active than you know.*

He's been talking to Bia.

Majesty's mouth thinned into a colorless line.

He does not have the... sway he once did, but not everyone knows that. Least of all the students. He has painted a target on your back and is covering for anyone who takes a shot at you or any of your classmates.

Who was missing? Even in his shock, Ifrit had registered that there had been an empty seat on the plane back.

Majesty's expression further stilled.

There was... a casualty.

Ifrit immediately ran through what he could remember of the ride back, but he couldn't place who was missing.

Who? And how?

You wouldn't know her. She was one of very few of my students who actually focused on the work at hand and did her best. Majesty's lip trembled and she pressed her fingers to it before she continued. *We are still waiting on the autopsy report, but at this moment it appears to have been self-inflicted violence.*

She killed herself? Ifrit shook his head. *You don't fucking believe that.*

No, I don't. Majesty pushed the cube back across the counter toward him. *Nor do I particularly trust the school anymore, ei-*

ther.

Ifrit stared at the offending metal and back up to her.

We don't have any way to fucking figure out what this is otherwise. This could help us find Aether, to find— The realization of whose secrets he'd almost just betrayed hit Ifrit like a jolt of electricity. He really needed to sleep, the bitter taste of self-hatred coating his tongue.

I know. Majesty, once so stoic, was displaying an unbelievable amount of pity in her eyes. Ifrit hated it, hated that *this* was who he had to go to for help. The void of Pressure's absence opened without warning, the well of grief yawning before him and threatening to swallow him whole. This wasn't right, none of it. He should be with her, telling her about all this shit, telling her how they'd found a piece of the puzzle. He should have someone who he could trust and tell about Kirin's siblings, who would get them back without condemning them, who would take the fucking piece of machinery and deal with it. Who wouldn't look at him like they were about to make something else be his fucking problem to solve.

The tears burned at the back of his eyes, and he wasn't quite sure how he kept them from falling. But he wouldn't cry. Not in front of her.

There is a researcher that you can trust. She turned to her computer, images reflected in her eyes as she scrolled. She had to pause and turn back to him when she signed, *he is young, but brilliant. And he's like you.*

The fuck is that supposed to mean?

He owes his position here to Pressure. Majesty turned back to face him, and Ifrit lost his composure as he saw that she was crying. *I am truly sorry, A—*

Don't. He was on his feet, looking away. When he finally managed to look back, a small, sad smile played across her face.

Alright. I just wanted you to know that you are not alone.

That was the final straw, causing the tears to fall, and he bit his lip hard enough to draw blood to keep it from wobbling.

I wish it had not taken so long for me to realize how right she was. Majesty didn't even try to wipe away the silver streaks on her face, wearing them like a badge of honor. A badge of redemption. *We were all kids once, and they teach us so young to hate ourselves. To hate each other. She was so much braver than I was to question it.*

Why now? Ifrit couldn't make himself sit down, couldn't make himself move closer.

Because my mistakes have been thrown into sharp relief. Because I see you, and your friends, and how hard you are working to make things better, instead of accepting things the way they are. And because Bán deserves better than I ever got.

It was painful to sit, like each step closer was through a thicket of thorns, but Ifrit eased himself into the chair and picked up the cube.

Who's this fucking researcher? Even when he placed it in his pocket, he could feel the dents from Kirin's fingers running along the side. It made him feel just a little calmer, like Kirin was there, sitting next to him.

Nwabudike Edozie. She painstakingly spelled out the name twice. *Your... large friend already knows him.*

The way she hesitated made Ifrit feel like she'd been about to say something else.

Do you have a fucking address or something then? We can't walk into the lab without authorization.

I believe you have someone who can make short work of that. Majesty actually gave him a real smile, a glimmer of conspiratorial humor in her eyes. For a moment, Ifrit understood why she and his mother had been friends, once. *He does not have another address. He is not allowed to leave campus.*

What? Why the fuck not?

Majesty suddenly looked at the door, her usual imperious mask in place.

"...conduct further once your temper is better." She had stopped signing, forcing him to turn his hearing aids back on with a frown. "For now, you are excused. I hope this does not become a regular occurrence."

"Yeah, I really fucking hope not too." Ifrit got up with real irritation, not needing to feign anything. Why was it that every time it felt like he was about to find out something, it was interrupted? He stomped over to the door and wrenched it open unceremoniously, only to come face to face with someone vaguely familiar.

She was willowy, pretty in a sort of ethereal way. Her hair was long, the tightly coiled curls pulled down by the weight of it. Everything about her screamed loveliness, begged the viewer to stop and stare, even made Ifrit's heart skip a beat despite his head crying out that something was wrong. When she gave him a slow, shy smile, he recognized her. The one who had hung back when Majesty's class attacked the year before. The one that Ness knew.

"Inanna, please, come in." Majesty's voice was cold behind him. "He was just leaving."

Recognizing her power seemed to lessen it, and Ifrit was able to continue on his way without a backward glance. He almost wished he did, as the door shut behind him, if only to see what sort of expression Majesty was wearing now.

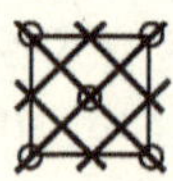

"Is anyone going to tell me what's going on?" Lilin hadn't questioned anything as she cloaked them in night to pass through the barrier, nor when she'd made the darkness deeper as they slid past a grad student who was yawning as they headed back to their dorm. But now that they were just outside the armorer's lab, she finally had developed a sense of curiosity.

"The less you know, the fucking better." Ifrit bit out, his jaw clenched so tightly that his muscles were getting sore. Yantra had insisted that it'd be easier with her there, but their group felt overly large, with the two of them, Kirin, himself, and Ness too, for some reason.

"That's fair enough." Lilin was content to accept that, which made Ifrit shoot her a faint look of distrust. Or tried to, as she was just another inky spot in the blackness, no different than the rest of them.

"If it makes you feel any better, this one is *almost* officially sanctioned." Kirin's voice came directly from Ifrit's right, though he didn't need it to know exactly where Kirin was. Not only did his invisible sense of space go fuzzy around Kirin, but their hands were firmly intertwined, the sight hidden by the shadow that surrounded them all.

"I don't even want to know what that means." Lilin laughed, a genuinely kind sound. Ifrit abruptly wished he'd hung out with her more, finding his shoulders relaxing in her presence. No wonder Kirin liked to talk to her so much.

"Alright, door's open." Yantra was vaguely off to the left, her image flickering in his head as a breeze blew through. It was safe for Ifrit to use his mien to this extent outside, but the open air fought against him as he tried to keep the gas in place.

"He really lives here?" Ness sounded troubled, but when hadn't she in the last few months? After meeting the woman she was spying on, Ifrit couldn't even blame her. Especially when some of the carbon passed right *through* her, like she wasn't even there. He really needed to mention that to Kirin.

"According to Majesty." Yantra's voice had an edge to it, one that Ifrit's own might have had just a few short weeks ago. He wouldn't have believed that she would become an ally so quickly, but with Shifter still appearing rarely, if ever, she was the only one they had.

"Should we head to the elevator?" Lilin was more nervous now that they were inside, where a cloud of moving darkness would be more conspicuous.

"No." When Yantra shook her head, Ifrit could follow the movement easier. He cursed silently and pulled the carbon closer around himself, where it could be suctioned away by Kirin. "The elevators are more closely watched. Stairs it is, unfortunately."

"Just when I thought we hadn't gotten enough exercise today." Ness was trying to sound cheerful, though it fell flat.

"We're about to get plenty, since he's on the twelfth floor." Yantra sighed as she opened the door to the stairwell. "And maybe we should go over what we're going to say when we get there? Is there any reason that we *should* trust that Majesty isn't trying to set us up?"

"I don't think he'd ever turn us in." Kirin sounded very certain. "He was willing to go against Valor, admittedly because of something in my acceptance requirements, but he was really determined to."

"And she wouldn't even have to fucking set us up." Ifrit was doing great at not taking Yantra's suspicion personally. "She could just say that we were up to something and that would be it, we'd be fucking done."

"Because it doesn't matter what we do, how good we do our jobs, we're still all one mistake away from being criminals." Ness wasn't even out of breath as they reached their target floor.

"That's why we're here." Kirin held open the door to let everyone walk through ahead of him. "To prove that we don't need their approval to make things right."

24

The Researcher

WITH THE WEIGHT OF everyone's gazes on him, Kirin awkwardly raised a hand to knock on the door. It was the middle of the night, so surely Nwabudike was sleeping, and the echo made Kirin flinch as the sound rolled down the corridor. What if there were other folks working late too? How would they explain it if someone else opened their door first?

As usual, his fears were unfounded, as Nwabudike opened his door with sparkling eyes, almost like he'd been expecting them.

"Come in, come in!" His enthusiasm was still intact at two in the morning, ushering the whole group inside without question. Maybe he really *had* known they were coming, as the space inside was cleaner than Kirin had ever seen it before, plans organized into their cubbies, his latest prototype neatly laid out on his workbench. The only other door in the room was propped open for the first time, a small, sterile-looking cot just visible. Kirin's heart sunk at the sight, part of him having hoped Majesty had been lying about this being a prison cell as well as a workshop.

"You seem... very awake." Yantra agreed with Kirin's assessment.

"Majesty stopped by to let me know that you had found some sensitive equipment that needed processing on your mission today." Nwabudike looked so happy at the thought of being trusted with something important that Kirin immediately felt bad for being party to the lie. "Would you all like something to drink? Or shall we jump right into it?"

He reached for one of his notebooks. There were more than Kirin remembered there being, and his chest stung as he realized this was all Nwabudike had. His work. Maybe Kirin *should* let him make modifications to his costume, just to give the boy some company.

"I don't know what she fucking told you, but we just need you to look into this." Ifrit released Kirin's hand for the first time to place the innocent looking cube on the table in front of them. Cleared of its usual detritus, the metal box felt more ominous, alone on the blank plane.

"Actually, we need you to look into that, and take a look at her." Kirin nodded to Ness, who frowned back at him. He offered an apologetic half-shrug, which was missed by Nwabudike, who was already circling Ness with interest.

"No problem, no problem at all!" Nwabudike shooed Ness over to the scanner in the corner. She stuck her tongue out at Kirin as the light booted up, the blue glow from under her feet making her look transparent. "I'll have the scan run while we discuss what you know of this."

"Only that it was on the belt of the head of Aether." Kirin leaned onto the table, feeling his back cry in protest. It *had* been such a long day, hadn't it?

"We think it was used to mimic some kind of mien." Yantra cut in, walking around the table to stand next to Nwabudike as he turned it over in his hands. "Most likely something to do with generating a high-pitched frequency meant to disable or injure other people."

"That is very specific, and also very unlikely." Nwabudike produced a small screwdriver out of somewhere and started poking at the edges of the cube. It was so odd to see him in thin linen pajamas, the lightness of the cloth contrasting with the darkness of his skin, both alien to the shiny gold of his braces. His hair had grown out, forming a dark halo around his head, making him look even younger than when they'd first met. It made his face rounder, softer, his joy so innocent as he worked on the new puzzle. "If this were intended to create such an auditory disturbance, there would need to be at least one perforated side to allow the noise to pass through, and there's no discernible amplification apparatus that would allow it to be so loud as to be damaging. I could still be wrong, but I wouldn't assume that's what this was doing at all."

"Do you have any idea what it *does* do?" Ness stepped off the scanner as it beeped, a tiny image of herself flickering in the corner.

"No, not the slightest. That'll have to wait until I can see inside." As he spoke, one of the sides popped off, revealing a nest of wires. "Oh, this is masterfully put together!"

He rushed over to the magnifier, placing the now open cube underneath. The screen lit up, parts outlined in glowing lines as they were identified by the program.

"The skill needed to do this level of detailed work is incredible. From the tiny misalignments in it, I'd say it was done by hand too, remarkable."

"Why would someone do this by hand if it's so detailed?" Lilin was perched on the desk, leaning over the drafting table to get a look at the screen.

"It could be that they have limited resources, or are simply on the move. The type of machinery you'd need to do this kind of fine work is unsurprisingly unwieldy to transport."

"We knew the second half, but you really think Aether doesn't have many resources?" Lilin frowned.

"All I can say for certain is that this isn't machine made. While some people do prefer to machine their equipment by hand, for something this intricate it would save a lot of time to have robotic assistance." Nwabudike pointed out a complex knot of wires. "That alone would take a week if I were doing it, and I am rather good at my job."

"I'd argue better than good, but I get your point." Kirin squinted at some of the names on the screen, trying to make sense of what he was seeing. "Can you tell what it *is* supposed to do now?"

"No!" Nwabudike looked incredibly pleased at the prospect. "Not yet, anyway. It truly is a puzzle. The computer is running the program on its chip now, and it will report back. In the meantime, shall we return to the second matter of business?"

He pulled up the scan of Ness on the drafting table, Lilin leaning back to stop the projection from getting cut off by her head.

"I assume the issue you're struggling with is corporeality?" Nwabudike pulled up a list of results from whatever the scanner measured and Kirin gave up trying to follow the conversation entirely. He found his gaze straying to the window that overlooked the atrium, the fountain in the center looking like a video playing on repeat more than something just beyond the glass. Moonlight streamed into the space from the panels in the ceiling, the dim lighting so different to the brightly lit walls in the tiny workroom. Kirin thought he saw a flicker of movement in the shadows, but his attention was drawn back to the group by Nwabudike exclaiming loudly.

"The pain is an interesting phenomenon, as it implies some separation from your physical state and yet you *bring* your body with you. The only true anomaly that the scanner was able to detect was on a molecular level, and combined with the discomfort, I think we can make a safe assumption about the mechanism of your mien."

"That's more than anyone else has guessed." Ness sighed. "Give me the bad news."

"Oh, no not bad, not bad at all! In fact, eminently solvable, with the right study. All matter in the universe vibrates at a certain frequency, yes?"

"I only have a high school level understanding of physics, so I'll take your word for it."

"An even easier way to think of it would be that when you interface with anything— person, object, the very ground you stand on— the atoms that make up *you* are pressing against the atoms that make up everything else. Atoms vibrate, which create heat which create energy which create us. The vibrational frequencies are fairly standard for most objects and for flesh, for cloth, so forth and so on. Still following?"

"I believe so." Ness spoke slowly, though Yantra next to her was nodding fiercely.

"*You* vibrate at a different frequency. I would have to speak with your armorer for their data from the beginning of the year, but I suspect that the more you use your ability, the more out of sync with the world you become. This would account for the discomfort you feel when utilizing it— you are getting perpetual rugburn from the air, the ground, everything as you become out of phase and therefore out of *known existence*."

"And if you're just vibrating wrong, you can create something to counteract that and help you stay stable." Yantra's eyes lit up as she looked at Ness. "It's complicated and not my specialty, but the theory isn't all that difficult to grasp. I could write a program to—"

"To measure the vibration of the standard person and match it?" Lilin cut in, looking at the magnifier. "Like that?"

They all looked up, to where indeed the computer had finished its analysis and was reporting something eerily similar.

"Odd." Nwabudike frowned as he expanded the report and read through it. "On its own, I don't see how this would do anything."

"Do we think she has a similar mien to Ness?" Kirin thought back, all the way back to Satol. To her in the tunnels, dancing away like gravity had no grasp on her at all. "It would explain how she keeps vanishing on us."

Ness looked discomfited by the thought.

"I told you. She definitely does not have a mien." Yantra bit her lip, fingers twining with her hair. She must have gotten caught on a snarl, as her head twitched as she pulled, hands ripped out and flat on the desk.

"I can run more tests." Nwabudike offered. "I would be hesitant to use the program that we found here, in case there is something that we can't see yet hiding in the code, but I could create a device with a blank program, that you could fill once you have a suitable program coded."

"Let's do that." Ness was more solid than she had been in hours, hope glimmering in her eyes. "How long do you think it'll take you to make?"

A knock on the door startled them all.

They all froze, except Nwabudike, who looked puzzled. He checked the time on his computer and his mouth dropped into an "o" shape. With one hand, he shooed them toward the bedroom door, using the other to minimize the scan of Ness, the readout, and whatever else he had been working on. He closed the front of the magnifier, hiding the cube from view, turning off the screen as well, though no one else could've possibly known what it was referring to. That left the rest of them to pile into the small bedroom, Ifrit the last to follow as he hesitated at the door, before Nwabudike sealed them in.

It wasn't as small as Kirin had feared, the bed pressed against a floor to ceiling window that overlooked the atrium, with a small closet at the end. A desk that was completely empty stood at the opposite side of the room, with a kitchenette taking up the wall opposite the bed. There was another door next to the closet that Kirin assumed would be the bathroom, but it was hardly bigger than his own dorm, not enough space to be confined to for days on end.

"Ah, Valor, I didn't see your request for repairs until just now. Luckily, I was up late today, so no worries at all!" Nwabudike's usually cheerful voice sounded strained, and they all went still at their teacher's name. Yantra held up her phone so they could all see the time— it was already three.

What the fuck is he doing here? Ifrit was trying and failing to hide his nerves.

"You are here for restitution. Check for urgent requests every hour to ensure you are doing your utmost for the people who have given you a second chance." Ifrit's shoulders raised at Valor's voice and Kirin pulled Ifrit to his side, as if he could protect him from the sound. "Fix these; I don't know why you keep giving me products that fail."

There was the sound of something metal being tossed onto the workbench, a crunk as if it were thrown, hard.

"What were you doing when it failed?" Nwabudike was back in his business mode, jangling sounds filtering in as he undoubtedly tinkered with whatever project he'd been given.

"That is none of your business." The coldness in Valor's voice made Ifrit flinch and Kirin pulled him closer, burying his face in Ifrit's hair.

"If I don't know what caused them to fail, I can't—"

A slam made them all flinch.

"I do not come to you for excuses. You should have been put down like a rabid dog when they found you, but you are here because they believe you to be some kind of genius. If I wanted excuses I would ask one of the sniveling idiots next to you for assistance. Prove to me you deserve to live or I will exercise my right to remove you."

Kirin nearly got them all killed, as he found himself reaching for the door before his brain caught up to him. Ifrit reacted quicker and held him back, shaking his head with wide eyes. Kirin's pulse was thundering in his ears, the thought of the innocent boy who was so excited to help being threatened just on the other side of the wall drowning out all rational thought. Ifrit put a hand on either side of Kirin's face and shook his head, his eyes terrified. It was his fear, and not any real desire for self-preservation on Kirin's part, that kept his hand from ripping open the thin barrier between him and Nwabudike.

"Understood." The word came out as nearly a whimper, which threatened Kirin's thin thread of self-control again. "I should have this repaired and back to you by the end of the week—"

"You'll have it done by tomorrow."

"By the end of day tomorrow." Nwabudike sounded near tears.

"Good." There was the creak of leather, the sound of a sharp slap on the back. "I'm so glad we're finally coming to understand one another."

And just as suddenly as he came in, there was the sound of the door opening and shutting, and Valor was gone.

Kirin didn't wait a moment longer to go in, finding Nwabudike's eyes wide with fear and his face streaked with tears, his gaze wild as it fell on them. He collapsed into himself, crying softly.

Lilin made it there first, ringing him in darkness that would smother the sensations all around him, her arms pulling him into a gentle hug as she stroked his back.

"That's it," she murmured softly, "let it out. He's gone now, and you're okay."

Nwabudike hugged her back gladly, Kirin joining them as softly as he could on the floor, laying a hand on Nwabudike's shoulder. When was the last time anyone had hugged him? And had he been dealing with threats like these alone this whole time?

"I'm sorry you had to see that." It only took him a few minutes to calm down, Ness coming back in from the bedroom silently with tissues she had procured from somewhere. Nwabudike took them gratefully, wiping off the snot and tears. "He usually... he usually isn't quite so aggressive."

"You don't have anything to apologize for." Lilin still held his hand, giving it a squeeze. "You didn't do anything wrong."

"He's right that I'm here for punishment though," Nwabudike sniffled. "It hardly feels like it most days because I do love the work. Maybe he's right to be cruel."

"He's like that to everyone, whether you've done anything or not." Ifrit looked pained. "You're just a fucking kid. You didn't do anything worth being treated like that."

Nwabudike offered a watery smile, accepting help to get back to his feet. His usually dark skin was still waxy, but his energy was coming back at least.

"You had asked how long the new model would take— only a few hours. I have a replicator I can use since none of the components are restricted. I can start it now and it'd be ready by morning." He turned back to his computer and Kirin tried to ignore how his hands were shaking.

"You don't have to get that done right away; you should do whatever Valor needs you to do first," Ness protested.

"It's fine; the work for him won't take long, it's just maintenance for a simple power enhancer. I think the issue is that he keeps overloading the capacitor, but, well, as you heard he never gives me a straight answer on what he was doing when it failed." Nwabudike's voice grew stronger as he focused on the task in front of him. "It's not terribly difficult, but I've learned that whatever timeline I give him he'll halve it at minimum, so I always tell him it'll take much longer than it should."

"How long has this been going on?" Kirin hoped his tone didn't betray his anger, though the look Ifrit shot him proved at least one person saw right through him.

"A month or so before the semester started." Nwabudike finished his adjustments and sent the design to the printer, the nozzles already gearing up and pouring metal. "I assume it was whenever they told him he was back to full duty. And he wasn't that bad in the beginning. Always condescending, but I've gotten used to that. I was the youngest student in my cohort; I've been dealing with people talking down to me for years. I don't really mind it, most days, since I get a lot more requests than the other technicians and it keeps me plenty busy."

"Are you really not allowed to leave?" Yantra had been strangely quiet, one of her fingers tracing the scar above her ear.

Nwabudike's face fell.

"They gave me a tracker, when I was allowed in." He turned his back to them under the pretense of checking on the fabricator, though it was whirring away steadily. "House arrest, they call it, but I am allowed outside and on some occasions into the hero sector. I don't live in the dorms, but I can go there too. I just can't leave campus."

"What fucking happens if you try?"

"Ah, the tracker shuts off the power to my braces." He was still turned away, though the slump in his shoulders spoke just as loudly as any expression would have.

"How old were you when you started... working here?" Lilin looked like she might cry, yet her voice was admirably free of any waver.

"I was fifteen." Nwabudike was finally satisfied the print was going to run without issue and turned back to face them. "That was two years ago."

None of them knew what to say.

"I would really love if you could stay longer, but I do have an appointment in just a few short hours and I've been stalling doing the repairs for too long." When the pause became too great, Nwabudike filled it with obvious reluctance. "In between my other duties I'll look into the materials and construction of the cube to see if it can give me any greater insights into its purpose. I should be able to ping Kirin to allow him in on the excuse of costume repairs once the new one is made, and then it'll just have to be programmed."

"If you upload your findings onto your computer I can help comb through." Yantra looked eager to offer. "I can also... I can chat with you on there too, if you get bored."

"I would appreciate that." Nwabudike's voice sounded small as they all shuffled up the step and into the corridor.

"And if you need help with... anything else, call me." It was empty, and Kirin knew it. Nwabudike could only contact him through the school's channels, and he could only pretend there were so many updates to a costume that hadn't changed since the year before. Maybe Kirin could give him his ID, so Nwabudike could get into the dorm in an emergency, and Kirin could just tailgate with his friends. But he doubted Nwabudike would accept it.

"I want you to know that I was very happy to get you assigned to me." Nwabudike's smile shone, even in the dark. "It was nice to feel like I had a friend, even if it was only a few days a month."

"I am your friend."

"And that is the best gift I've been given in a long time."

25

Gifts Given

IFRIT COULDN'T SLEEP.

He should've been exhausted— and he was, on some level— yet his brain just wouldn't shut up. Kirin's sibling. Aether. Valor. Now this armorer, trapped in his own lab. Every time he closed his eyes, the images just swam up. Bán. Something bad had happened to his little cousin, and he didn't even fucking know what it was. He knew how bad Valor was, he should've done something about it. Majesty. She was trying to make amends now, but could she make up for years of hate? Could anyone?

Kirin felt distant too. When they'd lain down to go to sleep, Kirin had almost refused to touch Ifrit until he'd put his head on Kirin's chest. Only then had he relaxed, burying his face in Ifrit's hair again. His breathing was slow and even, though his arm was still wrapped tightly around Ifrit's back.

Ifrit couldn't tell if he wanted to cry, or scream, or break something, or maybe some combination of all three. The scratches on his chest were now itchy and pulled as he breathed, and he regretted not asking Phoenix to help. As if summoned by the thought, a light flickered on in the common area.

It took considerable effort to extricate himself from Kirin without waking him, but Ifrit managed. He pulled on a pair of joggers and grabbed his ignition rings before he opened the door.

Phoenix was in the kitchen, heating up a bowl of saloona that Ifrit had made a few days prior. She looked up as he entered, offering him a tired smile.

“You want some?” The way her eyes flickered to her own door confirmed she’d snuck away from someone too, her voice low enough to not carry very far.

“I’m good.” Ifrit found himself drifting to the counter, not sure how to deal with this version of Phoenix. Especially not after how she’d seen him.

“You don’t have to look at me like that. Ad already is.” She turned away from him to stop the microwave before it went off. "I'm fine. Just tired.”

“You didn’t fucking heal for a minute today.” Ifrit wished he’d woken Kirin up for this. The fear was a bitter taste in his mouth. “I thought that I’d—”

“Sorry about that.” Phoenix didn’t meet his eyes as she shuffled around, grabbing a spoon and a glass of water. The shirt she was wearing was entirely too big, so it was probably Adlivun’s. “I didn’t mean to scare you.”

“I didn’t know you could fucking control it.”

“I can’t.”

“Then what the fuck was that?” Ifrit found himself about to cry, *again*. Fuck, he needed sleep. Sleep and maybe a break. Could he fake being sick and just not go to class for a week? Maybe he wouldn’t even tell Kirin it was a ruse just so he could feel taken care of for a little bit.

“Every power has its limit.” Phoenix lifted a shoulder in a shrug, like it didn’t particularly matter to her. “I can still help everyone else, it’s just… harder to help myself now.”

"Does that mean that you can—"

Phoenix silenced him by patting him on the back as she walked by, spoon in her mouth. The itching on his chest intensified and then vanished, proof that her healing of others was working just fine.

"Don't worry about it too much." She'd taken the spoon in her hand and waved it at him, as if that could make everything go away. "Just don't try to use me for target practice any time soon, okay?"

Before he could form any sort of response, the door to Kirin's room burst open, Kirin standing in the doorway breathing heavily. Phoenix used the distraction to sneak away, leaving the two of them alone.

"Sorry." Kirin's chest was still heaving, though his heartrate was visibly slowing now. "Sorry, I didn't mean to scare you, I just woke up and you weren't there and—"

"You don't have to apologize." Ifrit could see the sun already peeking up above the horizon, and decided he was in fact not going to class. It was just lectures, anyway. He pulled his phone out from his pocket and texted Clidna to come grab it before leaving it on the counter. "I couldn't sleep. Decided to fucking cut class, dropping this here so I don't get hit on attendance though."

"Okay." Kirin's eyes were still worried. He was too pretty like this, golden hair all a mess, one of Ifrit's shirts, and loose gym shorts. The scars that curled over his shoulders glittered, the sunlight quite literally sending sparkles glinting off them, decorating the walls with shimmering light. Ifrit felt a pull in his chest, wanting to run away right then, away from all the responsibility, from the horror, from the fear. He and Kirin could go somewhere, just the two of them, or maybe one or two of the less annoying assholes too, and they could just be happy. It was what Pressure had originally wanted for him, after all. To avoid all this.

"Hey, hey, it's okay." Ifrit hadn't realized he was crying until Kirin wrapped him up in his arms, holding him tightly. "Let's go back inside and we can talk about it, okay?"

Ifrit let himself be led, let Kirin fuss at getting him wrapped up in blankets and settled, Kirin only leaving to go back to the kitchen to get fresh water and a damp washcloth to help cool Ifrit's flushed face.

"Do you want to talk about what's been going on?"

"What fucking *hasn't* been?" Ifrit was on his feet suddenly, blankets forgotten as he paced. Kirin was still sitting on the bed, watching. "It's just… it's too much."

"I know."

"And I'm so tired but I can't sleep, and so fucking angry but I keep crying, and when it feels like we've helped one fucking person we find another struggling, and how can we fucking fix all of this?" The tears were dripping into his mouth so all he tasted was salt. "I thought we'd have a fucking year left before everything was suddenly our fucking problem and yet because motherfucking *Valor* is here I can barely get through the day and still no one is going to help us because they don't give a damn!"

"We have each other. That's nothing to scoff at." Kirin gripped the sides of Ifrit's face firmly, not letting him look away. Ifrit wanted to scream with their faces that close, when he could just reach out and *kiss* him, but that would ruin the one thing he had, the one source of comfort left to him. How having Kirin this close was both relief and utter torture. "We have Shifter. He might not be able to help much now, but once we're licensed, we'll be able to protect him better and then we'll have a good ally. And Majesty too, it sounds like, and she's powerful and connected. It's a lot but we can take it in small steps. And whatever you need Ifrit, I'm here."

"Adil." The name slipped out before he could stop himself, before he could think about it for a second more. But once he'd said it, it felt right. Majesty had almost called him by his name earlier, and he'd wanted to cry because it felt wrong. She might be willing to help, she might be ready to join their cause, but she wasn't the person he wanted to call for him. "My name is Adil."

Kirin went still, perfectly still. Even the air didn't move, proving he wasn't even breathing. His eyes were bright, but Ifrit couldn't tell what the emotion was behind them. They were searching, roaming all over Ifrit's face, like there was some secret there that could be peeled away and discovered.

"You don't— you don't have to tell me yours." Ifrit's throat suddenly felt tight, like he'd made a mistake. It was too real— too human— to give away his true name, instead of the ones they'd all been given. Kirin's hands were still holding him in place, and though the fan was running and the AC was on, Ifrit felt too warm, like his skin was on fire. "I can show you how to write it properly in Arabic... or we can just forget that I—"

"Adil." It was a whisper, Kirin's voice barely there. *"Adil."*

"Yeah?" Ifrit's voice came out as a croak, his breath hitching as tears choked him. The relief, the way his name sounded so *right* coming from Kirin, left him dizzy.

"Adil." Kirin said his name once more, and then he kissed him.

26

Entwined Trust

IFRIT—*ADIL*—WENT STILL under Kirin's hands, his cheeks still damp with tears. Kirin had the imprint of the last time they'd stood like this burned into his brain, the way their noses had rubbed, the chapped edge of Adil's lips, and this was nothing like that. Primarily in that Adil did not kiss him back.

The second it registered in his brain, Kirin pulled away, a pit of anxiety unfurling in his stomach. Ifrit's expression was pure surprise, his lips parted and his eyes wide. He hadn't reignited his halo, so it was only the wan light of the morning sun that colored his face, the crimson of his eyes deepened to maroon, the amber of his skin almost bronze. Kirin moved to take a step backward, but a hand shot out and grabbed his shirt in a fist.

"That... that wasn't to make me feel better, was it?" Adil's eyes were intense, pulling Kirin back in as they searched for an answer.

"No, I just—"

"And it wasn't because you feel fucking bad for me?"

"What? No, of course not—"

"And it really happened?" Adil's voice had gotten quieter, the hand buried in Kirin's shirt trembling slightly.

"Yeah." Kirin couldn't look at him now, instead staring at the floor, trying to hide his own misery. Adil was upset enough on his own; that was stupid, *Kirin* was stupid. Ness had been wrong, and Adil only liked him as a friend. And now he'd blown even that. "Look, I'm sorry, I should've thought—"

Adil shoved him hard enough that he hit the bed and lost his footing, dropping down to eye level, making them now nose to nose.

"The only fucking thing you need to apologize for is not doing it again." Adil grabbed Kirin by the back of the head, fingers entwined in Kirin's hair, and yanked him into a kiss.

It was Kirin's turn to be caught unaware, and it took him several seconds to react, wrapping an arm around Adil's back and pulling him in closer, savoring the softness of his lips. His cheeks were wet, but his hair underneath Kirin's other hand was soft, the flavor of his toothpaste lingering when they broke apart to breathe. Their chests were pressed together so tightly that Kirin could feel his own racing heart mirrored in Adil's, feel the way his breath ghosted past Kirin's lips and made him shiver, now that the sensation of Adil's mouth on his was brand new.

"Get it now, dumbass?" When Adil spoke, their mouths brushed featherlight against one another, causing goosebumps to rise on Kirin's arms. He nodded, if only so their lips would touch again. Though it had been fast, a chasm of yearning had opened in his heart with the contact, with the realization that *this* was what he wanted, that *Adil* was what he wanted, everything else be damned. When Adil started to pull away, Kirin stopped him this time, wanting to ask for more but not knowing how.

"We can fucking do that again, but not today, not right now." At Kirin's questioning look, he continued. "You picked a terrible fucking day, do you know that? It's been shit and I've been thinking about fucking kissing you for a whole *fucking year*. I don't want it to be associated with shit like today."

"Technically, everything except talking to Nwabudike was yesterday." Kirin really *was* tired, since now wasn't the best time to be snarky. Adil only smiled though, his lips bright red.

"We're going to fucking skip class *today*. Go put your phone outside so you're not marked absent." Adil was staring at him with open affection, the sensation so heady that when Kirin got up he tripped over his own feet. "I'm fucking tired though, so let's go to bed."

"Mhm." Kirin couldn't form a more coherent thought than that. He stumbled into the door and dropped his phone twice before he managed to get it on the counter. From the open doorway behind him, he could hear Adil laugh. *Adil.* He couldn't get over that.

When Kirin made it back inside, Adil had crawled back under the covers. He wasn't looking at the doorway and seemed to be internally debating something for a moment. He finally took his shirt off, folding it neatly. Kirin had to turn away as he felt his face flush, all the way to the tips of his ears.

"What are you waiting for?" Adil's voice sounded irritated, but it was to cover for the anxiety that hovered in the background. When Kirin looked up again, he found his blush mirrored in his friend's— was that the right word anymore?— face.

"Paper." The word popped into Kirin's head before he registered why. "You said you were going to show me how to write your name."

Adil blinked, as if he hadn't really expected Kirin to ask. And honestly, he hadn't planned to at first, but suddenly he was starving for any and all information about who Adil had been, where he'd come from, what his favorite memory was. All of it. Kirin wanted every bit of it.

When Kirin sat down and handed Adil the pen, he'd intended to watch how he wrote it out, to see the order of the strokes, to make sure he did it correctly. But he couldn't pull his gaze away from Adil's face, from the way his brows pinched together and his gaze grew intense as he wrote. How had Kirin not realized it sooner? He never could bring himself to look away from Adil when he did anything at all.

"Here." When Adil looked up, he realized that Kirin had been horribly distracted the whole time, and a cocky grin spread across his face. "What, am I that good a kisser that you can't fucking think anymore?"

"Yeah." Any price in pride that Kirin might have paid was worth the resulting blush that spread across Adil's cheeks again. He only got to see it for a second before Adil shoved a hand in his face.

"You can't fucking look at me like that." The mortification in Adil's voice made Kirin laugh out loud, the weight of everything vanishing, if only for a moment. "Just fucking give me a minute."

Kirin waited patiently for all of three seconds, and then pressed a small kiss to Adil's palm. He yelped like he'd been scalded and wrenched his hand away, leaving Kirin to topple into his lap, unable to stay upright from the force of his laughter.

"Fucking shut up, you're going to wake up Phoenix!" Adil resorted to covering his face with his hands, which Kirin pried away with a smile. Adil let out a strangled groan. "You *can't* fucking do that."

"Do what?" Kirin wasn't even trying to be obtuse, he was just marveling at the way that Adil's hands felt in his own, how much brighter the light seemed, how shy Adil had gotten. Nothing much had changed, yet so much had at the same time. He felt... buoyant. Unstoppable.

"How fucking long have you known?" Adil managed to look him in the eye, though his face was still flaming. Red *really* was his color.

"Known?"

"That you liked me."

"Oh." Kirin took a moment to tuck a stray curl behind Adil's ear, earning another vaguely choked sound. "Well, I think I've liked you for a long time now, but I just figured it out this afternoon."

"You fucking serious?"

"Yeah. Ness kind of had to kick my ass about it. Something about how I should've known the first time I wanted to kiss you."

"Your fucking dumb ass couldn't figure it out then?"

"It's all... new to me." Kirin traced the line of Adil's jaw, watching as he had the same effect as Adil had on him all those months before. "It's only ever been you."

Adil hit him in the head with a pillow.

"You *cannot* come to me the fucking *day* you figure out that you like me and just say all this sappy shit so easily! I have been suffering for fucking *months*, agonizing over if you'd be happy if I made a move, and then *day one* you just kiss me?" Adil fell back onto the mattress, covering his face again. "You... you fucking asshole!"

"Yeah, I'm the worst." Kirin pulled himself fully onto the bed, laying down next to Adil. "I should really have waited longer so I could perfect my longing gaze."

"You already did." Adil's voice was muffled, his face still hidden from view. "The way you'd look at me sometimes... I fucking thought my heart was going to stop."

"I'm glad it didn't." That earned another hit with the pillow, which unfortunately had been just a blur until it smacked into him. Some latent reflex had kicked in and crystallized the side of his head, shredding the thing and releasing stuffing all over the two of them. Adil felt the first of it hit and pulled his hands away from his face, pushing himself up to look at the downy rain. “And while I’ve only had a few hours to imagine it, this is better than anything I could’ve wanted.”

Adil waited only a moment longer and dragged Kirin down onto his chest, arms tight around Kirin’s waist. He buried his face in Kirin’s hair as the fluff rained down, making everything feel like a dream. A knot in Kirin’s chest tightened as part of his mind whispered that this *was* fake, that if he went to bed now, he’d wake up and everything would be gone. That the whole past year had just been that, a fiction, and none of this was real.

But Adil loosened his grip and allowed Kirin to pull back, to see the white dotting his jet-black hair, to start gently pulling the stuffing loose. To watch as Adil cautiously, anxiously reached out to do the same.

“This is real, right?” Adil whispered.

“It better be.” Kirin paused to play with a curl. “I’m glad my brain didn’t catch up fast enough to stop me because I’ve been worrying all day if it was taking advantage of you to sleep in the same bed knowing how I feel about you."

“You’ve been doing that for months, dumbass.”

“Yeah, but I was dumb then.”

“You’re dumb now.”

“Mm.” Kirin didn’t want to move at all, though the remnants of the pillow were finally settling down around them, but then he noticed the paper crumpled up on the bed next to Adil. “Oh, speaking of dumb, let me see that.”

He handed it over, and when Kirin made a grabbing gesture, Adil tossed the pen as well.

“You’re doing that really fucking wrong.” It took a few seconds, but Adil sat up and frowned at the paper, where Kirin was doing a terrible job of replicating what he’d written.

“Well, that’s because I’m not writing your name.” Kirin finished the last stroke and handed it back. "I wrote mine."

Adil practically grabbed the paper out of his hand, looking intently at the hanja.

"How do I say it?" He looked back up at Kirin with such wonder, such joy, like he'd been given a gift.

"Min-soo." It felt so strange to say it out loud, to hear his own name after so many months. He finger-spelled as he spoke, so Adil didn't miss it. "The 'soo' is the ending my parents used for all my siblings. I'm lucky that I got it at all, since not every family keeps it for girls as well as boys."

"It's your birth name?" Adil was already tracing over the letters, the lines becoming indented in the paper. When he spoke he looked up, his eyes shining.

"Yeah, it's gender neutral though it's more masculine." Kirin leaned back against the wall, feeling some stuffing tickling his elbows. "I guess my parents knew somehow."

The quiet scratching of the pencil stopped.

"Do you think we would've been friends?" Adil cursed softly after he spoke, his practiced lines a little more violent when he resumed. It was cute how he did that often, asking something so innocent and getting embarrassed about it. "When we were fucking kids, or whatever."

"Yeah, I think so." Kirin brushed the last of the white out of Adil's hair.

"I was real fucking different back then."

"So was I."

"And you still think—"

"I don't think there's a single lifetime where I wouldn't like you."

It was lucky that Adil hadn't reignited his halo as carbon flooded the air. Kirin laughed and Adil's blush deepened even further as he wrestled his control back, channeling the excess out to the window.

"I wish I'd fucking met you earlier."

"You've said that before."

"What, do you not?"

"I think I've only just realized how much I hate the prohibition on the photos." Kirin pressed against Adil's shoulder, taking the pen out of his hands. The lines that Adil had written were so fluid, almost like flames themselves in the way they curled and flowed. It was fitting, but hard to mimic for someone with as poor handwriting as Kirin. "I know I've seen one photo of you as a kid, but I wish I could see them all."

"Don't have any from before then." Adil leaned their heads together and started flicking Kirin's hand every time his script veered from the correct version. "Pressure took loads after though. Still got all that shit back at our house."

"And you'll let me see?"

Adil made a noncommittal grunt, not promising anything.

"Maybe we can visit your mom at some point, so I can see some of your shit too." He was being forcibly casual about it, but the way his eyes flickered was enough to convince Kirin that Adil really wanted to meet her.

The idea had never even occurred to Kirin of Adil coming into their house, sitting at their table, cooking in their kitchen. Maybe those old walls would actually feel like home that way. What would his mother do? Would she actually come out of her office? Would she look Kirin in the eye?

"I'd pay money to see you try on my old firefighter's jacket." Kirin shook off the memories, though one caught on the edge, a nearer one, something he'd shut away the year before. "Actually, I do have one photo I can show you."

Adil sat up straight, not even pretending to be disinterested this time.

It took Kirin a moment to remember where he'd put it, since he hadn't dared take it out again after the first few months.

Hadn't dared or hadn't wanted to? He put away the thought. He eventually found it tucked between the pages of a book, the very first book that Adil had lent him, one that he *had* read, just on his phone instead. The reflective surface of the photo was slightly fractured from the folds it'd suffered from being shoved in his pocket, though they looked less prominent now, like the pages had smoothed away the damage Kirin had done.

Adil crept up to Kirin's shoulder, already searching the picture for every detail.

"Your dad looks a lot fucking less terrifying here." Adil was attempting to keep his voice light, yet his hand was tense as he reached for the image. Kirin passed it over, all the faces ingrained in his mind already. Hyeon-soo's carefree laugh was captured there, nothing like the haunted visage they'd worn hours earlier.

"I'd imagine most people look less scary alive than dead." The sun was officially above the tree line, the light shining directly through the window and lighting up Adil's skin with gold. He looked so much more like a portrait than the faded photo clasped in his hands, so much more alive than that dim countryside had ever been.

"Was he..." Adil's voice faltered. "Was he always like that?"

Even as he looked back at Kirin with burning eyes, Kirin could see he was fading quickly. All his adrenaline gone, the softness in his gaze, the way his lashes trailed on his cheek as he blinked slower than usual; all the signs were there that he was about to pass out.

"Let's lie down before I get into that, okay?" And since his last attempt at being bold had paid off so spectacularly, Kirin did one of the things he'd always wanted to do. He took Adil's ignition rings off, letting the pads of his fingers trail up Adil's hands slowly. One hand he did, then the other, this time crystallizing the tips so that Adil could feel the gentle brush through his too-thick skin. Adil's ears went red as Kirin did, and he couldn't stop the smile that unfurled across his face as he pulled them both to bed.

As Kirin lay there, hair spilling across the top of the pillow and over the edge, Adil held the photo up to his face, crimson eyes flicking back and forth between the old and the new.

"Your hair was short back then. Can't even tell the fucking color."

"Mhm." Kirin touched Adil's hair as he spoke, running his fingers through the curls. "I started growing it out to hide the scars better."

"You shouldn't fucking hide them." Adil frowned. "They really are beautiful."

Kirin was spared from trying to respond to that by Adil remembering his earlier question.

"Your dad?"

He buried his face in Adil's neck, crushing the hand holding the photo between their chests.

"We were close." Would pressing a kiss to the side of his throat count as a violation of Adil's no-kissing-until-tomorrow rule? Kirin didn't want to push too far when everything was so new. Tomorrow was a bubble in his chest, a promise of hope and happiness and love, and he could wait to make sure it stayed that way. "I think that's why it was so hard."

Adil clumsily extricated one of his arms to wrap around Kirin, pressing them even more firmly together.

"Like I told you before, when I was little a few folks got it into their heads that I was a great way to make money. And where we lived... they didn't protect kids like me very well. My dad tried to report it to the police a few times, but they never did much. So we just moved around a lot at first. Hopping town to town until we found a place remote enough or unimportant enough that they didn't bother to follow. Only Hyeon-soo was born before we settled in, and they were still so little I don't think they remember much of it at all."

"Remind me to ask about all your other siblings' names." Adil's voice was slurred from drowsiness.

"I will." Kirin satisfied himself with giving Adil another squeeze, though the desire to kiss him again was strengthened by the way Adil snuggled closer. "Even after it seemed like the danger had passed, my dad was very overprotective of me, of all of us, but me especially. I think it's lucky that none of the others had their miens present until he was gone, because I think the stress of it would've sent him over the edge."

"The reason he was so against you using your mien..."

"He just didn't want me to be found again." Even though the sun was now shining fully, he closed his eyes, turning the world into shades of red and pink. It reminded him of Adil. "You telling me that he was just trying to control me made me realize it, I think. I'd already started thinking about how I could help other people like me, and even though it was a long time until I considered becoming a hero, I think he could see where that path would lead. He didn't like heroes generally, anyways. Always said there was a lot more good to be done by helping the people around you, instead of beating up someone you don't know."

"Maybe... I wouldn't have fucking hated him... entirely." Adil's breath was hot on Kirin's hair, each word an exhale.

"I think he would've loved you." For the first time, Kirin seriously considered asking Adlivun if she could still see his father around. Maybe they could meet. Maybe there was a way for Adil to get to talk to him, get to know him. Tears threatened to prick at Kirin's eyes, grief uncomplicated for the first time. "My mom would yell at you relentlessly, but that just means that she likes you."

"I'll... cook her... something."

"She'd like that. Hyeon-soo's a rotten chef, and they started cooking right after I started working full-time. I think one of the twins had started learning just so the food would be edible..."

"They won't... have to.... I'll take care of... all of you." After that last sentence, Adil's breathing slowed, all the tension finally dropping away from his frame. Kirin almost felt mad that he'd said something so sweet and then promptly *fell asleep* so Kirin couldn't even properly hug him. Alone, with a well of affection bubbling up so strongly, his tears finally fell. Maybe it was for the best that Adil was asleep, as Kirin couldn't even think of the words he would've said, any way he could've made Adil realize what that would mean to him.

Was that even possible? After graduation, could they go and collect Kirin's family, bring them somewhere close by, somewhere they could visit on the weekends? Hyeon-soo had proven that they were already compromised; could there be an exception where Kirin and Adil and his siblings could live together instead?

Tomorrow truly was made of hope. As something fragile fixed itself in Kirin's chest, something inside him whispered that there was a way out of this, that there was a path forward. As he watched the light climb up the wall, Kirin pressed a kiss to Ifrit's curls.

After all, it was already tomorrow, wasn't it?

27

Have Hope

When Ifrit woke up, Kirin wasn't there.

His heart plummeted to his feet immediately. He'd decided that yesterday was a mistake. That his family was more important. Would Kirin even still be at East Tech? Maybe he'd just left entirely, with Ifrit having ruined even their friendship with his want. He should've kissed Kirin more; he shouldn't have kissed him at all.

It was into this self-pity spiral that the door opened, Kirin walking in as quietly as he could, carrying a tray of food.

He was so focused on not dropping any of the dishes, his hair pulled fully up and back, his dark brows pressed together in concentration, that he almost dropped everything altogether when he noticed that Ifrit was awake.

"No, no, don't get up!" Kirin sounded upset. "I thought you'd sleep for longer."

Ifrit didn't let himself speak, the tightness in his chest hardly lifting as he watched Kirin bustle around, grabbing a stack of textbooks to prop up the food.

"I'll be right back." Kirin disappeared back through the door, leaving Ifrit to stare at the food laid out before him. It wasn't altogether odd for Kirin to cook for them, but he usually made simple foods, and while it always tasted good, it never looked fancy. But here were fluffy pancakes, fruit cut into stars, rolled omelets, and perfectly round rice balls all laid out neatly. It looked like it had come straight out of a picture from a magazine, not something that had been made in their shitty dorm kitchen.

Ifrit had been so focused on the food that he hadn't noticed Kirin return until he gently set down a cup overflowing with whipped cream.

"I know you usually go for coffee, but since the goal of today is to rest, I made hot chocolate instead." Kirin's smile was genuine, though there was a faint hesitation, a slight anxiety hidden behind it. "And I know you don't really like sweet things in the morning, but it's not really morning anymore, so I thought it'd be fine, but if you want something else I can—"

"How fucking long did it take you to make this?" That hadn't even been the question Ifrit wanted to ask; he'd intended to check if he'd hallucinated the night before, like he'd created the memory of Kirin kissing him all those months ago. Yet the words wouldn't come.

"Hm?" Kirin's eyes darted to the food like he'd forgotten it was there. "Only an hour or so, I haven't been up that long."

"This fucking looks incredible." Ifrit leaned forward slowly. "Where did you even get this shit?"

"I borrowed some ingredients from Dulu and Medusa, and the tray Ness uses for movie nights." Kirin shifted. "Do you like it?"

Fuck this man.

"Of fucking course I like it, but why did you do all this?" Ifrit heard his own words too late and rushed to correct them. "It's great and it looks fucking professional, but you didn't have to—"

"I wanted to." Kirin was *blushing*. That needed to be illegal. It needed to be illegal immediately. He always flushed so completely it made him *glow*. That wasn't fair. "We, um, well we're unlikely to get a pass off campus any time soon and even though we're stuck in the dorm all day I thought we could, I mean, if you wanted to, we could maybe..."

Kirin cleared his throat.

"We could maybe make this a date?" When he finally looked back up, the anxiety was back, his eyes flickering between Ifrit's own.

"I want to." It was ridiculous how buoyant Ifrit felt, how the pain in his chest could suddenly turn to joy, to something disgustingly warm and gooey. The way Kirin perked up, the smile that unfurled across his face, it was all too cute. Ifrit wanted to shove a pillow in his face so he wasn't blinded.

Instead, he turned to the food and stuffed his face, hoping his own red cheeks weren't noticeable.

It wasn't until after he'd devoured the entire plate of pancakes that he noticed Kirin wasn't eating.

"Aren't you gonna?" Ifrit gestured to the feast in front of them.

"I'll have whatever you don't want." Kirin shrugged, leaning against the foot of the bed and smiling. "You need the food more than me after yesterday, plus I snacked a lot when I was cooking."

If Ifrit hadn't been so hungry he would've absolutely protested, but after the first few bites, he'd realized he was starving. And everything was so *good* too. When the fuck had Kirin learned to cook like this?

As if reading his thoughts, Kirin answered.

"If you like stuff like this, I can make more. I used to work part-time at a café for a while; it's not all that hard to do." The casual mention of his former life was the only thing that felt different from any other day. Kirin had moved to the desk for a minute, pulling up some movie or another, or maybe one of the tv shows they'd been in the middle of watching. When was the last time they'd had a spare minute to watch anything?

"Only if you fucking show me how to do it too." Ifrit was glad Kirin was looking away, since it felt far too embarrassing a statement when Ifrit remembered *how* most cooking scenes in books went. Or at least the books that Lilin had recommended him when she'd found out they liked a few of the same romance authors.

"Anytime you want." Kirin finally made his way back to the bed, curling up behind Ifrit and resting his chin on Ifrit's shoulder. "You tell me when."

Ifrit didn't realize that finding out Kirin felt the same would make him *more* susceptible to goosebumps and not less, feeling them erupt on his arms when Kirin's breath brushed his cheek. Ifrit shouldn't have even been able to feel it, yet he was hyper aware of their closeness, of how one of Kirin's hands was resting idly on Ifrit's waist, the other at the edge of the bed with his fingers drumming.

Ifrit went to take a sip of the hot chocolate, trying to insist it was because the whipped cream was melting fast and not to give himself an escape, but Kirin stole it out of his hands. Kirin took a long sip, leaving him with a horrible milk mustache.

"You've fucking got shit on your face." *Don't think about helping him get it off, don't think about helping him get it off.*

"Oh, do I?" Kirin asked far too innocently.

"Mm."

"I would get it, but I don't have any hands to." Kirin lifted a shoulder in a casual shrug. Was that an invitation? Ifrit felt the tips of his ears burning.

"I can't fucking reach your face from this angle." His arms were trapped, true. And the other option... nope, that was way too cheesy. No way.

"You sure?" Kirin was *pouting*. Ifrit was going to put his head through the wall.

"I haven't brushed my fucking teeth yet." Ifrit was definitely blushing now. He hadn't even meant to suggest—

"I don't mind!" Kirin had the audacity to smile. Asshole.

"That's gross."

"You should know I'm kind of gross by now." Anxiety was back on Kirin's face, though he was hiding it well. Shit. Ifrit was being stupid again. It was fine. They could just... do this now.

Even though it had very much been Kirin's idea, he still seemed surprised when Ifrit kissed him. There was that moment of hesitation, that pause before the brain caught up, and then the pressure was returned, the taste of chocolate filling Ifrit's senses. Kirin must've put the cup down, as one of his hands came up to touch the side of Ifrit's face gently, oh so gently. When they broke apart, there was still cream on Kirin's face.

"You missed, I think," Kirin whispered, since they were just centimeters apart.

"Was this whole fucking bit just to get a kiss?" What did it say about Ifrit that he was hoping it was? He really was absolutely whipped. "You could've just fucking *asked,* dumbass."

"The food was just because I wanted you to eat." Kirin wiped the offending cream off his lip with his thumb and licked it, which made Ifrit grateful he'd already been red since his ears felt like they were on fire. "The hot chocolate was because you really shouldn't have coffee if you're trying to rest. But the whipped cream *was* me trying to get one, without having to ask."

How could he just *admit* things like that so easily?

"What do you want to do for the rest of the day?" Suddenly Kirin was moving away, sitting up taller and stealing a piece of pineapple. "I pulled up a few of your favorite movies, but we could read instead. I'm almost caught up to you in that one audiobook so we can talk about it."

"Why did you back up?" Ifrit really needed more sleep. His thoughts were slipping out too easily.

Yet Kirin looked delighted.

"I'm just going to put something on; I'm not going far."

Ifrit hated that he still wanted to protest, that just across the room *was* too far. But he bit his tongue and watched Kirin scroll through the options, a piece of his hair falling out of his bun and into his eyes. The mid-afternoon light cut across his face at an angle, making him even more golden than normal. How many times had Ifrit seen Kirin like that, seen Kirin give that quick smile over his shoulder, felt that painful tug in his chest? How many times had he forced himself to look away, to tell himself that his best friend didn't feel the same? And how was it at all possible that he'd been wrong and could have *this* now?

He was on his feet before he knew it, and Kirin didn't have time to form words before Ifrit grabbed his hair and pulled himself up to crush their mouths together.

Kirin responded faster this time, though in his surprise he stumbled slightly and fell onto the desk, making them the same height. Ifrit still tasted chocolate on Kirin's lips, smelled the sugar from the cream on his skin, but all that was secondary to the way their mouths fit together. Ifrit tugged, bringing him ever closer, feeling the hitch in Kirin's breath from the motion. Ifrit had *some* practice in kissing, but it had never been like this never— felt like his nerves had been set on fire, never felt so desperate or so *nice*, never made Ifrit dig his hands in like his life depended on it. Kirin's own hands had fallen onto Ifrit's hips, and from the gentle scratch, Ifrit knew before he opened his eyes that Kirin's would be opal white.

"Sorry!" Kirin's eyes were wide, fear chasing away yearning, though his lips were still bright red. "I didn't realize I had—"

Ifrit crushed their faces together, their noses bumping, biting off the words before Kirin could spiral any further. Kirin had a hand on Ifrit's shoulder now, as if considering pushing him away, but when Ifrit— not even intentionally— ran his teeth along Kirin's bottom lip it earned the smallest groan, and Kirin's hand fisted in Ifrit's shirt slashed the fabric as Kirin fought to regain control.

"You *can't* hurt me." When Ifrit finally ran out of air, he grabbed Kirin's jaw and smashed their foreheads together. "Don't fucking apologize, just don't *stop*."

The hair tie holding Kirin's bun had been pulled out, the light glinting off Kirin's hair as he stared at Ifrit in awe, despite the fact that *he* was the one glowing. Ifrit couldn't even *look* at him a second longer, pulling them back together, pushing Kirin further back onto the desk until his back hit the wall. Kirin— for someone who claimed to never have done anything like this before— was frustratingly good at it, not even having the fucking courtesy to be clumsy. He was slow and gentle, but Ifrit wanted to shake him until he lost his composure, until he felt as desperate as Ifrit did. But he was shoved away as Kirin's whole face crystallized.

"Sorry, sorry!" Kirin's skin returned to normal after a moment, his chest heaving. His hair was mussed, his cheeks bright red, his eyes still opalescent, patches of his skin shifting between diamond and rich ochre. "There's just— I mean you just give off so much carbon and normally I can regulate it but it's just... *really* hard to concentrate."

The smile Kirin gave him nearly sent Ifrit to his knees. It was one part shy, embarrassment seeping in, and the other absolutely adoring, his eyes shining in a way that had nothing to do with his mien.

"I don't fucking care." Ifrit put his hand on Kirin's shoulder, right over one of his scars, feeling the ridges through the fabric.

"Fuck, I don't care."

"I don't want to cut your lip." Kirin brushed the pad of his thumb over Ifrit's bottom lip, his eyes flickering up to Ifrit's before dropping back down to his mouth.

"I don't care."

"I do." Kirin's brows drew together. "I don't want to—"

Ifrit bit Kirin's lip.

Kirin both very clearly hadn't been expecting it, and from the way he clapped a hand over his mouth and the blush that spread all the way to his ears, he wasn't expecting to enjoy it so much. Or at least enjoy it so *loudly*.

"It's fucking *hot*, dumbass." Ifrit was having trouble thinking now too, and even though it was summer, he wished they'd left the window open to get a breeze. It was far too hot in there. "I don't give a shit if you're too fucking sharp, because I want to feel all of you."

Kirin looked like he might have finally understood when the door burst open.

"Fucking WHAT now?!" Ifrit whirled toward the door, temper flaring. Kirin was on his feet instantly, the edges of his arms subtly crystallizing as it took them a moment to register who was standing in the doorway.

"Clidna?" The worry in Kirin's voice was apparent. If she was there, something had to have gone wrong in class and—

"Oh, you're both here." Her voice came out wrong, too deep and without the dry edge she never noticed using. A moment later her face was gone entirely, freckles and round chin replaced by days old stubble and dark bags. "Yantra took care of the cameras then? I swear you kids can't keep your hands off one another."

In an instant, Ifrit remembered what the room looked like. Stuffing still clumped on the floor, food laid out neatly on the bed, Ifrit's shirt ripped, and Kirin's face red; it hardly took any brain power at all to realize what had happened. What had been happening before the door opened.

"These doors need better fucking locks," Ifrit muttered, at the same time as Kirin said, "Shifter."

His mien entirely released, Shifter looked like shit. He always looked like he hadn't gotten enough sleep— something Ifrit couldn't be sure was intentional or not— but now he also looked like he'd been hit by a car that was carting around dirt and garbage and then got dropped in a sewer.

"Has something happened?" Kirin was still flushed, but he dropped into hero mode effortlessly.

"Not yet." Shifter closed the door behind himself, eyes sweeping the room like there might be someone hiding in there with them. "And I hope to keep it that way as long as possible, which is why I'm here."

"Be less cryptic," Ifrit snapped.

"Have you made any progress on the assassinations?" Shifter's eyes flickered between them.

"We've got a way in, but she hasn't found out much yet." Kirin's tone was reconciliatory, which made Ifrit bristle more.

"But she probably fucking won't for a bit because one of Majesty's students just fucking died."

"What?" Shifter hadn't been expecting that. From the surprise on Kirin's face, Ifrit had forgotten to mention it to him, too.

"Was it the same as—"

"No. That's the weird fucking thing."

Shifter's anxiety wasn't as physical as Kirin's or Ifrit's. There were no hurried movements, no need to shake out the fear and energy. Instead, he went stock still, as if he was frozen in place.

"When was this?"

"Sometime yesterday. They were missing when we boarded

the plane back." Kirin smoothly filled in.

"And you knew everyone else's whereabouts at the time?"

"No, actually." Kirin sat back down on the desk, rubbing his forehead. "We lost track of everyone. There was a… blackout."

"They made a new fucking dead zone."

Shifter's face briefly went blurry.

"I see."

"Why?"

"There were three more coalition murders yesterday."

"Who?"

"You wouldn't know their names. They were all quiet members, diplomats, not outspoken, out of need. They were slated to speak at the upcoming Mien-User Summit."

"Isn't that soon?"

Shifter nodded.

"Too soon to find replacements?"

"In a manner of speaking." Shifter's eyes flickered around again. "They've asked me to fill in."

"Aren't you in fucking hiding?" Ifrit's annoyance was building again. If Shifter had just *been there,* Ifrit never would've had to talk to Majesty. Never would've had to sneak around, feel Valor's anger up close. "Is it really a fucking good idea for you to go to such a fucking public event?"

"If the coalition can push its goals at this congress, then yes, it would be a great idea. We have representatives from all major nations, and some of those countries with the most restrictive mien regulations are attending, all with the goal of providing new comprehensive policies that are more equitable. *This* is what Pressure was trying to accomplish, and if it takes me dying to make it happen, that's worth it." Shifter was only a few centimeters shorter than Ifrit, a change that Ifrit had never noticed before. Then again, Shifter had never gotten *angry* before, never tried to get into Ifrit's face before. He realized it too, his face softening as he took a step back. "I don't mean to sound accusatory, especially when I've kept you in the dark about all this, but it *is* worth it."

"What do you want us to do?" Kirin didn't fully step between them, but the way he positioned himself, he might as well have. It was strange how he managed to be so calming despite being so tall, so reassuring despite looking like he could rip a man in half.

"I need people I can trust." Shifter looked regretful. "But I still don't want to put you kids in the middle of this."

"We're already there." Kirin's voice was soft and sad. Ifrit couldn't stop himself from looking up, from seeing the melancholy that swept across Kirin's face.

"You're on the edge, just out of the eye." Shifter rubbed a hand across his face. "But you know, sometimes that's the worst place to be. Able to see it all and yet not do a damn thing."

"Do you want us to fucking guard the summit?" Ifrit was honestly surprised he hadn't asked sooner.

"There will be police." Shifter's tone was acerbic. "They've been less inclined to allow large operations within the city since last year."

"That's why it's us and not professionals." Kirin made it sound so reasonable. "Students, there as a symbolic presence as it was Pressure who created the idea of it in the first place. A ceremonial send off for her and what she stood for."

"That definitely could work." Shifter looked less tired suddenly.

"What sort of trouble are you expecting? The diplomats are coming here, aren't they? Since the island's isolated right now?"

"Aether is always a concern, especially since their movements have been so sporadic. They've been making it between countries with alarming speed and many of the politicians are bringing their own security. I wouldn't be surprised if half of the bodyguards in the audience are plants by the time they arrive on the island."

"Is that an educated guess or have you just been spending so much time with the fucking scumbags they tell you everything now?"

"I'm the coordinator, officially, which includes security measures. The city itself insisted on the police force, and I don't trust half the active heroes right now. Most of those I would've tapped have been found dead, and the others are trying to keep from presenting a target."

Kirin and Ifrit exchanged a look then, one that decided immediately they would not be telling Shifter about the attempt on their lives if he didn't already know.

"Wait, why the fuck are you the replacement for some country's politicians?"

Shifter, for the first time since Ifrit had known him, smiled.

Of course, Irit had seen him grimace before, and laugh a few times at Pressure's horrible dad jokes, but he'd never seen this sort of sad smile, one that was entirely self-pitying. He decided that he hated it.

"I grew up in Kazakhstan. The first few years of my career after college I made sure to get assigned there. I didn't come back here until Pressure asked, about eight years ago." Shifter didn't look at Ifrit, but he didn't have to. Ifrit could still remember the first day they met. "The victims in question, one of them was my cousin. She had a similar mien to mine, but couldn't control it. Spent her whole life not knowing what her true face looked like. And she was crushed so completely we couldn't even find out in death."

"I—"

"My country is kinder to people with miens than most. It's a harsh climate; we don't have time to be harsh with one another. Whoever did this, they knew that my people would not have backed down until they were heard." It took practice to notice when Shifter started to use his mien, but the way the glassiness of his eyes vanished suddenly was enough for someone who was looking. "They were willing to die for this, and I will make sure it wasn't in vain."

"It could be..." Kirin cleared his throat, looking at the ceiling instead of either of them. "It could be the opportunity we need."

"We're not going to leave a fucking opening—"

"Of course not." The flicker of hurt was gone from Kirin's face so quickly, but Ifrit hated that he could've even suggested it. "But I assume it'll be announced that you're taking their places? At least to the other diplomats?"

"This is an open forum, and open means that everyone who is speaking is listed by full name and country of origin." Shifter stood a little straighter. "My cousin, she was the last living family I had. I've already cleared it with the Hero Council; I don't have to step down even though my name and face will be revealed."

"Good thing you can fucking change your face." Ifrit didn't mean it.

"It should be good for you, too, if you ever need to do something like this." Shifter looked straight at Ifrit, dark eyes meeting red. "I have all the information about the coalition's plans at your house. Should anything happen, you'll be able to find it and all the contacts that I've made worldwide."

"*Nothing's* going to happen." The word came out as a hiss.

"If anyone tries anything, we can catch them." Kirin finished his thought from before. "Ness hasn't been able to get that much information from Inanna, and with this news it sounds like they're escalating. Ideally, we wouldn't have Shifter in the public eye at all, but since he's going to be anyway, we can stop all of this by stopping them now."

"And you really don't fucking think Aether is going to do anything?" Ifrit ignored the idea that they'd have to stop someone at all.

"They can't get here. The only way in is by jet and no other planes are allowed the week of the summit."

"We'll be prepared, even if they try anything." Kirin squeezed Ifrit's shoulder. "One way or another, these murders end in a week."

28

An Improvement

"...SO I TOOK ALL the scans I'd done on *you* previously, and then ran a few more on myself after sleeping, running, eating, so on and so forth, and then averaged all those frequencies to find one that I believe could work. I also did some basic research on if there are known differences between the vibrational frequencies of people of various genders, but there weren't any conclusive studies that pointed one way or another." Nwabudike proudly held out a new, undented cube to Kirin. "Bhuta Vahana Yantra has been terribly helpful in making final decisions and minor adjustments, and I believe we have it."

Ness materialized from nowhere, reaching out with shaking hands.

"How do I turn it on?" She looked nervous and tired, neither of which were surprising. They all did, recently.

"There's a thumbprint key on the bottom right on that face—yes, there you go!"

Nwabudike's exclamation was unnecessary as suddenly Ness was there.

Kirin had never really noticed the difference between someone being *there* and *mostly there* before, but when the cube lit up, Ness suddenly felt real, like he'd only been watching a movie before, and now the actors were right on stage before him.

Her hair was dark brown, curling around a round face in waves, light freckles dotting deeply tanned skin. Her eyes were brown too, but now that the distortion was gone Kirin could see the iris as distinct from the pupil. When she ran her hand down her face, then across the table and her sweater, tears gathered in her eyes, which looked impossibly crisp.

"Ness." She looked up at Kirin wordlessly, eyes wide. "Are you okay?"

"Yeah." She broke into a huge smile. "Yeah, I'm great."

"No side effects? No feeling of nausea, dizziness, pain, discomfort— anything?" Nwabudike circled her, looking for any spot that didn't look quite solid.

"No, no, it's—" Ness broke off with a sniff. "It's better than I could've ever hoped for."

"Don't be ridiculous, this is only the beginning!" Nwabudike's grin, now that he'd confirmed it was working, was effusive. "The design of the device isn't ideal, but without further study I didn't want to adjust it too much lest it effect the functionality. In the future, I hope to make it more wearable since you do need to have skin to skin contact to make it work. I'm envisioning bracelets on each arm and one on each ankle to spread out the load, and therefore make the mechanism smaller. The other issue—"

The color on the box blinked out.

"—is the power requirement."

Kirin had expected Ness to fade immediately, but she stayed largely solid, just the tiniest blur reappearing.

"That's okay— I just never thought anything would work." Her smile remained as she handed Nwabudike back the now dead-looking cube.

"I admit I don't think I could've thought this up so quickly if I hadn't been given an already mostly completed design, but there is almost always a way once you know to look." Nwabudike placed the cube on a charging block, the lights overhead flickering once, twice, before stabilizing. "As you can see, even running it for a short amount of time requires an enormous amount of power. I think the more spread out design could help alleviate this too."

"That explains why we kept finding Aether at generators." Ness pulled herself up onto the drafting table and sat down cross-legged. "Probably were trying to siphon energy to that."

"Also explains how the woman in white kept getting away." Kirin nodded.

"Yeah, did you have to reverse any of the mechanics to make it stabilize rather than disappear?" Ness looked over at Nwabudike.

"Oh, this on its own couldn't make anyone disappear." He shook his head. "And the program that I recovered was very similar to the one Bhuta Vahana Yantra created for your device."

"How much more energy?"

"Enough to power a city, certainly. To *match* with the universe is much easier than to go against it, and the requisite energy components for both reflect that. To change the vibration of billions of molecules— the amount that make up *you*— still requires great effort, but far less than if you were trying to force them out of phase. No, this was always intended to stabilize."

"Yantra was wrong then?" Kirin didn't believe it himself; whatever Yantra was holding back about what she knew, she seemed very convinced of it. "The woman in white has the same problem you do?"

"Unless she was using the generator to mimic my mien." Ness looked disturbed. "I don't recommend it though. I pulled Yantra with me *once* and she vomited."

"Following right in Futurus' footsteps." Kirin remembered that Nwabudike was still right there, though he was dashing back and forth, tinkering with various projects. "Did you fix your problem with them?"

When Nwabudike looked confused, Kirin gestured to his legs.

"You're practically running around and there's not even a sound."

"Oh!" Nwabudike looked pleased. "Yes, actually! I finally got approval from the school to upgrade them as a thank you for the contributions I've made lately. Although personally I think it was just because the poor folks on either side of me kept complaining about hearing me walk around while they were working. I've had the actual braces designed and built for months, but, well, if I try to change anything with the neural interface without approval, I get... shocked. To put it simply. It's a rather ingenious measure to ensure that I'm upholding my censure without needing to have me monitored constantly. It gives me my privacy and them their peace of mind, so who am I to complain?"

He shrugged as if that weren't a horrible thing.

"Neural interface?" Ness looked at him.

"Ah." Nwabudike flinched as if he realized what he'd said belatedly. "Oh, well, I don't suppose you'll think badly of me, though I'm not supposed to talk about it."

"Well, now you have to or it's rude." Ness was joking, though Nwabudike didn't seem to realize it.

"The braces. I designed them after I was paralyzed in an accident when I was much younger. Human experimentation, as you well know, is highly illegal, even if you are doing it on yourself. I was supposed to go to jail, but the university intervened and asked that I be placed under house arrest here, where I could still help advance world tech, though under close watch."

"You do it *yourself*?" Kirin couldn't help the horror that crept into his voice. "They don't get you a doctor?"

"Oh, no, not me." He waved Kirin over to the worktop and pressed a button. A panel in the ceiling moved, revealing multiple robotic arms with various tools at the ends. Several were conspicuously missing their digits, terminating in empty ports instead. "I have a recorded sequence that goes in here and it does it for me! I don't think I'd trust any doctor to do it anyway, it's very complicated if you can believe it. I'm only allowed all of my tools if I've given the school advance notice of precisely what I'm going to use them for— Kirin, you remember the day I reconnected your prosthetic— and then they are held for safekeeping until I get approval again."

"Cybernetics is an approved field of research though; why were they so worried about what you successfully did on your own?" Ness looked angry, though she was beginning to thin at the edges again.

"Branching the divide between man and technology is still not quite allowed, and with *how* people have been going about it, I don't entirely blame the government for being prickly. Just a few years ago there were reports of a whole school of children being experimented on being discovered, all without miens but attempting to replicate them. A far cruder option than what Futurus was running, especially since it was caught within five years of opening. I suppose the great fear is that I won't be content with just walking again and try to get my mien back, and then start giving it to other people."

"Wait, what?" Nwabudike looked at Kirin in confusion. "Get your mien back?"

"Oh!" He waved a hand as if it weren't important. "Before my accident, I had super speed."

"Just that?" Ness snorted.

"Yes, I'll admit I was disappointed. I wanted the ability to read faster or just not have to sleep, or best yet, be a technopath. I wasn't much of an outdoorsy kid so running very quickly wasn't as exciting for me as it probably should have been." Nwabudike turned back to his computer, idly waving a hand. "I just wanted to be able to walk and move about my lab with ease, but all these government folks, they're so obsessed with what they *think* you value, not what you tell them you do."

"That's definitely true." Kirin normally never tried to look at Nwabudike's notes, but a small handwritten scribble in the corner of the screen caught his eye. "What does that mean, there?"

The note read: *communicating with what?*

"Ah! Yes, that was something that I almost missed, and it wasn't until I was confirming the functionality of our replicated one that I noticed it." Nwabudike produced a tiny pair of pliers and used them to point. "This."

"Are we supposed to be seeing something?" Ness made Nwabudike jump as she suddenly appeared over his shoulder, looking at the scan he was pointing at.

"Yes and no. There is nothing that we would be able to see normally, however—" he enlarged a part of the image, magnifying it so many times that the surrounding wires began to look alien— "this is a microscopic transmitter."

"Can you trace back to what it's transmitting to?" Kirin's heartbeat picked up.

"I'm already working on it. The encryption is impossible for me to decipher, so I have Bhuta Vahana Yantra looking into it."

"She's very good." Ness smiled to herself.

"That she is." Nwabudike became thoughtful. "I don't suppose she'll crack it before you all move out though, will she?"

Ness and Kirin looked at one another, not sure how to respond.

"It should be an easy enough mission." Ness decided to put on a brave face, ignoring the stress they'd all been feeling as the weekend drew to a close. "There are plenty of us, and we're just the ceremonial back-up anyway."

"I still wish I could be of more help to you all, that I could help predict what Aether is planning." Nwabudike suddenly looked young to Kirin, like a child who had just woken from a bad dream. "I can't do much from in here—"

"You do more than enough." Kirin interrupted him, feeling his heart wrench as he recognized the helplessness in his tone. "All the help you've given— it truly can't be overstated."

"And you're the only one who has ever offered me hope before too." Ness squeezed his shoulder, flickering into existence again. "You can't put a price on that."

"Still..." Nwabudike looked at the screen again. "I'll get back to work on this from my end. You go out and save the world."

"You should stop by our dorm afterward." Ness had already vanished by the time Kirin thought to offer, mostly out of regret for having to leave so suddenly after they'd arrived. "We'd all love to see you there."

Nwabudike couldn't hide the longing that flew across his face.

"I... I'll see if I can come up with an excuse as to why I'd need to stop by. Maybe I can say we're doing regular testing throughout the day." He pulled up some schematics of Kirin himself, a few additions to the suit standing out in bright red. "Yes... I think I could find a reason to stop in."

"Don't be a stranger, then." Kirin only hesitated a moment before ruffling his hair, the afro bouncing gently after he let go.

Nwabudike's smile followed Kirin into the hallway as he headed back to his building full of friends, leaving behind that small room built for only one.

29

Oh Shit

THE HARDEST PART ABOUT dating in a college that expressly forbid relationships was trying not to jump your partner in public. And Kirin's hero costume did *not* help at all.

If Kirin had told Ifrit that he was adding red detailing to his costume, Ifrit would've been flattered but told him no fucking way. Instead, Ifrit had shown up to their meeting entirely unaware, and had been absolutely blasted by the sight of Kirin with his fucking *boob window cut-out* now delicately outlined in red as well as gold. And Ifrit knew for fucking *certain* that Kirin had picked the color, as it just so happened to be the same shade as Ifrit's eyes.

"Everyone in position?" Kirin, for his part, looked utterly calm and in control, his hair pulled back and his muscles rippling as he stretched out his back, one hand on his earpiece. The two of them were waiting for Shifter outside one of the tech buildings, while the rest of the class was already in position at the assembly hall. The smaller the entourage, the less attention they would draw, hopefully.

"*We're all set. Just waiting on you two.*" Yantra's voice came through as clearly as if she'd been standing directly next to them, which was to say, slightly muffled. Ifrit probably needed new hearing aids at this point, considering all the abuse his had put up with for the past year.

"Shifter's coming to us now, we'll keep you updated on our progress as we make our way there." Kirin gave Ifrit's arm one last squeeze before the door opened behind them. If they hadn't gone over the meeting place five fucking times, Ifrit wouldn't have known it was Shifter at all. He'd switched to very light, almost white, hair, watery blue eyes, and pale, pale skin. Ironically, despite looking positively geriatric, he seemed rested, for once.

"Diplomats arriving already?" Shifter's posture was tense, his eyes flicking back and forth as if he expected someone to dart out from one of the tech buildings and take a shot at him. That would be ironic, considering he'd insisted they meet there to avoid such a thing from happening.

"Yes." Yantra's voice crackled in Ifrit's ear.

"Yantra said yeah." Ifrit was scanning the paths as they walked, but so early in the morning there were few people milling about. It was just after the break of dawn, which felt too early to start an international congress, but apparently all parties just wanted to get it over with. A great attitude to have for a momentous occasion.

"Good." Shifter rarely did anything quickly, cautious to the point of irritation, but he was moving fast through campus, walking as swiftly as he could without breaking into a run. "What're the numbers on their security details?"

"At least two bodyguards per representative, but I wouldn't count on them in a fight." Yantra sent a ping to Ifrit's phone and he opened it only to find his lip curling in disgust. *"We better hope Aether doesn't show because if they pull their blackout act again, we're on our own."*

"They didn't." Kirin looked over Ifrit's shoulder and his face fell, his eyes flashing.

"They sure did." Yantra's voice was quiet now, and from the faint sounds Ifrit could make out, she seemed to be walking past a group of people. The thought of a crowd brought the first twinges of anxiety to Ifrit's stomach. A fight he could do. Crowds, maybe not.

"I'm not surprised." Shifter's voice pulled Ifrit's attention back to the present. "While most governments did seize the powersuits that Futurus created, they didn't destroy them. Why would they? It's a convenient and cheap solution to protect your politicians, cheaper than hiring real heroes whose prices are inflated by the virtue of very few licensed officials existing."

Ifrit only grunted in return, knowing it was far too early to be this pissed off.

They walked in silence the rest of the way to the gate, where an unfamiliar car was waiting for them. Ifrit felt his shoulders lower marginally away from his ears. He wasn't sure if he'd have been able to stand it if they were supposed to take Pressure's car, even though technically it was Shifter's now.

He was surprised further when Kirin got into the front seat.

"The fuck's he doing?" The words slipped out.

"Driving." Shifter reached out of the backseat and pulled Ifrit in, strong despite his outwardly frail appearance.

"But why's—"

"Considering we're here to prevent a potential assassination, it seemed like a bad idea to have a civilian driver." Kirin turned to look at them once, the way his eyes curved promising he was smiling. "I'm rather bulletproof."

As he turned back, Kirin slid a divider between the front and the rear of car, a dull tap showing how thick it was. No wonder they'd taken a different car; this one was reinforced.

"And you don't have a license," Shifter added rather unnecessarily.

"I live in a city, why the fuck would I need a license?" Ifrit crossed his arms and tried to ignore how childish that had sounded. Shifter, to his credit, didn't point it out and assumed a silent vigil at the window, posture tense as he watched the city roll by.

They took a meandering course to their destination, in part to assess the state of the city and in part to confuse anyone who might have been following them. The streets were still quiet, still sleeping, even as they pulled into the underground parking lot that was their rendezvous point.

Yantra and Ness were waiting for them, Yantra lowering the rolling gate the moment the car passed through.

"You'll get to see everyone as we go in, so I'm not going to bother giving you a rundown of everyone's positions." Yantra started talking before Shifter had even gotten out of the car. He was looking like himself again, though his dark hair was combed for once and— Ifrit noticed for the first time— he was wearing a suit. It felt... odd. "Dulu and Naddāha are already in the central room, though not everyone's seated yet. Most people are just bored, but there are some that are anxious. I've got the cameras tracking them, in case they know something we don't."

There was a ring of blue around her left eye, proving she was watching everyone inside even as they spoke.

"I'd be more concerned if everyone was relaxed." Shifter absently smoothed back his hair, though it was so tightly pulled back it made his forehead smooth. They were moving again, out of the garage and into the tunnel that would connect both to the subway and the assembly chamber. Even though he could see the light at the end as they turned in, even though this one was brightly lit, just *being* in a tunnel brought a tightness to Ifrit's chest. Yantra and Ness were walking ahead of Shifter, leaving Ifrit and Kirin to bring up the rear. It gave Kirin time to give Ifrit's hand a squeeze before they made it to the end.

Wyrm, Kapre, and Aïcha were all standing there, on guard. Kapre was on their knees, knuckles pressed to the floor and their head bowed, indicating their consciousness was in the very floor Ifrit was walking on. There was a grinding noise as they sealed the entryway Kirin and Ifrit had just come through, the only path that would be sealed so close to the chamber itself. Kapre had already sealed off the other tunnels running away from the circular room, but farther back, so any attackers would be seen and the three would have time to react before they were upon them.

Wyrm had added something to his costume, a very thin line of tubing that ran from his shoulders down to his hands, likely to take the venom from those barbs and turn it into an aerosol. The line ran in orange across his otherwise red suit, his white-blond hair on top making him look like a living flame. Ifrit strongly approved.

Aïcha was positioned facing away from the other two. Her hair had been braided tightly and then coiled back to keep it out of her view, since she faced the bigger two tunnels alone.

With just a nod their group moved past. Ifrit didn't envy the three of them, standing alone in that space, destined to stand for hours staring at those yawning tunnels.

Once they entered the main hall though, Ifrit thought that maybe he ought to be jealous that they got to stay in such relative peace.

The hall was designed in an old, classic style, with fluted columns bracketing the corridor as far as it could be seen, before it curved off around the main chamber. The ceiling was tall, over double Ifrit's height, but even that was less than half of what the great amphitheater would be inside. Everything was washed in white, from the stone walls to the coffered ceiling, and Ifrit felt the weight of it. This was the sort of place where people met and tried to live in an illusionary beautiful past, instead of ever trying to move forward into the future. It felt emblematic of what they fought against, the mountain of legislation that needed to be overturned to make life anywhere near fair.

A nudge at his shoulder told Ifrit he'd hesitated too long at the top of the stairs, the ghost of a touch as Kirin's gloved hand slid down his arm. Even though it had hardly been there, it grounded Ifrit, and let him follow Shifter into the fray.

When Yantra said that not everyone was inside, he'd been envisioning a mostly empty hall, a point where they could stand and watch the diplomats file in as the day went on. Instead, the hallway was crowded, people in suits talking loudly to one another while their bodyguards stood stoically by, harassed aides trying to walk through the throng to get outdoors to make a call that just *couldn't* wait, and the police officers posted at every entrance and exit making the airy corridor feel small and tight. No one gave Yantra and Ness half a glance— someone even ran straight *into* Ness, giving her a dirty look before moving on. Shifter was looking anxious again, eyes flickering side to side as bodies pressed in, until Ifrit stepped forward up to his side.

Even here, even in a room full of people claiming to fight for mien-user rights, Ifrit found himself with a large berth. The flame around his head danced; eyes flickered to the fire and then, almost unconsciously, people took steps away. A voice from a lifetime ago whispered in his head, reminding him that he didn't *really* need it anymore, that with Kirin he could have cut the *dramatics* and not made everyone around him uncomfortable. But a moment later, a different voice rang out in his head, his *real* mother's voice.

There's not a thing that you need to change. Pressure had told him that the first day he'd suggested he stop using his license, before he had good enough control that he could've done so safely. *It helps you. They can deal with it.*

With clearer eyes, he noticed something.

The people backing up didn't look fearful. They didn't look at him with disgust, or horror. Instead, the people moving out of his way looked at him with respect. When he looked around and met a pair of eyes, he received nods, smiles. His heart thudded in his chest. Maybe, maybe this would work.

Lost in his thoughts, Ifrit almost walked into Shifter's back as they paused at the door.

An officer was posted there, one he recognized. The nice lady from the aquarium, the one who'd given him her card. Nguyen, if her ID badge was correct.

"Well, look who it is!" She greeted him and Kirin warmly as they held out their student IDs for her to scan. Ifrit's eyes darted to Yantra and his suspicion was confirmed as a line of text scrawled over her eye just as the scanner beeped. "I hope your semester has been more restful than the start."

"I wouldn't say that." Kirin's eyes creased, his tone light. "But there's been a lot of good this year."

Ifrit hated the way his chest felt fluttery when Kirin shot him a wink. So much bad, and yet Kirin was thinking about the good. Asshole.

"I want you kids to know I was personally tasked with picking the officers for today." Her voice was quieter now, making it hard for Ifrit to process what she was saying with all the noise around them. "If anyone does anything out of line, you tell me, and I'll make them leave immediately."

Ifrit found himself speechless, but Kirin, as always, came to his rescue.

"Thank you." His voice was sincere. "And thank you for being kind."

"Somewhere down the line, I think a lot of my colleagues have forgotten that's how we're supposed to be." She straightened. "I'm one of the lucky ones, who wasn't run out for reporting. You can only do so much from the outside. Some change has to start from within."

Ifrit took his ID back wordlessly, not sure what he could say. This woman, this tiny fucking powerless woman, had so much more spine than half the heroes he'd grown up around.

"Get in there, kid." He hadn't realized Kirin had already gone ahead, but Officer Nguyen seemed to understand, smiling warmly. "Go watch them change the world."

Changing the world, it turns out, was painfully boring.

Shifter was on the tallest balcony— by request— but the voices from below carried. Ifrit almost wished they didn't; the acoustics in the room were perfect, the wooden panels dangling from the ceiling meticulously engineered to reflect the speaker's voice to even this remote corner. Ifrit and Ness were standing directly behind Shifter and the aides of the lost Kazakhstani contingent, the six of them the only people on the platform. Kirin and Yantra were on the other side of the room, Dulu and Naddāha on the middle balcony looking attentive. Kirin was on guard, his eyes narrowed, but Yantra's eyes looked distant, likely lost in all the information she was sifting through as the day went on.

It had been exciting, for the first hour. Ifrit knew that Shifter said this was a big deal, but people his age thought any progress was big. Yet the opening policy for the contingent was to discuss eliminating the prohibition on mien use in rental properties. Ifrit had seen Dulu's head pop up too, his eyes wide. Maybe this actually would be big.

Then the constituents had argued, had pushed and pulled,

changing language word by word. Diplomats from certain countries required clarification on *their* specific type of government housing, or on co-ownership, or any number of tiny details that hardly seemed to matter at all. Half the room looked as bored as Ifrit felt, and if he didn't plan on avoiding talking to her forever, he might have asked Naddāha to confirm if anyone in the top tier was paying attention at all. Actually, the final "secret" he'd kept holed in his heart was gone now, so maybe there was no reason to avoid her after all. When she turned and smiled at him the moment he had the thought, he decided that no, no he wouldn't. That shit was creepy.

But it was just... a boring mission. The most interesting things got was when Yantra would duck out of her position and ask everyone to manually confirm what their status was. Sometimes, depending where she stood, Ifrit could hear the mutterings of bodyguards, complaining about how long it was taking, and while he hated the bastards and their blood-tech suits, maybe they did have something in common after all.

Yantra had only just gotten into position again after their last check-in when she suddenly ducked out again. Ifrit saw her step away, saw the way her hand nervously reached for her hair to tug on. Even if he hadn't seen the anxious tic, he couldn't have missed the way her brow furrowed, not even from all the way across the room.

What was that? Kirin's eyes had locked with Ifrit's only a moment after Yantra had disappeared, so Ifrit signed rather than use their comms channel.

I don't know. He couldn't see Kirin's frown, but the way his eyes flashed promised it was there. *She didn't say anything.*

Ifrit swore under his breath and looked over at Ness, nodding to let her know he was going to step away. Her dark eyes were piercing, the only part of her easy to see as she blended into the background, and she watched as he left alone.

He hated it out here. They were separated from the larger ambulatory by a thick stone wall, and only the staircases placed at regular intervals punched holes in the featureless floor. The bodyguards were lined up out here, standing in clouds of black suits and blinking lights as Ifrit walked past. Not all of them, but most. The way their heads turned to watch him pass made their presence all the more hostile.

Walking through the hall to get to Yantra felt like it was taking far too long. Like Kapre was even more bored than he was and was stretching the floor to wrap back on itself, to make him pass the same group of suspicious faces over and over again until he was just marching in front of angry eyes forever. He refused to speed up his pace, to let any of them think that the was nervous.

"Hey Adlivun, can you check something for me?" Something about Yantra's voice felt odd, but maybe it was just the difference between hearing her through his headset like he had been all day and hearing it right in front of him now. She'd positioned herself the farthest from the bodyguards that she could get, neatly between two pairs and pacing across the width of the corridor.

"I just noticed a large group leave the school. Can you check who it was?" Yantra had been quiet for a moment, waiting for a response, but Ifrit hadn't heard anything on his comm. She must've opened a private channel; Ifrit's eyes flickered to the bodyguards around them, like they would know that Valor had forbidden them from doing so. He wasn't even on this mission, had been oddly willing to let Shifter take them out alone, but Ifrit wasn't about to complain about it.

"No, I can't tell who it is. They were using some kind of blocker on the cameras." Yantra was chewing on her lip, her knuckles white from the grip on her hair.

"Most of the rich fuckers keep blockers on them, so that they won't be caught in news footage." At the sound of Ifrit's voice, Yantra jumped. She hadn't even realized he was there. "Wasn't campus supposed to be fucking locked down today though? We agreed on that since the fucking jets are all there."

He muted himself in the general channel, so no one else could hear.

"What the fuck is this about? It can't just be the cameras."

She looked at the bodyguards around them, pulling Ifrit closer to the far wall to whisper.

"Nwabudike just messaged me. Said he traced the signal on the transponder. It's coming from the island. Can't narrow it down; it's pinging in multiple spots, likely to stop anyone from tracking it."

Dread started to build in Ifrit's chest.

"It's communicating with something in the fucking city?"

The way Yantra's lips pressed into a thin line was answer enough. But a patrolling officer behind them made her clam right back up.

"Kapre, can you double check that there's no movement on your side?" Yantra switched to the main channel, echoing in Ifrit's ears as her voice came through on his comm a moment later.

"There's no one in the tunnels." Kapre's dreamlike voice came through the headset. *"We're clear on our end."*

"Antaeus, anything out front?"

"We have clear line of sight down the street, nothing for a block or two."

"Wait." Kuafu spoke tersely. He had the better vantage point, having managed to hover with his mien, watching from six meters in the air. *"I see something further out. Roughly two dozen figures, moving toward us."*

Ifrit's heart thudded.

"Can you identify anyone?" Kirin's calm tone rang out in Ifrit's

ear.

"Not from this distance."

"From which direction?"

"It looks like they were coming from the school."

Ifrit and Yantra made eye contact.

"Get back in position," she said, wires lifting from her suit and forming a coiled rope, "and be prepared for anything."

Ifrit didn't waste time on his way back, breaking into a jog, ignoring the stares. He stopped worrying about giving anyone headaches, spreading carbon all over the hall, the shape of the space filling out in his mind. The staircases were painfully slow to fill in, the area around Kirin a void as always, but there was the room, there were the delegates. As he slipped back onto the balcony, he felt his shoulders lower marginally, just marginally. No one could sneak up on them, the subway tunnels were already closed. The rest of the class had the front entrance anyway; it was fine.

No sooner had the thought occurred than the ceiling caved in.

30

Into Action

KIRIN WATCHED AS IFRIT began moving before the ceiling had fallen more than a meter, the carbon he'd laced in the air rushing toward him as his rings clashed together and the building shook with a resounding boom. The plaster and stone and concrete was sent back into the sky instead of falling onto the screaming audience's heads. The force threw Ifrit backward, down into the floor. He rolled once and got to his feet, but the dent in the wood promised it hadn't been an easy landing. Delegates were scattering, running for the doors, and the sound of fighting came to life over their headsets.

"Majesty's class is here!" Medusa sounded panicked, no doubt from the attack on two sides. The dome collapsing must have been Bia's work, but Kirin couldn't see her, couldn't see anyone in the sky apart from Kuafu, who was already plunging down to support their classmates out front.

"Secure the targets before you come support us." Enenra managed to keep her tone steady, amidst the chaos. *"We can hold them for a few minutes."*

"Everyone, please remain calm." Naddāha's voice rolled through the room, bringing with it a wave of peace. "Head to the nearest stairwell and head down. There are heroes there who will guide you back to the school. Move quickly but calmly, there is no reason to panic."

Kirin felt the brush of her power too as he jumped down to the first floor, grabbing Ifrit by the arm as they plunged ahead of the delegates. There were meant to be police supporting the skeleton crew on the exterior, but they could see through the front windows that the street was empty of cars, police or otherwise.

"Who has eyes on Bia?" Ifrit demanded as they ran, having exited into the rear of the corridor. They had to push through the sea of bodies now, Ifrit careless as he pushed his way forward.

"Can't— see— her." Lilin was panting, like she'd been running. *"I've blacked out— the front of the building— so they— can't— see you."*

"Opening tunnel three now to start moving diplomats back to campus." Kapre's voice came through nervously, and Kirin couldn't blame them even though this was always the emergency plan. "We'll come back the moment they're secure."

"Shifter is a little sick but in the tunnels." Ness's voice felt thin. *"I'm heading back up now."*

"Ness, stay with him." Yantra was just ahead now, eyes flickering between multiple screens she had pulled up in front of her. "Aïcha, you come back instead."

"No, I'm not going to—"

"I'm on my way." Aïcha burst out of the stairwell only a moment later, skidding to a halt in front of the three of them. They all looked at each other, and then the black mass rolling against the window. Yantra gave a nod, and Ifrit exploded the glass.

Lilin dropped the darkness to show the chaos that had overtaken the front steps. The sky darkened and chilled as someone from Majesty's class raised their hands, calling for ice and snow. Two bruisers stalked toward Clidna, who barely opened her mouth at all before they were collapsing, clawing at their ears. Antaeus was on them in an instant, shrinking them to finger sized miniatures before tossing them into a small plastic pouch attached to his belt. Dulu shot out from the now open ceiling, lightning striking across the sky behind him. He beelined for the one calling the storm, hitting them at full speed and wrapping his wings around them as they both went down.

A speedster shot toward their group of four, and wires ripped out of the ground, tripping them before Aïcha was there, kicking them in the head and knocking them out with a single blow.

"Where's—" Ifrit didn't even finish the question before he was thrown to the ground by a blast of pure force.

"We never did get a chance at group combat, did we?" Bia didn't seem to realize that her side was losing as she made her grand entrance, floating leisurely down from above. Her appearance stalled the action for a moment, everyone watching her, Majesty's class— and a few others that Kirin didn't recognize— with pride and gloating, Pressure's with disgust. "Let's see who's really the best."

"You really are just a smug bitch." Goldhorn slapped Bia backward with a loose vine, emerging from their cocoon of branches now that the window was sealed tightly again. Bia's eyes opened comically wide as she was thrown past her own classmates. They all hesitated, clearly not sure how to proceed when their leader was down.

"Who even *are* you?" Bia's rage was incandescent as she got back to her feet, red spots high in her cheeks.

"Literally no one." Goldhorn threw the rest of Bia's cronies off the stairs, not one hair in their ponytail out of place. "You're just not that hard to beat."

Bia shot forward the same moment Ifrit did. He met her in midair and threw her backward again, isolating her from the rest of the group. For the first time in months, Kirin didn't feel the compulsive need to get to Ifrit's side, watching as he easily sent Bia to the ground with a small explosion, her screaming wordlessly at him. Kirin instead joined Yantra in disabling a man with a pair of extra arms, Kirin grabbing him by the torso and throwing him over his head, Yantra causing the wires in the sidewalk to rip through the concrete and pin him in place until Antaeus could come their way.

He was busy at the moment ducking blows from a gargantuan woman who caused wind to blow by after every swing, blood on his face from where she'd swept glass from the window across his face. Kuafu jumped onto her back from behind, covering both her eyes with his hands and flashing his power, leaving her blind. She tripped down a stair and Antaeus grabbed her chin, fitting her into his pouch just a moment later.

Adlivun was standing calmly off to the side, her eyes glazed white as shades spread out before her, wrestling down two students who hadn't even had time to fight back. Lilin and Enenra stood back to back, Lilin's face scraped as if she'd hit the ground hard, but her expression was calm as she squared off against a technopath working with an army of drones. Enenra turned to smoke and jumped, destroying each drone and confusing the students trying to attack Lilin from behind. Lilin shrouded the whole group in darkness and when it fell away, she was standing alone, surrounded by four unconscious bodies on the ground.

Dulu was flying back toward the group now, wings outstretched as he tackled Medusa out of the way of an attack from behind, Aïcha smoothly intercepting their attacker and knocking her to the ground as Antaeus ran by. Those he couldn't get to quickly were trapped by Goldhorn, who was striding through the fray untouched, horns glittering in the sunlight.

Kirin ran in to support Clidna, who had been identified as a threat and was surrounded, Yantra hot on his heels. He crystallized his ears as she opened her mouth to scream, crashing into two of the men next to her and throwing them back down the stairs. Yantra ducked as one of the remaining women swung at her, brandishing her whip and tying her enemy tightly before tossing her into Antaeus's path. Explosions erupted constantly as Ifrit held Bia back, isolating her from the rest of the class. Kirin straightened and turned back to see where he needed to go next, but there wasn't much for him to do. The last of the hostile combatants were being handled, none of his friends even breathing hard.

"Something's wrong." Ifrit was suddenly at Kirin's shoulder, Bia forgotten for the moment. She was angry at being treated as so little a threat that he had turned his back on her and was on the pair of them in an instant, but Kirin simply grabbed her by the leg and sent her flying, straight to Aïcha who kicked her in the head hard enough to keep her down. "We should get back inside, I don't fucking like this."

"Everyone, regroup in the tunnels! Yantra, can you let them know we're coming to cover the rear?" Kirin's voice carried easily.

Yantra nodded and put her hand to her ear, only to frown.

"Communication lines are down." The blue light appeared around her eye, making the concern on her face starker. "I didn't notice because of the fighting, but someone must have taken them out with an electrical pulse. There's nothing coming and going."

"And who were those other students?" Enenra surged toward them, coming back to full solidity only once she was right in front of them. "I didn't recognize some of them. Not to mention— wasn't the one Ness was talking to missing?"

"Maybe she just wasn't told? After all, Ness hadn't heard anything about this." Clidna's voice wasn't even a little raw, that was how easy it had all been. The feeling of wrongness grew.

"Inside— *now*." Ifrit's voice had gone hard, the way it always did when he was anxious.

"Not so fast." The voice came from above Dulu, and he flinched. He looked up, as they all did, to see Valor almost directly overhead. His costume was stained with gore, like he'd just come from a fight. He sent them all flying with a blast, scattering them across the steps. "Attacking your fellow classmates? I knew you were all worthless, but this is despicable, even for you. Wasn't attacking the congress enough?"

Light hit the side of the building, the blue and red flickering and making Kirin's heart plummet. Ifrit's face went pale, Kirin watching him from what felt like leagues away, though they were only a few paces apart.

"You never would stay *dead*, would you?" Valor's words were directed at Ifrit now. "You're a cockroach, a stain. To think that all these people had bought your little innocence act, had wanted to defend you."

"You're the one who was killing the coalition members." Understanding hit Kirin like a truck.

"My sister was deluded, *degraded* by her association with you." Valor ignored them all, descending slowly from the sky, bracers glowing on his arms. The bracers Nwabudike had made him. Bracers that amplified his strength to the level that his sister's had been.

The anger in Kirin's chest felt detached. Dangerous. Like he could tear Valor apart and not blink.

"She was perfect before you came along. She understood that powers are only for those who deserve them, not for the weak and the pitiful. That heroes are those who have proven they are *worthy* of godlike abilities, and that most need to be crushed to stop chaos from happening."

Valor landed with an audible thud, just a few steps away from Kirin, close enough that Kirin's fists crystallized, that his blood *sang* with the prospect of hurting the man who had hurt Ifrit. Had hurt Adil.

"You're insane." Ifrit's mask had broken from the attack, leaving him with only a thin cloth one in white. White and gold. His eyes shone from fear, his chest heaving.

"And you are finally going to die." Valor held out his hand in a familiar posture, in a gesture that Kirin had seen hundreds of times, something that the world had seen hundreds of times, but not from him. Never from the sidekick, from the weaker of the pair. The lines on his arms blazed as Valor lazily flicked his fingers toward Ifrit.

The force made wind blow, scattered the debris from the fight around in small whirls. Kirin looked down in surprise at the blood on his fist.

"*Kirin*." Ifrit's voice behind him made him turn, the terror palpable in just that one word.

"It's alright." His voice sounded dull to him, given that his head was still half encased in diamond. "I'm not hurt."

Another blast came, stronger this time, enough to shatter all the windows of the assembly hall behind them. But Kirin didn't move.

"What did you..." Ifrit had fallen, toppled backward as he braced for the attack to come. "How did you?"

Valor gasped again and tried, feebly, to remove himself from Kirin's grip. The more he squirmed, the more the sharp edges of Kirin's fingers cut his throat. Kirin watched the red droplets fall, still not sure how he'd gotten there. What had happened.

The sound of sirens finally reached him, the flashing lights upon them suddenly.

Kirin's momentary distraction let Valor send a blast down

toward the ground, breaking himself free of Kirin's grip. It cost him, leaving gouges in his throat, his collarbone. Blood dripped to the floor in great drops, rain that smelled like iron. Kirin wished it were a flood.

"Kapre, can you hear us?" It was a futile effort, but the sound of guns loading had made them all freeze.

Comms are fully down. Clidna shifted so her hands were visible to Kirin, her jaw firmly set. *Count us off and we run.*

"Three." Ifrit didn't look like he *could* run, his eyes locked on Valor, the way his hand was held out, the way he seemed to be *mocking* Pressure, tormenting a teenager to mimic her power. "We meet back at the school."

Her power.

"Two." Clidna spoke calmly, standing on Ifrit's other side, a mirror to Kirin. Goldhorn was flexing their hands, plants twitching at their feet, darkness bubbled from the torn open building where Lilin was half hidden, Medusa reached for her visor.

"*One*." Ifrit spat through gritted teeth— and shot straight up.

31

Wanton Destruction

IFRIT BLASTED INTO THE air while the rest of the class sprinted for the door. Kirin, instead, sprinted at the police.

Guns went off as he ran, but he was unstoppable, glittering as he charged straight for the line of cars that blockaded the street. Ifrit hesitated as his mind fought between wanting to stop Kirin and wanting to help him, but Kirin ignored the cops entirely, only using them to launch himself into the sky.

In two strides he was upon them, one jump and he was on the roof of a car, running across the rest as if the gaps between them were nothing, until he reached the last in the line and leapt. His feet hit the wall of a building first, and he crystallized them, stabbing straight into the concrete. He pushed *up* with his next step and his next, running across the side of the building, higher and higher, until he was above Valor's head, above where he floated, sending out wave after wave of force. The building shook once, twice, as Valor's wide blast hit unintentional targets, a metallic screeching filling the air as a section of a skyscraper fell away.

And Kirin jumped.

He threw himself right over Valor, crystallizing everything and letting himself fall. Valor desperately, helplessly tried to force Kirin off, to stop the relentless pull of gravity. A mere second before they touched the ground, he finally accepted that he wasn't going to win and threw himself to the side, rolling several times before coming to a rest. He was back on his feet in a flash, mask ripped off and teeth gritted. His eyes found Ifrit in the sky, where he floated high enough to stay out of the range of the police guns, frozen as he watched in horror. Kirin continued to ignore those same guns as they battered his back without causing a single wound.

Valor had a shield around himself, one that was clumsier than the ones Pressure had created. It wobbled and spun, bullets ricocheting off in every direction, striking some of the very police he'd called in to frame them. Officer Nguyen was running out from the building, just a speck below Ifrit, yelling at them to stop firing, and between their own losses and her words, they stopped, confused.

"Why are you protecting him?" Ifrit's attention was drawn back to Valor as he roared at Kirin. "Why can you all not see that he is an abomination?"

Kirin's expression was hidden for Ifrit as he strode forward, but something about his posture made Ifrit's blood run cold. There was an iciness to it, a *violence* to it that he'd never before associated with Kirin.

"The world *needs* to be protected from monsters like him! And if the world won't do it, *I* will." Valor shot into the sky, arms outstretched as he reached for Ifrit. Almost in a dream, Ifrit saw his rings click together, saw Valor flicked out of the sky like he was little more than an ant.

"Halt!" One of the police officers finally tried to intervene, but Kirin didn't turn around.

"You're all *sick*, but I know the cause." Valor had more control over his shield this time, his voice calmer. Ifrit felt sick, hearing the words echo across years. "It all started with *him*. All of it."

"Did you not hear me?" Kirin's voice was low and threatening, and if the wind hadn't carried the words to Ifrit's ears, he would've missed them entirely.

"It took *months* to get the bitch to let me be alone with him. Who knew she was both so smart and so stupid?" Ifrit tried to get Valor to shut up by firing on him, but the shield meant his flames were battered away without coming close to touching Valor. Valor was smiling now. "It was almost like she didn't trust me or something. Me, who had been her loyal partner for *years*. Abandoned, for some pathetic, disgusting *monster*."

Kirin swung on Valor, but his fist was stopped by the wavering bubble of force. Ifrit watched as the shield bent under the pressure, Kirin pushing forward just as much as it pushed back.

"Do you know what the most infuriating part was?" Valor was gaining confidence now that it seemed like Kirin was going to be kept at bay, his unhinged smile spreading across his face. "It was *too* easy. He just sat there. Let me hit him. Apologized. Acted as if he felt *bad* for killing thousands."

Ifrit was twelve again. He was tripping through Valor's backyard, apologizing, crying. His uncle was just behind, hands outstretched.

"I shouldn't have taken my time. I could've snuffed him out between my fingers like *nothing*, but I wanted him to feel fear. I wanted him to know why he was about to die. That no one would forgive him for what he did." Valor pushed forward, his cobbled together shield pushing Kirin back one step, two. "These politicians, the *coalition*, they all think that the world needs to forgive and move on. That creatures like *him* need to be treated like humans. But I know the truth. They corrupt and condemn and destroy everything around them. They need to be put down like the animals they are."

From above, Ifrit watched as Valor leaned forward, eyes

glinting madly as he bore down on Kirin.

"He might have gotten stronger, but so have I. And this ends *today.*" He slammed both his hands forward and Kirin was thrown backward over a police car as Valor shot toward Ifrit in the sky.

Worthless, pathetic, demon.

Had Valor laughed when he found out Ifrit's assigned name? Had he asked Majesty to put in a good word, push the school to make sure Ifrit knew he'd never escape the whispers? *Monster, murderer.*

The wave of force that skimmed his chest as he darted backward felt all the more vile knowing it was meant to mimic the one person who had never believed any of that about him.

"All you ever did was run." The voice came from his left, his worse ear. Valor always loved to stand there, to hide in Ifrit's blind spots, and then lash out from the dark. It was only that knowledge that sent Ifrit blasting backward, even in his panic, watching helplessly as a line of destruction sped from Valor's outstretched hand. Another building toppled a hundred meters away, the air tasting metallic from the particles torn free.

He had to bring Valor away from there, away from the busy parts of the city. But where wasn't busy? East City was packed to the brim with bodies, with movement and sound. He'd hated it at first, when he got his first hearing aids, how he went from silence to chaos, and he hated it again now. There were too many people who needed protecting and all Ifrit's mien was good for was destruction.

But Kirin could protect them.

The thought grounded him. Valor was afraid of Kirin— *Valor had tried to kill Kirin.*

Valor didn't notice the shift in Ifrit's posture, though they were now still, hovering dozens of meters in the air. He was saying something, some threat, some insult. Something to make Ifrit feel worthless and small. Ifrit didn't hear him.

The aquarium. The line scored in the floor right after Kirin threatened Valor. Their last several missions, Kirin always in the line of fire with far too few people as back up. Valor had marked him as a target, but he *failed.* He couldn't win against Kirin.

Could anyone?

Ifrit interrupted Valor's self-righteous monologue, speeding back the way they'd come. There was an alarmingly wide path of destruction to follow, an arrow carved into the ground, guiding him back toward home. And as if he never doubted that Ifrit would come back, there was Kirin, his hair catching the light breaking through the clouds, hanging off the side of a building, eyes trained on Ifrit.

They fought together enough that it didn't take more than a wave of Kirin's hand for Ifrit to know what to do. He sped up, the flames supporting and propelling him growing larger, his headache fading as the wind kept most of the poison out of his lungs. There was a straight shot down the middle, right beside the building that Kirin dangled from, an odd shadow clinging to the ground promising more of their classmates were hiding below. All Ifrit had to do was convince Valor to set foot in the trap.

Ifrit passed through the gap between skyscrapers, feeling the air shift around him as Kirin breathed, feeling his fire pulled to the side, eddies of carbon pooling around Kirin's body. For a split second, it was just them, Ifrit meeting Kirin's eyes. They were opalescent, practically glowing in the creeping sun, and curved upward at the corners in pride. And then Ifrit was slammed into from the side.

He'd underestimated how afraid of Kirin Valor was. Or maybe just how observant Valor was. They'd been moving at breakneck speed, so he'd thought Valor wouldn't even notice the figure on the building, and even if he had he'd assume there was nothing that Kirin could do. But he'd learned from last time and without Ifrit even noticing, had dodged around the structure entirely, catching up and hitting Ifrit right as he'd come around the corner. Valor's initial attack took Ifrit just under his ribs, slamming him into the windows across from where Kirin perched, too far for him to jump, but close enough to see everything.

"Did you think that ploy would work? I have been tracking all of you since the day I set foot at this school, I know all your little escapades, your plans." Valor had one hand squeezing Ifrit's throat, but Ifrit hardly felt it. He'd spent so much time choking that it seemed to have lost its hold on him. Instead, his brain was far away, connecting to tendrils of air that he shouldn't have been able to feel, disconnected as they were. Clumps of carbon were being pulled to and fro as he scratched at the hand holding him. The actual attack might not have brought him terror, but the face that was now so close to his own did.

Valor was saying something. His mouth was moving, but either the impact had damaged Ifrit's hearings aids, or his brain simply refused to listen, because he didn't hear a word. He focused on all the carbon he could release, on not looking away from Kirin for a moment. On keeping his free hand moving, spelling as fast as he could. He saw Kirin understand, saw the diamond that Kirin once hid creeping over his arms, his chest, his face.

"Are you listening to me, boy?" Valor slammed Ifrit against the wall again, cracks radiating out from where his head connected. Ifrit's cloth mask was still in place, so Valor couldn't see the smile that took over Ifrit's lips.

"No," Ifrit said, lifting his hand so that Valor could see the metal rings shining there, "I'm not going to listen to another fucking word you say."

Valor's eyes widened as Ifrit snapped, the spark from the rings colliding singeing his eyebrows once it caught. Valor's head turned, watched the thread of fire speed away, Valor's hand going out ineffectually to stop it. His hand clasped uselessly at empty air, and they both watched as the air around Kirin turned to fire, and he flew across the street toward them.

Kirin caught Ifrit with one arm wrapped around his waist, pulling him to Kirin's side protectively as Ifrit struggled to regain his breath. One of Kirin's feet was stabbed into the building to give him purchase, counterbalanced by the hand that was pinning Valor to the wall by his throat.

"Well, this feels familiar." Kirin's voice was cold. His fingers were ruby red, the blood underneath his diamond skin pulsing with anger. "What did I say about touching him?"

Valor had his head tilted back, keeping the arteries of his throat as far as he could from the sharp edges of Kirin's hand. Ifrit had to look away from the hatred on Valor's face, the disgust too familiar. Kirin didn't dare take his attention away from Valor, but his tightened grip promised he noticed.

They stood at an impasse for a moment. It gave Ifrit time to recollect himself, to resupply and reignite his flames, changing the angle to give Kirin some relief, as there was just the subtlest shake in his arms. Kirin glanced away from Valor for a moment, just a moment, to check that Ifrit was okay, and then they were falling.

Kirin, fucking impossible Kirin, had known. He'd reacted so fast, faster than Ifrit had even realized what was happening, and covered them both, so the force only threw them backward and didn't tear them apart. Ifrit sent a blast down, the burst of air pushing them back upright, and then maintained a constant flame to keep them from sinking lower. It was difficult, holding Kirin next to him and not beneath, but they faced Valor shoulder to shoulder as he pushed himself out of the fractured building.

"This is weakness!" Valor was truly mad now, his voice reduced to a hiss. "How could *you* stop me when you're too busy covering for each other's inadequacies? There is no hope that you could ever be reformed, so the right thing to do is to destroy you."

When Valor raised his hand, Ifrit found that he wasn't afraid. Kirin wasn't even tense, his shoulders relaxed, his hand in Ifrit's. He'd protect them, somehow. Had Pressure known, when she'd first interviewed him? Had she known that he could protect Ifrit, no matter what?

Even with all his trust in Kirin, Ifrit couldn't help himself cringing back, from bracing for the impact. But instead, he found silence.

True silence. He could feel the beating of his heart in his ears, but though he knew the wind was blowing steadily, knew that people were shouting in the streets, knew that sirens were wailing in the distance, there was nothing. And the lines running down Valor's arms blinked out.

There was a moment, a breath where everything was frozen as Ifrit's brain processed what he was seeing. As Valor's eyes widened when he realized there was no force bursting from his hand, no wave of pressure flattening the pair of them. Kirin's arm around Ifrit tightened imperceptibly as Valor began to fall.

Ifrit lurched forward slightly, not sure if he was trying to watch or trying to catch him, but Valor was far away now, growing smaller as he dropped, his mouth open in a scream that Ifrit couldn't hear. Even after a lifetime of torment, Ifrit made himself look away, couldn't watch and see the ground connect. See Pressure's brother splatter.

But when he turned away, turned to face the wall instead of into the city, his pulse quickened. The great barricade around the ocean usually glowed with lights, the windows of station workers dotting the metal. They were all black.

Ifrit brought them down to the ground fast, pressing his hand to the asphalt on the street. When he still didn't feel anything, he pressed his face down against the ground, hoping, praying that he'd feel that tell-tale rumble of machinery whirring away underneath their feet. There was nothing.

Lights still shone in the center of the city, but the entire outer ring was dark. As Ifrit watched, lights in the second began to die out.

"Get the politicians to their planes— *now*!" With his hearing aids dead, he had no idea how loud he was being. Why, fucking *why* had the city decided to use a building so far from the school? So far from the only way off the island? "We need to get them out of here before they can't leave!"

He and Kirin were already running for the assembly hall, the generator next to it now dull and gray, knowing there was no way to reach their classmates underground until they were out of the dead zone's reach. East City, a dead zone. What that entailed hit Ifrit like a wave. Was the city going to go under? No, it couldn't. The machinery was only needed to turn salt water into fresh, to keep the city on its migratory path. They just had to get the fucking diplomats out and it'd be okay. They wouldn't drown.

Pressure's house flashed in his eyes, another home that might be destroyed before this was all over. He shoved the thought away.

They'd landed quite close to the assembly hall, and within just a few seconds they were running up the stairs, getting close to the tunnels. They'd be able to hold out better there, where Aether could only attack from one direction. Kuafu would give them light, and they'd make the diplomats run the whole fucking way if they had to. This tiny attempt at progress wouldn't stop here. It couldn't.

He'd just about convinced himself that it'd be easy, even, to get everyone off the island alive when the generator next to them exploded.

32

Impossible Choices

KIRIN GRABBED HOLD OF Ifrit and tucked him safely away as they were both blown backward off the stairs. They skidded back a dozen meters, Kirin's diamond skin gouging into the pavement but hardly slowing them down. When they finally stopped, Kirin opened his eyes to see Goldhorn reaching out to haul him to his feet, their eyes locked on the burning remnants of the generator.

While they were focused on the fire, Kirin was focused on the one-armed figure striding out of it. How could they be here?

"Tunnels." His voice was hoarse, and he had to force himself to let go of Ifrit to sign. Even just having him an arm's length away felt wrong, though he knew Ifrit's hearing aids couldn't be working. "We get the diplomats off the island first, and then we'll deal with Aether."

Aïcha was there in front of him suddenly, winded for the first time that Kirin could remember.

"They're coming," she gasped, one hand to her chest. "I don't know how they got here; they came out of the generators, less than Satol but a few hundred at least—"

More than their fractured class could handle.

"The generators." Yantra turned to look at Kirin. "To recreate

Ness's power, they'd need enough energy to *power a city*."

"But Ness's power isn't enough to get them here, they'd need to—"

"To teleport." Kirin met Yantra's horrified eyes. "Or, to slip out of existence in one spot, and reappear in another."

"The signal wasn't bouncing around the island. When they blew up the generator *last year* they were planting transmitters, planting the signal that would pull them from *there* to *here*." Yantra was pale, bloodless. "They've been planning this all along."

"Where did the police go?" Lilin sounded scared. She had every right to since they'd been fired upon only minutes earlier, but though the police cars remained, all the officers had vanished.

"We'll just have to trust that they're on our side for now." Kirin started pushing everyone forward, though the generator still burned, the heat overwhelming even at a distance. "Get the diplomats *out*. Then we fight back."

That spurred everyone to action, and they were running again. Out of the corner of his eye, Kirin saw the figure silhouetted in flame turn, saw them track the movement, but he couldn't worry about that now. Someday, they'd know that he was doing this for them, too.

The air was stifling in the assembly hall, smoke curling through the shattered ceiling, walls bursting into flames as they made it down the stairwell. Medusa stumbled and screamed, Clidna grabbing one of her arms and throwing it around her neck in an instant. Right, it wasn't only Ifrit affected by the sudden outage; she couldn't see anymore.

They were only halfway down when an ominous crashing promised the building above was collapsing. Goldhorn turned from their position at the front and threw seeds, which expanded into a great net to hold the weight of the building until they were clear and out of harm's way. Even then, when the first section of wall collapsed, Kirin saw a few vines sag and even snap.

Medusa and Clidna leapt for it as Goldhorn's protection gave out entirely, the mass of concrete and plaster grinding itself together and covering them in a fine layer of dust. They stood there, coughing, staring incomprehensibly at the mass of material that blocked their way out.

"Well," Kuafu looked eerie as he spoke, the light from his hands casting his face in shadow. "They will not be following us that way."

"We need to fucking *move*." Ifrit's voice was overly loud, likely a product of both his inability to hear and his anxiety. "That fucking black out is moving and I don't think Aether waiting until *now* to attack is a coincidence. They want the delegation, they want to make a fucking example of it."

"They want the school, too." Wyrm spoke so quietly. "No East Tech, no more heroes. No heroes... Aether controls the narrative."

"Then let's fucking *move*." Ifrit didn't wait for anyone to reply, not that he'd hear it. His hands were curled tightly into fists, the tremor in his arms just barely visible. "We're not letting them take any of it."

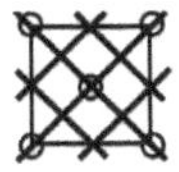

Even at a full run, they didn't catch up to the politicians until they were underneath the park, just at the edge of the tunnels' extents. The lights had flickered on just a few minutes into their dead sprint, but even that did little to calm Ifrit down, the lines of tension in his shoulders betraying his fear. Aether, in the city. Another tunnel. And...and Hyeon-soo nearby.

Kirin forced the thought away as daylight came into view, and with it the silhouettes of the group ahead. A few of the diplomats at the rear jumped at the sound of their arrival, bodyguards raising their hands or their weapons, but it was bright enough that their concern only lasted a few seconds. Wordlessly, they parted, allowing Kirin and his friends to make it through to the front. Ness, Wyrm, and Kapre had halted the group a few meters away from the exit, likely because Kapre had felt them coming.

"What's the plan?" Clidna was at his side, looking as unruffled as ever. Her posture was casual, relaxed. As Kirin looked around, he realized that most of their class did too, as they looked at *him*. Like he had some big idea to get them out of this mess. The thought made all his words lodge in his throat.

"We get to the jets." Ifrit smoothly took over for Kirin and gestured to their charges, to the people who had just minutes before been trying to lay the foundations for a better future. Would they still want to now? "Get them in the air and moving. The outer edges of the city are already in the dead zone, but the initial propulsion should be enough thrust to get them clear. But we need to move *now*."

"Just one problem." Ness appeared in front of them, one hand to her ear, image wavering in the bright light. "Aether's attacking the school. We don't have a clear path through."

"In the park?" Goldhorn stepped forward, rolling their wrists. "I'll give us a clear path. You all just need to protect me."

"We have to assume their goal is to take out all of the delegates; we'll be a walking target," Shifter warned.

"They can try to." Enenra answered, the lines in her suit shutting down as she shifted to smoke.

"But we'll be ready." Kapre was standing next to Goldhorn at the entrance, kneeling. Their head dropped for a moment before they stood. "There are two figures on either side of the tunnel exit. One about five meters away and armed with a rifle, the other to the right and poised to jump."

"I'll take the rifle, you take our jumper?" Kirin nudged Ifrit, who rolled his eyes.

"Like you have to ask."

Without another word, Kirin charged forward.

The gun went off almost immediately as he emerged, but the bullets glinted off his skin harmlessly. Ifrit had a blast ready and pushed the ambushing attacker backward, shooting off after them out of Kirin's sight. Kirin barreled straight ahead, to where the shots were coming from, more rapidly now and with less intention. Kirin was on them a moment later, placing his hands on either side of the barrel and swinging himself over the boulder they were crouched behind. He flattened them against the rock a moment later. They grabbed at the hand on their chest, eyes wide as they gasped. They didn't look old at all, maybe in their late teens. Kirin must have been crushing them from the way they were wheezing; had he broken their ribs without realizing it?

He almost pulled back, horrified, when they pulled a gun from a holster on the side of their leg and fired rapidly, until the trigger only made an empty clicking sound. The second weapon fell from their hand as it trembled, and they finally started to cry.

"Please." Their voice was hardly more than a whisper. "Please."

Kirin suddenly felt sick. He couldn't do this. Bodies laying broken underground filled his vision. He couldn't do it again.

Wyrm was at his side and gently touched the face of Kirin's attacker. He felt their body go rigid under his hand, Wyrm's paralytic taking effect far quicker than it should've.

"I think I might've—" Kirin's own voice was gone, suddenly, as if he couldn't bear to hear the words aloud. But Wyrm was already moving.

"There are more." He gestured for Kirin to follow.

Kirin spared one last glance at his would-be victim and set off at a run.

Goldhorn's work could be heard in screams around the park; the few who made it through to their group were swiftly taken care of, incapacitated, their progress not even stalled. The run through the park usually took Kirin and Ifrit only five minutes, but their charges were flagging now, and Kirin found himself carrying several who could simply no longer run. As he held them, the knot in his chest loosened.

The sounds of fighting grew louder.

Kapre stopped them at a fork in the road and collapsed, the ground under their feet rolling as they tried to check for the safest path, forgoing subtlety for speed. The seconds ticked by and Kirin put down the people he was carrying, feeling the pinpricks of someone's eyes on him. But when he turned and looked back the way they'd come, there was no one there, just trees swaying in the breeze. Over the treetops, the dead towers at the edge of the city loomed ominously. How far had it spread now? How much time did they have?

"They're at the main and service entrances." Kapre's voice was soft, but with the silence from the rest of the group, it carried. "A few dozen on both."

"Is the shield still active?" Kuafu strode up to them, his bright yellow costume shining in the dimming light.

"I think so." Kapre's voice grew even smaller.

"I can turn it off." Yantra and Ness spoke simultaneously and turned to look at one another. Both looked furious.

"I know how to shut down the system," Yantra insisted.

"But you'd need to access the controls yourself. I can just walk through the wall and shut if off from the inside." Ness was calm, calmer than Kirin had seen her in a long time.

"No. You said—"

"We can't fight through a horde of Aether agents and protect everyone. So it's *fine*." Ness stressed the word with a meaningful glance at their audience, which was quite large given the attendance at the congress. Yantra's chest heaved up and down like she was about to scream, but all she did was give a curt nod.

"We can't leave the school unguarded." Shifter's voice was harsh. "Aether would be able to get in just as quickly as we would."

"We'll head in through the front." Ifrit's voice was odd. "I can take care of the crowd there."

Kirin's pulse thudded slowly in his ears.

"There are almost forty people there," Kapre said, but Kirin felt like they were speaking from under water. The look in Ifrit's eyes, the way they were shining; he'd decided what he needed to do to keep these people safe. He'd probably made the calculation when he saw the line creeping toward them, saw their time start ticking down, down, down.

Ifrit was saying something now. The main entrance. They were talking about the main entrance.

Kirin could clear the main entrance.

They were arguing now. Shifter knew just as well as Kirin did what Ifrit would have to do. What it would *cost* Ifrit to do it. The diplomats didn't understand; they were watching with confusion and not a little frustration. Some were already starting to push back. But it was fine. Kirin could take care of it.

With no one watching him, he slipped back into the trees.

It was mechanical. One foot in front of the other, branches hitting his face as he went. He didn't feel them, didn't feel a thing. There was noise that was growing louder, the sound of people battering against metal, against electricity. There were screams, maybe from more of Goldhorn's traps. There were still some active, plants that reached out and grabbed at Kirin's ankles, at his arms. But his skin was razor-sharp and they snapped before they could slow him down.

None of the Aether agents even noticed when he stepped out behind them. They were so focused on the gate to the school, at trying to make a hole in the shield, through the wall, anything. They were spread out but sometimes in clumps, people wielding fire or weapons or currents or just their own strength. And then, by the gate, still in pristine white, was the woman he'd last seen pulling Yantra's hair.

That made it easier. Some small part of his brain wanted to believe that maybe, maybe if he just... *handled* her, he wouldn't have to do anything more. That would be it. Just one more. Yet when the first shout promised he'd been seen, he knew it was a lie.

They were fast. He couldn't even see their face. In the end, he didn't even have to do anything. They shredded themself against his skin so quickly he could almost pretend it hadn't happened. Almost. Their blood soaked through his shirt, turning him scarlet.

They were still screaming. Still alive, for now. This would not be quick and painless and bloodless like it had been at Satol. This time, he would have to see what he was doing. This time, there was no pretense that they were just unconscious.

He wished they would fall unconscious.

Only a few turned away from their task to attack him, the others still slamming themselves against or firing into the shield like that would do something. Maybe they had been relying on someone to take down the barrier, to let them in. They were hardly making progress the way they were going. He kept his eyes forward, letting his body return any attacks that were hurled his way. He didn't let himself look when his attackers suddenly stopped fighting back.

A woman turned away from the wall and threw something at him. It looked like nothing at first, just a small trinket. When it got within a meter, it expanded into a full spear, hitting him square in the shoulder. It bounced, but before it made it far, he caught it with one hand. The woman who threw it took a few staggering steps back, her eyes flicking to the tree line before someone yelled at her. Her eyes snapped to Kirin, then to the man who was yelling. He was hovering several meters in the air, just above the wall itself, his focus on the shield as twin blasts of energy radiated from both his hands. She was shaking her head, stumbling backward still. The man raised one hand, his intention clear as his anger shifted from the barrier that wasn't breaking to the woman who was. There was the barest crackle of electricity between his palms before the spear erupted from his chest.

Kirin didn't even remember throwing it.

The blood splattered across the woman's face, her eyes opened in horror. She was far away, too far away to hear him speak. But he did anyway.

"Please, run."

Whether she heard him or not, she listened.

When the man's body collapsed on the ground, Kirin finally had the attention of the rest of the group, except for the woman in white. None of the faces he was met with looked familiar, and half looked far too young to be involved with something as horrible as this. He couldn't... he couldn't do this.

But if he didn't, Ifrit would have to.

"Please, back away from the gate." Kirin made his voice louder, stepping forward with his hands raised. Several of the younger members flinched as they saw the blood coating his gloves, his chest, his arms. Could they tell from that far away that it wasn't his? Or maybe... maybe it was the scene behind him that they were looking at. “If you leave now, you won’t be hurt.”

“Oh *please*.” It was the woman in white speaking, though she didn’t bother to turn her head. Her hands were moving over a keyboard, wires running up to the keypad for the gate. “Everyone knows heroes have no ability to keep their word.”

“I suspect I do right now.” Kirin couldn’t be sure how far behind him the class was. A few seconds? Maybe a few minutes? They might have been worried that he’d been grabbed by an Aether agent they hadn’t seen and paused to look for him. He hoped they had. He didn’t want them to see this. “The police are busy with the rest of you in the lower city. And until someone can reverse what you’ve done, they’ll be distracted a good while longer. Right now, it’s just me and you. I need to get through that door and you’re in my way. If you get out of it, I’ll have no reason to find you.”

Some of the young ones were wavering, he could see it. His heart burgeoned with hope. He could save them. He could get them to leave.

“For now, maybe.” She still wasn’t looking away from her work, wasn’t even concerned that everyone around her had abandoned their own efforts. “But what happens when you have what you want, hero? When you stop us evil villains and yet you *know* we’re still out there? When you’re ordered to come after us?”

“Then I’ll be bad at my job.” Kirin had found this sliver of hope, and he wasn’t letting it go. It grew as he realized there *was* a face he recognized in the crowd. “You know it. You know I never came looking for you.”

The boy shifted uncomfortably, but he wasn’t wearing a mask, wasn’t covering his face at all, so Kirin was *certain* it was the boy from their first mission of the year, the one he’d let run.

"You... you didn't." The boy spoke hesitantly. "But it doesn't mean you *won't*."

"That's true." Kirin thought he could hear someone coming through the trees, someone getting closer. "But I can tell you what will happen if you don't leave. I *will* kill you. Because if I don't, someone else has to. We just need to get through that gate. There's already so much damage control that needs to be done; if you aren't here when the police show up, no one will know."

The members of Aether were spread out before him in a semi-circle, none of them willing to step any closer to him, none of them willing to step in their fallen comrades' blood.

"I don't *want* to do this." Kirin's voice broke on the word, and he couldn't stop tears from falling. "I don't have a choice. Please, *run*."

"You made *your* choice!" The woman in white was suddenly up, her laptop abandoned as she turned and screamed. "You abandoned us and sided with *them*, with the people who *kill* us! And now you're shocked that you're expected to? You're horrified with the fact that you're expected to do the job you signed up for?"

Kirin cringed backward. She wasn't wrong. He'd known it from the praise he'd gotten after Satol, known it from the way the news had only spoken about the deaths on Aether's side as *good* and *deserved*. Known it from the way he clung onto Ifrit. From the need to prove to himself that it was worth it. And it was. But somehow, that wasn't enough.

The older Aether members smelled weakness. They moved closer, the blood on the ground making each step louder with the sharp slap of boots against liquid. More tears fell from Kirin's eyes as he crystallized his skin. He wouldn't even have to move. They'd simply lunge at him and die from the contact. Was that any better?

But it never came.

Kirin should've used his mien on his eyes. He never did, he was too afraid, but he would've rather been unable to see what befell the crowd in front of him. He'd seen Pressure's mien at work, but from a distance, or censored on TV. He'd never imagined what it would look like for someone to be hit with the force of a speeding train. Now he knew.

He turned his head to find Valor limping toward him, one hand still outstretched. The attack hadn't even been meant for them, had it? It'd been meant for Kirin.

"Where is he?" Valor didn't look at the woman in white, the only one unscathed from the attack, didn't look at the dozens of people he'd just killed with an errant wave of his hand. His eyes were bloodshot, his throat torn. He looked like he'd just clawed his way out of a grave, which was just as well. He was supposed to be dead; the fall should've killed him without the power he'd forced Nwabudike to create. It had still done damage, just not enough.

Kirin was still frozen in shock. He'd activated enough of his mien that he remained unmoved as Valor threw blow after blow at him, his enhancer working again now in the center of the city. Valor was advancing slowly, blood dripping sluggishly from his dragging leg, a constant barrage of invisible attacks shredding the trees behind Kirin, but Kirin himself untouched. One of the blows even tore away a corner of Kirin's costume, peeling away the blood-stained cloth to reveal not a single wound underneath. His mask was ripped clean off, both the one that Nwabudike had so painstakingly designed, and the plain cloth underneath.

It was strange that he could be standing so still and yet his mind was miles away. Ifrit's discomfort with the idea of his cuts vanishing suddenly made so much sense. How could Kirin still be untouched around all this death? How could he still be *whole* after the number of people he'd killed? This was fitting, this horror, seeing these people cut down in front of him without being able to do anything. After all, was he any better?

Valor had stopped a few meters away, still too afraid of Kirin to come any closer. Or maybe it was because his wounds were finally enough to stop him from moving. His left leg looked mangled, the left arm unmoving by his side. The way he was leaning— his ribs were broken. The pain he must have been in, to keep walking in that state... how much did he hate them to drag his broken body this far?

"Why won't you BREAK?!" Valor let out an inhuman scream that echoed meaninglessly in Kirin's mind. "I know you can; the other one did! So why won't you?"

That did translate. Kirin's gaze snapped up to meet Valor's, and the movement made Valor *flinch.*

"What did you say?" When Kirin released his mien to talk, a wave caught him across the cheek and opened a gash that coated his jaw in blood. The stinging pain was helpful, clearing away some of the noise in his brain. Or maybe that was just the returning anger.

Valor took a faltering step back, his ankle noticeably giving out and forcing him to hold his ground when he so clearly wanted to run. How dare he be the one who got to run, when he was the one who created the whole situation? Someone who was actively out there making everything worse? Kirin's mind quieted as he realized this time, this time there was no fear that maybe the person on the receiving end might not deserve it, that maybe they didn't have a choice to be facing him down. Valor had made his choices, and Kirin had now made his.

There was a noise from the tree line, but Kirin didn't turn. Instead, he counted in his head. Valor could only fire off a blast of force every two seconds, and the angle was always the same. Slowly, adjusting his feet, Kirin turned his body so he was facing

Valor head on. The older man was sweating profusely, his face slick with water and blood. Kirin had never bothered to look at his face much, but it was carved with years of cruelty, his beady eyes furrowed even now with anger. No, Kirin wouldn't feel bad about this.

Valor seemed to realize what was about to happen at the same moment Kirin began to move. With a roar of fury and pain, Valor raised his left hand to meet his right. Kirin breathed in, pulling all the carbon from the air that he could, his mien flickering across his body as he ran. He was four steps, three away from Valor, pulling back his fist and crystallizing each and every knuckle, ready to strike the side of Valor's ribcage, right where the ribs seemed weakest, when Valor's gaze shifted.

There was just the barest flicker of fire in the corner of Kirin's vision, but Valor saw it too. His hands swung to the side, aiming for where Ifrit had broken free of the trees, where *Adil* would be standing defenseless. Kirin didn't think. There was no other choice to be made. He dropped his mien and jumped, arms outstretched, as Valor fired.

It was with relief that Kirin felt it tear through his chest.

33

Living Nightmare

IFRIT EMERGED FROM THE trees and into a scene from his worst nightmare. Valor, still alive. Kirin, covered in blood and running toward him. For a moment, neither of them reacted to his presence, both focused on the other, Valor's mouth open in a scream, Kirin's forced shut by his mien. But then, they turned.

Valor's face fell into a grim smile and if Clidna hadn't been right behind him, Ifrit would've blasted himself far back into the minimal cover of the remaining trees. Instead, he stayed frozen in place, a perfect target as Valor's hands swung his way, the air rippling in front of them as it contracted in preparation to fire. Was Phoenix close enough? Would there be enough of him to even put back together?

Instead, something worse happened.

The blast caught Kirin in the chest at point blank range. There was a loud crack as *something* split, Kirin thrown backward almost to Ifrit's feet, facedown and unmoving. The ground had been covered in blood already, but Ifrit didn't fail to notice the puddle spreading further as Kirin lay there, one arm trapped by his body, the other draped across his face and hiding it from view.

Phoenix darted forward, her eyes wide; Adlivun grabbed her

arm and pulled her back just before a line was scored in the ground separating her from Kirin.

"I said," Valor hissed, "no healing unless I say so. You haven't forgotten that, have you?"

The whole class was there, spread out among the trees. Clidna was prepping from the way his hearing aids buzzed, the air around Kuafu's hands turning hazy, Aïcha stretching her neck and giving him a nod. But Ifrit couldn't move. Kirin was too still. He couldn't be... he couldn't. He *couldn't.*

"Ifrit." Adlivun was looking at him, her eyes intense. "I don't see him."

Ifrit's eyes flickered back to Kirin, chest heaving as he tried to contain his fear. Kirin wasn't gone yet. His eyes landed back on Valor, wounded and angry, but just one man. Phoenix was only a few meters away. It didn't matter that it was Valor in the way. If anything, that made it easy.

Because *no one* was going to take Kirin away from him.

Valor registered the change in time to throw himself to the side as Ifrit blasted forward, the class scattering around him. Clidna started whistling and Valor fell to the ground covering his ears, throwing up a hand in response. She dropped to the ground to avoid the arc of power, a tree toppling to the ground behind her.

Kapre was next, opening the earth beneath Valor's feet, holding him for just a moment before the dirt erupted outward, Valor clawing himself up. Lilin sent a cloud of darkness rolling over Valor, leaving him unable to find a target, but he just started attacking at random, catching Adlivun in the shoulder. She fell and Phoenix tripped in her hurry to turn around, slipping on the bloodied ground as she grasped the bigger woman's ankle.

Goldhorn was advancing, their shield made of plants being rapidly hacked away, though Valor's attacks were slowing. Ifrit was hovering in the air above Valor, and from his vantage point he could see Naddāha next to Goldhorn, her eyes calm as she looked up at Ifrit. Wyrm was advancing too, rubbing his hands along his shoulders to build up his paralytic poison, but it was all going to be for nothing as Valor wasn't being swayed by Naddāha's power, he was just preparing for something bigger. Force's preferred attack, the one that had made her so untouchable, the sphere of power she could send ripping out away from her. Ifrit could stop it. He just had to point. He had more than enough carbon, he could do it.

He could do it.

So why couldn't he?

Valor was distracted by the appearance of one of Adlivun's shades, an echo of Phoenix that was quickly blasted back into oblivion. Enenra appeared within striking distance, but three bursts in rapid succession sent her scattered to the wind, her suit lighting up as she desperately tried to pull herself back together. Medusa was walking forward with her mask up and eyes wide, none of Valor's attacks able to touch her, but she was still far off and making slow progress as she tried to ensure she didn't hurt any of their classmates. Phoenix was still scrambling toward Kirin, but Valor knew what she was trying to do, firing at her whenever she got even halfway close. The way she flinched when they nearly landed reminded Ifrit of how slowly she'd healed the last time she'd been dealt a fatal blow.

And then Valor had his hand around someone's throat. *Ness's* throat. She'd been able to sneak up on him, but she was still so small. He held her with one hand, shouting something that Ifrit couldn't hear. Ifrit glanced out at the city, hoping to see someone, anyone, coming to their aid, but all he saw were dead buildings, only a few blocks out from the park. They had no *time*.

A scream of pain brought him back to the fight going on beneath his feet, and he looked down to see Ness bodily thrown away from Valor as they fuzzed back into existence. Valor sent off two surface level blasts that knocked the whole class back as he vomited. He was *down,* Ifrit had to strike *now.*

But as Ifrit raised his hand, his fingers were shaking. He hadn't… he hadn't killed anyone since Satol. He hadn't used deadly force *intentionally* ever. Even if it was Valor, his muscles wouldn't listen.

When Valor finished heaving, he sat back on his haunches, looking up at the sky. He saw Ifrit just floating there, watching, and he smiled again.

"You know you deserve this." Valor raised both his hands, wincing as he did, blood running down his left arm. "That's why you never run far."

Ifrit felt a tear track down his cheek. The carbon was already pooling around Valor; he could see the whole landscape in his mind. His classmates, his *friends,* trying so hard to stop Valor, to get all the people hiding in the trees off the island and to safety, Valor's victims littering the ground and Kirin—

The air moved. It churned, densifying into something that Ifrit couldn't control. He felt it solidifying, elongating, his brain struggling to understand how that could happen, *what* was happening. There was a haze— Lilin's doing— a threat hidden in the dark. Valor was so focused elsewhere that he forgot to watch his back.

Ifrit felt the release, felt the path carving through the air. It was going to miss, it was going to—

The tip of the spear erupted from Valor's chest, the attack he'd been building passing Ifrit like a light breeze, barely ruffling his hair. Valor looked down at the offending weapon, not comprehending what he was seeing. The sun was fully out now, and the spear glistened in the light, not just from the viscera covering it. Blood dripped from the corner of Valor's mouth as he tipped over, Ifrit dropping to the ground not more than a second later. Valor raised his hand in one final attempt, but a hand grabbed the spear where it protruded from his back, knocking Valor down as a foot was planted on his back.

"No more." Kirin sounded near tears as he grabbed the shaft with both hands and wrenched it out. Valor collapsed, and Ifrit knew he'd never move again. He found himself staring, staring at how small Valor looked now, how old. He was just an empty vessel, drained and broken. "Are you okay?"

Kirin was looking at Ifrit, hand outstretched as if to touch his face. Kirin's gloves had been lost somewhere, his palms cut and bleeding, and he stopped a handspan away as if he was afraid of getting blood on Ifrit's face. Ifrit couldn't speak, didn't know what he *could* say, but he pressed his cheek to Kirin's hand, before a shout got both of their attention.

"She's in!" Antaeus was yelling, pointing at the front gate of the school. The tech section was still buzzing with light, but that meant they could *see* it. The shield was down. And the woman in white was already through the wall, heading straight down the paths that would lead to the hero section.

"Alright, go, move, head to the jets!" Kuafu was ushering the diplomats out of the woods at a run, flashing Ifrit a knowing look that he hated.

"Everyone, fan out." Kirin's expression shuttered as he turned to the class, calling out orders. "Aether will be coming from the service entrance, majority in front. Kapre, have Wyrm support you and give me updates on numbers and locations. We're this close, we're not going to fail here."

The class burst into action, the fastest racing ahead to keep the lead. Kuafu shot Ifrit one last look before he moved to join them. Ifrit spared one more glance for Valor, checking that he really was dead. Then, to be extra sure, he snapped his rings together and set the corpse to char.

34

Under Attack

WHEN THE FIRST AETHER agent attacked Kirin, he froze.

His hands felt sticky and tight with dried blood, his every move causing the flakes to drift off, a trail of rose petals that whispered of what he'd done. The students fleeing campus gave him a wide berth, a stream breaking around him as he marched forward mechanically, not hearing the words they were saying, not seeing the looks they gave him. There was only forward. There was only the next task. That was all he could do.

It was so strange that he'd been waiting for the next attack, and yet when it came, he was ready to just take it. He wanted to rest. They weren't going to be able to do much anyway, young as they looked, *scared* as they looked. Maybe just enough to knock him out, to let him lie down and the people to walk over him until it was over. That wouldn't be so bad. In the end, he didn't need to move at all.

The shining wave of energy hit at their feet, sending the two teenagers trying to attack Kirin sprawling, tossing them several meters away where they scrambled to get back to their feet. Goldhorn secured them with an errant look, the grass growing long and tough enough to bind them to the ground. The hero section was flooded with bodies, Aether and students, professors and staff all spilling across the grounds, locked in combat or running from it as best they could. Pollen, one of the other professors, was flitting between combatants, stinging the trespassers and freezing them, giving her overwhelmed students time to breathe. Phantasm was even farther back still, amorphous shapes swarming out from her position, most of them pulverized under gunfire.

"Move, move!" Shifter pushed Kirin forward, shoved him into motion as their arrival began to attract notice, the mass of bodies breaking into a run now that the final barrier between them and safety had fallen. Kapre knelt down, the ground beneath Kirin's feet lifting up and stretching out, a bridge connecting them to the roof, to where the jets sat innocently, right there in view. Bodies were already climbing onto the pathway, figures starting to line up and form one last push to keep them from escaping. Kirin tasted the carbon coating his tongue, felt the air change as Dulu summoned his wings. Clidna clicked her tongue and Kuafu's hands ignited, as they crashed into the fray.

Kirin's body wouldn't obey, his mien refusing to activate, but his arms still knew how to throw a punch, his shoulders just as good at shoving people out of the way, soft flesh or hard rock. Ifrit cleared most of the advancing enemies, a simple blast detonated a few meters in front of them, the pressure from the explosion sending them careening backward and over the sides of the rock hewn ramp. Kuafu slapped his hands on the path, arcs of heat racing along invisible veins, causing attackers to back up, to stumble, unsteady enough to be knocked aside as Lilin pushed past. Dulu flew ahead, grabbing enemies at random and sending them back down below, sowing chaos in their ranks that left openings for Clidna to exploit, chunks of rock sheering off and away with the unwitting victim atop them.

Aïcha led the charge, hooves clattering against the stone,

opening a clear path wide enough for several people to run through, kicking her way through the now shattered line. Ness appeared much farther down, behind the enemy, scaring them enough to turn their backs, vanishing the moment she had their attention. Yantra swept in after, wires tearing out of the disaster simulator's windows— they were now practically on top of it— and tying down those in her way. Medusa marched ahead with purpose, her pace unimpeded, eyes open and forward, not changing her gaze as Naddāha disposed of the frozen enemies in her path. Wyrm paralyzed the rest, and then they were there, on the roof.

"First ship, everyone in! As many as you can fit!" Shifter's voice rang out, authoritative, before he was grabbed from behind. Faster than any of them could move, he produced a knife from a sleeve and stabbed at the arm holding him, elbowing the owner hard enough that they dropped back over the edge of the roof. "MOVE."

The diplomats did not need to be told twice, running for the closest jet, the bay open wide and ready. Aether agents were pulling themselves over the parapet, guns blazing, ready to take out who they could, but a glowing whip sent them back the way they came, Yantra staring after them with wide eyes as if just realizing what she'd done.

"I—"

"There you are, you *bitch*." The woman in white was there. She'd come from the opposite side of the roof, everyone turning and squaring off, the politicians still piling into the passenger hold, even as the door began to close.

"You too." Shifter grabbed Lilin, who was closest to the on-ramp, and tossed her into the ship just as it raised too high for anyone further to board.

"What?" Kuafu started forward, but they all froze as the engine started, and the jet began to rise.

Even the Aether agents on the roof stood still, watching the white hot propulsion engines kick into gear, watching the jet go higher and higher and higher until it was a speck the size of Kirin's thumb in the sky. Over the comms, Kirin could hear Lilin yelling, hear her pounding on the metal in anger, begging them to let her go back down.

The jet shot forward and plummeted, growing larger by the second as it dropped in its path toward the wall. Kirin felt his heart in his throat as the barrier loomed ahead of the craft, as the hull of the ship dipped ever closer to that great reaching hand around the city. One second. Two. He couldn't tell the angle, couldn't tell if they were going to make it. Three. Four.

The jet skimmed cleanly over the wall, a sliver of horizon still visible as it made it. Another second and it disappeared from view, having dropped behind the metal behemoth, Lilin's audio long since lost. Kirin's lips parted in horror, waiting to hear the sure to follow splash.

Instead, there was a boom, and the jet shot back into view, heading for the far distant land.

A wordless cry of success erupted from the civilians behind him, from the people who realized that there *was* hope for making it out alive. The crowd resumed its mad dash for the remaining jets and Kirin turned his attention back to the woman in white.

"You think a few powerless people can stop us?" Her tricks from all their fights before seemed to have been used up; the woman offered no signs of preparing to fight. "This is only the beginning."

"Why are you doing this?" Yantra stepped up beside Kirin, her face a mask of sadness. "What do you gain?"

"Everything we ever wanted." The earlier passivity was a bluff, the woman lunging forward now, hands out as she reached for Yantra. Yantra reared back, not expecting the attack. Suddenly Ness was in the space in between them, her arm a blur in front. In the moment between Ness landing her blow, a gun went off, a puff of air rolling over Kirin, making his hair blow.

Yantra went down, the woman in white falling from the gaping wound in her chest that Ness had inflicted. Kirin's head snapped to the side and he saw, impossibly, Nwabudike standing next to the stairwell, his eyes wide with horror.

"No, it was only..." He dropped the weapon— something that looked like a modified air cannon— to the side, one hand going to cover his mouth in horror. "It shouldn't have hurt anyone else, it was only supposed to affect..."

"Yantra, wake up!" Ness shook Yantra's shoulders, her head rolled to the side. "Yantra!"

"Keep moving!" Shifter wrapped a hand around Antaeus's collar this time, throwing him bodily into the next jet. It took off, less than half of the crowd that they'd started out with safely on their way out of the city. Wyrm's head snapped around, away from the two men he was fighting, the distraction costing him as he was sent over the edge, only saved from dropping to the ground by a timely intervention by Dulu.

"What did you do?!" Ness screamed at Nwabudike, gathering Yantra's prone body in her arms.

"It was only supposed to affect—"

"Constructs," Ifrit said, looking down at the woman in white, whose abdomen was torn open to reveal wires and metal surrounding her beating heart.

35

Someone's Responsibility

THE ROOFTOP WAS EMPTYING rapidly, Ifrit maintaining explosions around the perimeter of the roof to keep enemies off it, to hold their position until the last of the diplomats could board their jets and get free of the hellscape that East City had turned into. The first lights in the park were shutting off, the coming dusk as the sun bent ever downward heightened by the lampposts shuttering as the wave of blackouts crept nearer. Ifrit forced himself not to look into the city, forced himself not to look at the once that had once been so bright and full of light, forced himself to not feel like he was failing his mother a second time.

A flash of bright blue in the corner of his eye caught his attention.

Majesty? He hadn't seen her, hadn't spotted her among the teachers, hadn't seen her with her class. But when he turned and looked, really looked, the figure was too small to have been her, though that was certainly her bright blue hair.

Bán.

"What?" At the exclamation, Kirin's head snapped up, his gaze following Ifrit's.

"What're they—"

Bán saw them. Ifrit knew they did. They were so far away,

near Majesty's office, but the stark red coating their face was clear.

"I'll be right back." Kirin gripped Ifrit's arm, only for a second, and then he was gone, jumping off and down, landing with a thud that shook the building. Ifrit looked behind him, saw only two jets left to load, and shot after him.

The fighting was still dense on the ground, students being overwhelmed by the brutality of the force, by the guns and the desperation of their attackers. Ifrit separated the groups, scattered the attackers with explosions where he could risk them, focused mostly on catching up to Kirin's shining back as they both converged on Bán.

"Are you hurt?" Kirin didn't wait for an answer as he scooped them up, Bán wrapping their too thin arms around his neck. "This blood, is it yours?"

Bán answered by glowing, releasing a curtain of energy that separated them from an attacker that Ifrit had failed to notice coming up from behind. Ifrit recognized the shimmer, recognized the mesmerizing, awe-inspiring depth to the light, a weaker form of the very light Majesty employed.

"Let's get you out of here." Kirin turned to the disaster simulator, just in time to see the bridge they had taken crumble, finally succumbing to the damage sustained during their rush.

"No!" Bán pushed away, almost succeeding in shoving out of Kirin's arms. "You have to help her!"

"Help who?" Ifrit felt his mouth go dry, remembering suddenly that Valor had shown *up* already covered in blood.

"My mom." Bán pointed a tremulous finger toward the building behind them, to where a trail of blood lead from Majesty's office.

"Get them to the roof." Kirin held Bán— Pressure's *family*— out to Ifrit, who found he couldn't move. "I'll go get her, okay?"

The look in Kirin's eyes. The resolute sadness there. Neither of them suspected he'd be finding Majesty alive.

"She was... she was finally protecting me." Bán finally started to cry. "She said... she wouldn't let him take me. Never again."

Ifrit found himself accepting the weight of his cousin, but still unable to move as Kirin darted into the building. They stood still within the curtain that Bán had created, the fighting ceasing whenever someone stared at the gently shimmering light. Ifrit didn't know what to say. He didn't know what to do, how to explain who he was, if Bán would even remember him. If Bán would want to know that they might be the only two left.

Kirin reemerged a moment later, Majesty laid out unconscious in his arms. Ifrit couldn't make himself look closer, couldn't stare too hard at the dripping wounds on her back. Her mask was off, her unlined face visible, pale as snow and still.

"Let's move." Kirin's face gave nothing away, crystallizing the backs of his arms as he broke into a run, the barrier ahead of him breaking just before he made contact. Outside, the fight raged on, Ifrit shooting ahead and clearing a path, up the wall and onto the roof in seconds. He dropped Bán down, turning back to help Kirin, ignoring the way Yantra was so still on the floor.

Kirin was already climbing the building, stabbing one of his hands into the side and jumping, doing his best not to jostle Majesty as he did. That gave Ifrit's heart a painful twist— was there a chance she wasn't gone? He wouldn't have been trying to be so gentle if she was, would he? Ifrit reached for her wordlessly, Kirin passing her off just a moment before someone jumped up and tore him off the wall.

Ifrit almost dropped Majesty, one arm reaching for Kirin even though he was already too far. Kirin hit the ground with a crack, rolling over and pushing himself to his feet slowly. He wasn't hurt, was he? Why was he moving like that? Like every motion cost him great pain? Kirin's eyes flickered to Ifrit, the meaning in the look clear. *Go, get safe.* Ifrit looked down, looked at Majesty *still breathing* in his arms, and darted up to the roof, depositing her at Phoenix's feet before leaping back down himself.

Fire rolled out beneath him to cushion his fall, just opposite Kirin. Kirin's attacker didn't pay any mind to Ifrit at all, ignored the flames that licked at their side, eyes only on the man who looked oh so similar to them.

"Min-soo." They said Kirin's name like hope, like a curse. "I'm sorry."

"What have you done?" Kirin's voice trembled. "And what have they done to you?"

"I couldn't keep them safe." Hyeon-soo choked. "I'm sorry hyung, I tried."

"It's not your fault." Kirin moved forward, to hug them, to comfort them, his posture relaxed, his guard down. Hyeon-soo let him hug them, wrapped their arm around him, before Ifrit noticed the needle in their hand.

"Kirin!" He lurched forward, the only thing he could do sliding his hand under the weapon, feeling the tip scrape against his skin.

Kirin shoved Hyeon-soo away, grabbing Ifrit and jumping back so hard that his back collided with the wall. Ifrit, trapped in Kirin's arms, felt his head swim, the ground tilting slightly under his feet. He staggered, falling against Kirin's chest, trying to clear his thoughts.

"What did you do?"

"I'm sorry!" Hyeon-soo was fully crying now. "I need to save them! And you left!"

"Get us up." Kirin's voice was rough in Ifrit's ears. "I'll direct, just get us out of here."

Ifrit knew he used too much power, knew he'd released too much carbon, but Kirin was good as his word, and they crashed back down upon the roof. Majesty was up now, hugging Bán one more time before she handed him to Shifter, standing in the bay of the final jet. They were all there, the whole class loaded in. The armorer was the lone figure on the roof, his afro blowing in the wind from the last take off. The lights were out now halfway to the school, the fighting dying as the defenders were subdued. Bodies lay piled around campus, students, teachers, innocent staff all dropped like flies, and for what?

"Get in." Kirin was talking to the armorer, who stood above the woman in white, his weapon at the ready. Yantra had been moved inside the jet, still unconscious, Ness whispering as she touched Yantra's face.

"Someone needs to stay." The kid was stubborn, even in his addled state Ifrit could see the set of his jaw, the fearful determination in his eyes. "With the power out, someone needs to figure out how to get fresh water to the city. And the farms are mostly underground; they rely on grow lights and rotating which crops are topside, people are going to run out of food fast—"

"It doesn't have to be you!"

"He's right." Majesty wasn't boarding. "The city needs someone to protect it. It won't be pretty. It will be messy and violent. Which is why we need all hands to be figuring out a way to reclaim the city, to stop what Aether has done. There are millions of people who live here, who will go hungry if this isn't reversed."

Ifrit's head swung back out toward the city proper, toward the small house nestled far out of sight. Fires burned intermittently throughout the outer ring, some creeping closer as he watched. There were screams, sounds of violence, but no sirens, no one going to help. He turned and looked back at the jet, where the last of the people he trusted to put things right were waiting, were leaving.

"Someone does have to stay." His own voice sounded distant. Kirin turned and looked, tear tracks carving clean lines down his bloodstained face. "I'll stay."

"No." The word sounded like it was torn from Kirin's throat.

"I need to stay." Now that he said it, the dread fell away from him. This was his home. This city, the school. The first place he hadn't been treated like shit. He couldn't abandon it. "I need to protect *her*."

And his mom. The pictures she had insisted on taking, the walls covered with memories from the years, the only photos that remained of her as a person, not a hero, not a monument. If he left, he might come back to it gone, all gone, destroyed as if it was never there.

"Adil." Kirin pressed their foreheads together, tears dripping from his nose onto Ifrit's face, pressing his lips to Ifrit's forehead. "Okay. It'll be protected."

"But you—" Ifrit felt the burning lines escape from his eyes, trace down his cheeks— "you need to go. I need to know you're watching Bán."

Kirin raised Ifrit's eyes to his own, sadness and acceptance filling them. Kirin never would say no to Ifrit, would he? Ifrit knew it was unfair to ask, knew it would have been worse if he asked what he really wanted, asked Kirin to stay by his side, to stand with him as everything burned around them. Kirin would've said yes, and Ifrit had already taken so much from him. He'd *seen* Kirin's face when Kirin realized Valor was dead, seen Kirin's face after he had cleared the front entrance. Kirin had lost so much protecting Ifrit; this was all Ifrit could do for him. Beg him to go.

Maybe if there was time Kirin would've argued. Maybe if there was time Ifrit could've been swayed, could've agreed to be selfish. But now, seeing Kirin covered in blood, seeing the way his eyes looked shattered, Ifrit just wanted him safe.

"Adil." Kirin pulled down Ifrit's mask, pressing their foreheads together one last time as the engines started behind them, as the jet started to rise, hovering just high enough to allow them to jump. "I love you."

Kirin pressed his mouth to Ifrit's, Ifrit grabbing the torn edges of Kirin's shirt and pulling him close, memorizing the way that Kirin felt, the way that his hands held Ifrit delicately, like Ifrit might break, the way that his arms crystallized slightly and dug into Ifrit's waist.

"I love you." Kirin pulled back and looked Ifrit in the eye. "And I'll be waiting."

Just before the door to the jet closed, Kirin threw Ifrit inside.

36

Too Far

"No!" Ifrit's fist slammed against the metal, and he reached for the carbon in his veins, ready to blow the ship open, ready to destroy their only way off the island to get back to Kirin, to stop him from doing this, but there was nothing there. Through the thin strip of glass in the gate Ifrit could see Kirin looking up at him, his whole body shimmering diamond in the last light of the sun, all the carbon he had stolen protecting him from a barrage of gunfire as the remaining Aether agents crested the building, Majesty sending out waves of dazzling light that kept attackers spinning away from the armorer, now exposed. "Kirin!"

"Ifrit." Naddāha was behind him, one hand on his arm. "He was never going to come."

Ifrit wanted to hit her, to shake her and make her lose that pitying look, that helpless wobble in her lip. He turned and looked down again, Majesty and Kirin now back to back, the armorer nowhere in sight. Someone reached the woman in white on the ground, shrinking as the jet shot up, up, up. Ifrit couldn't get himself to look away, couldn't stop watching the shining figure who had his head turned toward the sky.

He wanted to collapse. He wanted to fall to his knees and scream, but that would mean he would have to stop looking, and he would miss the last glimpses that he might ever get of Kirin, his Kirin. He hadn't even said that he loved him back.

"I'm sorry." Kirin's voice crackled through his headset. *"Please don't be mad."*

"I'm going to be fucking furious if you don't get here right now!" Ifrit punched the wall again, hoping Kirin could hear the sound, would realize that Ifrit needed him there, needed him to be okay. "Dulu can get you, he can fly down and—"

There was a scuffle, the sound of someone grabbing Kirin's comm and tearing it away. They were too high up now to see who it was, to see anything other than tiny shapes dotting the roof, the engines powering up as the jet prepared to launch itself over the dead city.

"*Ness*." A new voice hissed through the comm, Naddāha going stiff where she still touched him. *"It's time to bring me what I asked for."*

Three things happened at once.

Naddāha lunged for Ness, where she still sat cradling Yantra on the floor.

The moment Naddāha touched Ness's arm, the three of them vanished from sight.

The jet shot sideways, Ifrit's last glance out the window of the trio plunging down toward the roof, a tiny glittering shape jumping up to catch them.

Ifrit's stomach was in his mouth as the cabin tilted, as they all slid back against the wall separating them from the cockpit, as the plane dipped nose down and the jet slid into free fall, still shooting for the wall. This was the last chance, the final opportunity for him to stay, to stand with Kirin and fight. There was a window looking in, the view from the pilot's seat a grim one as the ocean loomed larger and larger out front. Ifrit felt a hand on his shoulder, another on his back, turning to see Clidna and Medusa on either side, both staring out with him.

Clidna was crying silently, her eyes only sliding to his for a moment, just long enough for him to see that she was hoping for the same thing; that she wanted to stay too. Shifter was in the corner, trying and failing to hide his sorrow, not looking at any of them, burying his face in his hands.

The barrier still grew closer. They were lower, this time, than any of the other jets had been. Ifrit let himself believe it, *chose* to believe it. They weren't going to make it. They would crash and it would hurt, but Goldhorn was there, they'd be okay. And then he would run, he would run all the way back to Kirin, yell at him. Scream at him. But Kirin would forgive him, because Kirin would understand. Kirin deserved to be safe, and if he wouldn't go the easy way, Ifrit would keep him safe himself.

The bottom of the jet screeched, scraping over the very edge of the wall, bouncing them up slightly, just slightly, just enough to give the engines time to reignite before they hit the water.

As the propulsion kicked in and shot them toward land, Ifrit fell to his knees and wept.

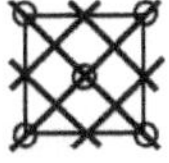

"You understand what you're being assigned."

"Yes."

"And if you accept, you will receive no back up."

"I understand."

"We have been unable to get any signal into or out of East City except for the one we have shared with you. You will be going in blind."

"I understand."

"The mission is simple. With your team, you are to accomplish three things. Firstly: find the device that Aether is using to turn the city into a dead zone and destroy it. Secondly: free

East Technical Institute and any remaining researchers inside it."

"I accept."

"Thirdly..." The head of the Hero Council leaned forward, looking down at Ifrit and his friends. "We need you to kill the head of Aether."

Ifrit didn't flinch. He knew what he'd done as the weeks turned into months to get them to offer him the mission, and what they would ask of him once he got it. It would all be worth it, all of it, once he got Kirin back.

"With pleasure."

The Aftermath

"ANY CHANGE?" MIN-SOO SAT down hard, feeling the barely healed skin on his chest pull.

"Not yet." Naddāha looked up at him wearily, rubbing sleep from her eyes. They'd been swapping on and off for days now, keeping a watch around the clock. The city was in shambles, the police resorting to brutality against anyone and everyone they suspected of being related to Aether. Aether, for their part, were holed up in the school, the only area on the island that remained lit, night and day. Stores were emptying rapidly, water becoming scarce.

"I swung by the second ring." Min-soo pulled out some wilting herbs, offering her a sprig of mint to chew on. "I think we should start there."

Naddāha nodded absently, still watching Yantra, who looked like she was just sleeping peacefully. If one ignored the blood-stained bandages wrapped around her head.

"Shouldn't it have worked by now?" Her voice cracked slightly, before she smoothed her facial expressions back over. "Maybe it was more than we thought."

"I can't say for sure." Nwabudike rolled into the room, his wheelchair catching as always on the rough threshold of the door. "Without my tools, it is guesswork. But this is the best chance we've got."

Naddāha nodded again, her eyes distant.

"If I could just get *close* to Ness—"

"We tried that already." Min-soo shook his head.

"They're keeping her too close, for now." Nwabudike winced as he tried to stand, and failed. He was still getting used to being wheelchair bound again. "We just need to wait."

A light knock on the far door startled them all, Naddāha most of all. She practically jumped, so unused to people sneaking up on her. She rubbed at her forehead, shaking her head.

"You two are too similar; I can't even tell your *feelings* apart."

With the confirmation it was okay, Min-soo forced his tired legs to push him to his feet, limping as he walked through their makeshift sickbay to the room where Nwabudike counted and recounted the food they had left. The metal door had a thick steel pipe across it, which Min-soo lifted with a grunt, allowing Hyeon-soo to rush into the room, pressing the door closed quickly behind themself.

"It's getting harder to sneak away; they're getting more and more paranoid as the police are getting more aggressive." Between the four of them, Hyeon-soo looked the most well-rested, though they still looked haggard. "We'll have to figure out a new way of passing along messages soon, if things keep going the way they're going. No one knows what to do, but they're looking for *her*."

They nodded to Yantra, so pale on the table.

"Why?" Nwabudike knew better than the rest of them why, but Min-soo insisted they didn't tell his sibling everything. Naddāha was convinced they were on their side, but he couldn't shake the feeling that they were over-eager to help. They had been so willing to hurt anyone before; the change was jarring, suspicious.

"I don't know. Just that the top people are all out looking for her." Hyeon-soo cleared their throat. "Including... including your friend."

"They have her going out alone?" Naddāha's head perked up, casting Min-soo a knowing look.

"Not yet. That pretty woman they got to defect from the school, she's still keeping her on a short leash. Seemed to think she wouldn't need to soon, though."

"That's good." Naddāha took a deep breath, looking at Min-soo. "That's good."

"What's your plan?" Hyeon-soo looked at Min-soo, their eyes hopeful. "We should act now, right? While they don't have a leader?"

Min-soo didn't answer, unable to look at them, striding instead through the room and out to the hallway they slept in, the piles of blankets arranged along the wall. He pressed the heels of his hands to his eyes, breathing deeply. They needed to understand that they couldn't *trust* him, that he couldn't do anything to help. He only hurt.

"Kirin." Naddāha gently took his elbow. "I know you're beating yourself up over everything. But you did what you had to. He's safe. Now you need to focus on keeping yourself safe. You promised him, right? That you'd be waiting?"

Min-soo didn't trust himself to speak, one hand already in his pocket, folded over the picture he'd stolen, something else to feel guilty about.

"Focus on the problems at hand. What's the first thing we need to do?" She coaxed him back into the main room, where Hyeon-soo and Nwabudike were waiting, where the steady drip of the IV was the only sound.

"Water." He took a breath. One thing at a time. "We need to figure out how to get water. The city is going to die of thirst before hunger, and you can't water crops with saltwater."

"Good." Naddāha patted the seat next to the table, seating herself by Yantra's feet. "How do we do that?"

"We find whatever they used to knock out the power with and turn it off." A voice croaked. They all turned to see Yantra's eyes open, still pale as a sheet but conscious, a small smile curling her lip. "We turn that power against them, and *we* control the city."

"You're awake!" Nwabudike once again tried to stand, falling back and then quickly wheeling himself into their kitchen to get her some water.

"Don't push yourself." Min-soo tried to stop her as she pushed herself up to sitting, but she batted his hand away. When one hand went to her head, she looked at him with fear, but when she failed to find judgement in his or Naddāha's eyes, she relaxed.

"The police aren't going to protect the people," Naddāha said quietly. "And we know Aether won't either. They need someone who is going to keep them safe, whether it's the legal way of doing things or not."

Min-soo met her eyes, the knowing look she had.

"And maybe," Yantra coughed once before continuing, "maybe if we do it here, maybe we can show the world there's a better way. Maybe we don't just keep the city safe, maybe we fix it."

They were both looking at him. There was hope in their eyes, reflecting the opportunity that he had been too blind to see. Too caught up in his own head. But who was he to try it?

"Just think of it." Naddāha took one of his hands, pressing it between her own. "A city where everyone is safe to be who they are. We could do that."

"Just the three of us?"

"You'd be surprised how many people want to leave Aether." Hyeon-soo chimed in. "Most people are there because there wasn't another choice. They couldn't make it into the school. They couldn't blend in with everyone else. They did what they had to."

"C'mon Kirin." Yantra gave him a full smile, her lips so chapped one of them cracked. "Let's give everyone something to come back to."

Min-soo looked at them, then at the photo he'd subconsciously pulled out of his pocket. At Adil, years younger, trying to hide a smile as Pressure threw her arms over his shoulders.

"Yeah," Kirin agreed. "Let's give them something to come back to."

Acknowledgements

This book was wrenched out of me kicking and screaming, fighting me the whole way through. Accordingly, there are so many people who helped me through the process, and put up with my unending whining, for which I am eternally grateful.

Firstly, as always, I have to thank Sam, for being my chapter by chapter beta reader, who keeps me motivated and politely doesn't complain when I send her a chapter only to say "wait, I hate it now, I'm rewriting." This book, much like the first book, truly wouldn't exist without you and I hope you know how much I appreciate your feedback as a reader, and our weekly phone calls. I love you so much and cannot wait until I finally get to visit you and Jennifer.

Next, to all my beta readers. A special shoutout as always to Mini, for sending me all your thoughts as you read; to Reid for reading and then immediately hyping it to everyone you talk to; to Mira for being a rat about it which makes me feel quite accomplished indeed; for Jennifer who still refuses to tell me what she thought of it; to Janna who read the book so fast and then immediately proceeded to send me incredible art of my stupid boys; and to AJ, because yes you are supposed to be there and I truly appreciate you. And a shoutout to one of my ARC readers Asher, for not only reading book one, but being so passionate about my boys, that you reached out for book two. That did really make my day I hope you know. Readers like you make it all worth it.

I've already started to, but I do need to send many, many thanks to the incredible artists I've had the privilege of working with. A huge thank you to Mariska for creating the beautiful cover of this book. You always manage to capture exactly what I want to portray and I appreciate your attention to detail so much. Loona, as always you are a delight to work with and I love your enthusiasm for my characters and the silliness we get up to as you send me progress. And a second thanks to Janna, for so beautifully rendering my boys. Seeing them come to life in a traditional medium really is something different, seeing the care and time you put into painting them touched me so deeply. In the realm of second thanks, Reid and Mira need to be here as well for all your drawings and doodles that I hoard and put all over my walls.

Then I have to thank all my incredible writing friends. To the Wayward Writers group, a sincere thank you for the constant hyping and helping, and for the wonderful community you've all helped create. To Irene, for being such a help with book one, and an inspiration for the launch of book two. To Sam (Silberberg, this time) for being one of my biggest cheerleader, and Jessica for always thinking of me when support trains come along! And, a new addition to the team, thank you so much to Zen for editing not only Hot-Blooded, but retroactively getting Warm-Blooded into shape as well! I promise I will use fewer "thens" in the future.

As always, my thanks and love to my incredible partner Jordan for keeping me fed and reminding me to sleep. If you didn't stare sadly at me when I was trying to write late into the night I probably would've stayed up later and been more miserable which would've resulted in a worse book. So yes, this book couldn't have happened without you, because you help me and that goes very far you silly.

And my final personal thanks goes to my silly lil bunny. Thank you Chomp for eating my bad drafts and for making every day be a good one. You cannot have a bad day if you start it by reading with a tiny 3 lb (1 kg, and change) bunny.

But a huge thanks to everyone reading this, to everyone who read book one and decided it was worth continuing. To everyone who has left a review, a comment, or just mentioned the book to a friend. I really do appreciate all of you, and I can't wait for you all to see what I have in store for book 3.

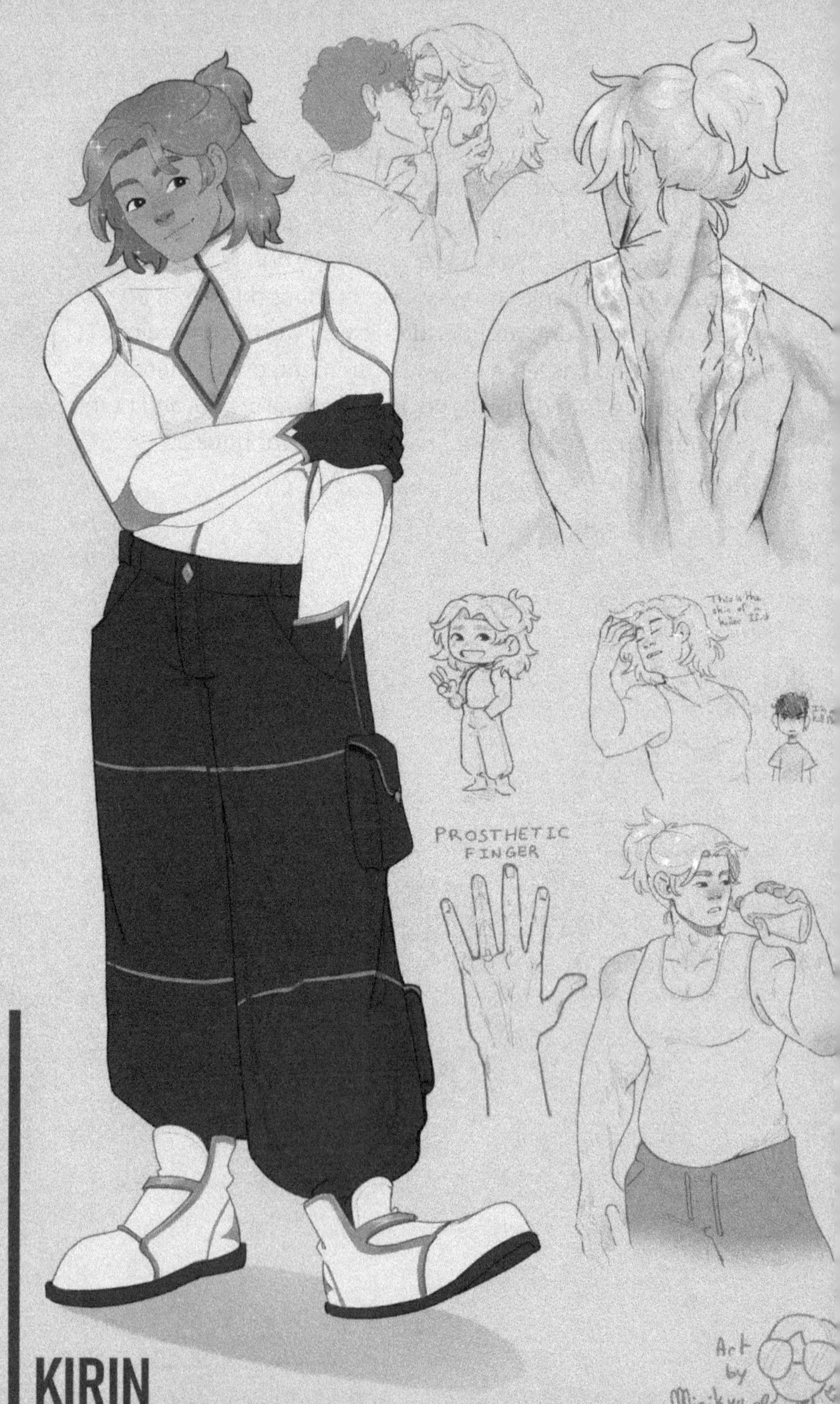
PROSTHETIC
FINGER
KIRIN
Art
by
Minikyu

IFRIT
IGNITION RINGS
padded
steel toed
Art by Minikyu

OTHERS

Ness

Kuafu

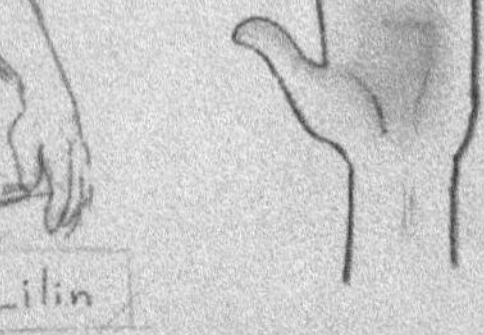

About the Author

J is far less interesting to talk about than their adorable rabbit, Chomp. They have kindly provided a photo of him below for your viewing pleasure. They are the author of *Warm-Blooded* and *Hot-Blooded*, the first two books of the Carbon Chronicles trilogy.

www.ingramcontent.com/pod-product-compliance
Lightning Source LLC
Chambersburg PA
CBHW031946011225
36165CB00001B/1

* 9 7 9 8 9 9 0 9 4 9 2 4 9 *